ALIX JAMES

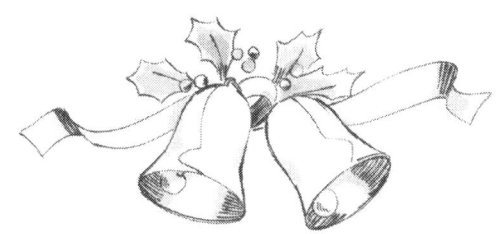

THE
Scotsman's Ghost

OR HOW TO WRECK
A YULE PARTY

A PRIDE & PREJUDICE CHRISTMAS VARIATION

Cover Design by GetCovers.com
Cover Image Licensed by Period Images
Background image licensed by Shutterstock

Blog and Website: https://alixjames.com/
Newsletter: https://subscribepage.io/alix-james
Book Bub: https://www.bookbub.com/authors/alix-james
Facebook: https://www.facebook.com/ShortSweetNovellas
Twitter: https://twitter.com/N_Clarkston
Amazon: https://www.amazon.com/stores/Alix-James/author/B07Z1BWFF3
Austen Variations: http://austenvariations.com/

Contents

One

Darcy

I LOATHED COUNTRY ASSEMBLIES.

The room was stifling—far too small for the number of people packed in there. And yet, I could not find it in myself to make an excuse and leave, though I had conjured no fewer than six in the last ten minutes. My patience had already been tested beyond its limits. The heat, the noise, the suffocating stench of roast meats and cheap perfume—it was a kind of assault on the senses that made one question why one agreed to leave London at all.

I stole a glance toward Bingley. He was entirely absorbed in some light conversation with a local family, his smile bright, his eyes alight with the easy charm that always seemed to work for him, no matter the company. Charles Bingley could find something to admire in the plainest of towns or the most vapid company, and somehow, he could not seem to find a single word of criticism for any of it.

This was Meryton. A provincial town with provincial people, where the height of entertainment was watching people humiliate themselves at one of these so-called "gatherings." It was an absurd spectacle—overly bright dresses, all lace and ruffles in colors so garish it was as if the entire countryside had turned out to celebrate a jest only they found amusing.

I shifted my weight uncomfortably, the polished leather of my boots catching on the worn floorboards, and resisted the urge to roll my eyes. This was beneath me. And yet, here I was.

It wouldn't do to abandon Bingley, of course. He was far too kind for his own good, and I doubted the poor fool would know what to do with himself without a steady hand guiding him through these situations. He saw good in everything—and everyone, apparently. It was charming in its own way, but also reckless. He refused to acknowledge how deeply out of his element he truly was here.

Across the room, Caroline Bingley stood with the practiced air of someone who believed she was above it all. Which, frankly, she was—though she took every opportunity to remind others of it. She cast her icy gaze across the room, scanning it like a hawk searching for prey, while tossing yet another veiled insult toward her brother.

"These assemblies are so very... quaint, Charles. One must admire the simplicity of country life, of course. Simple amusements for simple people, wouldn't you agree?"

I almost pitied Bingley for the way his smile faltered, but he caught himself before the comment could do any real damage. That was the way of it with Caroline. Her insults came wrapped in fine lace, soft enough to seem like compliments unless one truly listened. Bingley, as ever, did not listen.

I caught his eye, and he shot me a pleading glance—a silent request to engage with the locals or, at the very least, offer him some kind of escape from his sister's barbs.

Not tonight.

I had had my fill of shallow conversations with people who only wished to know me for my fortune or name. I hadn't come to Meryton to mingle with the locals—I had come because Bingley was too easily charmed by novelty and needed someone with sense to keep him grounded. Now, I wondered if it was too late.

Still, I could not leave. Not without appearing rude, though I do not know why it bothered me that I might make enemies in this town. It was not as if I would be staying long.

It was then that I noticed Bingley moving toward me, his eyes bright with excitement as he seemed to sweep through the crowd with ease. I should have known he was plotting something. Bingley was like that—he would make twenty new acquaintances in a matter of minutes and somehow remember them all the next day. I could already sense where this was going, and it filled me with dread.

"Darcy!" he called, a bit too loud for my taste, though no one else seemed to notice. "You've been standing here long enough. I've someone I want you to meet."

I glanced around, hoping he might mean anyone other than that brunette I had spotted earlier this evening. She had been laughing with her sister—the blonde Bingley had danced with... twice. Surely not *her*, of all people. The last thing I wanted was to be used as a sort of fourth for some misguided double-matchmaking endeavors this evening.

But no. Bingley was already steering me through the crowd, and there was no mistaking the direction we were headed.

My stomach clenched as we approached. The lady stood near the refreshments table, her eyes sparkling with laughter as she spoke to her companions. Indeed, there was an ease about her that I could not ignore, no matter how hard I tried. She seemed utterly at home in this room full of people I could barely stand to be near.

Bingley was grinning like a schoolboy as he approached her, oblivious to the tightening of my jaw.

"Miss Elizabeth Bennet," Bingley said cheerfully, "may I present my friend, Mr. Fitzwilliam Darcy?"

Miss Elizabeth turned toward us, her gaze flicking to mine with an unreadable expression. If she was surprised or displeased by the introduction, she hid it well, offering a small curtsey and a polite smile.

"Mr. Darcy," she said pleasantly, though I could detect the slightest hint of irony in her tone. "We are already acquainted."

Her gaze settled on me, and I felt a sharpness there that was unmistakable, even as she kept her expression demure. She was judging me. Again.

I returned her polite nod. "Indeed, we are." In fact, I was acquainted with the lady, her preposterous mother, her gossipy aunt, her uncle the solicitor, all *four* of her sisters, and sadly, not her brother. Because... ah, that was right. She did not have one, which meant the daughters were scouring the landscape for loose males all the more diligently.

Bingley clapped his hands with pleasure. "I thought as much! Well, no harm in reintroducing friends, eh?"

I resisted the urge to contradict him, though I knew any attempt would fall on deaf ears. Instead, I kept my expression neutral, doing my best to ignore the increasingly satisfied look Miss Elizabeth was casting in my direction.

"I hope you are enjoying the evening, Mr. Darcy," she said, almost as if she were preparing to dismiss me. "Assemblies such as these must be quite the novelty for you."

Ah, there it was. The needle, subtle but unmistakable. I had known this was coming from the moment Bingley dragged me over. In fact, I had noted a glint in the lady's eye earlier this evening when we were introduced, and my guess was right. She was the village wit.

Perfect.

I gave a small, tight smile. "They are certainly... lively."

Her brow lifted in response, the corner of her mouth twitching as though she were trying very hard not to laugh. "Indeed," she murmured. "I suppose one could call it lively. Though you do not appear to be enjoying it overmuch."

"I assure you," I replied, keeping my voice flat, "I am tolerating it with perfect equanimity."

That seemed to amuse her even more. Her eyes danced with something I could only interpret as triumph, as though she had expected exactly that answer. "Well, I am pleased to hear it. I should hate to think you find our company wanting."

"Miss Elizabeth," I said stiffly, "you should not presume my thoughts."

"Oh, I wouldn't dream of it, Mr. Darcy."

There was a brief, awkward silence before Bingley cleared his throat. Apparently, this conversation was not going as he had envisioned.

"Well, Darcy," he said, clapping a hand on my shoulder with a force that nearly made me wince, "I shall leave you to it, then. Miss Elizabeth, I hope you'll save me a dance later."

She smiled at him, genuinely this time. "Of course, Mr. Bingley."

And then he was gone, leaving me alone with her, standing awkwardly by the refreshment table as the conversation—and my discomfort—lingered in the air.

Miss Elizabeth's smile faded slightly as she glanced toward the dancers. I should have taken the opportunity to excuse myself, but curse it all, I couldn't think of another place in the room to stand that would not be worse.

"Do you not dance, Mr. Darcy?" she asked suddenly, breaking the silence.

I blinked, caught off guard by the question. "I do," I answered curtly, "though I find it more agreeable in certain settings."

Her lips quirked. "Certain settings?"

I gestured vaguely toward the crowded dance floor, where couples were stumbling through the movements with varying degrees of success. "A room less crowded. More... select company."

Her eyes narrowed, and I immediately regretted my words.

"I see," she said slowly. "Then I suppose you find our company here somewhat lacking in refinement."

"That is not what I meant," I said quickly, though the damage was done. She knew exactly what I meant. Of course, she did.

"No?" she asked, her voice light but her gaze sharp. "Then what did you mean, Mr. Darcy?"

I had no answer that would satisfy her. So, I did what any sensible man would do in such a situation. "Miss Elizabeth," I said, bowing stiffly, "if you will excuse me."

I didn't wait for her reply.

Elizabeth

I SUPPOSE IT WOULD have been too much to hope that Mr. Darcy might find some excuse to leave early.

I had noticed him, of course. How could I not? He loomed near the back of the room, his expression inscrutable but distinctly unwelcoming. His eyes scanned the assembly as though he were cataloging every last one of us—and finding us all thoroughly beneath his notice. He stood apart from the merriment, barely engaging with those around him, though all evening, Mr. Bingley had been attempting, with almost painful determination, to pull him into the fold.

It wasn't working.

I turned away from the sight of Mr. Darcy, letting my attention drift back to the more pleasant scene unfolding before me. Mr. Bingley was dancing with Jane, and she looked beautiful—flushed and smiling, though I could see the tension in her posture whenever Lydia's giggles rose above the music. My youngest sister had already made quite the spectacle of herself this evening—laughing too loudly, flirting too boldly—and Jane was doing her best to ignore it.

I felt my own face heating at the memory of Mama's remarks earlier. She had practically thrown Jane at Mr. Bingley, as if that would secure him for more than just a dance. It was mortifying, and Jane, bless her, had simply smiled through it all.

Mr. Darcy's disapproval had been written all over his face. He hadn't said a word, but I'd caught him watching us, his brow slightly furrowed, his gaze drifting over my family as if weighing each of us in turn. I supposed he found us lacking. I couldn't fault him for that entirely. The way Lydia was carrying on—and Mama, for that matter—I could hardly deny we were putting on quite the performance.

Still, Mr. Darcy's quiet disdain rankled. He seemed to think himself above the room. Above us. Above everything.

And yet... for all his superiority, I couldn't help but notice that he never once allowed himself to truly slip. His posture was impeccable, his coat perfectly tailored, his expression carefully neutral, no matter how ridiculous the evening became. While others flitted about the room, laughing too loudly or stumbling through a dance, he remained still.

Controlled.

Almost unnervingly so.

It made him all the more absurd, really. To stand so stiffly amidst such chaos, to guard himself so carefully against the prospect of enjoyment. How exhausting it must be, to never allow oneself a moment's unguarded amusement.

As I wandered toward the refreshment table, I caught a glimpse of Kitty and Lydia at the other end of the room, practically hanging off the arms of two soldiers, their laughter ringing out above the music. I winced, glancing toward Jane, who was clearly doing her best to ignore the spectacle. If she was embarrassed, she would never show it.

But I wasn't quite as patient. I could only imagine what Mr. Darcy made of the scene. Why I cared, I had no idea. What did it matter to me if he was a prig? But I still noticed.

He was near the fireplace now, standing perfectly still, his eyes flicking across the room as though cataloging every flaw in the evening. And yet, something about him remained so... steady. I found myself studying him in spite of myself. He was so unlike any man I had ever met—so fastidious, so very controlled, even in a setting like this where most men would have grown frustrated or bored.

My father, for instance, had long since retreated to a corner of the room, where he could sit in peace, nursing a glass of wine and casting the occasional amused glance at Mama's efforts to herd my sisters like a determined sheepdog. But Mr. Darcy? He remained in the thick of it, though he hardly participated. He was like a marble statue, observing, never reacting.

I supposed I should find it irritating—his insistence on remaining aloof. And yet, there was something strangely fascinating about it.

"Lizzy!"

I turned just in time to see Charlotte approaching, her face flushed with exertion from her recent dance. She smiled as she reached my side, following my gaze toward the refreshment table, then across the room to where Mr. Darcy stood, still glowering at the crowd.

"He doesn't look as though he's enjoying himself," Charlotte remarked quietly, her smile fading.

"No," I said, unable to suppress a smile of my own. "I don't think Mr. Darcy was made for country assemblies."

Charlotte shook her head. "Or any sort of assembly at all. How can a man be so disagreeable? And with Mr. Bingley as his friend, no less!"

"Perhaps that is why Mr. Bingley is so eager to befriend everyone else. He must balance out the company he keeps."

Charlotte chuckled at that, though her eyes flicked back toward Mr. Darcy, her expression thoughtful. "Still, there's something about him, isn't there?"

"Something unpleasant, you mean?"

"No, something... steady. You can't quite shake the feeling that he's always in control."

I raised a brow at her. "You find that appealing?"

"Not appealing, exactly." She frowned, considering. "But intriguing. He doesn't seem the type to let anything get the better of him, does he?"

I glanced back toward Mr. Darcy. He was watching Mr. Bingley and Jane dance, his expression as impassive as ever.

"He doesn't," I admitted. "But he also doesn't seem the type to enjoy anything either. Where's the fun in that?"

Charlotte shrugged, her smile returning. "Perhaps he finds enjoyment in other things."

I doubted that very much, but I kept the thought to myself. We had spent enough time analyzing Mr. Darcy for one evening. Whatever his faults—and there were many—I could at least be grateful that he was no threat to Jane's happiness. Mr. Bingley, for all his good nature, seemed unlikely to be swayed by the opinions of his stiff-necked friend.

The evening wore on, and the room grew even more crowded, the air thick with the mingled scents of sweat, perfume, and the increasingly warm bodies pressing closer together. I stayed by Charlotte's side for much of the night, grateful for her company—and her good humor, which made it far easier to ignore the more embarrassing behaviors of my family.

At one point, Jane and Mr. Bingley passed by us, both of them glowing from their second dance, and I smiled at the sight of my sister so obviously happy. If only we could escape Mama's loud declarations long enough to let Jane's natural grace shine through.

And if only Mr. Darcy weren't there to witness the whole evening.

I glanced back toward him one last time just as he turned away from the dance floor. Our eyes met briefly—his expression as hooded as ever—but there was something in his gaze that made me pause.

For a moment, I thought he looked almost... tired. Not the disdain I had seen earlier, but something far more ordinary.

I quickly looked away, unsure what to make of it.

Two

Darcy

"Y ou know," Bingley said, staring at his plate with a dreamy smile, "I believe I have never met a more amiable woman than Miss Bennet."

I nearly choked on my tea. Amiable was one word for it. Passive might have been another. But before I could remark on his absurd infatuation, Caroline Bingley swept in to fill the gap.

"Yes, Miss Bennet is charming, of course," she purred, carefully buttering a piece of toast as though she hadn't been rolling her eyes the entire night before. "So elegant, so composed."

Composed? I glanced at Bingley, half-expecting him to challenge the blatant exaggeration, but he just nodded, eyes shining like a schoolboy. Nothing about that entire family was *composed*. Apparently, he and I had been at two entirely different assemblies.

Louisa Hurst hummed in agreement, adding, "It is unfortunate, though, about the rest of her family."

Caroline Bingley's knife clattered to the plate with a bit too much enthusiasm. "Yes, it is rather difficult to overlook their... boisterous nature. And that mother of hers—dear me, you could hear her voice echoing across the room like a town crier."

I could feel Bingley's distress rising beside me, so I stared harder at my plate and let the sisters continue. There was no need for me to interject. They would do enough damage on their own.

"And those sisters!" Miss Bingley's voice had dropped to a scandalized whisper, though we were hardly in the company of anyone who cared. "That youngest! Lydia, was it? Absolutely wild. Flirting with every man in uniform—"

"Young girls are lively," Bingley interrupted. He was grasping at straws now. "Miss Lydia was just... youthful enthusiasm. It's perfectly harmless."

I nearly rolled my eyes. One more assembly like that, and Miss Lydia Bennet would likely be causing a scandal that would be heard of from here to London.

"Harmless," Miss Bingley repeated with a delicate sniff. "Well, I suppose you're more forgiving than I, dear brother. I only wonder how Miss Bennet can manage to stand out amidst such a... lively family."

I let Caroline Bingley's words hang in the air and pretended not to hear them. Bingley sighed, looking mournfully at his plate as if it might offer him a solution.

"Darcy," he said suddenly, turning to me as though I could save him from the conversation, "you must have noticed Miss Bennet. Was she not the very picture of elegance last night?"

I looked up from my cup, slowly. The cold tea wasn't going to save me from this, apparently. "She was pleasant."

"Pleasant?" Bingley echoed, looking at me as if I'd said fire was hot. "Well, of course. More than that, though. She's delightful."

Miss Bingley's smile tightened. "Delightful, yes... as long as you can overlook the rest of Meryton's rather provincial charms."

"Provincial charms," I muttered under my breath, eyeing Caroline across the table. I wasn't sure whether I was impressed or irritated by her ability to turn snobbery into an art form.

But before anyone could continue the debate over Miss Bennet's superiority despite her family, the door creaked open, and a servant entered, carrying a letter on a silver tray. He crossed the room with the expression of someone who had interrupted one too many of these charming breakfasts and handed it to me.

I frowned, unfolding the letter and reading it over, my mood shifting from mild irritation to outright confusion.

Fitzwilliam Darcy, Esq.
Darcy House, London and Pemberley House,
Derbyshire
Dear Mr. Darcy,

I write to inform you of an unexpected develop-
ment regarding the estate of an elderly widow,
one Miss Isobel McLean, with whom you may
not be acquainted. Her passing last month has
brought to light a connection to your family, and
as such, you have been named the beneficiary of
certain assets and properties under her estate.

This matter requires your immediate atten-
tion, and I urge you to travel to London as soon
as you may to review the legal documents and
finalize the transfer of inheritance. Please come
at your earliest convenience so that we may dis-
cuss the particulars.

Yours faithfully,
John ArthursonSolicitorArthurson & Wilkes,
London

I flipped the letter over as if the back of it might contain further enlightenment, but alas, it was as blank as it was when I broke the seal. A relative I had never heard of? No... I squinted at the letter again. It only said she had a "connection" to my family, which could mean anything under the sun. What in the world...?

"Bad news?" Bingley asked, leaning forward with the kind of wide-eyed curiosity I found mildly alarming.

I folded the letter slowly and placed it next to my plate. "It seems I'm required in London."

Bingley blinked. "London? Whatever for?"

"A matter of inheritance," I said. "From a connection I was not even aware of."

Caroline Bingley raised a brow. "A relative you didn't know? How... strange."

Strange didn't even begin to cover it. McLean? That sounded Scottish, but I had no Scottish relations. That I knew of. But I wasn't about to launch into the complexities of my family tree over breakfast, especially not in the company of Caroline Bingley, who had made it clear that she wished to become a branch in said tree.

"It seems the situation demands my attention," I continued, doing my best to sound as though the whole thing didn't perplex me as much as it did. "I will send for my carriage and leave at once."

Bingley's face fell, and for a moment, I wondered if he might actually pout. "But Darcy, you'll miss the shooting! We've been planning it for weeks!"

I glanced toward the window, where the grey sky had taken a distinctly menacing turn. "The weather promises rain," I said, more to save myself than to comfort him. "I doubt there will be much sport today."

Bingley looked as though he might argue, but one glance outside and his shoulders sagged. "Well, still. It's only a passing shower, I'm sure. You won't be gone too long, will you?"

I took another sip of coffee, considering the letter that lay neatly folded beside me. "I should return by tomorrow, or perhaps the day after next."

Caroline Bingley sighed. "I do hope your business will not detain you too long, Mr. Darcy. We should all feel terribly bereft without your company."

"I'm sure you'll manage," I said, allowing myself the smallest flicker of a smile.

Louisa Hurst laughed lightly. "At least you'll be spared any further... local amusements today."

I couldn't argue with that. The thought of escaping Meryton, if only briefly, was one small consolation.

"Well," Bingley mused, "at least we'll have calls to look forward to, eh? I daresay we shall be full of visiting neighbors, and we shall start calling on our new acquaintances."

A pity I was going to miss that. I stood, pushing my chair back with deliberate calm. "I will prepare for my departure."

Bingley mumbled something about bad timing and poor luck as I excused myself, but my thoughts were already elsewhere. As the door clicked shut behind me, I couldn't help but glance once more at the letter in my hand.

A connection I'd never heard of. Inheritance matters that couldn't wait.

London called, and for once, I was glad of it.

Elizabeth

"I DON'T KNOW WHY you insist on rifling through these old things, Lizzy," my father's voice sounded from the doorway, sounding half-amused and half-exasperated.

I looked up from where I sat cross-legged on the floor of his library, surrounded by books and a few scattered papers I had pulled from the shelf.

"I like history," I replied, without any real guilt. "And you hide all the interesting things in here."

He raised an eyebrow. "It's not hiding. It's *my* library, and I would rather it stay that way."

I grinned, holding up a dusty old book I had just uncovered. "Is this a personal favorite? 'A Complete Account of the Families of Hertfordshire'—sounds positively riveting."

"Thrilling, I assure you," he said dryly, stepping further into the room. "If you enjoy reading about long-dead people with too much land and too little sense."

"I do enjoy that, actually," I said, flipping through the brittle pages with care. "Though I must say, your taste in reading is a bit... practical. You don't have any scandalous letters tucked away in here, do you?"

Father gave me a look over his spectacles. "If I did, I certainly wouldn't tell you."

I let out a mock sigh of disappointment and set the book aside, reaching for another stack of papers. "You must have something of interest to hide in here. Some secret will? A forgotten fortune?"

"What I have in here," he said pointedly, "are old estate records and documents you likely have no business reading."

"That's what makes them interesting," I said with a grin, holding up a particularly aged-looking paper. "Look at this—it's from the year 1700! I'm practically touching history."

"You're touching something dusty," he corrected, stepping closer to peer at the paper in my hand. "And most likely irrelevant."

"Is it?" I squinted at the document, trying to make sense of the elaborate script. "What is it, then? Some kind of land agreement?"

Father sighed. "That, my dear, is a very old lease agreement for a tenant farmer. Hardly riveting."

"Maybe not to you," I said, glancing at it again. "But I find it fascinating how everything is so... connected. The land, the families, the history of it all."

"If you'd been born a son, you'd have made an excellent steward, but a rather useless master. Far too inquisitive for your own good."

"I'll take that as a compliment," I said brightly, rolling up the paper and setting it aside.

Father moved to sit at his desk, shuffling some of the papers I had displaced. "You know, Lizzy, not everything in this library is meant for idle curiosity."

I shrugged, unrepentant. "Perhaps not. But you leave it all lying about as if you're waiting for someone to discover it."

"I leave it all lying about because no one else is usually fool enough to wade through these old ledgers and documents."

"Foolishness or curiosity?" I asked, smiling at him. "There's a fine line between the two."

He chuckled softly, shaking his head. "One you seem determined to dance upon."

I reached for another book, my fingers brushing the worn leather cover. "There's so much history in these pages," I murmured. "All these names and events, shaping everything around us, even now."

Father leaned back in his chair, watching me with an indulgent expression. "And what is it you hope to find in all this history, Lizzy?"

I paused, thinking about it. "Maybe I just want to understand how things work. The estate, the land... why we're all tied to it the way we are."

"And here I thought you only cared for novels."

"I'm more complicated than you give me credit for," I said with a smirk, turning the page in the ancient book I had picked up.

"So you keep reminding me." Eventually, he sighed again, a long-suffering sound I'd heard many times before.

"You really should leave these things alone, you know."

I grinned. "I'll take it under advisement."

Three

Darcy

THE RAIN HAD STARTED up again by the time I reached Arthurson & Wilkes. Fitting, I thought. Of course, it would rain on the day I was dragged away from the comforts of Netherfield for some inheritance I didn't even know existed.

The office was unremarkable. Dark wood, old volumes lining the shelves—what one might expect from any respectable solicitor in London. A man behind the desk looked up as I entered, giving me the kind of look that said he was used to dealing with men of means but found them all rather tedious.

"Mr. Darcy," he said, standing quickly and giving a brief bow. "John Arthurson. Please, do sit."

I did not sit. "You sent for me about an inheritance."

His lips twitched into something like a smile. "Indeed, sir. The matter concerns a recently deceased connection of yours—one Miss Isobel McLean."

McLean. The name didn't spark the faintest recognition. I stared at him, hoping this was some ridiculous mistake. "I don't know anyone by that name."

Arthurson nodded as though this was perfectly expected. "No, I didn't imagine you would. Miss McLean was quite an elderly lady, passed just last month at the age of eighty-three. The connection is somewhat distant, but the legalities are clear. She was... shall we say, an associate of your grandmother's."

I frowned. "An associate?"

"Yes, it seems your grandmother—on your father's side—had a brief friendship with Miss McLean before her death. The details are not necessarily clarified, but we do have a record of Miss McLean living in Derbyshire some twenty years ago." He cleared his throat. "It's a rather convoluted connection, but Miss McLean named you in her will as a beneficiary, as you are your grandmother's closest living descendant."

I straightened, crossing my arms. "And what, exactly, am I inheriting?"

He rifled through a few papers on his desk before pulling out a document. "Primarily some personal effects, a modest property near Edinburgh, and a few heirlooms. It's not of any significant monetary value, but the will was quite specific in naming you as the recipient."

I resisted the urge to roll my eyes. "Why me?"

Arthurson coughed. "It seems your grandmother left quite an impression on Miss McLean in her later years. She had no close family left, and as a mark of her esteem for your grandmother, she chose to pass on what remained of her estate to you."

So, I was being handed down a collection of ancient relics from some woman I'd never met, purely because she once liked my grandmother. Wonderful.

"And the heirlooms?" I asked, wondering if this was going to involve some ancient piece of furniture or worse—a collection of cats.

"Yes, there's one in particular mentioned in the will," Arthurson said, pulling out another document. "A brooch. According to the inventory list, it's a white rose brooch—a piece of jewelry Miss McLean treasured and kept from her family's history. There's some... sentimental value attached to it, I believe."

A brooch. Just what every gentleman longs to acquire. I could almost hear Caroline Bingley's shriek of delight at the thought of a new bauble to pin to her gown.

But there was something odd in the way Arthurson said it. *Sentimental value.* A brooch hardly seemed the sort of thing a solicitor would put much weight behind, unless...

"You seem hesitant," I said, narrowing my eyes at him. "Is there something else I should know?"

He shifted uncomfortably, avoiding my gaze for a moment before answering. "Well, there are some... unusual stories attached to the brooch. Nothing official, of course. But there were rumors—local legends, you understand—about its significance. Some say it's been passed down through the family since the Jacobite Risings."

I raised a brow. "Jacobite?"

Arthurson nodded. "Yes, sir. The McLeans were known to have supported the Stuart cause, and the brooch is thought to have belonged to a member of the family who was lost after the Battle of Culloden. Some say his spirit lingers—though, of course, that's just superstition."

I stared at him, waiting for him to admit he was joking. When he didn't, I let out a short laugh. "You mean to tell me this brooch is supposedly haunted?"

Arthurson cleared his throat again. "That's one way of putting it, sir."

"Absurd," I muttered, turning to look out the window. The rain had picked up, pounding against the glass. It matched my mood.

"Yes, well, I'm certain there's nothing to be concerned about," Arthurson added quickly. "Most of these old family heirlooms come with some kind of legend. It's purely decorative, I assure you."

Of course. Because what else could this day possibly throw at me? A haunted brooch, a friend of my grandmother's I'd never heard of, and now some nonsense about Culloden ghosts.

Still, the sooner I dealt with this, the sooner I could return to Netherfield and be done with it.

"I'll take the brooch," I said shortly. "And the rest of the inheritance?"

"We'll arrange the details for the property transfer in due time. But for now, the personal effects, including the brooch, are already here in London. I can have them sent to your residence at your convenience."

I nodded. "Do that. I'll review the rest when I return to Pemberley."

Arthurson gave a small bow, clearly relieved the meeting had concluded. "Very good, Mr. Darcy. If you have any further questions, you know where to find me."

I took the letter from his desk, pocketing it without another glance. The sooner I left this office, the better.

The idea of returning to Netherfield suddenly seemed far more appealing than it had that morning.

And perhaps this time, the rain would let up.

Elizabeth

"IT IS SUCH AN honor for Jane, of course," Mama was saying as she bustled around the sitting room, holding up first one and then another sample of ribbon beside Jane's gown to see which suited it best. "An invitation to dine at Netherfield! And only a day after the assembly. You see, Mr. Bingley is quite taken with her!"

I watched Jane as Mama darted around, issuing instructions as though preparing her for a royal engagement rather than a simple dinner. Jane smiled and nodded in all the right places, but I could see the faintest hint of hesitation in her eyes.

"You *do* want to go, don't you, Jane?" I asked, watching her carefully.

"Oh, yes," she said quickly. "I'm looking forward to it."

But there it was again, that flicker of uncertainty. I knew she liked Mr. Bingley, of course—who wouldn't? He was all charm and smiles. But dining at Netherfield, with that gentleman's cheerful presence sadly absent this evening, wasn't likely to be the most relaxing evening. Especially when one took into account that Caroline Bingley could be as sharp as her gown was fashionable.

"It's only a few miles," Mama continued, adjusting Jane's bonnet as though it were a crown, "and a fine day for a ride. You shall go on horseback."

I blinked, glancing at the window where the sky had taken on a distinctly gray hue. The clouds were thick and dark, promising rain that might begin at any moment. "On horseback?"

"Of course," Mama said. "The carriage is too much of a bother for such a short journey. Besides, a little ride will give her a healthy glow! Jane always looks loveliest with a bit of color in her cheeks."

I shot Jane a look, and she gave me the faintest smile in return. She knew better than to argue with Mama once she had her mind set on something. I, on the other hand, had no such restraint.

"It looks like it will rain," I said, more firmly this time. "Perhaps the carriage would be a better option."

"Nonsense, Lizzy!" Mama replied, dismissing me with a wave of her hand. "The rain won't start for hours. And besides, a bit of fresh air will do her good."

A bit of fresh air? More like a thorough soaking. But before I could say anything more, Jane was already stepping toward the door, her riding gloves in hand.

"I'll be well enough," she said. "It's not far, after all."

I sighed, knowing this wasn't a battle I would win. Jane was too good-natured to protest, and I could hardly argue with both her and Mama in the same breath.

"Well," I said, following her to the door, "at least wear your warmest cloak. If it does start to rain—"

"I'll manage," she interrupted, giving me a gentle smile. "I promise, Lizzy. It's only dinner."

Only dinner. Yes, but dinner at Netherfield, with the weight of Mama's ambitions hanging over her like a cloud just as heavy as the one outside.

"Very well," I muttered, though I wasn't satisfied. "But if you catch a cold, I'll never forgive Mama."

Mama's voice floated from the sitting room, as if she could hear every word despite being across the house. "Jane, don't dawdle! You mustn't be late for such an important engagement."

Jane gave me a quick, rueful look, then stepped out into the brisk air. I watched as she mounted the horse with practiced ease, the sky already darker than it had been mere moments ago.

"Be careful," I called after her. She waved, offering me one last smile before urging the horse forward.

I stood in the doorway for a long moment, watching her figure disappear down the lane. The wind had picked up, rustling the leaves in a way that made me even more uneasy.

"Well," I muttered to myself, "this ought to be a disaster."

Darcy

T HE CARRIAGE ROLLED TO a stop outside my townhouse, and I stepped out into the afternoon air. I had hoped the rain would ease by now, but it seemed London had no intention of obliging. The streets were wet, and the sky remained a dull gray, though the steady drizzle had at least turned into a fine mist.

The door opened before I even had time to knock. Mrs. Hodges, my housekeeper, was already standing there, hands folded, ready for whatever instruction I might give.

"Welcome back, sir," she said with a small curtsy. "Shall I have the kitchen prepare a full supper for you this evening?"

I paused in the entryway, shrugging off my coat and considering her question. The familiar smell of my own home and the quiet warmth of the house were inviting enough, but I was annoyed enough after wasting an entire day, coming to London just to claim a few silly baubles. The sooner I got my carriage turned around, back for Netherfield, the sooner I could forget about this whole blasted day.

Before I could answer Mrs. Hodges, there was a firm knock at the door. A footman promptly stepped forward to open it, revealing a man in a dark coat holding a large, neatly sealed box. He bowed slightly before speaking.

"From Arthurson & Wilkes, sir," he said, glancing between me and the footman as he stepped inside.

I stared at the box. The contents were inside—the brooch, the other items from Isobel McLean's estate. I had no desire to open it just now to look. In fact, the idea of sitting alone in the quiet of my study, rifling through the belongings of a woman I had never met, seemed like the worst possible use of my afternoon.

If I left now—immediately—I could be back at Netherfield just after dark. I'd miss supper, but Bingley wouldn't mind, and frankly, I would rather that than trouble Mrs. Hodges to make up my room for just one night. Besides, then Georgiana would hear I was in town and I would have no peace until I called on her and Lady Matlock, smoked some cigars with my uncle, got dragged to the club with Richard...

I made my decision. "No need for supper, Mrs. Hodges. I'll be leaving again shortly."

She blinked, clearly surprised, but only nodded. "Very good, sir. Shall I have your room prepared for your return?"

"That won't be necessary." I glanced at the box once more. "Have this placed in my carriage. I'll look through it later."

Mrs. Hodges gave another curtsy before signaling for a footman to handle the task. I turned away from the door, stepping into the house for only a brief moment to collect my things.

I had planned to rest here, spend a night while attending to other matters in town, but now I found the thought of staying in London unbearable. The house felt too quiet, too empty, and I was too irritated with the contents of that box. The idea of sitting alone, poring over old relics and trying to unravel some distant family connection to a woman I didn't even know—it all seemed pointless.

"I'll be leaving straightaway," I said. "No need for further preparations."

"As you wish, sir," she replied. "Shall I have a basket readied for you?"

"No need," I said, already stepping out into the misting rain. "I'll manage."

The box was loaded into the carriage, the horses already stamping impatiently as I climbed inside. I settled into my seat, glancing briefly at the sealed package sitting on the opposite bench. It sat there, unassuming, a simple wooden box. Someone's entire life, their most prized possessions. And now they were mine to dust. I sighed.

As the carriage jolted forward, I forced myself to look away. The rain began to tap softly against the windows, and I settled back, determined not to think of what was inside until I had to.

The sooner I returned to Netherfield, the sooner I could put this ridiculous business behind me.

Elizabeth

THREE HOURS LATER, I found myself sitting in the drawing room, my needlework abandoned beside me as I listened to the steady drum of rain against the windows. It had started only half an hour after Jane had left, and I could feel a knot of anxiety tightening in my chest with each passing minute.

"She's not back yet?" I asked, for what felt like the tenth time, glancing toward the door as though expecting her to materialize out of thin air.

Mama, who had been sitting by the fire with her sewing, looked up with a frown. "Of course not, Lizzy. She's dining at Netherfield. I'm sure they've kept her for some conversation or perhaps even a little music. Mr. Bingley is quite attentive, you know."

"Mr. Bingley was not even to be there, Mama. Miss Bingley's note said he was dining with Colonel Forster this evening."

"Oh, but surely the ladies have detained her at least until his return. Like enough, they are all singing and playing until the gentleman comes home."

Or she's drenched, chilled to the bone, and stranded somewhere along the road, I thought grimly, but didn't say.

I stood, pacing across the room to peer out the window. The rain was coming down harder now, turning the lane into a muddy mess, and I cursed under my breath. If Jane was not chilled or feverish after her first ride through the rain, the second—in the dark—would finish her off. Why hadn't I insisted on the carriage?

"She'll catch cold," I muttered, more to myself than anyone else.

Mama sighed, setting aside her sewing. "Lizzy, you worry too much. You will see, all will be well! And even if she does catch a small chill, it will hardly harm her. Why, Mr. Bingley will probably insist on nursing her back to health himself!"

I rolled my eyes but said nothing, returning to my seat by the fire. Mama's matchmaking fantasies knew no bounds. To hear her tell it, a little cold might be exactly the thing to seal the match. Still, my stomach twisted in worry, and I found myself glancing at the door every few minutes, hoping Jane would return before the night grew any worse.

Four

Darcy

THE SKY WAS WELL into dusk by the time the carriage rolled up the long drive to Netherfield. The faint glow from the windows spilled out into the darkening landscape, giving the house a warm, almost welcoming appearance. I was tired, sore from the hours spent in the carriage, and more than ready for a quiet evening without interruption.

As I stepped down from the carriage, a footman approached to take my coat and offer assistance. "Have this box taken up to my room," I said, gesturing toward the large wooden crate being unloaded from the back. "Be careful with it. Dratted thing is likely to fall apart."

He nodded and set about the task without a word.

I made my way inside, expecting the quiet of a late evening, but instead, I was greeted by Bingley bounding into the entryway with all the enthusiasm of a man who had forgotten what exhaustion felt like.

"Darcy!" he exclaimed, his face lighting up with surprise. "We weren't expecting you back tonight. Thought you said you meant to stay in town."

"Changed my mind," I said, brushing off my gloves and handing them to the waiting servant. "It was a simple matter. I'd rather return here than linger in London over something trivial."

Caroline Bingley and Louisa Hurst appeared from the drawing room, both offering slightly too-bright smiles of greeting. I could tell by the way Caroline's eyes gleamed that she had been hoping for a different outcome to my absence—perhaps one that involved all of them returning to London after me, and her playing hostess in my house.

"Mr. Darcy," Caroline cooed, moving closer. "You must be utterly exhausted after such a sudden trip. But we are ever so pleased to have you back so soon."

"Yes," Louisa added, glancing over at her brother. "You've missed quite a lot."

"I'm sure," I muttered, more to myself than anyone else. I had no doubt that whatever trivial events had occurred in my absence, Bingley and his sisters would make far more of them than they deserved.

Bingley clapped a hand on my shoulder, steering me toward the sitting room. "Come, Darcy, have a drink with us before you head upstairs. You must tell us all about this mysterious inheritance of yours. You had me intrigued when you left!"

"I doubt it's anything worth mentioning," I replied, though I allowed myself to be led toward the decanters.

"But you never know!" Bingley poured a generous amount of brandy into a glass and handed it to me. "Old estates, strange relatives—it sounds like something out of a novel."

"It's neither strange nor worth any great excitement," I said, accepting the drink. "Someone connected through my grandmother. The inheritance amounts to little more than personal effects."

"And yet, you went to London for it," Caroline remarked with an arched brow, clearly hoping for something more sensational.

I took a sip of the brandy, letting the warmth spread through me. "Yes, and now I'm back. That's all there is to it."

Bingley laughed. "Well, you've missed quite the dinner in the meantime. We dined with Colonel Forster, the local militia commander. Good fellow, quite a few stories. Hurst particularly enjoyed him."

Hurst, who had appeared in the doorway just moments earlier, gave a sleepy nod from his position by the fireplace. "He has a taste for good brandy," Hurst said lazily. "That's enough for me."

"And the ladies?" I asked, raising an eyebrow as I glanced toward Caroline and Louisa. "I'm sure you had your own amusements."

Caroline's smile stretched a little wider, and I could tell she had been waiting for this part of the conversation. "Oh, indeed. We had the pleasure of inviting Miss Bennet to dine with us earlier today."

I could see Bingley's expression brighten instantly at the mention of her name, but it was Louisa who continued the story, her tone far more amused than it should have been. "Poor Miss Bennet arrived just as the heavens opened. Absolutely drenched."

Caroline nodded. "She arrived on *horseback*, of all things, just before the rain came pouring down. Completely soaked and chilled to the bone. Naturally, we couldn't let her return in such a state."

"So, you put her up for the night?" I asked, though I already knew the answer.

"Of course," Caroline said, waving her hand dismissively. "We've only just sent word to Longbourn not half an hour ago. I expect her mother will be overjoyed at the situation."

That much was certainly true. I could already imagine Mrs. Bennet crowing with triumph, no doubt convinced that this was all part of some grand plan to ensnare Bingley for her daughter.

Bingley, of course, looked entirely too pleased with this turn of events. "I'm glad we could offer Miss Bennet shelter. It's the least we could do after such an unfortunate accident."

I said nothing, though I felt the familiar tug of annoyance. It was hardly an accident that Mrs. Bennet had sent her eldest daughter out into the rain on horseback. The woman was shameless in her ambitions. But I kept my thoughts to myself and finished my brandy.

"Well," I said, setting the glass down, "I appreciate the welcome, but I believe I'll retire for the evening."

Bingley stood, smiling warmly. "Of course. You must be exhausted after the journey."

Caroline tilted her head, watching me closely. "Are you sure you won't stay up a little longer, Mr. Darcy? We've missed your company terribly."

I gave a brief nod toward her and Mrs. Hurst, keeping my tone polite but firm. "Perhaps tomorrow. Good night."

Without waiting for further protest, I left the room and headed up the stairs, the long day finally catching up with me. As I reached the landing, the footman was already outside my room, the wooden box from Arthurson & Wilkes placed carefully by the door.

The thought of going through its contents was exhausting in itself. But for now, it could wait.

I TOSSED AND TURNED for what felt like an hour, trying to ignore the dull ache in my lower back. Too many hours in that blasted carriage, bouncing on uneven roads. And the brandy, though welcome at the time, had left my head muzzy and restless. Sleep was an impossible prospect.

With a groan, I rolled out of bed, stretching slowly in the dimly lit room. My muscles protested with every movement, stiff from being held taut in a rocking carriage over bad roads. I braced myself against the bedpost, trying to relieve the tightness in my back.

I glanced around, hoping something in the quiet stillness might lull me into some kind of comfort, and my eyes landed on the box. The one from the solicitor.

It sat there, as unremarkable as the inheritance it supposedly held. I hadn't the energy to care about it earlier, but now, with sleep nowhere in sight, it seemed a better distraction than pacing the room like a restless ghost.

I padded over to the box, the floor creaking beneath me as I bent to lift the lid. It gave way easily, revealing a collection of old items, each more underwhelming than the last.

I sighed, rubbing my temples, and started picking through the contents.

First, a few yellowed papers—receipts for some sort of... bread? Stew? Old letters, none of which seemed remotely interesting. I skimmed over the dates. Nothing out of the ordinary. Some were written in the faded hand of a person long dead. Others looked like deeds or records of some minor transaction, no more intriguing than a pile of estate ledgers.

Next, a small portrait. It was cracked along the edges, the face of a woman barely visible under the wear and grime. I stared at it for a moment, wondering vaguely if this was Isobel McLean herself or some other forgotten soul in the McLean family. There was no name, no inscription.

I set it aside, leaning back and rubbing the tight knot of muscle at my shoulder. The night was eerily quiet, the faint ticking of the clock the only sound.

I reached back into the box, almost wishing I hadn't bothered. There was nothing remarkable here, nothing that explained why I had been summoned to London. It was simply the debris of a life long ended, and none of it had anything to do with me.

Finally, I spotted the brooch, sitting at the very bottom of the box. It was small, barely the size of my palm, and almost seemed to glow faintly in the low fire light. The white rose symbol was unmistakable, delicate, and intricate despite its age. I picked it up, turning it over in my fingers. It felt oddly cold.

As I examined it, I felt a sharp sting.

I cursed under my breath, dropping the brooch. A small bead of blood welled up on my finger where I'd pricked myself on the point of one of the rose's metal thorns. How ridiculous—an old piece of jewelry, sharp enough to draw blood.

I moved to wipe the blood away, but then something strange happened. A chill swept through the room, sudden and biting, despite the fire still burning low in the hearth. My vision blurred, the room tilting slightly as if the very air had shifted around me.

The brooch on the floor seemed to pulse, as though it were alive.

What the devil had Bingley put in that brandy? I shook my head to clear my vision, but when that did not work, I stumbled backward, my body heavy and sluggish. The room had grown darker, the shadows pressing in on me, but before I could make sense of it, a figure appeared. It was sudden—there, in the blink of an eye.

A man, tall and wild-eyed, rushed at me with outstretched arms. His face, twisted with fury or madness, locked onto mine.

"A bloody sassenach!" he bellowed.

The cold hit me like a wall. My heart lurched in terror, my legs buckled beneath me, and then—nothing.

I CAME TO WITH my face pressed against the cold wooden floor. My heart was pounding in my ears, and for a moment, I wasn't entirely sure where I was. The memories were hazy—flashes of cold, a voice shouting, and... a man?

I pushed myself up, wincing at the stiffness in my body, and glanced around the room. The brooch was lying a few feet away from me, perfectly still and completely unremarkable.

For a brief moment, I just stared at it. Then I looked down at my hand. There it was—a small, red mark where the thing had pricked my finger. I ran my thumb over it, half-expecting some other sign of what I had seen. But there was nothing. No cuts, no bruises, no indication that I had just... fainted?

I pushed myself upright, still breathing heavily. The room felt colder than it had been before, but my head was clearer. The brandy. That *had* to be it. Probably a bad lot—I would speak to Bingley about improving the quality of his cellars. I had been half-asleep, over-tired, and muddled from bad drink. It was preposterous, really. I never faint.

Feeling slightly ridiculous, I rubbed my face, trying to shake off the lingering disorientation. Was I feverish? My skin felt like the sticky residue of perspiration, but that was it. No warmth, no obvious sign of illness.

"Get a hold of yourself," I muttered, glancing around the room as though the shadows themselves were listening.

I moved to pick up the brooch, the papers I'd scattered across the floor, and tried to convince myself that nothing had happened. Because nothing *did* happen. The cold air in the room was simply my imagination—a draft from the chimney, perhaps. The strange figure I had seen—well, that had to be the brandy playing tricks on me. It was nothing.

But just as I stooped to gather the rest of the scattered papers, the door swung open, and in walked... well, I'd no idea who, precisely.

A man, just as I'd seen before—tall, broad-shouldered, and every bit as out of place as I had feared. But this time, he was carrying a bottle of something amber-colored, and before I could so much as process what was happening, he sniffed the bottle with a look of disdain.

"It's no' verra good, this stuff," he said, his voice thick with a Scottish accent. "But I s'pose it'll do."

I froze, my hands still halfway to the floor, staring at the man. My breath caught in my throat. This was *not* the brandy.

He stood there, completely at ease, glancing around my room as though he had just stumbled into it for a friendly chat. He looked like something from a bad theatre production—his clothes worn and faded, his hair wild and untamed, and his face... Well, his face was almost bored.

"Who the devil are you?" I demanded, my voice sharp, though I wasn't entirely sure it wasn't shaking too.

He raised an eyebrow, as if my question had been unworthy of his attention. "Who the devil are *ye?* Ye've got a lot of nerve, askin' me that in *my* room!"

I blinked, trying to make sense of the situation. "What—no, this is *my* room. You—you're the one who's—"

"Aye, I'm the one," he interrupted, waving his hand as if to dismiss my entire train of thought. "And now ye've gone and brought *me* here, too. So, let's nae waste time arguin' about whose room it is, eh?"

I gaped at him, unable to find words for a long moment. I glanced toward the door. Was I still fainting? Was this some twisted dream?

He sighed, apparently unimpressed by my silence, and pulled out the chair at my desk, plopping down into it as if he owned the place. "So, who are ye, then?"

I stared at him, still crouched half over the floor, my mind too numb to think of anything clever. "Darcy," I muttered. "Fitzwilliam Darcy."

He gave a nod, eyeing me with mild disdain. "Aye, a proper name for a proper sassenach. Ye've the look of someone wi' more titles than sense."

That stirred something like pride or dignity, or perhaps just stupidity in me. I straightened. "I hold no titles, sir, but I will have you know, the D'Arcy heritage is a proud one, all the way from the Normans who—"

He leaned back in the chair, shaking his head with what could only be described as disappointment. "I ken no' but here I am, saddled wi' an Englishman. Of all the folk to get tied to, it had to be a sassenach who faints like a lass in a church pew." He shot me a look as if my fainting had been a personal offense. "A Scot would've stood his ground."

"I— I fainted?"

"Aye, ye did." He seemed quite amused by this fact, leaning back in my chair with a smirk. "Down like a sack o' potatoes. No' even a wee fight."

My legs wobbled slightly beneath me as I backed away from the stranger. I finally found my voice, pushing past the numbness that had kept me frozen. "You're trespassing," I said, standing up straighter and feeling a spark of my old self return. "I'll wake the household if I must. Call the footmen. You'll be thrown out on your ear before you can say another word."

"Aye, is that right? Gonna wake the whole house for a wee tantrum, are ye?" He crossed his arms, his eyes dancing with amusement. "Go on then. I'm sure the footmen would love to see ye blubbering aboot ghosts at this hour."

I bristled at his tone. "I don't blubber, and I don't believe in ghosts."

He raised an eyebrow, smirking. "Then what're ye so worked up aboot, lad?"

My mouth opened, but no words came out. It was maddening, how casually he sat there—in *my* room!—as if my threats were nothing more than an idle game.

Then, as if to prove his point, he leaned over and casually swept his hand through the wood of the table beside him, his fingers sinking into the solid surface as though it were made of water. My heart stopped, and I hardly know how I kept from crumpling again as he pulled back, producing a pen knife as if from thin air. He inspected it lazily, then tossed it onto the table with a soft clink. "That'll serve ye well."

I stared, my pulse pounding in my ears. That was *not* possible. Was it? It *wasn't*... right?

"Ye see?" Ewan said with a grin. "Ye're havin' yerself a fine wee tantrum, and fer what? Ye canna throw me out."

I slapped my own face—hard enough to feel the sting, as if that would somehow wake me from this madness. But when I opened my eyes again, he was still there, looking more amused than ever.

"You're not real," I said firmly, my voice shaking only slightly. "This... this is absurd. I'm imagining all of this."

He sniffed the bottle again, pulling a face as if I'd just insulted his honor. "Aye, well, if I'm no' real, then I've got nae business drinkin' this swill, do I?"

I shook my head, my hand tightening on the back of the chair to steady myself. "Who *are* you?" I demanded again, my voice rising with the frustration of being completely unmoored.

The man tilted his head, considering me for a moment. "Ewan," he said finally, as though I should have known all along. "Ewan Douglas Malcom McLean."

My blood ran cold. *McLean*. Isobel McLean.

I gaped at him, my throat tight. "Mclean... The brooch..." I whispered.

His eyes glinted. "McLean, ye've got it, lad. There's nae wrong with your hearing."

I stared at him, my mind struggling to make sense of what was happening. "But... you're dead," I said slowly.

He raised his bottle in mock toast. "Aye, tha's the long an' short of it, lad."

And then I did the only thing a sensible man could do in such a situation.

I sat down hard on the bed, rubbing my face with my hands, and muttered, "I need more brandy."

Five

Elizabeth

I WOKE EARLY, DESPITE a night of restless tossing, thanks to a nagging worry in the pit of my stomach. Jane had not returned. The rain had come down hard the night before, and though we had received word that she was staying at Netherfield, I couldn't help but imagine her shivering in a strange room, her cold getting worse by the hour.

Throwing back the covers, I quickly dressed and hurried downstairs, hoping for some news. The early morning light filtered weakly through the windows as I reached the breakfast room, only to find my mother already seated with Lydia and Kitty, conspiring about something.

"She's certainly staying another day," Mama declared as if it were the most obvious thing in the world, her hands fluttering over her tea cup. "You mark my words, Lizzy, this is all for the best. What could be more advantageous than Jane falling ill at Netherfield? Mr. Bingley won't be able to help himself—he'll be bound to offer every comfort and kindness!"

I stared at her, incredulous. "She's ill, Mama. And no doubt uncomfortable in a strange house. How can you be so certain this is for the best?"

Mama tutted, waving her hand as if I were fretting over nothing. "Oh, nonsense, Lizzy. Jane is perfectly well—just a touch of a cold. And she's with Mr. Bingley! Do you know how many girls would give anything to be in her position?"

"Yes," I muttered, grabbing a piece of bread from the table. "But those girls aren't shivering in some drafty guest room with a cold."

Lydia, far less concerned than I was, giggled. "Perhaps Mr. Bingley is already by her bedside, offering to sponge her forehead."

My patience thinned. "Enough, Lydia. This is no laughing matter."

"Honestly, Lizzy," Mama interjected, setting her cup down with a clatter, "you worry too much. A girl must make the most of every opportunity, and Jane is doing just that—whether by chance or design. Mr. Bingley is as good as smitten!"

I pressed my lips together, debating how much I should argue. There was no point in reasoning with my mother when she had already decided that Jane's cold was somehow a victory for the Bennet family.

"Has anyone heard from her this morning?" I asked, hoping to divert the conversation back to something useful.

"Not yet," Mama replied, sounding far too pleased with herself. "But I'm sure news will arrive soon. They're likely all fussing over Jane as we speak!"

I sighed, pushing back from the table. "If there's no word by mid-morning, I'll walk to Netherfield myself to check on her."

Mama's eyes widened in alarm. "Walk? You'll do no such thing! What will people think—especially Mr. Bingley—if you appear at Netherfield all flushed and untidy?"

I raised my eyebrows. "What will people think if Jane is left there sick and I do nothing? I'll be perfectly well, Mama."

"You most certainly will not," she declared, her voice rising with a mixture of frustration and disbelief. "It's far too improper. And in this weather? You'll be soaked to the bone before you even arrive, and then I shall have *two* sick daughters!"

"But Mama, are there not *two* single gentlemen there?" Kitty pointed out.

"If the other even counts as a gentleman, and I shan't give him that much credit. Mr. Darcy is not worth suffering a cold for. No, Lizzy, I absolutely forbid it. You will die and have nothing to show for it."

"I've walked farther in worse weather," I retorted, already moving toward the door. "Besides, Jane may need me."

Mama made one last attempt to protest, but I was already reaching for my bonnet. I couldn't sit idly by and leave Jane to the care of the Bingley sisters—who, while polite, had never struck me as the nurturing type. Jane would at least have the comfort of her family in her misery.

Darcy

I WOKE WITH A pounding in my skull, my mouth as dry as sand, and the distinct sensation that something was terribly wrong.

For one, I was lying face-down at the foot of the bed, wearing breeches and a rumpled shirt for some reason, my head resting uncomfortably on top of the covers like some discarded piece of baggage. My limbs felt stiff, and my stomach churned with the unmistakable queasiness of too much brandy.

I groaned, dragging myself upright, and immediately rubbed my head. The ache in my temples flared painfully, and I pressed my hands harder against my scalp as though I could knead the headache out of existence. What on earth had happened last night?

Flashes of strange images crossed my mind—dark shadows, a wild-eyed man, and... what had he been saying? Something about lousy whisky? Nonsense. Complete and utter nonsense.

I let out a ragged sigh. It had to have been the brandy. Far too much of it. I had not thought I drank that much—just a nightcap with Bingley—but there was an empty bottle on the floor.

That must have been what happened. I'd imagined it all. Had too much to drink and imagined it all. No wonder I felt like I'd been trampled by a horse.

"This is absurd," I muttered, my voice rough from sleep. "Just a wild dream."

I swung my legs off the bed, stumbling slightly as I stood. My body protested every movement, aching from being twisted in an awkward position for what must have been hours. Too much drink. Too little sense. I should have known better than to let Bingley talk me into staying up for that nightcap.

Still grumbling to myself, I staggered over to the basin. A good, stiff splash of cold water on my face would surely clear the last remnants of this ridiculous dream. I leaned over, doused my face, and wiped my eyes with a towel.

But when I glanced up at the mirror, my heart nearly stopped.

There, reflected behind me, was the wild-eyed man again—Ewan, if I remembered that part of the dream correctly—looking over my shoulder with an almost curious expression.

I froze, every muscle locking up in terror. For a split second, I told myself this couldn't be real. But when he raised an eyebrow, I screamed.

Not the dignified, stern kind of shout one might expect from a man like me—oh no. This was a full-throated, soul-leaving-my-body sort of scream, the kind usually reserved for surprise proposals and armed highwaymen. I bolted for the door, my feet sliding on the floorboards, limbs flailing. All thoughts of composure, breeding, and every shred of decency went flying out the window.

"Ach, lad! There's nae need to keen like a banshee!" his voice trailed after me, but I was too busy fleeing for my life to care.

Out into the hall I ran, my untucked shirt billowing around me, bare feet slapping against the floor in a manner I was sure would haunt me later. I didn't care. I just had to get out.

I reached the landing and there he was, standing at the bottom of the stairs like he'd been there all along, arms folded, face full of complete boredom.

"Yer no' gonna outrun me, ye know," he called up, looking for all the world like he was lecturing a child about stealing jam.

I let out a sound somewhere between a yelp and a very manly grunt—no one would ever call it a squeak, certainly not—and spun around, charging back the way I came. The panic bubbling inside me surged like some wild animal, and reason had completely fled the scene, much like I was trying to.

"Ye'll wear yersel' oot, lad!" Ewan called, his voice infuriatingly casual, as if this were all a bit of morning exercise.

I pelted down the corridor, headlong into the next staircase. This was absurd. This couldn't be happening! Ghosts weren't real, and even if they were, they had the good sense to remain in tragic ballads, not in my bedroom.

But then, halfway down the stairs, I skidded to a halt. Ewan was standing at the bottom again, looking far too pleased with himself. This man—this ghost—was popping up like an unwanted relative at a dinner party.

"Ach, come, Darcy, this is gettin' a wee bit daft." He gave a long-suffering sigh, as though he were speaking to a child having a tantrum over vegetables. "Ye'd think ye'd ne'er laid eyes on a spirit afore."

I let out another undignified yelp and darted down the hall, heart hammering in my ears—or was that my pride, beating itself to death after this series of humiliations?

This was insanity. Complete, unadulterated madness. But still, I had no desire to be seen by anyone else in this ridiculous state. The servants were stirring already, and the very idea of Mrs. Nicholls spotting me, barefoot and wild-eyed, tearing down the hall like a madman, made me consider launching myself out of a window.

I didn't have the courage for that, though, so I did the next best thing.

I spotted the service staircase, hidden away near the far end of the hall. I lunged for it like a man lunging for the last lifeboat on a sinking ship. Flinging open the door, I threw myself down the narrow, creaking steps two at a time. There wasn't much space to maneuver, but it wasn't like I was doing much thinking anyway.

"Ach, runnin' off now, are ye? Ye'll nae get far, lad. I'm stuck with ye, like it or no'!"

I wasn't listening. I couldn't be. If I slowed down for even a moment, I'd have to face the fact that my life had taken a sharp, deeply unwelcome detour into the world of ghosts and curses. Either that, or it was the worst hangover I'd had since university.

Down the stairs I went, hurtling myself toward the back of the house. Each step groaned beneath my weight, and I could practically hear the house mocking me for my complete and utter lack of dignity. But I kept going. I had no other choice.

The moment I hit the stone floor, I slammed open the door to the servant's entrance and practically fell out into the cold morning air, my feet skidding on the wet ground. I clung to the side of the house, gasping, hair sticking to my face in an undignified and, frankly, sweaty mess.

The chill of the dawn hit me, sharp and biting, and I stood there, panting like a hare that had just escaped the hounds. I had never been so grateful for fresh air in my life, but I also had never been more utterly, completely, certifiably done with everything.

"I'm going mad," I muttered to myself. "That's it. I've lost my mind."

But I didn't dare look behind me. If that horrid Scotsman appeared again, I'd likely faint outright, and that was a humiliation I wasn't ready to face just yet.

Elizabeth

T HE MORNING COULDN'T HAVE been more beautiful. The rain had washed everything clean, leaving the air crisp and the sky a brilliant blue, dotted with a few
lingering clouds. The trees, rich with autumn colors, glistened with drops of water, and
the smell of damp earth filled the air as I walked. My shoes squelched occasionally in the
mud, but otherwise, I was perfectly comfortable.

Mama had been completely wrong. There wasn't a drop of rain in sight. The only
danger I faced was the mud beneath my feet—and perhaps the odd look I might get for
cutting across the fields to reach Netherfield more quickly.

I rounded a small grove of trees, the great house just coming into view, when—

A man came hurtling across the lawn, arms flailing, shirt untucked, and with no
waistcoat or jacket, screaming at the top of his lungs.

It took me a moment to realize it was... good heavens, it was *Mr. Darcy!*

His breeches were muddy, his hair in wild disarray, and his chest heaved as he ran.
I stood frozen in place, blinking at the sight before me. Was someone attacking him?
I squinted into the distance but saw... no one. There was not a soul to be seen except
for Darcy, fists pumping like a bellows, his face pale as though he had just seen the devil
himself.

"Get away from me!" he thundered into the empty air, skidding around a bush with
all the grace of a madman in flight.

I stood rooted to the spot, my mind racing to catch up with what my eyes were seeing.
Surely, there was someone after him. There *had* to be. But no matter how hard I squinted
into the distance, I saw... nothing. No one.

I stared, mouth slightly agape. I had seen Mr. Darcy look many things in the one evening of my acquaintance with him—aloof, brooding, proud—but this was... unexpected. He rounded a bush, skidding slightly on the wet ground, and suddenly found himself face-to-face with me.

We both froze.

His chest heaved, and his wild, panicked eyes locked onto mine. For a long moment, neither of us moved. I opened my mouth to say something—what, I wasn't sure—but the words died in my throat as he straightened, attempting to look dignified despite the mud and the fact that his shirt was barely hanging on his shoulders. His hair clung to his forehead, his shirt flapping and covered in mud. He looked utterly... undone.

I blinked, trying to make sense of the situation. And then I blushed because, well... his attire hid very little.

"Miss Bennet," he rasped, trying to smooth his hair with one hand, though it did little good. He tugged at his shirt as though that would magically restore some shred of dignity. "Good... good morning."

I blinked. "Good morning to you, Mr. Darcy." I glanced around the empty lawn. "Ah... out for some exercise?"

His nostrils flared. "Do I look like a man out enjoying some sport this morning?"

I pursed my lips. "You look like a man running for your life. I only ask because... well... *who* exactly were you running from?"

His eyes darted wildly over my shoulder, and without warning, he let out a high-pitched yelp, pointing just past me. "Him!" he cried, his voice cracking. "Right there!"

I whipped around, my heart surging against my ribs in sudden terror.

There was no one. Just an empty lawn, the trees swaying gently in the breeze. I turned back to him, eyebrows raised. "Mr. Darcy... there is no one there."

His eyes went wide as though I had just suggested the moon was made of cheese. "What do you mean, no one? He's—he's standing right there!" He jabbed his finger toward the empty space behind me, his face flushed with panic. "Look! He's—"

He stopped short, his jaw dropping.

I glanced over my shoulder again, seeing nothing but open air. "Mr. Darcy... have you perhaps taken ill?"

Mr. Darcy let out a strangled sound and pointed even more frantically. "He's—he's gone! He was just standing there, I swear! Right over your shoulder!" He backed up a step, his eyes darting around like a hunted animal. "Where did he go?"

I looked at the empty space, then back at Mr. Darcy, who was now pressing a hand to his forehead like a man trying to wake himself from a nightmare. "You're certain there's someone after you?"

"Certain?" he nearly shrieked. "He was right—oh no. Oh, no, he's back. He's—"

Mr. Darcy's eyes widened in horror, and before I could ask another question, he pointed directly at me, his voice dropping to a horrified whisper. "He's behind you again."

I stiffened, feeling a shiver run down my spine. "Behind *me*?"

"Yes!" he exclaimed, eyes bulging as he took another step back. "He's standing right over your shoulder, staring at—good God, he's peering around your face and down... Back I say, sir! You *will* respect the lady's dignity... Egad, how *dare* you, sir!"

I wheeled around so fast I nearly tripped over my own feet, but again, there was nothing. Not even a whisper in the treetops.

Mr. Darcy let out a pitiful groan, clutching his hair. "Why can't you see him?" he moaned, more to himself than to me. "He's right there, I swear. He's—he's looking at you! He was going to touch your hair!"

I stared at him, half-expecting him to collapse on the spot. "Mr. Darcy," I said slowly, "there is absolutely no one standing behind me."

Mr. Darcy's breathing quickened, his eyes flicking back and forth as if the invisible man were playing a game of hide-and-seek. "He's gone again!" he gasped, staring at the empty space over my shoulder. "*How* does he keep disappearing? And why am I the only one who sees him?"

I blinked, utterly baffled. This was not the Mr. Darcy I had met at the Assembly. The proud—conceited, even—impossibly self-assured and utterly in-control-of-the-world man I'd seen at the ball was nowhere to be found. Instead, he looked like a man on the brink of complete collapse, shouting at invisible attackers in his half-buttoned shirt and mud-covered breeches.

"Mr. Darcy..." I began carefully, "are you quite sure you haven't—"

"I'm *not* mad!" he blurted, his voice high-pitched and frantic. "I'm not! He's here—I swear, he's here! He was just—right—"

He froze, his eyes locking onto something just over my shoulder again. His face drained of color, and he took another stumbling step backward.

I swallowed hard, glancing behind me one last time, seeing nothing but trees swaying in the breeze. "Perhaps I should fetch someone for you..."

"No!" Darcy all but shouted, his voice cracking. "No one else can see him, they'll think I've lost my mind! But I swear, he's—"

And then he threw his hands up in frustration, practically shouting at the sky. "Away with you!"

Once again, I turned to see absolutely no one.

Darcy froze again, his eyes darting wildly to the side as if something—or someone—had just appeared next to him.

"Leave me alone!" he barked, swatting at the empty air beside him. "I said—get off! Unhand me, or I shall... No, I will *not* go to... leave me be!"

I stared, my mouth falling open. *Who* was he talking to? And... was he punching something? It looked for all the world like his fist was making contact with a wall of empty air.

He took a step back, eyes widening as if this invisible tormentor were inching closer. "I swear, if you touch me again—"

Darcy staggered, throwing his hands up as though fending off an unseen attacker. "I said get away from me!" he practically howled, his voice strained and high-pitched.

Then, with one final yelp, he spun around and bolted—sprinting across the lawn like a man chased by wolves, his untucked shirt flapping behind him as he disappeared around the side of the house.

I stood frozen, staring at the space where no one had been, watching Darcy's retreat with utter disbelief.

Six

Darcy

I STUMBLED AROUND THE corner of the house, barely keeping myself upright as my legs threatened to give out beneath me. My lungs burned from running, my head swam with confusion, and my entire body felt like it was one wrong breath away from expiring completely. I needed to get back to my room—back to safety.

For a moment, Ewan had vanished. That small mercy allowed me to breathe, but just barely. My hands still trembled, and I was fairly certain my legs wouldn't hold me much longer.

I reached the stairs, my hand gripping the banister like a lifeline, when I heard it—Caroline Bingley's voice drifting from the hallway. My heart nearly stopped. Of all the people to find me in this state, it had to be *her*. I pressed myself against the wall, trying to steady my breathing, hoping against hope that she wouldn't turn the corner.

"Has anyone seen Mr. Darcy this morning?" Her voice echoed closer, and I could hear the scrape of her shoes on the floor. "I haven't had the pleasure of speaking with him yet today."

Pleasure. The word made me want to scream again.

My body locked up. I wasn't sure if I would faint or simply crumble into a heap right there, but I could not—*would not*—let Caroline Bingley find me. My shirt was still half untucked, mud caked my breeches, and I had the bedraggled look of a man who had been wallowing with the pigs. No doubt my aroma was equally distinguished. If Caroline Bingley saw me like this, the news would reach London by dinner.

I pressed my back to the wall, heart hammering in my chest, every muscle tense. Ewan McLean, thank Heaven, had chosen this moment to disappear. Or maybe he was never really there. A small grace, though I had no illusions it would last.

Miss Bingley's footsteps paused, and I held my breath, waiting.

After what felt like an eternity, they resumed, fading in the opposite direction.

I exhaled shakily and bolted up the stairs two at a time, stumbling through the door of my room and slamming it shut behind me. I leaned against it, gasping for breath, my hands trembling uncontrollably.

For a brief moment, I allowed myself to relax. I was alone. No Scottish nuisance, no ghostly figures popping up behind me. Just the blessed, quiet solitude of my room.

But then the humiliation of what had just occurred hit me like a blow to the gut.

Elizabeth Bennet.

Of all people to witness my disgraceful flight across the lawn, it had to be her. The one with the razor-sharp wit and speaking eyes that were positively laughing at my discomfiture. I closed my eyes, groaning as I slumped against the door. Of course it was her. It figured that she *would* be the one to see me unraveling like a lunatic.

But... at least it hadn't been Caroline Bingley.

Miss Bennet was a country girl—no one would listen to her. She could say whatever she pleased, and society would barely blink. But if Miss Bingley had seen... I shuddered. I would have been the subject of gossip from here to London for the next decade.

Or she would use it to blackmail me into marriage. Quite frankly, I'd rather have the gossip.

Shaking all over, I pushed myself upright and took stock of my appearance in the mirror. My shirt was torn and smeared with mud, my breeches filthy, my hair drenched and sticking out in every direction as if I'd spent the morning wrestling with demons—which, frankly, didn't feel far from the truth.

I didn't waste another second. I stumbled over to my hair trunk, yanking it open with clumsy hands, and began stuffing clothes into it without rhyme or reason. I needed to leave. *Now.* London, Derbyshire, the Orient—*anywhere* but here. I couldn't wait for a footman or explanations. I had to be gone before Ewan McLean appeared again or, worse before Caroline Bingley sniffed me out.

As I crammed the last of my shirts into the trunk, I heard a sharp knock at the door.

I screamed. Again.

My knees buckled, and I clutched the edge of the bed to stop myself from collapsing. *No.* Not again! I couldn't take another confrontation with—

"Darcy?" came Bingley's voice from the other side of the door. "Are you hurt?"

I exhaled in relief, nearly sinking to the floor. It wasn't Ewan. It was Bingley. A real, living, breathing human being. I could handle this.

My heart was still racing, but at least I wasn't about to face another ghost. Thank Heaven.

"Darcy?" came Bingley's voice again, far more urgent now. "Are you—er—alive in there?"

I hauled myself to my feet, gripping the bedpost like it was the only thing keeping me upright. "Yes! Yes, I'm... here."

The door creaked open, and Bingley stepped in, taking one look at me—mud-smeared breeches, shirt hanging out, hair as if I'd been struck by lightning—and stopped dead in his tracks.

"Good heavens, man," he said, blinking. "What happened to you? You look like you've been trampled by a herd of cows."

I straightened up, but my legs were still shaking beneath me. "Cows? No. No cows," I stammered, trying to smooth my shirt—though that was a futile effort. "I was... startled. That's all."

Bingley raised an eyebrow, clearly not buying it. "Startled? Darcy, I could've sworn I heard a scream. A rather... high-pitched one."

"I do *not* scream," I snapped, though I could hear how unconvincing I sounded. "I was... surprised, that's all. Surprised."

Bingley blinked again, his gaze flicking to the half-packed trunk behind me. "Surprised into packing your things without even waiting for a servant? Were you 'startled' by your shirts and cravats?"

"No," I muttered, shoving a crumpled cravat into the trunk with far more force than necessary. "I simply thought it best to... return to London. Yes. Important matters. Cannot delay."

"London?" Bingley's frown deepened, and he stepped further into the room, hands on his hips. "Darcy, what's this about? You only came back last night! The weather's cleared up, and Hurst and I were planning to go shooting this morning."

"Shooting?" I repeated, half dazed, as I glanced out the window. The sky, of course, was a perfect blue, and the trees shimmered in the sunlight like nothing strange had happened at all. "Yes, well, I'm sure you and Hurst will manage without me."

Bingley's eyes narrowed. "Are you sure? You look..." He searched for the word. "You look like you've been running across the fallow fields already this morning."

If only he knew. My head was pounding, my hands were trembling, and every part of me wanted to escape this house before Ewan popped up again to haunt me.

"It's just... the matter of the estate," I said weakly, stuffing a pair of boots into the trunk. "Can't leave it unattended for too long. Must get back to Derbyshire."

Bingley was not convinced. "You didn't mention anything pressing before you left for London yesterday."

I groaned inwardly. "Well, things change. Urgently. There's business. Papers. People waiting." I was rambling now, and Bingley's concerned frown was only getting deeper.

"Darcy," he said slowly, "it's a beautiful day. The rain's cleared, the countryside's fresh, and Hurst and I were hoping for a bit of sport. I daresay some fresh air would do you good."

Fresh air? Fresh air was what got me into this mess, tearing across the lawn like a madman while a young lady looked on, no doubt thinking I'd lost my mind, and probably scandalized by how much of me my clothing did not cover. The village wit, no less, with the sort of tongue that could scald my dignity a dozen different ways before noon.

I shuddered.

Bingley, oblivious to my inner turmoil, kept going. "And besides," he added with far too much enthusiasm, "I've just had word that Miss Elizabeth Bennet has arrived to visit her sister."

Miss Elizabeth. The very last person on this earth I wanted to face again.

I felt my face pale, the trembling in my hands worsening. "Miss Elizabeth?" I croaked.

"Yes!" Bingley said brightly, either ignoring or missing the absolute horror in my voice. "You must join us in greeting her. It would be most improper not to."

Most improper. How about most *insane*? I was about to have a complete collapse, and he wanted to stand around exchanging pleasantries with *Elizabeth Bennet?*

"Surely... surely that's not necessary," I stammered. "After all, Miss Bennet has come to see her sister, not us. We wouldn't want to disturb them."

"Disturb them?" Bingley laughed. "Nonsense. She'll be pleased to see us. Come, we'll make a day of it. Some shooting, a pleasant visit with Miss Bennet. It'll be just the thing to lift your spirits!"

Lift my spirits? The only thing that would lift my spirits was getting as far away from Netherfield as humanly possible. But I couldn't leave without making myself look even more ridiculous than I already had.

"Right," I said weakly, my voice barely holding together. "A day of it."

Bingley beamed. "Excellent! I'll have the footmen bring down your things, and we'll head out to the lawn in just a bit. Miss Elizabeth is with her sister now, but we shall greet her in the drawing room after she has satisfied herself. I do hope she will find Miss Bennet somewhat recovered since last evening."

I nodded, my stomach twisting into knots. *Elizabeth Bennet.* Again. I'd barely survived the last encounter, and now I had to face her *again*.

But at least that wretched Scotsman was nowhere to be seen. For now.

Elizabeth

I DESCENDED THE STAIRS with a knot in my stomach. Facing Mr. Bingley's sisters wasn't high on my list of enjoyable activities, but Jane needed me to play messenger, and unfortunately, these were the people I had to deliver the news to. My brief meeting with them at the Assembly had been enough to assure me that the warmest thing about them was the fireplace they were sitting next to.

As I stepped into the drawing room, there they were—Miss Bingley and Mrs. Hurst, sitting like two finely dressed sphinxes, looking as if the greatest effort they'd made that morning was lifting their teacups. Mr. Hurst was there too, slumped in a chair, presumably pretending to be asleep so no one would ask him anything too taxing. He had all the air of a man who contributed absolutely nothing to the world except snoring.

"Miss Bennet," Miss Bingley said, her voice a careful mix of civility and complete disinterest, "how is your sister this morning?"

I smiled as politely as I could manage. "Not well, I'm afraid."

Miss Bingley's eyebrows rose just enough to suggest she was mildly interested, but not so much that it would wrinkle her perfectly powdered forehead. "Oh dear," she said with the kind of concern one might express for a misplaced glove. "I do hope she recovers swiftly."

"I'm sure she will," Mrs. Hurst added, although she didn't look sure of anything, least of all Jane's fate. "And, of course, if her condition worsens, we'll send for the local apothecary. I trust there is one?"

I clasped my hands behind my back, trying to ignore their not-so-veiled slight about our village. "Ah, yes. His name is Mr. Jones. He is quite competent."

"Yes, Mr. Jones," Miss Bingley echoed, her fingers gliding delicately along the rim of her teacup. "We wouldn't want her to suffer unnecessarily."

The word "unnecessarily" hung in the air, and I couldn't help but wonder what level of suffering would qualify as "necessary" for these women. I smiled again, tighter this time, and nodded.

"Thank you," I said, fully aware that their offer to call the apothecary was about as heartfelt as a garden statue. The way they spoke, you'd think they were offering to save the nation.

I shifted uncomfortably, glancing toward the door as if some magical rescue might appear. It was clear they weren't planning to offer anything more helpful than that. They looked perfectly content to sip their tea and hope Jane either recovered or discreetly perished without disturbing their breakfast.

The thought left me feeling rather cold, and worse—there was something else on my mind, something much stranger and far more unsettling.

Mr. Darcy.

The sight of him earlier, sprinting across the lawn like a man possessed, still made the hair on the back of my neck prickle. Was he mad? That was the most logical conclusion, given how he'd behaved. And yet... there he was, upstairs, presumably roaming the halls in his usual brooding manner. If Jane wasn't already feverish, I'd worry she might catch madness simply from being under the same roof as that man.

Just as I was contemplating this disturbing possibility, the door opened, and in walked Mr. Bingley, smiling as brightly as ever. He was a walking sunbeam, all charm and ease.

"Miss Elizabeth," he said warmly, "how is your sister this morning?"

I gave him the same report I had given his sisters. "Not well at all, I'm afraid."

Unlike the ladies, Bingley's face immediately fell into genuine concern. "Not well? That won't do at all," he said, frowning. "I'll send for the apothecary right away. Mrs. Nicholls will know whom to send for."

Finally, someone with a pulse.

But before I could express my thanks, Bingley added, "And of course, you must stay with her, Miss Elizabeth. We wouldn't want her to be bereft of the comfort of her family. I'll have your things sent for at once. You should be by her side."

I blinked. Stay *here?* At Netherfield?

Before I could think of an appropriate response, my eyes drifted to the door—where, as if summoned by some dark force, Mr. Darcy appeared.

I tensed immediately. He was still pale, his eyes darting nervously around the room like he expected someone to leap out and throttle him. His pupils were blown wide, and he flinched every time someone so much as moved a teacup. If anything, he looked worse than before. The man was shaking, for heaven's sake, and it wasn't from cold.

I didn't want to be anywhere near him.

But Jane needed me, and I couldn't leave her here, sick and vulnerable, while I fled back to Longbourn. It was bad enough she had to endure Caroline Bingley's tender mercies. The last thing she needed was to be stuck in a house with Mr. Darcy, who was clearly on the verge of some kind of mental collapse. What if he snapped and went about murdering people in their beds?

Still, I forced a smile. "That's very kind of you, Mr. Bingley," I said, even as my insides screamed *"Get out while you can!"*

As I glanced around the room, I caught Miss Bingley and Mrs. Hurst exchanging a quick look as if they were silently communicating some unspoken dread. They weren't the only ones.

Mr. Darcy, who had been standing in rigid silence, suddenly gasped. Yes, *gasped*—like a man who'd just been told he was going to be executed at dawn. His hand shot up to his cravat, yanking at it as if it had just turned into a hangman's noose.

Without a word, he turned on his heel and fled the room.

Fled.

Mr. Darcy, the most composed, aloof man I had ever met—at least, he sure seemed that way at the Assembly—had just sprinted out of the drawing room as if the devil himself were after him.

I stood there, dumbfounded.

Bingley chuckled awkwardly, glancing after his retreating friend. "Darcy has been acting... rather distressed this morning. Quite a lot on his mind, I shouldn't wonder. And a deal of travel, and... I'm sure he'll be back to himself soon."

"Distressed" didn't begin to cover it. I wasn't sure if I should be more concerned about Jane's fever or for Mr. Darcy's state of mind.

"Right," Bingley continued, clearly trying to salvage the moment. "I'll speak to Mrs. Nicholls about your things, Miss Elizabeth. You should be settled in no time."

He gave me a polite bow and hurried after his friend, leaving me standing in the drawing room, staring at the door in complete disbelief.

What on earth had I just got myself into?

Seven

Darcy

THE BROOCH SAT ON the bedside table, taunting me. It was a cursed little thing, gleaming smugly like it knew what it had done. I stared at it, my pulse quickening—not with fear, I told myself, but with frustration. Yes, just frustration. That was all this was.

I picked it up gingerly, turning it over in my hands as if by examining it from every angle, I might convince myself that none of this had actually happened. Maybe I'd had more to drink than I remembered. Maybe I'd hit my head on the carriage ride back from London. That would be logical. Sensible. Not like the mania I thought I had seen earlier.

No, no. It was nonsense. I was overworked. Tired. Exhausted, really. What I needed was sleep, not to be obsessing over this brooch. I could feel my pulse in my throat—practically knocking my cravat loose with how hard it was hammering away, like I was some country schoolboy caught misbehaving.

And then, as if he had been waiting for me to give in to the absurdity of it all, he was there.

Out of nowhere. Again.

"Aye, there ye be," Ewan drawled, propped up in my favorite chair like a king of nothing, bottle in hand, his legs crossed as if he had all the time in the world. He didn't just appear—he materialized, casually, as though being summoned to haunt a man's bedroom was the most natural thing in the world.

I dropped the brooch—flung it across the room, really—and backed up so fast I nearly tripped over my own feet. "*You!*" I blurted, choking on the words, pointing like a fool. "How did you—*where* did you—"

"Still twitchy as a cat in a thunderstorm, are ye?" he said, taking a long swig from his bottle and wiping his mouth with his sleeve. "Ye'd think ye'd be used tae it by now."

Used to it? The man was a ghost. Or... or a hallucination. Or—blast, I didn't know what he was, but "used to it" was the furthest thing from my mind.

I swallowed, trying to rein in the shock, but failing spectacularly. "How are you doing this? Appearing like this?" I managed to say, though my voice had taken on a rather embarrassing note of hysteria. "It's—it's not possible."

Ewan raised an eyebrow, as if *I* were the one making things difficult. "Aye, I'm here, am I no'?"

"Yes, but *why?*" My pulse was going again—this time, I swear, it was trying to escape. "You just... show up whenever you please, with no warning, no—"

He cut me off with a wave of his hand, dismissing me like I was some fretting child. "Ach, steady yersel, will ye? Yer heart's about to beat its way out o' yer coat."

I blinked. *Steady myself?* My nerves were shot to pieces. Calm? I hadn't known calm since he'd first appeared out of thin air, and now I was meant to just... *accept* this?

My eyes landed back on the brooch, which glinted on the rug between us. "It's that, isn't it?" I asked, motioning toward the cursed thing, my mind racing. "That's what's causing this—this madness."

That was it. All I had to do was get rid of it! I lunged for it before Ewan could respond and flung it out of the open window. I heard it make a 'clink' on the iron railing outside as it fell.

Ewan glanced down at his hand, and devil take me if he was not rolling the thing about between his fingers. *How?* I had just flung it...

"This wee thing?" He squinted at it and held it up to the light. "Aye, could be. Bonny Prince Charlie." He toasted the air, then put his bottle to his lips as if paying tribute to another ghost. Oh, bollocks, I don't know. Perhaps he was.

"*How?*" I demanded.

Ewan shrugged. "Ye nicked yer finger on it, did ye no'?"

I stared at him, completely baffled. "What does that have to do with anything?"

He swirled the liquid in his bottle, looking thoroughly bored. "Blood magic, lad. Och, it's always the blood wi' these things."

My mind was reeling. "Blood? What on earth are you talking about? Blood magic? What are you, some—some fairy tale?"

He took another swig, his eyes narrowing at me like I'd just insulted his entire clan. "Fairytale?" he said, his voice dripping with savagery. "Ye think I'm some daft fairytale? Lad, what's in yer Sassenach books isnae worth the paper it's scribbled on! Ye nicked yer finger, let a wee drap o' blood, an' here I am—same as it's been fer centuries. Maybe ye ought tae crack open a proper book now an' again."

I blinked at him, my brain firing off half-formed thoughts at lightning speed. This could *not* be real. There had to be some explanation. Ghosts don't just show up because of a drop of blood! For heaven's sake, if they did, I should have been haunted by an entire battalion of them when I cut my head open climbing rocks as a boy.

"And what, exactly, am I supposed to do about it?" I asked, my voice shaking. "How do I—how do I get rid of you?"

He gave me a slow, deliberate grin that made me want to tear out my hair. "Why'd ye want tae get rid o' me? Aye, I'm only just gettin' started tae enjoy mesel', so I am."

"*Enjoy yourself?*" My hands were shaking now, and I had half a mind to throttle him—if only I were certain he wasn't going to vanish the moment I tried. "You've been dead for mercy knows how long, and now you're here, *haunting* me, and you're telling me that you're *enjoying yourself*?"

"Ye've got it," he said, raising the bottle in a mock toast. "Ach, ye can stop yer bawlin', lad. I'm here, an' I'm no' budgin'."

I blinked again, my mind racing back to the brooch. "The brooch," I muttered, pacing the floor. "It has to be the brooch. If I... if I get rid of it..."

Ewan chuckled, an infuriating sound that grated on every last one of my nerves. "Aye, good luck wi' that. It's no' that simple, ye know."

"What do you mean, 'not that simple'?" I stopped pacing, my pulse galloping as I contemplated impending disaster. "What is simple about *any* of this? Give me that thing!"

Ewan shrugged and opened his palm. I wasn't taking any chances this time. Into the fire grate it went, into the very hottest part of the flames. With any luck, that bright silver would send up a scorching smoke within seconds that...

"I've telt ye, ye cannae be rid o' it 'cause *I* cannae be rid o' *it*." Ewan held out his hand, still brandishing that blasted brooch.

That was when my knees buckled. My head was swimming, and I wanted to be sick all over the carpet. But by some small miracle, I found my voice. Or at least a raspy whisper. "*How* are you doing that?"

"It's blood magic, ye daftie. Ye think ye can chuck that brooch out a window an' be rid o' me? Aye, I wish. Then maybe I'd get mesel' a proper Highlander instead o'..." He gave me a once-over, curling his lip. "*Ye.*"

I stared at him, my mouth opening and closing, utterly speechless. This couldn't be happening. This was some nightmare—yes, that was it. Any moment now, I'd wake up and laugh about it all.

"I'm losing my mind," I muttered, pressing my fingers to my temples.

"Nay, lad," Ewan said, grinning like the cat who'd caught the canary. "But ye're stuck wi' me, ye are."

"And how long," I ground out, "will that be?"

He took a slow, deliberate sip of his whisky. "Could be forever. Could be a few days. Depends, doesnae?"

"On what?" I snapped, desperate for anything to cling to. "And how on earth are you able to drink that? Aren't you dead?" I strode forward and snatched the bottle out of his hand, then sniffed it. It was real—the bottle had weight and shape, it was cold to the touch and still half full of some awful-smelling foulness.

Ewan's eyes darkened. He moved faster than I expected, lunging forward and yanking it back with a grip like iron.

"Are ye mad, lad?" he growled, his voice low and dangerous, far more threatening than I'd ever heard it. "There's nae a more foolish thing in this world than layin' yer hands on a man's whisky. Ye want trouble, eh? Because that's how ye get it."

I just stood there, my fingers slack, and my hand open limply as he took another drink. "You... *you're dead!*" I cried. "*How* are you drinking?"

Ewan shrugged. "Ach, who's tae say? Nae rules set down, ye ken, but I'm right glad o' a bit o' drink just now. Ye're enough to drive a man tae it."

I groaned, throwing myself into the nearest chair and staring up at the ceiling, my heart still thudding like it was trying to dig its way out through my ribs. Every rational bone in my body screamed that this wasn't possible—that none of this was possible—but the ghost lounging in my chair with a whisky bottle said otherwise.

"Why..." I started, my voice tight, "...can nobody else see you?"

Ewan grinned, the kind of grin that made me want to throttle him. "Ach, now there's a question, eh?"

"Yes!" I snapped, my temper fraying. "That's exactly the question."

He swirled the whisky around in the bottle, leaning back in my chair like he owned the bloody thing. "Well, lad, I reckon it's 'cause ye called me up wi' yer blood. It's yer doin', after all. No' like I'm hangin' aboot fer a bit o' fun."

"That's not an answer! I need to know this. *Why*," I asked, forcing my voice to remain steady, "can't anyone else see you?"

He shrugged. "Maybe 'cause they didnae go jabbin' their fingers on some auld bit o' metal." His eyes sparkled with amusement as he took another swig. "Or maybe I just like tormentin' *ye* more. Gad's teeth, but ye're a toffee-nosed heid bummer."

My fists clenched. "So, I'm the only one cursed to deal with you?"

He just shrugged and took another pull from his bottle.

I groaned, rubbing my face with both hands. This was utterly insane. I was losing my mind, that was the only explanation.

Before I could spiral any further into my own misery, Ewan's voice cut through my thoughts. "But I've a wee question fer ye, lad."

I didn't look up. "I'm not interested."

"Ah, but ye might want tae be, ye ken. An' who was that bonnie lass ye near knocked o'er on the lawn?"

I froze. Slowly, I raised my head to find Ewan staring at me, an eyebrow arched with far too much interest.

"Who?" I asked, though I knew exactly who he meant.

"The lass," he said, waving the bottle like a man giving orders. "Dark hair, sharp tongue on her, aye? Looks like she can handle hersel', that yin. Ye ken the lass I mean."

"Miss Bennet?" I replied, trying to keep my voice neutral. "What of her?"

He grinned, leaning forward. "Och, she's a bonny one, isnae she? Caught me eye, she did. Bold lass, by the looks o' her. Not one o' those simperin' flowers ye see around here, but wi'..." He gestured with his bottle, pantomiming a woman's... er... shape. "That's a pair of sweet—"

My stomach dropped, and I moved to cut him off before he could blurt out whatever Scottish obscenity he was about to utter. "That is entirely inappropriate!"

He let out a bark of laughter. "Aye, well, what care I aboot yer Sassenach manners, eh? A Highland man kens fine how tae admire a bonnie lass when he claps eyes on one."

My hands clenched into fists at my sides, the color rising in my face. "You will *not* speak of Miss Bennet that way."

Ewan raised an eyebrow, his grin widening. "Och, have I struck a nerve, have I? So, she be *yer* lass, then?"

"You will not speak of *any* lady in that way, not merely Miss Bennet! Her honor," I said sharply, standing straighter, "is not for you to question."

I blinked, suddenly aware of just how absurd this situation had become. I was lecturing a ghost—or a figment of my imagination—about a lady's honor. Her honor! As if that mattered to him, or as if he could do anything about it. Was I truly standing here, arguing with a man from another century about propriety?

Before I could dwell on the ridiculousness of it all, Ewan leaned back, his grin growing wider.

"Aye, an' I'll wager she's got plenty more tae her name, eh? That spark in her eyes—ye ken that's somethin' special, don't ye, lad?"

I glared at him, my blood boiling. "It is indecent. *You* are indecent."

He waved me off, still chuckling. "Och, save yer preachin', Sassenach. I've seen more decency in a pigsty. But that lass—she's a canty one. Wouldnae mind learnin' a thing or two aboot her."

My jaw clenched so tightly that I thought my teeth might crack. "You will do no such thing," I growled, my voice shaking with anger. "You'll leave Miss Bennet *entirely* out of this."

Ewan gave me a sly look, but thankfully, he didn't push any further. Instead, he stood up, the bottle still clutched in his hand. "Ach, I'll leave ye tae yer sulkin'. Got better things tae dae than sit here listenin' tae yer greetin'."

I blinked. "More important things? You're *dead*."

He grinned again, tipping his bottle in my direction. "Aye, but I'm not lettin' that stop me." He turned toward the door. "Think I'll see if yer cook's got anythin' worth drinkin'. Or eatin'."

"You can't just—" I started, but before I could finish, he was gone, vanishing into thin air as if he had never been there.

I stood there, frozen, staring at the empty space where he'd stood only moments ago. *Gone.* Again.

But he'd be back. That much was certain. He'd be back, and no amount of yelling or scolding was going to change that.

My fists unclenched, and I pressed my hands to my temples, pacing the floor in front of the bed, trying to force my mind to work through the madness. What could I do? I couldn't tell Bingley or anyone else in this house. They'd think I'd gone mad—and maybe I had.

Was I mad? Hallucinating? Had I somehow conjured this nightmare myself?

I ran a hand through my hair, trying to find some shred of rationality in all this. The brooch. It had to be connected to the brooch. But why?

And why *me?*

Eight

Elizabeth

I HAD HOPED TO slip into the library quietly, just long enough to select a book for the evening before joining the others in the drawing room. Jane was resting at last, her breathing soft and steady, but after spending most of the day in her room, I longed for a distraction. A good book was exactly what I needed.

The library at Netherfield was a peaceful room, normally. But the moment I stepped inside, I realized it wasn't empty.

Mr. Darcy was already there, standing near the back shelves, frantically pulling down one book after another, examining their spines with all the intensity of a man searching for money he had hidden somewhere, or a cure to some terrible disease. He flipped through the pages of each volume briefly before shoving them back in place, only to repeat the process with the next.

I nearly turned around and slipped out the way I'd come, but I hesitated. He hadn't noticed me yet, and he was clearly preoccupied. Perhaps I could simply choose my book and leave without much interaction.

But just as I began to step away, Mr. Darcy turned sharply, as though he'd been pricked in the breeches by a sewing needle. His eyes were wide, and his breathing was still a bit too rapid for my comfort. He looked pale, though not as alarmingly so as earlier that day.

There was a tension in his posture, but it wasn't as frantic. He offered me a bow, though it was more a reflex than anything polite.

"Miss Bennet," he said, his voice tight but civil.

For a moment, I weighed my options. I could leave now—there were plenty of other books to read in the drawing room. But something about his current state intrigued me. He looked... lost. Panicked, even. And yet, strangely harmless in that moment.

After a brief hesitation, I returned his bow with a slight nod, deciding that a few minutes wouldn't hurt. I turned back to the shelves and began scanning for something suitable. His eyes followed me for a moment before he returned to his frantic search, his hands moving faster now as he flipped through more volumes.

"There are a few here you might find interesting," he said suddenly, his tone more casual than I expected. "That green volume on the second shelf—historical essays. Or perhaps the blue one near the end, third shelf, travels in Italy. And if you prefer fiction, there's a collection of stories, dark cover with gold lettering, just to your left."

I blinked, surprised by his unexpected recommendations. "Thank you, Mr. Darcy."

I pulled out the green volume he'd mentioned, more out of curiosity than anything, and glanced toward him. He was back to pulling books off the shelves, though his movements were no less frantic. After a moment of silence, I couldn't help myself.

"What exactly are you looking for?" I asked, clutching the book to my chest.

He didn't turn around but muttered, "A book on myths. Legends. Nonsense."

That was unexpected. "Legends? I wouldn't have thought such a subject would interest you."

He gave a short, humorless laugh. "I'm just as surprised as you are, Miss Bennet."

I studied him for a moment longer, feeling an odd mix of curiosity and unease, but the tension in the room was too thick to linger.

"Good evening, Mr. Darcy," I said, and before he could respond, I slipped out of the library.

Darcy

I PACED THE LENGTH of the library, the book clutched in my hand like it held the secrets of the universe. I flipped it open, read two lines, and snapped it shut again. The idea of retreating to my room, locking the door, and burying myself in Scottish myths was tempting—tempting in the way jumping into a freezing lake seemed like a reasonable option when one was on fire. But even the thought of pretending to relax felt absurd. I hadn't had a moment's peace since Ewan barged into my life, and now I was grasping at straws—no, at books—hoping one might explain how I'd come to be haunted by a dead Scotsman.

But I had spent far too much time alone today. Between the hours of pacing my room, being haunted by an infuriating ghost, and now hiding in the library, I was beginning to wonder if being around others might stabilize whatever remained of my fragile sanity.

And then there was Elizabeth Bennet.

The way she had looked at me just now—like she was contemplating whether I might leap at her at any moment. *Terrified*. That was the word. Terrified of *me*, of all people! If she went about spreading tales of Mr. Darcy of Pemberley behaving erratically, looking pale and wide-eyed, heaven only knew what gossip would start. The last thing I needed was more rumors about my temperament.

No, perhaps some company would be good for me. If Elizabeth Bennet could see me seated, reading calmly, acting like any rational gentleman ought to, maybe she'd reconsider whatever nonsense she might be imagining.

With that thought, I tucked the book under my arm and made my way to the drawing room, silently steeling myself against whatever lay in wait. Ghosts or no ghosts, I would behave like the model of calm, collected civility.

When I entered the room, the scene was as predictable as ever. Miss Bingley and Mrs. Hurst were gathered around a card table with Mr. Hurst and Bingley, the former looking bored out of his wits and the latter delighted as usual. Miss Bingley cast a quick glance my way, her lips curving into that familiar, predatory smile. Thankfully, she returned her attention to the cards without comment.

Elizabeth was seated by the fire, a book already in her hands, her expression focused. I could only hope she wouldn't glance my way too often, lest she catch me doing something involuntary and... alarming. I chose a chair as far from the card game as possible and settled in, opening my book with every appearance of nonchalance I could muster.

The first page hadn't even registered before I felt it: the unmistakable presence of Ewan McLean.

Of course. I should have known better than to think I could have one moment of peace.

He appeared casually—so casually that for a moment, I imagined the others might notice him strolling about. But no. There he was, completely invisible to everyone but me, pacing around the room and sniffing at the company I kept.

"Ach, they're a right scunnerin' bunch, eh?" he said, his voice low but just loud enough to make me jump and nearly drop the book. "That blonde one—" he nodded toward Miss Bingley—"she's got a face on her like she's sniffin' somethin' foul. Right bunch o' bletherin' gowks, this lot."

I closed my eyes briefly, willing him to leave. *Now.*

Of course, he didn't.

Instead, Ewan wandered over to the card table, peering over Bingley's shoulder, his eyes narrowing in mock concentration. "Och, lad, ye call that a bluff? Might as well be holdin' up a sign sayin', 'Help yersel' tae all my coin.' He's near flashin' his cards aboot like a bletherin' eejit."

I gritted my teeth, silently praying he'd keep his voice down. But since I was the only one who could hear it... well, perhaps it did not matter.

He moved to Mrs. Hurst's side next, chuckling under his breath. "She's tryin' tae play coy, but she's got the worst hand at the table, the poor lass. No' that she'd ken it. She's too busy pretendin' she gives a toss."

Mr. Hurst barely stirred from his spot, barely paying attention to the game at all. Ewan grinned and leaned in closer to him. "Ach, now here's a sight," he whispered. "The man's sittin' on a winnin' hand, an' he doesnae even ken it. Ha! He could walk away wi' the lot if he could stay awake long enough tae notice."

I bit my lip to keep from groaning aloud. Ewan was having the time of his afterlife, and I was moments away from losing my mind.

He circled back to Miss Bingley, who was frowning down at her cards like they had personally insulted her. "Och, an' this yin," Ewan went on with a smirk, "her face is gettin' tighter wi' every toss. She's tryin' tae bluff, but she's as subtle as a cannon blast. Ye could read her mind fae the doorway."

I gripped my book harder, trying to look engrossed in the pages in front of me, but I wasn't reading a single word.

And Ewan, of course, wasn't done. He sidled up to Bingley, shaking his head in mock dismay. "Now he's the only one havin' a grand time, the poor lad. Nae strategy, nae idea he's bein' outplayed by his ain sister. Here's a man who finds joy in everythin', even losin'."

Ewan wandered away from the card table, clearly losing interest in the players, his eyes locking on Elizabeth, who sat by the fire with her book. I tensed at the look on his face. Nothing good ever followed that look.

He began to saunter over toward her, and I knew—*knew*—he was about to say something inappropriate. I silently prayed he wouldn't, but what was the use?

"Now that," he murmured, just loud enough for me to hear, "is a sight worth seein'."

I nearly crushed the spine of my book as I fought the urge to shout at him. Of course, that would do no good. It would only make me look mad. But the way he was hovering over Miss Bennet—no gentleman, alive or dead, should behave this way.

"Get *away* from her," I whispered, fighting to keep my voice low.

Naturally, he ignored me, stepping closer to Elizabeth, tilting his head like he was admiring some sort of portrait. "Och, she's got a look, doesnae she? There's somethin' in those eyes…"

I clenched my teeth. "I said *get away.*"

"Mr. Darcy?" Elizabeth's voice broke through my frustration. She was peering at me over the top of her book, a delicate brow arched in confusion. "Did you say something?"

Blast.

My heart almost stopped as I scrambled for an excuse. "Ah… no. Just… reading. Aloud. To myself."

Her brow arched higher. "I see." She clearly didn't, but she went back to her book, though with far more suspicion than before.

Meanwhile, Ewan was practically standing over her now, inspecting her like she was an exhibit at the Royal Academy. He even twirled his finger in a loose spiral of hair until she twitched absently at the tickle of it—as if a draft from the door had swept it aside—and flicked the ringlet back into place herself.

"There's somethin' aboot her," he said softly. "The eyes... aye, reminds me of—"

"*Shut up,*" I hissed, hoping Elizabeth didn't hear me this time.

"Mr. Darcy?" she said again, now more curious than confused. "Are you... quite well?"

My mind flailed for something, anything. "Perfectly," I said, far too quickly. "Just... enjoying my book."

Her expression told me she was definitely not convinced.

Ewan, naturally, had no sympathy for the situation he was making worse. "Elspeth," he murmured, completely oblivious to my rising panic. "My Elspeth."

"*Who... what?*" I hissed, barely managing to contain myself. Oh, I was not going to stand for this madness! Was he now claiming he *knew* her? This was too much.

Elizabeth shifted in her chair, her eyes narrowing. "Who what?" she asked, tilting her head like she was trying to catch me in some sort of trap.

I blinked rapidly, trying to think of something clever. "Oh, nothing," I said, forcing a smile. "Just... reciting something."

She gave me a long look, clearly suspicious now. I could almost see her calculating how quickly she could leave the room if I started talking to myself again.

Ewan, completely oblivious to the chaos he was causing, leaned in closer to Elizabeth, shaking his head as if marveling at some long-lost memory. "Aye, there's a fire in her, lad. Just like Elspeth. Ye dinnae see it?"

Oh, so he was not claiming to know her, but that she *reminded* him of someone. That... no, that was not better. I squeezed my eyes shut for a moment, silently begging for this to end. "She is *not* your Elspeth," I whispered.

"Ye canna deny it," he said, ignoring me as usual. "Aye, she's a bonny one! What're ye doin' over there, lad? If ye had even half an eye, ye'd be over here where ye can reach—"

My knuckles were white around my book. "Get *away* from her!" I muttered, my patience on the verge of snapping entirely.

"Darcy?" Bingley's voice interrupted the chaos in my head, loud enough to make me flinch. "Something amiss?"

I snapped the book shut, desperately trying to force a calm expression onto my face. "I'm quite well, thank you," I lied, my voice strained to the breaking point. "Just... deep in thought."

Bingley gave me a curious look, his eyebrows knitting together in confusion. He clearly wasn't convinced and seemed on the verge of pressing further when Miss Bingley jumped in.

"Oh, Brother," she said, waving her hand dismissively. "Mr. Darcy often appears pensive when he is thinking on matters of great importance. His mind is far too noble to be occupied with trivial things. It's quite natural for him to appear a little distant in company."

For once, I couldn't even muster my usual irritation. I shot her a brief, almost grateful glance before returning to the book in my hands. Miss Bingley—defending me. The irony was not lost on me, and yet, at this moment, I'd take any excuse that spared me from further scrutiny.

But Elizabeth Bennet—the look on her face was enough to make me want to sink into the floor. She wasn't fooled. Not by Miss Bingley's flattery or my forced composure.

I cleared my throat and gave a stiff nod. "As Miss Bingley says... just thinking."

She stared at me for a moment, her eyes narrowing slightly as if trying to decipher *what*, exactly, I was thinking. No doubt, she already thought me strange after our encounter in the library. Now, this only added to her growing suspicions. She didn't buy a word of what I was saying, and frankly, I couldn't blame her. I wouldn't trust me right now, either.

Ewan, though, was still staring at her, and my frustration only grew. "She cannae even see me," he said, grinning. "It's a right laugh, eh? Admirin' her, an' she's nane the wiser."

"Get *away* from her!" I whispered again, my temper barely in check.

"Relax, lad," he said with a wink. "She's nae yer problem—more's the pity."

"Mr. Darcy?" Elizabeth interrupted again. "What are you doing?"

I realized too late that I'd been glaring daggers at Ewan, who was standing beside her, and she had caught me mid-glare.

"Ye might want tae stop starin' at her like that," Ewan chuckled. "Yer Sassenach charm's no' exactly doin' ye any favors."

I cleared my throat, forcing my expression into something resembling calm. "Just... thinking. Deep thoughts. About... Scottish myths, and the fools who believe them."

She didn't look remotely convinced. In fact, she looked ready to bolt at the slightest provocation.

Meanwhile, Ewan leaned in closer, still smirking. "Ye'd best watch yersel', lad. A lass like that doesnae come around often. Ye might want tae keep an eye on her."

I could only stare back at him, my frustration mounting. "Get. Out," I whispered one final time.

He chuckled, stepping away as though he'd won some battle only he was fighting. "Aye, I'll leave ye tae it. But mind what I told ye, eh?"

With that, he vanished, leaving me standing there, gripping my book as though it were the only thing keeping me tethered to reality. I stole a glance at Elizabeth Bennet, who was still watching me like I might burst into flames at any moment.

It took everything in me to force a smile and return to my book. But I knew—I *knew*—my sanity was hanging by a thread.

Nine

Darcy

"**W**HERE'S THE BLASTED ANSWER?**" I growled, shoving my chair back as I rifled through the old pages of *A Tour in Scotland*. The book thudded against the desk as I tossed it open, my finger tracing the lines, desperately searching for something—anything—that might help.

"Ye ken, that's nae gonna work, aye?" Ewan's voice echoed from the corner, but I didn't look up.

I ignored him, teeth grinding, hoping Thomas Pennant, a man who'd traveled Scotland in the 1770s, might have written down some foolproof way to send a Highland ghost packing. There had to be something in here about how to rid myself of this curse.

"Ye're wastin' yer time, lad," Ewan drawled. "Pennant's a Sassenach. What does he know aboot the likes o' me?"

"Let's see," I muttered, ignoring him as I skimmed the index for any mention of ghosts, spirits, or anything remotely useful. "Superstitions of the Highlands..." I turned to the relevant page and began reading.

It didn't take long before I hit a passage on the "Second Sight"—the peculiar Scottish belief that certain individuals could foresee the future, often predicting death or misfortune. There were mentions of ghostly visitations, particularly those of men who had died in battle, and spirits lingering over unfinished business.

Of course. There was always unfinished business.

I sighed, running a hand through my hair. "Spirits of the deceased are said to linger until their souls find rest," I muttered aloud, reading Pennant's rather clinical explanation. "They haunt those connected to their past, often appearing to demand retribution or to seek justice for a wrong unavenged..."

"Aye, that's me, right enough." Ewan was no longer across the room. He had suddenly materialized on the other side of the desk, peering down at the book as though it were some quaint novelty. "I always said ye English like yer books more than yer women."

I glared at him but kept my focus on the page. "Do you mind?" I asked sharply. "I'm trying to figure out how to get rid of you."

Ewan snorted. "Ye think some Sassenach writin' about Highland ghosts has the answer, dae ye? Ha! Bet he never set foot in a proper Scottish hoose. Likely had a few too many ales in Edinburgh an' started ramblin' aboot the 'mystical' hills."

I scanned further down the page. "'Highland ghosts often appear tied to objects of personal significance—belongings of the deceased, which they seek to reclaim in order to sever the spiritual bond.'"

I paused and glanced at the brooch resting innocently on the bedside table. That *had* to be it. Somehow, my pricking my finger on it had woken Ewan, and now I was stuck with him until... well, that was the question, wasn't it?

I looked back at the book. Pennant continued, listing ways ghosts could be laid to rest. Unfortunately, it wasn't as simple as destroying the object.

I sighed again. "It says here I need to help you 'finish your unfinished business.'" I glanced up at Ewan. "Do you even know what that is?"

He scratched his chin, clearly amused by my predicament. "Aye, that's a fine question, lad. But what's the fun in tellin' ye?"

"You don't even know, do you?"

He gave me a shrug that was far too casual for my liking. "Maybe I dae. Maybe I dinnae. I'm enjoyin' seein' ye squirm."

I closed the book with a thud. "So, what? I'm just supposed to let you haunt me indefinitely while I play detective? What did you do, murder somebody?"

Ewan didn't respond right away, and for a moment, I thought he'd actually left. I glanced back to find him staring off, his expression briefly clouded. But then he shrugged, his usual indifference settling back into place.

"Eh, maybe. Could be somethin' like that." He rubbed his chin thoughtfully, as if the idea of unfinished business was a mildly interesting curiosity, not the reason for his eternal haunting.

I narrowed my eyes. "Maybe? That's it?"

He shrugged again. "Who cares? Ye think I've spent me afterlife wonderin' what's keepin' me here? If I'm here, I'm here. If I'm no', I'm no'."

I pinched the bridge of my nose, fighting the urge to slam the book shut. "So, you don't even know if there's something you need to finish? How did you die?"

Ewan curled his lip. "Culloden. On a Sassenach blade."

I swallowed. No wonder he did not care for me. Egad, what if I told him my cousin was a colonel in the Regulars? That I had a great uncle who fought in that battle? I... no, that did not seem like such a good idea, after all. I couldn't figure out how to get rid of him, so it seemed impolitic to make him hate me any more than he already did.

"Well, there go all my ideas." I'd been hoping for a clue, a hint—anything that might give me direction. But no, I was stuck with a ghost who didn't care in the slightest whether he stayed or left.

I skimmed the text again, looking for some practical advice. "It says here that spirits can be bound to objects—like the brooch." I glanced over at that *thing* sitting on the desk, the thing that had started this whole nightmare. "But it's not as simple as just getting rid of it. Apparently, there's something more to it. Something tied to your past."

Ewan leaned over, peering at the brooch like it was some boring trinket. "Aye, that's ma brooch, sure as. Bonny, ain't it?"

I shot him a glare. "'Bonny' isn't exactly the word I'd use. The thing was a seditious commodity. Probably illegal just to own."

Ewan frowned and nodded, conceding my point. "Weel, ye pricked yersel' on it, so now we're tethered, aye? Reckon bad luck flows in yer blood, lad."

"Or it's just bad luck being around you," I shot back.

He let out a laugh. "Aye, that too."

I rubbed my temple, the beginnings of a headache forming. "So, let me get this straight. You're going to keep haunting me, and you don't even care if I figure out what's keeping you here?"

Ewan leaned back against the wall, crossing his arms again. "Nah, no' really. I'm havin' a braw time, an' ye're just makin' it all the merrier, ye ken."

I closed the book with a thud and threw myself back in the chair. "Fantastic. I'm haunted by the most unhelpful ghost in history."

"Could be worse," Ewan said with a grin. "Ye could be dead like me, lad. At least ye've got a bed tae sleep in, and, if ye'd give yerself the trouble o' it, you could feel the warmth of a lassie's—"

I stood abruptly and began pacing the room, my mind spinning. "This is absurd. According to Pennant, Highlanders believed spirits would appear during storms, or in the dead of night, sometimes in dreams. You, however, appear whenever you feel like it and make yourself perfectly at home."

"Aye, well, that's true," he said, sounding quite pleased with himself.

I rolled my eyes and returned to the desk, sitting heavily. I stared at the book, trying to will some piece of information to jump off the page and save me from this nonsense.

"Here," I said, reading aloud again, "Many Highlanders believe that spirits linger where they are wronged, seeking justice or completion of a vow left undone in life. Only once these tasks are fulfilled can they cross over into peace."

I glanced up. "Does that sound familiar to you?"

Ewan's expression faltered, just for a second, but it was enough to catch my attention. He quickly masked it with a laugh. "Maybe. Or maybe I'm havin' a laugh watchin' ye fret over that book, like it's gonna wave a wand an' fix all yer troubles."

I sighed and closed the book again, leaning back in my chair. "You're insufferable."

"Aye, but I'm also yer problem," Ewan shot back, leaning on the desk with a grin. "Instead o' buryin' yer nose in books about ghosts, why don't ye get on wi' livin', lad? Go chase after the lasses. That one wi' the sharp tongue an' those bonny eyes would be—"

I shot him a glare. "The real world would be much easier to navigate without a dead Highlander criticizing my every move."

"Och, ye'll get there, lad. Or I'll stick around long enough tae make ye wish ye'd sorted it sooner."

I resisted the urge to throw the book at him, knowing it would pass right through. Instead, I leaned back, closed my eyes, and tried to remember what life was like before a ghost had taken up permanent residence in my life.

Elizabeth

T HE EVENING HAD UNFOLDED predictably enough. Miss Bingley, with a smug little smile, had settled herself at the piano and begun to play—a performance designed, no doubt, to impress a certain Mr. Darcy. Well, she was welcome to him, the madman.

I sat by the fire, half-listening to the music and bouncing my foot along with the rhythm, more amused than anything. Miss Bingley was decent at the piano, but there was an air of over-rehearsed perfection about it that left no room for real enjoyment.

I glanced around the room. Mr. Bingley, of course, was beaming, happy to encourage any activity that didn't involve people talking over one another. Mr. Hurst was dozing, as usual, and Mr. Darcy... well, Mr. Darcy was being his usual stiff, inscrutable self. Or so I thought, until I noticed something strange.

His posture, always so rigid, was even more so tonight, if that were possible. He sat straight as a rod, his jaw clenched, his eyes darting around like a man looking for an escape route. And then he... twitched.

Not a graceful shift, mind you, but a sudden jerk, as if someone had whacked him in the back of the head with a shepherd's cane.

I blinked, watching in fascination as his whole body seemed to be locked in a silent struggle. One moment he stiffened further, as if trying to resist some unseen force, and the next, he jerked again, this time almost rising out of his seat and then pushing himself backward again.

What on earth was happening?

Just as I was about to gesture to Mr. Bingley to witness this strange display, Mr. Darcy lurched to his feet, his face set in what could only be described as a mask of shaking resignation. He took a toe-dragging step forward, then another, his shoulders tipped backward and his entire body moving as if it were being pushed along by invisible hands. I barely had time to process the absurdity of it before he was standing directly in front of me.

"Miss Bennet," he said, his voice strained, "would you do me the honor of dancing the reel?"

A dance? With Mr. Darcy?

I stared up at him, half-expecting him to retract the offer immediately. His expression was a study in discomfort, as though he were bracing himself for an unpleasant task. His eyes flicked toward the piano, then back to me, and I could have sworn he looked... apologetic.

What in heaven's name was going on?

There was a long pause in which I seriously debated the risks of saying yes or no. If I accepted, I'd be touching him—and he was clearly unhinged. But if I refused... well, what if he really was mad? I didn't want to provoke a man in the middle of some bizarre fit.

"Yes," I said, a little too quickly. "Of course."

Miss Bingley's hands hit the piano keys with a bit more force than necessary, and her smile dropped faster than a stone in a well. That, at least, gave me a flicker of satisfaction. But that flicker vanished as soon as Mr. Darcy held out his hand, and I realized that I had no choice but to take it.

His grip was firm, but not unkind, though his whole body seemed as tense as a bowstring. He led me to the center of the room, where we took our places, and I tried not to think about how this man—this impossibly confusing man—was about to hold me for the next several minutes.

The music began, and we started to dance.

At first, it was exactly as awkward as I feared it would be. His movements were stiff, mechanical, and I could feel the tension radiating off him like steam from a boiling kettle. His eyes were focused somewhere above my head, as though he couldn't quite bring himself to look at me, and I found myself holding my breath, convinced that at any moment, he might flee the room entirely.

But then, something changed.

After a few measures, his posture eased—ever so slightly—and his movements became smoother. His hand, which had been gripping mine as if he were trying to avoid being dragged into the sea, relaxed. By the time we reached the middle of the dance, Mr. Darcy had transformed into something unexpected.

He was... graceful.

I blinked in surprise as he spun me gently, his steps confident, his hands steady and—dare I say it—almost tender in the way they guided me through the movements. The tension was still there, simmering beneath the surface, but he was no longer fighting the dance. In fact, he was keeping up with me with remarkable ease.

"You're quite the dancer, Mr. Darcy," I said.

He glanced at me then, and for a moment, I saw something in his eyes that made my breath catch. It wasn't the rigid, distant look I'd come to expect from him. No, this was different—focused, yes, but softer. As though he were actually seeing me, not just enduring me.

"Thank you," he said quietly, and there was a sincerity in his voice that startled me.

As the reel picked up rhythm, I couldn't help myself. I began to add a few flourishes to the steps—playful claps and lively footwork. To my astonishment, Mr. Darcy didn't miss a beat. He matched my steps effortlessly, even adding a few flourishes of his own. Mr. Bingley even started clapping along from the sidelines.

It was... fun. There was no other word for it. Somehow, in the midst of all the confusion and stiffness and awkwardness, Mr. Darcy had become not only a competent partner, but an enjoyable one. And the way he was looking at me now...

No. No, I couldn't trust that look. The warmth in his eyes, the gentleness of his touch—it was all a trick of the light. Or perhaps I was misreading him entirely. After all, this was Mr. Darcy. The man who had done everything but run from my presence just a few days ago. I couldn't believe he was now dancing with me as though he... liked me.

As the final notes of the song played, we came to a stop. Mr. Darcy released my hand slowly, and for a moment, he looked at me as if he wanted to say something. But whatever it was, he swallowed it back, the discomfort creeping back into his posture.

He bowed stiffly. "Thank you for the dance, Miss Bennet."

"Thank you, Mr. Darcy," I replied, still trying to make sense of the man standing in front of me.

He nodded once and then retreated—no, bolted—back to the sofa, where he sat as stiff as a statue, fixing his gaze firmly on something across the room. He didn't move for the rest of the evening.

And I was left standing there, feeling as though I had just danced with a man I would never truly understand.

Ten

Elizabeth

THE MORNING AIR WAS crisp, the sun shining bright enough to make everything feel a bit less stifling. After spending most of my time indoors, either keeping Jane company or attempting to survive Miss Bingley's conversation, a walk through the gardens felt like freedom. The scattering of golden leaves across my path was a refreshing change from the cloying conversations that seemed to follow me at every turn inside Netherfield.

I rounded a corner of the path, hoping to prolong my escape from the house, when—of course—I spotted Mr. Darcy heading straight toward me. He was staring down at the ground as though it had personally offended him, completely unaware of my presence.

I considered turning around—quickly—but the gravel beneath my foot had other ideas. A twig snapped loudly.

His head jerked up as if he'd been yanked by an invisible string.

"Miss Bennet," he blurted, sounding less like a greeting and more like a man staring into the maw of a sudden thunderstorm.

"Mr. Darcy," I replied, trying not to laugh at how startled he looked. He blinked at me, then glanced around as though unsure what to do next. He wasn't running or cursing at shadows, so I supposed that was a good sign.

We stood there—me staring at him, him staring at... everything else. Neither of us spoke, and if there's one thing I loathe more than awkward silences, it's awkward silences with Mr. Darcy.

"It's a lovely day for a walk," I ventured, hoping to break the stalemate. "Isn't it?"

"Yes," he replied, his voice flatter than a week-old biscuit. "Lovely."

I was beginning to wonder if he'd lost the ability to have a normal conversation. His eyes darted around, almost as if he was looking for something—or, more likely, trying to avoid looking at me. Was he hoping I'd vanish into the bushes if he stared hard enough at them?

"Are you... enjoying your stay at Netherfield?" he asked, as though someone had prompted him from offstage. The words came out stiffly, as if speaking them pained him.

"Quite," I said, though if I were being truthful, "surviving" would have been a better word than "enjoying." I had hoped for a bit more peace and less Mr. Darcy glaring at furniture.

His gaze flicked back to me, then off to the side again, and we resumed our silent standoff. The man looked about as comfortable as a cat in a room full of rocking chairs.

"Forgive me," I said, curiosity finally getting the better of me, "but you seem... unsettled, Mr. Darcy. Is something troubling you?"

He blinked as if I'd suddenly appeared out of nowhere, and his expression shifted so quickly I thought I might have imagined it. "No," he said, though the edge in his voice made it clear he wasn't fooling anyone. "Everything is perfectly under control."

Ah, yes. Perfectly under control. That explained why he looked like he'd been cornered by a pack of wild dogs or—knowing my luck—was bracing for someone to jump out of the hedges with a broadsword.

"You're sure?" I pressed, my eyebrows lifting. He was practically vibrating with whatever thoughts were rattling around in his head. For someone who claimed everything was under control, he certainly didn't seem calm.

"I am," he said, with the enthusiasm of someone trying to convince themselves they hadn't just spilled tea all over their best coat.

I tilted my head, studying him for a moment. He still wasn't looking directly at me. Instead, his gaze kept wandering to the trees, the sky—anything that wasn't my face. I half expected him to apologize to a bush at any moment.

"Well, if you're quite sure," I said, letting the words trail off as I took a step back. This entire conversation was a disaster, and I wasn't sure how to rescue it.

Mr. Darcy nodded sharply as though agreeing with himself. "Yes. Quite."

I began to walk past him, certain I should leave before anything stranger happened. But then, just as I was about to escape, he spoke again.

"Miss Bennet?"

I paused, half-turning back to him. "Yes, Mr. Darcy?"

He stared at me for a moment, his lips parting as if he was about to say something important. But then he snapped his mouth shut, blinking rapidly, and whatever it was, he seemed to abandon it.

"Enjoy your walk," he said stiffly, sounding as though the words had physically hurt him.

I blinked at him, unsure whether to laugh or feel concerned. "Thank you. And you as well."

I didn't wait for a response. Instead, I hurried down the path, glancing back only once to see him still standing there, staring at nothing in particular like he was waiting for the ground to swallow him whole.

Darcy

T HE MOMENT ELIZABETH BENNET turned her back, I all but bolted down the garden path. What the devil had I been thinking, standing there like some sort of tree, my mouth moving but saying nothing? I practically fled to the farthest corner of the grounds, willing my legs to carry me as far from that awkward mess as possible.

"Ach, ye run like a hare wi' its tail on fire!" came the familiar brogue, and before I could even groan, Ewan appeared out of nowhere, strolling alongside me, his arms crossed, a look of pure disappointment on his face. "After the way that lassie danced in yer arms last night?"

"*You* made me do that!" I snapped. "A reel... what the devil, man?"

"Aye, an' ye almost looked like a man for a moment there. A pity ye turn tail in the daylight. Blind fool, ye are, lad. A fool, an' a coward, tae."

I clenched my jaw and kept walking, eyes fixed ahead. Maybe if I ignored him, he'd disappear.

"Ignorin' me now, eh? Aye, that'll fix everythin'," Ewan continued, undeterred. "Ye get a lass like that lookin' ye in the eye, an' ye skitter off like she's got the plague! Where's yer backbone, man?"

"I didn't skitter," I muttered, quickening my pace. "I merely... departed. Sensibly."

"Sensibly?" Ewan threw his head back and let out a bark of laughter. "Ye've got the sense of a sheep herdin' itself into a river! She was right there, lad! Bold as brass, and ye ran! What kind o' 'gen'leman' does that?"

I rounded a hedge, determined to put distance between us, though I knew it was pointless. He was dead; I wasn't getting away.

"A wise gentleman," I snapped. "Who knows when a situation is too far gone to salvage."

Ewan shook his head, keeping pace with me, his boots making no sound against the gravel. "Ye're aff yer heid, lad. Ye had her interest—an' that's more than most men'll ever get. But instead o' takin' the chance, ye ran off wi' yer tail between yer legs like some green lad meetin' his first lass."

I stopped, turning to face him, my patience officially gone. "What would you know of being a gentleman? You've spent most of your time barging into my life, hovering like a cretin over women who can't even see you, and making indecent remarks."

"Och, I see. So ye're a master o' manners now, are ye? Tell me, lad, how gentlemanly was it when ye stood there gapin' like a fish in front o' Miss Bennet, sayin' nothin'? Eh? Aye, thought so."

I groaned, running a hand through my hair. "I didn't know what to say! She... catches me off guard."

Ewan snorted. "Aye, catches ye off guard 'cause ye're too busy hidin' behind yer precious propriety. Always those books wi' ye. Ye wouldn't ken what tae dae wi' a real woman if she slapped ye across the face."

I glared at him. "I suppose your idea of a fitting encounter with a woman involves inappropriate comments and lurking about like a lecherous specter?"

"A lecherous specter!" Ewan laughed again. "Ach, that's a fine joke, comin' from a lad who scarpers at the sight o' his own shadow. Naw, lad. Ye've got tae stop thinkin' an' start feelin'. But ye wouldnae ken much aboot that, would ye?"

"I feel plenty," I snapped, probably too loudly. A nearby gardener glanced in my direction, and I quickly coughed, pretending I'd swallowed a bug. "I 'feel' quite well, indeed."

Ewan raised both eyebrows now, looking thoroughly unimpressed. "Aye, ye feel plenty, do ye? Then why's it ye're standin' there wi' yer neck straighter than a ship's mast whenever she's about?"

"That's enough," I growled. "I am handling things. Quite well, in fact."

"Ye couldnae handle a sheep wi' a stick if it were standin' still."

I bit back a sharp retort, taking a deep breath. "And what exactly do you propose I do? Go back there and declare myself like some lovesick fool?"

"Why no'?" Ewan shrugged. "At least she'd ken ye're alive, instead o' wonderin' why ye keep runnin' fae her like she's got claws."

I groaned again, exasperated. "You have no idea what you're talking about."

"Dinnae I?" He shot me a sideways glance, arms crossed. "If ye had even half the fire that lass has, ye'd ha' wed her by now, nae doubt."

I stopped dead in my tracks, staring at him. "*Wed* her?! We aren't even courting! Egad, I don't even *like* her."

"Oh, aye?" He tapped his chin, looking thoughtful. "Well then, if there's nae objections, I reckon I might just—"

"You will leave the lady alone!" I cried. "Last night was more than enough meddling!"

He grinned and set his fists on his hips. "No' when a lassie fancies a man."

"Fancies... She can barely stand to be in the same room with me!"

"Because ye act like ye're terrified o' her!" Ewan fired back. "Aye, lad. Ye've got all the charm o' a wet mop, an' ye run like one too. If ye'd stop bein' such a stubborn Sassenach, ye'd see the lass looks at ye more than ye think."

I felt my mouth open to argue, but nothing came out. He was grinning, clearly having the time of his life, while I stood there, thoroughly rattled. The worst part? He wasn't entirely wrong. She *was* the only one at Netherfield who even noticed me—truly *noticed* me—enough to see that something was amiss.

A pity she thought I was barking mad.

"I am not discussing this with you anymore," I muttered, turning sharply and marching back toward the house.

Ewan's voice followed me, as irritatingly cheerful as ever. "Aye, run along now! Back tae yer books, yer ruminatin'. Maybe one day ye'll grow a spine!"

I didn't stop, but I could feel my teeth grinding. If I were not careful, I'd be the first person in history to die from sheer annoyance.

Darcy

"How is Miss Bennet this evening, Miss Elizabeth?" Bingley asked, his eyes bright with concern as he leaned forward slightly. "I trust she is recovering well?"

Elizabeth set down her spoon before replying. "My sister was in excellent spirits earlier, Mr. Bingley. I expect we shall return to Longbourn tomorrow."

Bingley frowned. "Tomorrow? Surely, you could both stay a little longer. Another day or two to fully recover might be best. Do you not agree?"

Elizabeth's eyes flicked—almost too quickly—toward me before settling back on Bingley. "I'm confident my sister is well enough to return home," she replied. Her tone was firm, but I couldn't help noticing the slight shift in her expression. Did she think I might object? Or had my presence been the reason for her eagerness to leave?

Better she should go. One less complication for me to fight myself over.

I kept my gaze fixed on my wine glass, reminding myself to breathe. Ever since that cursed conversation in the garden, I'd found myself... *noticing* too much. The way Elizabeth Bennet tilted her head when she laughed, the way her eyes held a spark of something sharp and intelligent when she said something witty. Which she did with regularity, and I think I was the only one at Netherfield who even perceived half the clever things she said. Caroline Bingley had no idea that Elizabeth Bennet was laughing at her more often than not, because she had a sweetly devious way of turning her slights to sound like compliments to vain ears.

And I was fascinated.

I stared down at my plate, suddenly very aware of how insidious this attraction to her had become. Whatever it was that drew my attention to Elizabeth Bennet, it was dangerous—utterly unwanted—and growing harder to dismiss.

Worse than that... it was ever in my face, because even when the lady was not in the same room, I still had that wretched Highlander apparition urging me to do and think things unbecoming of a gentleman. "*She looks at ye...*" he had claimed.

As if Elizabeth Bennet would be caught within half a mile of me if she had any alternatives. If she *did* look at me, it was because she had every reason to believe I was mad as a hatter!

But there I was, allowing myself to watch her. The way she laughed softly at something Bingley said, the way her fingers brushed absently against the tablecloth, the way she met every exchange with a keen wit that belied her playful nature. She truly was... remarkable.

For a blissful moment, Ewan was absent, leaving my thoughts and admiration uninterrupted. I leaned forward slightly, debating whether I should actually say something to her. Something benign, harmless, to provoke her to look my way and tilt her head just so when she replied.

Something that wouldn't make her think I'd gone off the deep end again.

"So, Miss Bennet," I began, clearing my throat awkwardly, "I trust your stay at Netherfield has been... tolerable?"

Her eyes shifted toward me, and in that brief glance, I realized I'd said the wrong thing. What the devil was wrong with my question? Clearly, *something* had provoked her, and not the way I had hoped. Her brows arched, and a faint smile tugged at her lips, though I suspected it was merely out of politeness.

"Tolerable?" she repeated, her tone light but sharp. "I daresay it has been more than *tolerable*, Mr. Darcy. I do hope my sister and I have not been a burden." There it was—that gentle reproach that made me wonder if she'd misinterpreted my every word, or if I simply didn't know how to speak around her.

Bingley had always been oblivious to nuance, and he proved it again. "A burden! No sense. It is a pity you are going so soon. I have used my time poorly, it seems, for I have been meaning to ask someone, and surely you must know—have we any festivities in Meryton to look forward to this autumn? I imagine there must be certain local traditions."

Elizabeth's smile warmed as she considered the question. And, I noted, she was careful to avoid looking at me.

"Oh, there are many—I suppose not that different to any other town. Autumn fairs are quite common, as are harvest suppers. The tenants often gather, and there's always a good deal of music and dancing. In winter, we have caroling and feasts to celebrate the season. Mr. Bingley, I expect you'll have your tenants to entertain at Netherfield?"

Bingley's eyes lit up. "Indeed! I hadn't given it much thought, but a proper gathering for the tenants sounds delightful."

"Oh yes," Elizabeth added. "It's quite traditional here—landowners usually host a gathering of some kind. It brings the community together, particularly as the colder months set in. And, of course, December brings even more delights."

"Ah, lovely," Miss Bingley put in. "Christmas in the country. How quaint. I shan't imagine we shall be here long enough for such... celebrations. Such a pity."

Caroline's eyes slid toward me, a subtle attempt to gauge my reaction, but I remained silent. I could feel Elizabeth's gaze lingering on me as well, though her interest, I suspected, was far less flattering.

"Do you not think, Caroline?" Bingley asked. "I cannot think where else we would be. I have every intention of passing the winter here, and I think it all sounds wonderful! Fireside games, music, perhaps a bit of mistletoe, hmm? Oh, Miss Elizabeth, I saw a pond I fancied would be perfect for skating. Do you... and, er... your sisters skate?"

Elizabeth laughed. "I do, Mr. Bingley, though not well, I'm afraid. But I imagine my sisters would be delighted at the prospect."

Bingley grinned. "Then it is settled! We shall have skating, and you must join us!"

I was nodding along, mentally begging the conversation to stay on the cheerful topic of skating, when I caught sight of movement by the sideboard. My heart sank.

There he was—Ewan, plucking a glass of claret as if he were the honored guest of the evening. He lifted it, examined it like some connoisseur, and took a hefty gulp, his face twisting into an expression of exaggerated disdain. "Och, Christmas... what a miserable time o' year. Cold, dark, and filled wi' folk singin' as if that'll keep the snow away. No' to mention all the daft superstitions. Could hardly walk a step without someone wailin' about spirits lurkin' in the shadows. As if the cauld wasn't bitter enough already!" He paused, looking thoughtfully at the glass in his hand. "Still, this claret's no' as terrible as I thought. For English swill."

And with that, he ambled off, glass in hand, like he owned the place.

The glass. I blinked and gripped my fork so hard it could have snapped. What the devil was he *doing?* What would everyone else see if they should happen to look toward the corner of the room? Hurst, for one, had a perfect view from where he sat, but he was paying far too much attention to his own glass to notice any... anomalies.

I risked a glance around the table. No one else seemed to notice. Not the floating glass. Not the rogue Highlander sampling the Bingleys' best claret. They were all still absorbed in their conversation, blissfully unaware that a ghost was casually reminiscing about haunted holidays while helping himself to their wine.

"Mr. Darcy?" Elizabeth's voice jolted me back into the present, and I nearly knocked over my own glass. She was looking at me, expectant. "Surely you've experienced many grand Christmases in the country?"

Christmas. I released a shaky breath. *Right.*

"Oh, yes," I stammered, scrambling for a coherent thought. "Christmas... of course. Though, I must say, Pemberley has fewer... er..." *Ghosts? No, do not say ghosts.* "...traditional festivities than Meryton seems to, by your description."

"Truly?" she asked. "I would have expected such a grand estate as I have heard Pemberley is to be the very heart and soul of the local festivities."

I swallowed, doing my best to not let my eyes dart to the far side of the room, but instead, fixing them on her face. "Not since my mother's passing, Miss Elizabeth."

"Ah, to be sure!" Caroline Bingley agreed. "Perhaps someday, Mr. Darcy, you will remedy that tremendous loss."

I tried to offer a thin smile. The old me would have done... something. Probably made some pithy remark. But just now, the only thing I was thinking of "remedying" was a certain wine-sloshing intruder.

Ewan wandered to the far side of the room, claret in hand, mumbling to himself like an old man lost in his thoughts. "Aye... no' like we had back home... Elspeth... always somethin' at Christmas, wasn't it?... Yule log... och, that was the stuff. None o' this English... prancin' about. Spirits, aye... but not... no, just stories, mind. Always stories..."

He stopped, took another swig of claret, then sniffed at the glass. "Hmph. No' as bad as I thought... but could use a proper drink..." He wandered further off, grumbling, "Ghosts... aye, no real ones... jus' stories. Still... would make things interestin', eh?"

I was half convinced that if I didn't move, didn't breathe, the claret glass might just remain unnoticed by the others. But every muscle in my body was twitching, and I was desperately trying not to stare at the floating drink.

Elizabeth, however, seemed to notice my discomfort, tilting her head just slightly. "Deep in thought, Mr. Darcy?"

I forced a smile—probably the least convincing one I'd ever mustered. "Just... reflecting on my own country Christmases, Miss Elizabeth. Perhaps I have not appreciated them fully."

She raised an eyebrow but said nothing, while Bingley launched back into his enthusiastic ramblings about the pond and skating, and then, I think he said something about hosting a ball.

"I say," Hurst exclaimed, "where is that footman?"

I froze, my eyes rolling to the corner where Ewan had been standing. He was gone, and the glass with him... by whatever mercies prevailed.

Bingley looked about curiously and then frowned. "Indeed, I had not noticed. He must have stepped out. Something amiss, Hurst?"

Hurst pointed to the sideboard, where the bottle of claret and all those glasses had once stood ready to replenish the ones on the table. "Shoddy business, this. The wine is all gone."

Eleven

Elizabeth

THE MORNING OF OUR departure from Netherfield had finally arrived, and I could not remember the last time I had felt such overwhelming relief. While Jane had been the perfect patient, slowly regaining her strength, the rest of my stay had been something akin to a fever dream. And the strangest part of it all was, of course, Mr. Darcy.

He had spent the last few days lurching from one awkward interaction to the next, and I still couldn't make heads or tails of him. At dinner, I would catch him glaring—not *at* me, precisely, but just past me, as if something dreadful lurked over my shoulder. His eyes would dart back and forth like a man watching a duel no one else could see. If anyone else noticed this behavior, they certainly didn't say a word. And on the rare occasion someone did seem to notice, Miss Bingley would wave it off with one of her insufferable explanations.

"Oh, Mr. Darcy is always so very deep in thought," she would say, with that saccharine smile of hers. "His mind is simply elsewhere."

"Elsewhere" was the understatement of the century.

The most uncomfortable encounter, by far, had been in the library yesterday. A rainy afternoon, and both of us had wanted to read—simple enough—but the air had felt as thick as porridge. He'd fidgeted the entire time, flipping pages and scowling at the book as if it had wronged him. Every now and then, he would look up and glance at me—or near me—with that same intense, searching expression, as though waiting for me to do something… unexpected.

I'd asked if he was enjoying his book.

He'd nearly dropped it, stammered something incomprehensible, and promptly resumed glaring at the spine like it had insulted his ancestors.

It had been a long few days.

As Jane and I made our way downstairs to the waiting carriage, I felt lighter with every step. The suffocating atmosphere of Netherfield, the endless politeness that masked so many undercurrents, and—above all—Mr. Darcy's increasingly strange behavior, were all things I would be happy to leave behind.

I glanced at Jane, who, though still pale, was clearly much improved. She smiled at me, her calm and serene demeanor a stark contrast to the whirlwind of confusion I'd been living in. At least one of us had had a normal stay here.

When we reached the hall, the others were there to see us off. Miss Bingley and Mrs. Hurst stood with their usual expressions of polite detachment, though Miss Bingley was doing her best to appear genuinely concerned for Jane's health. Mr. Hurst seemed to be staring off into the distance, probably lost in a dream about the next meal. Only Mr. Bingley seemed sincerely glad for Jane's recovery, stepping forward to offer his warmest wishes for her swift return to full health. He was the one beacon of normalcy in this odd household.

And then there was Mr. Darcy.

He stood a little apart from the others, hands clasped behind his back, his posture rigid as ever, but… different. For the first time in days, he wasn't glaring at invisible threats, wasn't flinching or darting nervous glances everywhere. Instead, he looked at me—*really* looked at me—as if I had something he wanted but couldn't bring himself to ask for.

It was strange, unsettling even, but there was a flicker of something else in his expression too—something that almost resembled… interest? No, not quite. Curiosity, perhaps. Disapproval, probably. I couldn't say for certain, but whatever it was, it made me pause.

For all the oddity of his behavior, for all the discomfort he had caused me, I found myself feeling a shred of sympathy for him. This was not a house full of particularly warm or understanding people—apart from Mr. Bingley, who was lovely but oblivious to anything more nuanced than polite conversation. Whatever mental malady Mr. Darcy suffered from, it clearly wasn't something the others had noticed or cared to comment on.

As Jane stepped into the carriage, I heard Mr. Bingley's voice again, full of genuine concern. "I do hope you'll recover fully soon, Miss Bennet. Your health is of the utmost importance to us all."

Jane smiled warmly at him, and he gave a small, almost bashful bow before stepping back.

Then it was my turn.

Mr. Darcy approached, his eyes meeting mine with that same strange intensity I'd noticed earlier. There was something flickering behind them, something unreadable but definitely there. He bowed, far more formally than I'd expected him to manage, and for a brief moment, he held my gaze longer than was proper. And for once, he did not swat at shadows or jump at the sound of his own voice.

I wasn't sure what to make of it. His expression was... softer than usual. Less guarded. Almost... vulnerable?

But just as quickly, he straightened, his usual air of aloofness snapping back into place like a lock clicking shut. Without another word, he turned and walked away, leaving me standing there, more confused than ever.

As Jane and I settled into the carriage, I couldn't help but feel a strange mix of relief and curiosity. Relief to be leaving the oddities of Netherfield behind, yes, but curiosity about what, exactly, had broken inside Mr. Darcy to make him behave in such a manner.

Whatever it was, I could only hope it wasn't contagious.

Darcy

"YOU'RE OFF YOUR FORM, Darcy. Missed that shot by a mile," Bingley said with a grin, reloading his fowling piece while I fumbled with mine.

"I wasn't aiming for anything," I muttered, though the truth was I hadn't even seen the birds take off.

Bingley gave me a look like he didn't believe me, but he was too cheerful to care. "What's got you so distracted? You look like you're still at Netherfield in body, but the rest of you is somewhere else."

"I'm here, Bingley," I said, lifting the fowling piece to scan the horizon for movement, though it was clear Bingley was less interested in shooting and more interested in talking.

"Well, I'm not," he continued, unbothered by my terse response. "My thoughts are still very much with Miss Bennet."

Of course, they were. I sighed, finally lowering the piece and giving him my full attention. "You barely spent ten minutes with her the entire time she was here."

"That's where you're wrong, my friend." Bingley's smile only widened. "I saw plenty. More than enough."

"You hardly saw her at all," I countered. "She was bedridden for most of her stay."

Bingley shook his head. "That's exactly why I'm convinced that she is the one, Darcy! Seeing her in her illness was the best possible test of her character."

"Her illness convinced you she's the one you wish to marry?"

"Absolutely!" Bingley stopped walking, clearly gearing up to make his point. "Think about it. People show their true colors when they're at their worst—when they're tired, unwell, or uncomfortable. Miss Bennet was patient, kind, and sweet, even while she was unwell. I spoke with all the maids, you know. She never complained, never asked for special attention. If she can be like that when she's ill, imagine how wonderful she must be when things are going well."

I pinched the bridge of my nose, half in disbelief, half in resignation. "You're jumping to conclusions based on a few days of observing her while she was incapacitated."

"Not at all," Bingley argued. "It's when people are at their lowest that you truly see them, Darcy. Miss Bennet showed me exactly the kind of woman she is—graceful, even in adversity. If that's not a good sign, I don't know what is."

I had nothing to say to that, at least not without sounding like I was tearing down Jane Bennet, who, despite my reservations, had done nothing wrong. Bingley was far too enthusiastic to listen to reason anyway.

As we resumed our walk through the coveys, I found my thoughts turning to my own recent struggles. Ewan had been nothing but adversity since the moment he appeared, and I couldn't exactly say I'd handled it all with grace. In fact, I had probably failed every test of character thrown my way. Not that I cared about offending *him*. Ewan wasn't a person; he was a nuisance. Still, my behavior... well, it left much to be desired. Especially in front of company.

Particularly in front of Elizabeth Bennet.

The thought of her crept in, unbidden, and my viscera started to crawl. But hang it all, she was the only one who seemed to notice or care about my... troubles over the past few days, while the rest of the household was blissfully oblivious.

If I were to use Bingley's measure, she was kind, too, in the way she cared for her sister without a hint of complaint. And as much as I tried to avoid it, I couldn't deny that I found her appearance... striking. Her eyes, especially. They had a way of looking right through me, as if she saw more than I was willing to show.

Not that I would ever admit that. Not to Bingley. And certainly not to Ewan.

"You've gone silent again," Bingley said, giving me a nudge. "Still thinking about something?"

"Only about how you'll explain to the world that you've decided to marry a woman after observing her from across a sickbed," I replied, dodging the true direction of my thoughts.

Bingley laughed, unfazed. "Oh, Darcy, you think too much. That's your problem. You wait for things to be perfect, but life doesn't work that way. Sometimes, you just know."

"And sometimes, you end up shackled to a nightmare," I retorted dryly.

And as we continued through the fields, I couldn't help but wonder if, in some small way, he was right.

Elizabeth

T HE MOMENT THE CARRIAGE wheels churned up the gravel outside Longbourn, the familiar chaos of home washed over us. Before the driver had even pulled to a full stop, the front door flew open, and Lydia's voice rang out like a bell.

"They're here! Finally!"

Lydia bolted down the steps with Kitty on her heels, both of them nearly tripping over their excitement. Behind them came Mary, holding a book in one hand and looking as though she had dragged herself away from it under great duress.

Lydia reached the carriage first, flinging the door open so forcefully I half expected it to come off its hinges. "Jane! Lizzy! Tell us everything!" She seized my hand and nearly yanked me out of the carriage in her eagerness. "Did Mr. Bingley propose yet? Oh, I *know* he did. He must've!"

Kitty, breathless and wide-eyed, bounced beside her. "Did he, Jane? Or was it someone else? Oh, you have to tell us!"

Jane, pale but smiling as ever, shook her head as she descended gracefully. "No, nothing of the sort, I'm afraid," she said, though the blush that crept into her cheeks at the mention of Mr. Bingley didn't go unnoticed—least of all by Lydia.

"Oh, he will soon enough," Lydia declared, with all the certainty of someone who had never been wrong in her life. "Isn't that right, Mama?"

Mama, who had been hovering in the doorway, rushed forward, flapping her hands like a mother hen, seeing her chicks return to the nest. "Oh, my poor Jane! You look so pale! Mr. Bingley had better make good on his attentions after all you've suffered, I'll say that much! Did they feed you enough at Netherfield? Were the rooms warm enough? And the company—well, I don't doubt the company was tolerable, but oh, if only Mr. Bingley had been quicker about it!"

"Mama, I'm perfectly well," Jane insisted, though her soft voice was almost lost under the tide of our mother's fretting.

At last, my father appeared in the hallway, wearing his usual expression of wry amusement, as if the entire household were some great entertainment put on just for him. He didn't rush forward like the others but simply raised an eyebrow as we came inside.

"Well, well," he said, "Jane, it is good to see you on your feet again. And Lizzy, it seems you've returned just in time."

Jane and I exchanged confused looks. "In time for what, Papa?" I asked.

"To meet Mr. Collins. He'll be arriving by evening, and I confess I'm on the edge of my seat to discover if the man has any sense whatsoever. Though I dearly hope not."

I blinked. "Mr. Collins? Your cousin, Mr. Collins? I hadn't realized he was coming."

"Oh, yes. You're in for a treat. You may recall, my dear, that my esteemed cousin is now a parson, and the man who will inherit this house when I'm gone. He has come to avail himself of the opportunity to look over his future inheritance." He delivered this news with the same casual tone he might use to describe the weather.

The room went silent for a moment as we all took this in.

"I hope he's tall," Kitty muttered.

"I hope he's handsome," Lydia added, her eyes gleaming with the possibilities.

Mary cleared her throat as if she had already prepared a sermon on the virtues of cousins. "It is fortunate, indeed, to meet such relations. The fact that he is a parson is quite fortuitous, for he shall be a man of principle. I, for one, shall look forward to hearing his opinions on important matters."

Jane offered a diplomatic, "I'm sure we'll find Mr. Collins perfectly agreeable."

"Oh, I've no doubt that he will be far from all expectations, Jane," Papa said.

I simply sighed. "Well, let's hope he's not a complete bore."

"Not to worry," Papa said with a gleam in his eye. "If he's anything less than perfectly absurd, I'll be sorely disappointed."

With that unsettling prospect hanging in the air, I grabbed Jane's arm. "Come, Jane, let's get you upstairs. You need some rest before we have to entertain the heir to Longbourn."

Jane protested that she was perfectly well, but when Lydia and Kitty cried that Jane should stay and tell them all about Mr. Bingley, she relented and allowed me to lead her upstairs. Once we were safely in her room, I shut the door behind us and ran the bolt.

"Now," I insisted, "to bed with you, Jane. You are already pale from a cold ride in the carriage, and this evening promises to be equally taxing. You ought to preserve your strength."

She chuckled but let me guide her to the bed. "Lizzy, you've done nothing but look after me for days now. You needn't fuss over me anymore."

"Perhaps not," I replied, fluffing the pillow behind her as if it were my mission in life, "but I'm going to fuss anyway. After all, you've only just recovered, and you've been through enough without dealing with all this chaos downstairs. Now, rest."

"Rest," she repeated, her smile widening. "Lizzy, I've hardly been able to stop you from hovering over me this whole time."

I laughed, though I wasn't ready to give up my role as the responsible sister just yet. "Not hovering, Jane—merely keeping an eye on you."

"And here I thought you must have spent the entire time at Netherfield tending to me," she said, teasingly. "Though I suppose you *did* have many hours to spend with the others in the house."

I hesitated, half-wondering how much I should tell her, but Jane's warm expression made it clear she was genuinely curious. "Well, yes," I said slowly. "There were many hours with the others."

"And how did you find them? What are your impressions, after spending so much time with them?"

I settled myself at the foot of the bed, resting my hands on my knees. "Well, you can imagine how Mr. Bingley was," I began, carefully observing Jane's reaction.

As expected, a soft blush rose in her cheeks, and her eyes brightened. "Yes?"

"He was every bit as good-natured and agreeable as you would hope," I said, watching her expression soften with each word. "If anything, his manners were even more pleasing under his own roof than they were at the Assembly."

"I am not surprised," Jane said quietly, and I could hear the smile in her voice.

I couldn't resist teasing her a little. "Oh, I'm sure you're not. And as for the rest of the household—well, that's where it gets interesting."

Jane's brow furrowed slightly, though the corners of her mouth twitched. "Go on."

"The sisters," I said, leaning in, "are precisely what you'd expect—polished, yes, but with a constant air of superiority hanging around them like bad perfume. Miss Bingley spends most of her time either fawning over Mr. Darcy or making veiled remarks about how everyone else in the country is dreadfully provincial."

Jane chuckled softly. "Surely they cannot be that bad."

"Oh, trust me, they can be. Mrs. Hurst is hardly better—content to watch her husband nap while she drops comments like she's casting stones at anyone not born to fortune."

Jane shook her head, still unwilling to think ill of anyone. "I'm sure there is kindness somewhere in them."

I shrugged. "Perhaps. I'm not sure I'd want to spend the time it would take to find it, though."

"And what of Mr. Darcy?" she asked after a pause. "What impression did you form of him?"

I straightened slightly, for I'd been saving the best—or rather, the most bewildering—for last. "Well," I began, hesitating for effect, "I suppose I should tell you all about what really happened at Netherfield."

Jane's expression shifted from curious to concerned, as if she already half-guessed what was coming. "Lizzy, what do you mean?"

I leaned in, lowering my voice as if what I was about to share were some kind of dark secret. "Jane, Mr. Darcy is... odd."

Jane's brows knit together in concern. "Odd? In what way?"

I sighed, settling back against the bedpost. "Where do I even begin? He is the most rigid, uncomfortable man I have ever met. The moment I set foot at Netherfield, he barely looked at me. He spent most of the time glowering at everything and everyone—until, of course, he wasn't."

Jane tilted her head. "Wasn't?"

"Yes," I said, narrowing my eyes in confusion as I remembered the bizarre shift in his behavior. "One moment, he was the stiffest man alive, and the next... well, it's hard to explain."

"Please try," Jane urged, her soft smile not quite masking her growing concern.

"Well, you remember how he looked at the Assembly—so proud and distant, I could've sworn he'd snap if one more person tried to talk to him."

"Yes," Jane said, "though I'm sure he was simply not at ease."

I let out a short laugh. "Oh, I thought the same thing, but no. There's more. Jane, you didn't see him on the lawn before I came into the house. He screamed. *Screamed*, Jane, and then tore off like a man running from some terrible creature."

Jane's eyes widened in surprise. "Screamed?"

"Yes! I thought he was being chased by a pack of wolves. But no, there was no one. *Nothing*. And after that—oh, after that, he did the strangest thing of all. He asked me to dance one evening. When *nobody* else was dancing."

Jane blinked. "He did?"

I nodded. "He approached me with all the grace of a man who was being dragged by a team of horses. He practically stumbled across the room and then asked me if I would dance with him—stiff as a board."

Jane was clearly struggling to process this. "*Mr. Darcy* asked you to dance?"

"And not just any dance. We danced a reel, Jane. And do you know what happened next?"

She shook her head, looking even more perplexed.

"He relaxed. He was stiff, like someone was holding a pistol to his head, but then halfway through the dance, he... loosened. And not only that, he became a better dancer than I would have expected. He even smiled at me—twice! And by the end, I could've sworn he enjoyed it."

"Perhaps he did."

I scoffed. "I think he must've had some sort of fit. Or maybe it's just his nature to be strange. But then—" I paused, trying to make sense of it all. "The way he looked at me, Jane. It wasn't... normal. He looked at me like he was trying to figure something out. I am sure he disdains me mightily, but there were these strange times when it was almost as if—well, as if he was attracted to me."

Jane gave me a knowing look. "That's hardly impossible, Lizzy."

"Impossible or not," I said quickly, "I don't trust it. The man behaves erratically. One moment, he's glaring at the world and cursing at shadows, and the next, he's practically dancing a jig. If I didn't know any better, I'd say he's mad."

"Perhaps he is simply trying to find his place among strangers."

"Oh, Jane," I said, shaking my head with a laugh. "You wouldn't speak harshly of Napoleon Bonaparte himself!"

She smiled and shrugged. "I only think we should be cautious in our judgments. Mr. Darcy may surprise you yet."

"He's already surprised me, but I can't say any of it has been pleasant," I replied, leaning back against the bedpost. "If there's more to him, I'm not sure I want to find out."

Twelve

Elizabeth

"LIZZY, DO HURRY UP!" Lydia's voice rang out ahead of me as she and Kitty scurried down the road, their bonnets already askew despite having just left the house. "The officers won't wait forever!"

"They're hardly waiting at all," I muttered under my breath, quickening my pace to catch up. If my sisters could only summon half this energy for household tasks, our home would be a far more pleasant place. But alas, the mention of redcoats seemed to summon a frantic enthusiasm that nothing else could.

Behind me, Mr. Collins lumbered along, out of breath.

Oh, right. Mr. Collins. The walk to Meryton the next day might have been pleasant—if not for our houseguest.

It was Papa's fault. Mr. Collins had arrived the evening before, as expected, and he had been just as ridiculous as anyone could have hoped. So ridiculous was he that, this morning, when Kitty and Lydia proposed a walk into the village to cleanse our palates somewhat, Papa agreed that sounded like a fine notion. And he compelled Mr. Collins to offer to escort us.

He trundled along beside us, puffing out his chest like a rooster on parade, all while spouting endless praise for Lady Catherine de Bourgh, a woman none of us had ever heard of before last night, but about whom we now knew everything—from how she took her tea to her opinions on garden sculptures. I couldn't quite decide if I pitied or despised him for his mindless devotion.

"And you must know," he said, gesturing vaguely toward the landscape, "Lady Catherine always recommends a brisk walk as a remedy for the constitution. It is an activity that improves both body and spirit."

"Of course," I said dryly, exchanging a glance with Jane, who was clearly trying her best to keep a straight face. "A walk always does wonders." It might do a wonder or two for Mr. Collins, at least, for he could hardly manage to talk and move his feet at the same time, as both seemed to demand all the air in his body.

Kitty and Lydia, trailing a few steps behind, were already giggling. Mary, however, was nodding along, probably thinking this was exactly the sort of thing she'd read in one of her moral books.

"I daresay," Mr. Collins continued, oblivious to the barely concealed laughter behind him, "that Lady Catherine herself would find this village quite charming. She is, of course, a woman of unparalleled taste and judgment, and I feel certain she would take an interest in the welfare of the local inhabitants."

The way he spoke of Lady Catherine, you'd think she was the ruler of half the country and not some distant benefactor of his. I opened my mouth to make some biting comment but thought better of it. He seemed beyond reason, and it was hardly worth the effort.

I sighed, wishing I could shake Mr. Collins' company, but it seemed bothersome men were to be my lot this month. Another, far more vexing figure kept lingering at the edges of my thoughts—Mr. Darcy. His manner even more imposing, his behavior, even more baffling. One moment he seemed determined to avoid me, and the next, he looked as though he were on the verge of saying something important, only to think better of it. If he disliked me so much, why did he always seem so... double-minded when I was around?

"Lizzy!" Kitty called again, dragging me out of my thoughts. "Don't dawdle! We might miss them!"

"Miss them?" I hurried to catch up. "We don't even know if they'll be in town."

Lydia tossed her head. "If they're not in town, we'll wait. They have to come through eventually." Lydia's logic was about as flawless as her embroidery—which was to say, nonexistent.

"If only you applied this level of perseverance to your music lessons," I quipped, earning a giggle from Kitty and an eye roll from Lydia.

"Music won't secure me a husband, Lizzy," Lydia replied, tossing her head dramatically. "But a red coat might!"

Behind us, Mr. Collins caught up somewhat. "Miss Elizabeth, while I admire your light-hearted spirit, Lady Catherine would never approve of such frivolity. A woman's chief duty, as Lady Catherine has often remarked, is to secure the admiration of *respectable* men through modesty and propriety."

"Well, Mr. Collins," I said sweetly, not turning around, "I imagine Lady Catherine must be a paragon of both."

Kitty leaned in, her voice barely above a whisper. "He doesn't realize you're mocking him."

"Of course not," I muttered back. "This Lady Catherine of his wouldn't allow it."

Lydia turned again, already scanning the horizon. "But speaking of respectable men, we're bound to find Mr. Denny in town, and maybe that *handsome* officer too!"

"Ah, yes," I sighed. "The officer whose name you've forgot but whose face you remember all too well. When did you see this mythical being?"

Lydia giggled. "Two days ago, Lizzy, when you were wasting away at Netherfield. And who cares for names when the face is so agreeable?"

Kitty's gasp interrupted any further debate. "Look!" she cried, pointing ahead. "There he is now!"

Sure enough, a man in a red coat was standing by the village shop, chatting amiably with Lieutenant Denny, one of Lydia's favorites. The stranger had the easy posture of someone well accustomed to admiration—and the second he spotted us, his expression brightened into a smile that could have melted butter.

Lydia, never one to waste an opportunity, picked up her pace. "Denny!" she called, waving her hand as if they were the closest of friends.

"Good afternoon, Miss Lydia," Lieutenant Denny replied with a grin. "I see you've brought company." He turned to the man beside him and, with a conspiratorial wink, added, "May I introduce you to my friend, Lieutenant Wickham? He is newly arrived to our regiment."

"Lieutenant Wickham," Lydia repeated, her eyes shining with delight. "How wonderful to meet you!"

Mr. Wickham tipped his hat with an air of practiced smoothness. "The pleasure is mine, I assure you."

I studied him for a moment, noting the ease with which he carried himself. There was something undeniably charming about him, and I could see that Lydia and Kitty were both already smitten.

"And how are you finding Meryton, Mr. Wickham?" I asked, feeling the need to break up the ridiculous display of girlish infatuation from my younger sisters.

"Quite well, I must say," he replied. "It seems a lively little town. And, of course, I can already state with absolute certainty that the company is excellent."

Lydia giggled, and I had to suppress an eye roll. It was all too easy to see why they were taken with him—he was every bit as affable as Mr. Bingley but with the added allure of a uniform.

Before I could formulate a proper response, the unmistakable sound of hooves approached, and I turned just in time to see Mr. Bingley and Mr. Darcy riding toward us.

"Good afternoon, Miss Bennet!" Mr. Bingley called as he approached, his face lighting up. "And Miss Elizabeth! A fine day for a walk, is it not?"

I inclined my head politely. "It is, indeed, Mr. Bingley."

Mr. Darcy, however, said nothing, his gaze locked firmly on Lieutenant Wickham. The temperature between the two of them seemed to drop at least ten degrees. Mr. Darcy's expression, never particularly warm, now looked positively icy.

I stole a glance at the lieutenant, curious to see how he'd react to the arrival of our most enigmatic guest. Darcy was perfectly cracked, but I was the only one who ever seemed to notice.

The change in his demeanor was subtle but unmistakable. Wickham's easy smile faltered for just a moment, and his gaze darkened as he locked eyes with Mr. Darcy. For his part, Darcy's posture stiffened immediately, his jaw tightening as if he'd been hit by a sudden chill.

The two men stared at each other for what felt like an eternity, though not a word was spoken. The way they were glaring at each other, you'd think someone had stolen the last biscuit at tea.

Mr. Bingley, unaware of the silent battle being waged beside him, waved cheerfully at us. "I am terribly delighted to see you about and well again, Miss Bennet. I trust your parents are also well?"

Jane smiled warmly and made some polite answer, but I could barely focus on the pleasantries. My gaze flickered between Wickham and Darcy, both of whom seemed frozen in place. It was like a staring contest where neither man realized there wasn't a prize.

And then, something snapped. Without a word, Darcy turned his horse and rode on, Bingley casting a confused look between us before following.

As they disappeared down the road, I finally exhaled—apparently, I'd forgotten how to breathe for the past minute. My heart wasn't pounding from the walk; it was more the realization that whatever history those two had could probably fuel an entire three-act play.

Mr. Wickham, for his part, seemed to brush it off. He turned back to us with that same charming smile, though I noticed the grimace hadn't entirely left his face.

"Well, ladies," he said, all charm as if nothing at all had happened, "I trust the rest of your afternoon will be just as pleasant."

"Of course," I replied, though my brain was practically doing cartwheels.

What had just passed between those two? And why did Mr. Darcy look like he was about to combust the moment he saw Wickham?

Darcy

"I AM NOT GOING to punch him," I muttered, glaring at my horse's ears.

"What was that, Darcy?" Bingley turned to me, all cheer and confusion as usual.

"Nothing," I growled, adjusting the reins. My horse snorted, probably sensing that I was on the verge of losing my mind.

Behind me, I heard the distinct, sloshing sound of liquid being tipped back. Ewan was perched backward, completely at ease, on my horse's rear end—again—and from the sound of it, he was halfway through an entire bottle of claret.

"Lad," he slurred, swiping his mouth with the back of his hand, "if ye had a lick o' sense, ye'd turn yersel' around, get off that horse, an' knock that smug look clean off that bloody lobsterback's face."

"I am *not* punching anyone!" I hissed through clenched teeth, trying to focus on anything other than the walking disaster at my back.

"But he was talkin' to yer lass!" Ewan gesticulated, swaying slightly, and I've no idea how he didn't upset my horse. "I saw ye an' that redcoat exchangin' glares like ye were scrapin' o'er the last bit o' haggis. Ye'll feel better after ye give him a proper thrashin'."

"Quiet!" I hissed under my breath. I'd got used to the notion that nobody else could hear him, but with him blathering on like that, I could hardly hear myself. And right now, my "self" was the only thing keeping me from jumping out of my skin.

Bingley glanced over at me. "Did you say something, Darcy?"

"No," I said quickly, plastering a smile on my face. "Nothing."

Ewan, of course, wasn't done. "Och, an' that lass—Elspeth—dottin' on him like he's some kind o' prince. Redcoats, aye, nothin' but a plague on decent folk, an' now he's tryin' tae steal yer lass right out from under ye."

"For the last time, she is not *my* lass!" I muttered, mostly to myself, but apparently loud enough for Bingley to hear. "And her name is not Elspeth!"

"What's that, Darcy?" he asked, frowning slightly.

"I said 'not my glass,'" I lied. "No need to stop for a drink, Bingley."

Bingley blinked, confused. "Er... I wasn't suggesting that we—"

"Ye ken," Ewan cut in, "If I were ye, I'd've decked that redcoat right there an' then. Proper punch tae the face, lad. Show him what's what."

"I'm not decking anyone," I snarled under my breath, while Bingley continued to talk—still entirely oblivious.

"Oh-ho! So ye *do* have some fire in ye, lad!" Ewan crowed, louder still. "'Bout time, too! Thought ye'd lost all yer spine—strangled by that fancy cravat ye're so fond of."

At that exact moment, Mrs. Long waved us down on the road. "Mr. Darcy, Mr. Bingley! So good to see you both!" she called out, her smile too wide for my current level of patience.

I forced another tight smile. "Mrs. Long."

Bingley stopped to chat—blast his good manners—while Ewan leaned in even closer over my shoulder. "What in the blazes does this auld moggie want?" he barked, loud enough that I was certain Mrs. Long would hear.

"Mr. Darcy, I was just wondering if you might attend our little gathering next week—oh, how wonderful it would be to have both you and Mr. Bingley there!" Mrs. Long simpered, completely unaware of my growing urge to flee.

"Yes, of course," I answered, barely registering her words.

"Oh, splendid! You know, I thought I saw you speaking to Lieutenants Denny and Wickham—he is new in town, you know, and what a charming young man!"

"'Charming?'" Ewan mimicked in a high-pitched sing-song. "That red-coated serpent? He's charmful as a nettle in yer boot, he is."

For once, I agreed with Ewan. "Charming indeed," I mumbled.

Mrs. Long beamed. "I knew you'd think so! I always say—"

"Aye, turn that horse 'round, lad, an' gie that redcoat a proper thrashin'! What're ye waitin' on, eh? A bouquet o' flowers? Ye don't let a man like that sniff 'round yer lass wi'out leavin' him wi' a fist tae remember. Go on, show him what a real man does when his pride's on the line, instead o' sittin' there like a feart wee mouse!"

I ignored him. Creditably, I thought. I doubt Mrs. Long even noticed my face twitching.

Ewan, apparently annoyed that I wasn't paying him enough attention, leaned down and poked my horse sharply in the flank.

The horse bucked sideways, nearly throwing me off balance.

"Darcy! Are you well?" Bingley cried.

"Yes!" I snapped, shooting a glare at the invisible nuisance behind me. "Perfectly so."

Ewan chuckled, clearly pleased with himself. "That'll put the fire back in ye, sure enough."

Mrs. Long looked startled. "Oh, Mr. Darcy, do be careful."

I smiled again, though it felt like my face might crack under the strain. "Of course. Good day, Mrs. Long."

As we finally started moving again, Ewan stuck the whisky bottle inside his coat, which, I hoped, meant that no one else could see the blasted thing. "Ye cannae just sit there, lad. That redcoat's sniffin' about, an' here ye are, like a wee mouse at a feast. Get yersel' up an' put him in his place!"

I gritted my teeth but managed to say nothing this time.

As we rode further down the road, more villagers waved and called out greetings. I could hardly keep track of who was speaking anymore. Bingley, of course, jumped in with his usual charm, saving me the trouble of saying anything remotely civil, while I tried to resist the urge to throttle my own horse just to make a quicker escape.

Bingley had wanted to ride into town today on some pretense of asking the butcher about a roast pig for the ball he meant to have. It was an errand that could have been better managed through his cook, but I suppose Bingley felt better about taking the matter in hand himself, and so I was obliged to wait for him outside the shop, praying against disaster and feeling like a sitting duck on the streets of Meryton.

"Ye ken," Ewan said, as though we hadn't just been through this, "if I were still breathin', I'd handle that lad mesel'. No' a soul would trust a redcoat further than they could fling 'im. An' that lass o' yers—aye, I'd keep a keen watch on her. She's a bonny one, that. No wonder yer redcoat cannae keep his distance."

"She's not mine!" I hissed, but of course, that was exactly the moment Mrs. Philips happened to pass by.

"Mr. Darcy?" she asked, squinting at me.

I cleared my throat, praying for the ground to swallow me whole. "Mrs. Philips. Good day."

She opened her mouth, her eyes round, and then grasped her skirts and hurried away.

Perfect. Now, even the busiest body in town had reason to think me fit for an asylum. Thank Heaven Bingley was returning to his horse now, and we could be on our way!

Before he was quite back in the saddle, I was already turning my horse for Netherfield, but the sight before me made my blood run cold. Colonel Forster and Lieutenant Denny were heading our way, and right behind them—just my luck—was Wickham. The moment I saw him, my blood pressure spiked. That same infuriating smile plastered across his face as he casually chatted with the officers.

"Och, look there, lad," Ewan shouted, still far too loud. "There's the redcoat who's put the sour on yer day. Well? What're ye standin' there for? Get down there an' show him what a Darcy's truly made of! I hope it's no' porridge in yer veins, lad."

I ground my teeth and stared straight ahead.

Colonel Forster greeted us first with a brisk nod. "Mr. Bingley, Mr. Darcy. Fine day for a ride."

Bingley beamed. "Indeed, Colonel! Quite a fine afternoon! Lieutenant, Wickham. Perfect weather, wouldn't you say?"

Perfect? There was nothing perfect about this.

Wickham's eyes found mine, his grin faltering just slightly. "Mr. Darcy," he said, tipping his hat with false politeness. "Fancy seeing you again so soon. I had not expected to encounter you in Hertfordshire."

My jaw clenched. "Wickham."

That was all I could manage without growling.

Ewan leaned in over my shoulder, practically bouncing with glee. "Go on, lad! Ye can dae better than that! Give him a right jab tae the nose! Knock some sense intae that red-coat!"

I said nothing. Just clenched the reins harder.

Unfortunately, Ewan—thoroughly drunk and now determined to be "helpful"—reached over and gave my horse a sharp slap on the hindquarters.

My horse, understandably startled, exploded into motion.

Before I could react, we were off like a shot. I clutched the reins with white-knuckled desperation as the horse leaped full six feet in the air, then bolted down the street, weaving through carts and market stalls, scattering villagers like leaves in a windstorm. And Ewan, blast him, was holding on by my waist with one hand, twirling his Balmoral with the other, and crowing like a lunatic.

"Darcy!" Bingley's voice echoed behind me, full of panic, but I couldn't respond. I was too busy holding on for dear life.

We careened in a haphazard loop around the village square, where Colonel Forster and Lieutenant Denny were still standing on foot, probably thinking they'd find shelter beside the bulk of Bingley's mount. Instead, they got me—on a runaway horse—barreling straight toward them like I was leading a cavalry charge.

Ewan leaned in closer, cackling like the deranged menace he was. "Now that's more like it, lad! Ye've finally got some fire in ye!" And he... egad, he kept spurring the horse right in the flanks, making the poor brute buck and bolt all the harder.

"I'll kill you!" I shouted, though no one could hear me over the thunder of hooves and the shrieks of bystanders scrambling to get out of the way.

"Nae, lad, I'm already dead. Haud yer hats!" And he walloped my horse's rump again.

Just when I thought the situation couldn't get any worse, my horse bucked down a narrow side street—straight into a low-hanging laundry line.

I ducked just in time, just barely avoiding garroting myself as sheets and petticoats whipped across my face. The horse kept going, now tangled in linens, and all I could do was cling on, half-blinded by someone's very floral... garment.

Forster and Denny had to dive out of the way as I thundered past, narrowly avoiding flattening them both. Wickham, of course, just stood there, arms folded, watching the entire scene unfold with barely-contained amusement.

By some miracle, I managed to yank the reins hard enough to bring the horse to a trembling, humped-up, and quivering stop—right in the middle of the square, where half the village had gathered to witness my public disgrace. My heart was pounding, my face flushed with humiliation, and I was still covered in someone's laundry.

Colonel Forster was brushing dirt off his coat, and he did not look amused. "Mr. Darcy," he said, his voice tight with anger, "is everything... under control?"

I glanced at my poor horse, still tangled in bedsheets, and then up at the crowd of stunned onlookers. "Yes, Colonel," I muttered, barely managing to keep my dignity intact. "Perfectly."

"Oh, aye," Ewan slurred from behind me, still perched on the horse like some drunken pirate. "He's just gettin' warmed up, lad! Never seen a man enjoy a ride?"

I could feel the eyes of the entire village on me—Colonel Forster, Lieutenant Denny, Wickham, and half the townspeople—all watching as I peeled someone's garments off my head and struggled to get control of my horse and my sanity.

"I... I am... perfectly well," I forced out, though my grip on the reins told a different story. "Just... a bit of a mishap with the horse."

Forster's eyes narrowed. "A mishap?"

Behind me, Ewan grabbed my shoulder and rocked me as he shouted in my ear—"Coward, are ye, lad? Blamin' the horse now, is it? Run the blighter down like ye mean it!"

I could only imagine what everyone else thought they were seeing, with my body twitching and rocking uncontrollably for no apparent reason.

"It seemed more than a mishap to me," Wickham said, his voice full of faux concern. "Are you sure you are well, Mr. Darcy? Perhaps we ought to summon a doctor?"

Before I could answer, Ewan gave my horse another playful slap, causing it to rear up slightly. Ewan, the bloody devil, should have slid off backward, but he hooked an arm about my neck, choking me as he dangled there. I clung to the horse's mane and barely managed to stay in the saddle, much to the absolute horror of everyone watching.

Forster, now clearly on edge, turned to Bingley. "Mr. Bingley, do you often have... incidents like this with Mr. Darcy?"

Bingley looked flustered, glancing between me and the colonel. "Er... no. No, not at all. Darcy's usually... quite composed. This is... um... unusual."

"Unusual," Forster repeated, not looking convinced. He glanced back at me, clearly wondering if I was on the verge of losing my mind—or worse, endangering public safety.

Meanwhile, Ewan sat back, took another swig from his bottle, and winked at me. "Ye're welcome, lad. Keep that bloody lobsterback on his toes!"

I could already hear the whispers starting around the square. *There goes Darcy—he's not quite right, is he? Did you see the way he almost ran down the colonel?*

Wickham's smirk deepened as he clearly enjoyed every moment of my public humiliation. If I wasn't already plotting Ewan's second demise—again—I'd be planning Wickham's.

"Well, Darcy," Wickham said, his voice smooth as ever, "I do hope you'll be in better spirits soon. It would be a shame if your... 'mishaps' continued."

I was going to kill him.

Or Ewan.

Or both.

Thirteen

Darcy

THE IDEA OF LEAVING Netherfield had grown more tempting by the minute. After that disaster in Meryton—the awkward encounter with Wickham, the townspeople staring like I'd just declared myself the local madman—I had little reason to stay.

I'd already packed half my belongings, my hand lingering over the last few cravats to fold. London beckoned like a warm hearth on a cold night. At least there, I could put some distance between myself and Wickham, not to mention the other problem. Not Ewan... I already knew that running back to London would avail me nothing there.

But I could get away from Elizabeth Bennet.

A ball. Of all the things Bingley could have arranged, this was the worst. The prospect of spending an entire evening in a crowded room, trying to pretend that everything was normal while a Scottish ghost floated around causing chaos? It was enough to make my stomach churn.

So, I had no intention of lingering around, waiting for the worst. I could easily come up with an excuse—urgent business, an estate matter, or a sudden family obligation. Anything to avoid the inevitable embarrassment that awaited me. Ewan would undoubtedly find some way to humiliate me in front of everyone, and frankly, I'd had enough public scrutiny to last a lifetime.

I even started framing my excuse to Bingley. *My sister Georgiana is missing my company—it is with utmost regret that I must...*

But no sooner had the words formed than I heard a familiar noise. The window creaked open behind me, followed by the unmistakable sound of muddy boots hitting the floor.

"Goin' somewhere, lad?" Ewan's voice came from the direction of my bed, sounding far too relaxed for decent conversation.

I turned, and there he was—a second ago, he'd been crawling in through the window, and there was a muddy path to prove it. But in the blink of an eye, he was sprawled across my bed, boots off, claret in hand, his feet—bare feet, which had no business being in my room—propped up on one of my pillows. The scent of stale ale and mischief clung to him like a second skin.

"I'm leaving," I spat. "Going back to London."

"London, eh?" He took a swig from his cup. "Aye, I always wondered if that London was as grand as folk say. Leavin' yer lass behind, are ye? That's brave, lad. Admirable, truly."

I gritted my teeth. "Elizabeth Bennet is not—she's not—"

"Oh, aye, sure she's not." Ewan waved me off. "But yer runnin', aren't ye? Thought ye were made o' sterner stuff."

"I'm not running. I'm—getting away. There's a difference."

"Aye. The difference is, one's what a proper gentleman does. The other's what a coward wi' his tail tucked does."

I turned, glaring at him. "And what do you suggest I do? Stay here, with you haunting my every move, embarrassing me in front of half the town?"

"Could do that." Ewan shrugged. "Right then, London it is. Yer family's in town, right? Wee sister o' yours, she's there too?"

I froze, the trunk's latch half-closed in my hand. *Georgiana.* I hadn't even considered that.

Ewan's grin softened, almost thoughtful. "Aye, thought that'd catch yer ear. I've been wonderin' what yer sister's like. Must be somethin', growin' up with ye. Might be worth a wee visit tae see if she's got that same stubborn streak."

I stiffened, my pulse quickening. Georgiana didn't need that—didn't need him or the chaos he'd bring. And she didn't need to see her older brother, her closest relation and defender, disintegrate before her eyes.

Ewan scratched his chin, frowning like he was deep in thought. "Ach, but ye know, it's easier wi' ye around. Yer a bit o' fun, if I'm honest. I'm startin' tae get used tae it—this place, these folk. A Highland spirit like mesel' needs a bit o' routine after all these years."

I tensed, my thoughts still on Georgiana. "And if I don't stay?"

"Och, then I'll be wanderin' aboot, tryin' tae make sense o' yer grand London. But who's to say? Could be more trouble than it's worth. I'd rather stick wi' ye here, keep things as they are, eh? I've no mind tae be stirrin' things up wi' yer kin. No sense complicatin' it more than it needs tae be."

He wasn't threatening—just pointing out that, as maddening as he was, things could be worse if I left. Egad, what if the earl or my friends in London saw me acting... out of sorts? Nothing sort of a social catastrophe!

Perhaps... I was better off here for now.

Elizabeth

THE HOUSE WAS IN an uproar. Mama burst into the room like a general delivering news of victory, waving an invitation in the air. Her eyes were alight with the kind of excitement that always made me brace myself for what was coming.

"A ball! At Netherfield! Mr. Bingley has invited us all! Oh, Jane, you know this is a great honor to *you*, above all!"

Kitty and Lydia erupted into delighted squeals, already bouncing in their seats like children promised sweets.

"Finally!" Lydia cried. "Oh, we must go into Meryton today! I need ribbons—no, a whole new gown!"

Kitty was practically beside herself with glee, clutching at Lydia's arm. "Who do you think will be there? Do you think the officers will come?"

"They must! They simply must!" Lydia declared, spinning around as if the room couldn't possibly contain her excitement.

Jane blushed and smiled, a far more serene expression than the madness overtaking the younger girls. Her eyes, though, were full of anticipation. Mr. Bingley had clearly set her heart aflutter, and this invitation was only feeding the flames.

Beside me, Mary frowned. "A ball is hardly necessary, given the state of the country. Should we not focus on more serious pursuits?"

Mrs. Bennet waved Mary off with a flick of her wrist, too far gone in her excitement to listen to such notions. "Nonsense! A ball is exactly what this family needs. Jane, my dear, this is your moment!"

I sat back, watching the chaos unfold, amused but mildly exhausted already.

"It is most generous of him," Mr. Collins declared, oblivious to the fact that no one was listening. "And I trust that the evening will be as grand as those held at Rosings Park, where Lady Catherine often entertains with the highest elegance."

I bit the inside of my cheek to keep from laughing. The idea of a Netherfield ball resembling anything Lady Catherine would deem "elegant" was as likely as a pig sprouting wings.

"And, of course," Mr. Collins added with a knowing look in my direction, "I shall be most delighted to dance with you, Cousin Elizabeth."

Oh, joy—a preordained dance with Mr. Collins, who would likely trip over his own feet while reciting Lady Catherine's virtues. I gave him my most polite smile, hoping it conveyed just the right amount of reluctance.

Before I could respond, Lydia bounced out of her chair. "We must go to Meryton! I must see the officers—especially Mr. Wickham! He'll want to know about the ball!"

Mama clapped her hands. "Yes, yes, go, girls! You must be the first to spread the news!"

As if we weren't already halfway out the door.

T HE AFTERNOON SUN GREETED us as we made our way toward Meryton, the anticipation of the ball buzzing around us. Lydia and Kitty were already discussing the merits of various officers, barely pausing to take a breath.

"We simply must ask Mr. Wickham if he'll attend," Lydia declared, grabbing Kitty's arm. "Do you think he will? Oh, I hope he will!"

I half-listened, my thoughts wandering to what the evening might hold. There was, of course, the matter of Darcy. How in blazes would *that* twitchy fellow survive something as chaotic as a ball? Perhaps he would leave for London before it arrived.

It wasn't long before we spotted Mr. Wickham and his fellow officers walking toward us. Lydia wasted no time rushing up to them, her excitement spilling out like a waterfall. Lydia's squeal nearly shattered the windows.

"Mr. Wickham! Have you heard the news? A ball at Netherfield!" she exclaimed.

Mr. Wickham smiled warmly. "A ball? I had not heard. How delightful."

Kitty practically jumped in place. "You must come, Mr. Wickham! It wouldn't be the same without you!"

Wickham glanced at me then, his smile still in place, but something flickered behind his eyes—hesitation, perhaps. "But I have not been invited."

"Oh, surely you will be!" Lydia cried. "You know he must invite *all* the officers. You will come if he does, will you not?"

"I'm not sure if I should attend, Miss Kitty. I understand Mr. Darcy is in residence at Netherfield, and Darcy and I... well, let's just say our history makes such events somew hat... complicated."

"Complicated?" I echoed. "How so?"

His smile remained, but there was a tightness to it now. "It's a long story, Miss Elizabeth. Suffice it to say that Mr. Darcy and I are not the best of friends."

"I could have guessed that much from your greeting last week," I said with a laugh. "But surely you won't let him stop you from attending?"

Wickham gave a noncommittal shrug. "I hadn't planned to, no."

I glanced at my sisters, still chattering away, and I couldn't resist stepping closer and asking the question at the fore of my mind. "You must know the gentleman rather well, then?"

Mr. Wickham chuckled. "All my life, I'm afraid. You see, my father was the steward at Pemberley. Darcy and I knew each other as boys."

"Really!" Oh, now, here truly was an excellent source of information. I lowered my voice. "Perhaps you would be the right man to ask, then. I must admit, I've found Mr. Darcy's behavior rather... odd, since arriving in Hertfordshire."

Wickham raised an eyebrow. "Odd?"

"Yes," I said, a little more eagerly than I intended. "I've seen him act in ways that make me wonder if he's... well, if there's something wrong with him."

Wickham chuckled softly. "I wouldn't presume to say, Miss Bennet. Though, you're not the first to observe such things."

"Do you mean to say he's always been... this way?"

Wickham's smile turned a little sharper. "Mr. Darcy has always been... difficult to understand. Some might say it's pride, but others—well, others might call it something else entirely."

"I find myself perplexed by Mr. Darcy. There's something... unsettling about him. I can't quite put my finger on it."

Wickham's eyes gleamed with interest, and his lips curled into a grin that was just a touch too eager. "Ah, Mr. Darcy. Yes, he does have that effect, doesn't he?"

"I don't suppose *you've* noticed anything... off about him?"

He leaned in slightly, lowering his voice as though he were about to share some great, scandalous secret. "*Off?* Miss Bennet, you have no idea."

I raised an eyebrow, intrigued despite myself. "Do go on."

Wickham chuckled, clearly enjoying the attention. "Well, I suppose it's no secret that Mr. Darcy and I are not... on the best of terms, but I hardly think I am unique in thinking him less than a gentleman. In fact, just a few days ago, there was quite the spectacle in town."

My curiosity sharpened. "Spectacle?"

He leaned back, the picture of nonchalance. "Oh, yes. Mr. Darcy came tearing through Meryton on his horse, nearly knocked over half the market stalls, and all but ran over Colonel Forster. His horse was out of control, and Darcy—well, let's just say he wasn't exactly in control of himself either."

Lydia gasped, her hand flying to her mouth in delighted horror. "He ran over Colonel Forster?"

"No, no," Mr. Wickham corrected, his grin widening. "But he certainly looked like he was trying to. Poor Mr. Darcy was a sight. I've never seen a man so... flustered."

I blinked, trying to picture the usually rigid, proper Darcy in such a state. "Flustered?"

"Oh, yes," Mr. Wickham nodded, feigning sympathy. "Sweating, red-faced, muttering to himself. I believe I even heard him threatening his horse. Now, did you ever hear of such a thing? You'd have thought he was possessed."

Lydia giggled, and Kitty covered her mouth to hide a grin, but I frowned, something twisting uncomfortably in my chest. Possessed? Muttering to himself? This all sounded vastly familiar.

Mr. Wickham must have sensed my hesitation because he leaned in again, lowering his voice conspiratorially. "It's all rather unfortunate, really. The poor man's clearly... not quite right in the head."

The words hung in the air for a moment, and for the first time, I didn't find Wickham's easy charm amusing. "You think he's... mad?"

Wickham shrugged, his expression far too casual. "Well, I wouldn't go that far, but let's just say he's... *eccentric*. Everyone has their quirks, of course, but with Darcy... it's more than that. He's always been a strange fellow, but lately... well, let's just say I'd keep my distance if I were you."

Lydia and Kitty exchanged gleeful glances, clearly thrilled by the idea of Darcy being mad. But I found myself frowning, feeling a pang of... pity? Surely not. And yet...

I couldn't help but remember all the strange things I'd witnessed at Netherfield. Darcy's odd behavior, his stilted conversations, the way he looked at me as though he wanted to say something but couldn't. Could it be true? Was he really losing his mind?

"Is he quite safe to be around?" I found myself asking.

Mr. Wickham's face grew thoughtful. "I should not think him dangerous unless you choose to believe... whatever he is saying. Goodness knows what that might be."

I forced a tight smile. "I daresay it is a pity you will not be at the ball, then. I would very much like to hear your thoughts on how he comports himself there."

Just then, Lydia interrupted. "Oh, please say will you come, Mr. Wickham! We simply can't have a ball without you!"

Mr. Wickham's hesitation vanished, replaced by his charming smile. "On second thought, Miss Lydia, I think I shall attend. It might be worth seeing how the evening unfolds after all."

Darcy

I SAT HUNCHED OVER my desk, surrounded by an ever-growing pile of books, each one more useless than the last. I was in the middle of scratching out yet another letter to my solicitor, hoping for something—anything—that would explain this madness.

The window creaked open behind me.

At first, I thought it was a draft. Maybe the hinges were loose. But then I caught the faint smell of whisky and wet earth.

"Ach, yer books whisperin' sweet nothin's to ye again?" came Ewan's voice, far too close for comfort.

I whipped around, only to find Ewan—half through the window, his boots muddy, with a grin on his face like this was the most natural thing in the world. One leg was already inside, the other dangling outside as if he were just taking his sweet time.

"What are you doing?" I snapped. "You've got to be the most—"

"Comfortable, aye," he finished for me, hauling himself fully inside. He dusted off his coat, though the mud on his boots remained annoyingly intact. How did a ghost... oh, blast, what was the point in wondering about it anymore?

"Thought I'd stretch me legs. House gets cramped, ye know?"

I didn't know. At all.

I glared at him as he made himself right at home, strolling across the room with his usual swagger, wiping his muddy boots on my carpet as if it were a welcome mat.

"Get off that," I growled, feeling my blood pressure rising.

He gave me an innocent look. "What? It's no' like ye use it for anythin' other than collectin' dust."

I pinched the bridge of my nose. "You know, if you stopped distracting me with this... nonsense, maybe I'd actually make some progress figuring out why you're still here."

"Progress, eh?" Ewan said, plopping into the chair by the fire, boots still firmly planted in the middle of my rug. "Aye, ye look like yer gettin' somewhere. Must be riveting stuff, lad."

I wanted to throw something at him—preferably one of the heavier tomes.

"Why don't you make yourself useful and actually tell me what happened at Culloden?"

He ignored me entirely, picking up one of the books on the desk and flipping through it lazily as though the subject of his unfinished business was the last thing on his mind. "So, this is how ye spend yer nights. I'd go mad."

"Funny," I muttered, "I thought I was already there."

Ewan tossed the book aside, glancing out the window he'd just crawled through. "Ye ever think about somethin' other than yer precious cravats an' letters, lad? What about the bonny lass, eh? Ye've got eyes. Pretty thing like her, brown hair, a smile like she's got all yer secrets tucked away. Reminds me of—ach, never ye mind."

"Miss Bennet?" I asked, more alarmed by how casual he was about it. "Why do you keep bringing her up?"

"Because she knocks ye right off yer pins. Ye think I've got better things tae do than watch ye blunder about like a calf findin' its legs? Well, I dinnae, so why shouldn't I go on about the lass?"

I bit back a retort, mostly because my head was still reeling as dizzily as it had the evening we had danced. The fact that he was lingering on Elizabeth Bennet—on her—set my teeth on edge. "You stay away from her."

He grinned, slow and mischievous.

"I'm serious, Ewan."

"Aye, and so am I," he said, stretching his legs and letting out a long sigh as if this conversation were nothing more than a pleasant diversion. "Ye should be thankin' me, lad. If I hadnae given ye a wee shove, ye'd still be sittin' there, glarin' at the lass. Or that redcoat. Maybe both."

"If you hadn't shoved me, I might have passed for sane, but all such hopes are now out the window!"

"Well, ye weren't exactly takin' the lead, lad. Took a wee bit of encouragement."

"You... meddled in affairs that are not yours!"

"Meddled? Is that what ye call it? I prefer to say I was givin' ye a wee push in the right direction."

I clenched my fists. "If you keep meddling in my affairs—"

"Ach, ye'll what? Threaten me, will ye? I'm already dead, ye daftie, remember?" He chuckled, taking off his boots and propping them up on my desk, the smell hitting me like an attack.

How could I smell a ghost's feet? It made no sense, but here it was—an undeniable assault on the nose. "For heaven's sake, put those away!" I snapped, recoiling from the scent.

"What's the matter?" he said with a smirk, wiggling his toes like some kind of barbarian. "Afraid yer fancy English manners cannae stomach a wee taste o' real livin'?"

I buried my face in my hands, half in disbelief, half in frustration. "I cannot believe this is my life."

"Well, ye best get used to it," he said, lounging back like he hadn't a care in the world. "I'm no' goin' anywhere, lad. No' till ye sort yersel' out."

"And what exactly am I supposed to sort out?"

"I dinnae ken," he said before belching loudly. "Now, if ye don't mind, I'm off tae find somethin' a bit more excitin' than yer books. Maybe that bonny lass..."

Before I could even think of a reply, Ewan strolled right back out the window, leaving behind a muddy mess and the faint scent of whisky and regret.

Fourteen

Darcy

I STEPPED INTO THE cramped little bookseller's shop, the door creaking ominously behind me. It was the kind of place that reeked of dust and moldering paper, with shelves packed so tightly they seemed to sag under the weight of volumes that hadn't been touched in years. A far cry from the sort of establishments I was used to, but desperate times, and all that...

A bell jingled, and an older man emerged from the back, wiping his spectacles on a cloth. He squinted at me like he hadn't seen daylight in a while, or customers of my rank. "What can I do for you, sir?"

I cleared my throat, uncomfortable already. "I'm looking for books on... Scottish history. Myths, superstitions, that sort of thing. Anything on Culloden, perhaps?"

He blinked. Clearly, that was not the sort of request he got every day. "Culloden, you say?" His voice had that dubious tone people used when they were trying to figure out if I was serious. "Not much call for that around here, I'm afraid. Mostly got sermons, farming manuals, the odd novel. Plenty of those, actually. Can't say I've got much in the way of ghost stories, though."

Ghost stories. Of course, that's how it would sound. I resisted the urge to groan. "I'm in a bit of a hurry to find this material. Is there any way you could order something?"

He scratched his head, his face screwed up in thought. "I suppose I could try."

"I will make it worth your while," I said, sliding a coin across the counter.

He took it up with an appreciative smile. "Well, now, that will certainly grease the wheel, but even at that, it will take some time. London has its share of booksellers, but you know how it is, asking for small, specific orders like that. It's never quick."

Not quick. That was the last thing I wanted to hear. The thought of another week at Netherfield, dodging Wickham, avoiding Elizabeth Bennet, and dealing with Ewan's constant interruptions made me want to walk right out of Meryton and keep going. But still, I asked, "And there's no one nearby with a collection that might include such material?"

The bookseller chuckled, shaking his head. "Well, now, there's one man I can think of. That Bennet fellow, over at Longbourn. Buys more books than anyone I've ever seen. Got a whole room full of them. He's bound to have something. Might be worth asking him."

Bennet. Was I to be forever chasing Bennets?

I stared at the bookseller, unable to stop my jaw from clenching. Mr. Bennet. Of all people. I barely knew the man, apart from the few social interactions forced upon us, but worse—far worse—was his daughter. The last thing I wanted was another awkward encounter with Elizabeth Bennet, the woman who already believed I was unstable. Perhaps she wasn't far off at this rate.

The bookseller was still smiling at me as if he'd done me a great favor. "Of course," he added, "You may have to charm him a bit, and he's no respecter of a fat purse. Can be a tricky fellow, that one."

Tricky? If he was anything like his daughter, he would be a complete menace to my sanity.

I nodded, thanked him as politely as I could manage, and left the shop, my head already pounding with the thought of what I'd have to do next. The streets of Meryton were relatively empty, the autumn breeze rustling the leaves on the trees as I made my way toward my horse. Longbourn, it was. Every step felt heavier than the last.

How did one approach a man like Mr. Bennet? He was the sort of man who held no one and nothing in any sort of awe. My name and rank meant nothing to him. He would be just as likely to let me wait on his pleasure outside in the rain, just because he could—well, that was until his wife discovered me and took pity on me. With my luck, I would end up with a debilitating chest cold and a dangerous fever that necessitated my staying under his roof, nursed by the tender mercies of Mrs. Bennet and her plethora of daughters.

But no, I had no need to invent such fantastical fears, for the reality was terrifying enough. The real obstacle was not Mr. Bennet or his wife or even his raucous youngest daughter. The moment I set foot in that house, I would have to face *her* again. Elizabeth Bennet, with her sharp wit, her knowing looks, and that ever-present smirk that made me question everything I said. The woman had already witnessed me at my worst, and if I knocked on her father's door to beg for books about Highland ghosts, it wouldn't exactly improve my standing.

But what other choice did I have? I had to find answers, or I'd never rid myself of—

"Ach, ye look like yer walkin' to the gallows."

I swung into the saddle and stared straight ahead, my pulse spiking. "I might as well be," I muttered through gritted teeth.

Ewan was suddenly sitting backward on my horse's neck, arms crossed and staring at me. "Where ye off tae, lad? Gonna go ask yer lass's da for help? Och, that'll go well."

"Egad, you smell foul," I grumbled. "How the bloody devil do you *smell?*"

He wrinkled his nose and got a vague expression. "I reckon the same way *ye* do. Wi' my nose."

"Get off my horse!" I thundered.

And he actually did. I couldn't say where he went, but I didn't care. I spurred my horse into a gallop—not that it would do any good—but a woman carrying a basket was giving me the strangest look as she passed, and I had made myself "odd" enough in town.

He only laughed and kept up. I couldn't see him, but I could hear his boots clunking along beside my horse. "Dinna be so sour. Yer makin' a right fool o' yerself, ye know. What's the worst that could happen? Bennet might spin ye some tale about Highlanders and laugh ye out the door. But ye'll get tae see the lass. Aye, an' that's no' the worst fate, is it?"

I kept riding, refusing to rise to the bait. But my hands were clenching tighter on the reins with every stride.

And then, just as I turned the corner near Longbourn, I saw her.

Elizabeth Bennet.

I pulled my horse up so quickly his hind feet locked and slid on the slick road. All thoughts of asking Mr. Bennet for help evaporated. All sense of composure vanished. And for the first time in days, I wasn't thinking about books, or ghosts, or Highland superstitions. I was thinking about how quickly I could get out of there before she saw me.

Ewan, naturally, saw her too. "Aye, there she is. Lookin' like a storm in a teacup, ready tae rattle yer cage again."

"Shut. Up," I muttered, trying desperately to avoid making eye contact with her as I changed course, pretending I had somewhere else to be.

But she was already heading my way.

And there was no escape.

Elizabeth

I T WASN'T AS THOUGH I was actively seeking out Mr. Darcy, but there he was, sitting in the saddle stiff as a post by the corner of the road, looking like someone had told him his horse just insulted his mother. What *did* this man have against horses?

I couldn't exactly avoid him—well, I *could* have, if I hadn't been spotted already, but there was a limit to how uncivil I could be, even to Mr. Darcy. And so, as fate would have it, we were walking directly toward each other, his face growing tighter with each step.

Wonderful. I always like starting out a walk by getting waylaid by the local lunatic.

"Miss Bennet," he greeted me, with the same strained courtesy as always. The man couldn't have looked more uncomfortable if he were being measured for a noose.

"Mr. Darcy," I replied. He looked... well, agitated wasn't the word for it. Agitated was too mild. He looked like he was either going to burst into flames or collapse into a pile of anxious, brooding stares.

"Are you out for a pleasure ride, Mr. Darcy?" I asked, trying to mind my manners, even though I wasn't quite sure why I was making the effort. "It's such a fine day."

He blinked at me, as if he'd forgotten how conversations worked. "A... ride? Yes. Yes, I was just... riding. At a walk. A pleasure ride."

"Oh, good," I said lightly, resisting the urge to sigh. It was clear he hadn't been walking anywhere. His horse was dripping sweat and still blowing, and Mr. Darcy was practically pop-eyed and twitching like a hare that had just seen its own doom.

And, for not the first time, I wondered if it was because of *me.*

An awkward silence followed. He shifted in the saddle, glancing around like he was half-expecting something to jump out and bite him. And I, trying my best to keep the conversation alive—for reasons unknown even to myself—blurted, "You'll be attending the Netherfield Ball, I suppose?"

His face twisted for a second, like I'd just slapped him. The Netherfield Ball—a simple question, I thought. Naturally, he would attend, because he was a guest at the house... unless he thought to spare us all the bother of watching him swat at shadows and take himself back to London. But judging by his reaction, you'd think I'd asked him to dance with a tiger.

"Y-yes," he replied slowly, though his voice was taut. "I will."

I smiled as best I could. "And I expect Lieutenant Wickham will be there too. He did mention it when he called the other day."

If Mr. Darcy had looked uncomfortable before, he now resembled a man who had just been told he was about to be thrown off a cliff. His jaw tightened, and for a moment, I was sure he was going to snap his riding whip in half.

"Lieutenant Wickham," he said, and that was all.

Nothing more.

Just *Lieutenant Wickham*, as if the name alone caused him physical pain.

I watched him carefully, growing more and more bewildered by the second. Lieutenant Wickham hadn't spoken truly ill of Mr. Darcy the other day, but something was clearly brewing between them—something more than just a casual dislike.

"Is there—" I began, unsure of how to navigate the conversation any further without accidentally making the man combust on the spot, "—some... history between you and Lieutenant Wickham, Mr. Darcy?"

His eyes flicked to mine, and for a moment, I thought he might actually say something useful. But instead, he pulled his horse a step back, nodded stiffly, and said, "Excuse me," before whirling his mount and galloping off like a swarm of bees was after him.

I stared after him, my mouth half-open in disbelief. That was it? That was the extent of our conversation? He'd barely spoken ten words to me before bolting like a fox in the briars.

"Well," I muttered to myself, watching his tall figure disappear around the bend, "he's certainly not getting any less strange."

Poor Mr. Darcy. As mad as a hatter, and possibly more uncomfortable in his own skin than any person I had ever met. But still, I couldn't bring myself to dislike him.

I sighed, shaking my head. He wouldn't harm anyone. Of that much, I was sure. But if he kept behaving this way, the whole town would soon agree that Mr. Darcy of Pemberley was not quite right in the head.

And for reasons I couldn't quite explain, the thought made me pity him.

"L IZZY, DO YOU THINK there will be mistletoe at the ball?" Kitty asked, her voice full of hopeful mischief as she twirled about the room, her ribbons flying behind her.

"Lydia, it is only November. I certainly hope not," I replied, laughing at the thought. "Besides, with all those officers in attendance, I fear there would be no safe corner left in the room for any woman over the age of fourteen."

Kitty giggled, but Jane tried to turn our conversation in a more respectable direction. "Oh, Lizzy, you know it will be a lovely night. Mr. Bingley will ensure everyone enjoys themselves."

"And I'm sure he will," I said, "especially if a certain Miss Bennet is in attendance." Jane's blush was as predictable as it was charming.

We had been talking of the Netherfield Ball for days, and it seemed as if the whole town was abuzz with excitement. The chance to see all our neighbors dressed in their finest, the music, the dancing, and perhaps a moment of stolen romance for some lucky young lady—all the makings of a perfect evening.

Charlotte, seated near the fire, chimed in with her usual practicality. "I'm more excited about the food, to be honest. I hear Netherfield's cook has outdone herself with the preparations."

"Oh, Charlotte! Must you always be so sensible? I had hoped you would swoon over the prospect of dancing with every eligible bachelor in Meryton."

Charlotte snorted. "I'll leave the swooning to Lydia."

I grinned, but before I could respond, Charlotte leaned in with a conspiratorial air. "Actually, I've heard some rather interesting gossip about the guest list."

"Oh?" I feigned indifference, though I was always keen to hear the latest news.

Charlotte glanced at the door to ensure no one was listening, then lowered her voice. "Papa was in town the other day, and he overheard some of the men talking about Mr. Darcy."

I blinked. "Mr. Darcy? What could they possibly have to say about him?"

"Well," Charlotte said, leaning even closer, "it seems Mr. Darcy had quite the... episode in town a while ago."

I raised an eyebrow, already half-expecting whatever it was. "I believe I already know this rumor, but what did the gentlemen say?"

"They say he was seen acting very strangely—something about his horse nearly throwing him off, and then he started talking to himself."

My eyes widened in disbelief, though a laugh threatened to escape me. "To himself? In public?"

Charlotte nodded, her face as serious as ever. "Yes, and Colonel Forster himself had to intervene. Some of the townspeople are starting to wonder if Mr. Darcy is entirely... well, you know."

Kitty gasped, her eyes widening in excitement. "You mean they think he's mad?"

I groaned. "Oh, Kitty, don't be so dramatic. Mr. Darcy is not mad. He's..."

What? What *was* Mr. Darcy? Odd? Eccentric? Brooding in the most mysterious and puzzling way possible?

He was certainly something.

But as I thought about that strange encounter with him on the road, I couldn't deny that the man had a knack for making even the most straightforward conversations unbearable.

Still, it was one thing to be odd. It was another thing entirely to be dangerously unpredictable and a menace to society. And despite his many faults, I couldn't believe that Mr. Darcy had crossed into the realm of true madness. No. He was far too controlled for that.

"Well, whatever he is," I said with a sigh, "I'm sure Mr. Darcy will manage to endure the ball without causing a scene."

Charlotte smirked. "Perhaps, but I wouldn't place any wagers on it."

"Oh, come now," Jane objected. "Mr. Darcy may be reserved, but he is a gentleman. I'm sure we've misunderstood whatever happened in town."

"Misunderstood?" Charlotte repeated. "Jane Bennet, there you go again, defending everyone whether they deserve it or not. He nearly trampled a man in the middle of Meryton."

"He did *not* nearly trample anyone," Jane protested. "He's just…"

"Misunderstood?" I finished for her, grinning. "I daresay that's the best excuse yet."

"I don't care if he's 'misunderstood' or as cracked as King George," Kitty declared, already bouncing on her feet again. "I only care that the officers will be there—and Mr. Wickham!"

"And I care that there's snow in the forecast!" I added with a generous helping of fake excitement. Anything to change the subject. "I overheard Mama talking about ice skating on Christmas Eve. Perhaps we'll have enough ice this year to make it a proper party."

"Oh, I hope so!" Jane said, her eyes lighting up at the thought. "Remember last year, Lizzy? The whole village turned out."

"I remember. I nearly broke my neck when Kitty crashed into me."

Kitty huffed. "It wasn't my fault! *You* skated into *me*."

"Ah yes, that's what I recall," I said dryly. "But let's not repeat the performance this year, shall we?"

We all laughed, all thoughts of mad neighbors and scandals melting away. The ball, the upcoming Christmas festivities, the promise of winter fun—it was enough to push thoughts of Mr. Darcy's oddities to the back of my mind.

For now.

Fifteen

Darcy

I WALKED INTO THE ballroom, already regretting my life decisions. The noise, the heat, the endless stream of people talking at me—I'd had more pleasant experiences being thrown from a horse.

Bingley, naturally, was grinning from ear to ear, delighted to be playing host, while Caroline Bingley hovered nearby, fluttering around him like an overfed butterfly. But my attention, as much as I tried to avoid it, was drawn elsewhere.

Elizabeth Bennet.

She had arrived with her family, and somehow, without doing much at all, she had managed to become the only person I could see in the room. This woman was becoming a problem. A *serious* problem.

Across the room, I spotted her laughing at something Bingley said to Miss Bennet—her eyes sparkling, her smile wide—and suddenly, the ballroom felt stifling. I tugged at my cravat.

I needed air.

"Aye, that'll do ye wonders. Can't breathe 'cause ye're gawkin' at her again, are ye, lad?"

I didn't even flinch. I should have known better than to hope for an evening without Ewan's interference. Every time he appeared, it was like an invisible punch to the gut. And yet, it seemed I was building up some sort of tolerance for gut punches.

"Would ye just speak up tae the lass? She's had her eye on ye for weeks, ye daft fool."

"She has not."

"Oh aye, 'cause ye're the grand expert at readin' folk, aren't ye now?" Ewan rolled his eyes, leaning against the wall near the refreshment table.

Bingley caught sight of me and waved from across the room. "Darcy! Over here!"

I gave him a brief nod. Perhaps I should feign illness now...

Ewan, naturally, followed me as I crossed the room, his hands casually tucked behind his back like he was going for a pleasant evening stroll. It was eerie how Charlotte Lucas passed right through him, but he managed to stomp on the toe of some red-coated lieutenant until the young man yelped and spun round, looking accusingly at his inebriated comrade.

"Stop that!" I hissed under my breath.

"Ye'd best pick up yer pace, lad. That bloody redcoat's havin' words wi' yer lassie now. He'll be charm-in' the shoes right off her feet afore ye ken it."

My stomach flipped, and I glanced quickly in Elizabeth's direction. Sure enough, there he was—Wickham, all smiles and smooth words. Elizabeth was looking up at him, her expression a mixture of admiration and amusement.

Blast.

Wickham *dared* to come *here?* Tonight? I hadn't realized my fists were clenched until Ewan clucked his tongue next to me.

"There it is again—the bloomin' scowl. Ye've all the subtlety o' a cart wi' a busted wheel, but that's about *all* ye've got. Where's yer spine, man? D'ye need me tae send out a search party fer it?"

I reached for a glass of wine from a passing tray, resisting the urge to throw it in his direction. Instead, I took a long drink and tried to compose myself.

"Ye could at least say somethin', lad. A kind word, maybe? Or crack a wee joke? She's one fer a laugh, that lass."

I swallowed the wine with more force than necessary. "I'm not discussing this with you."

"Aye, then I'll take it on meself! Look at her! Even that cursed redcoat hasn't put her off, an' the man's got all the depth of a puddle."

I finally shot him a look of warning, but Ewan just winked. "What? Just makin' an observation, lad. Aye, if I had yer face an' half yer coin, I'd be dancin' circles round the lass."

"I beg you," I whispered sharply, "stop talking."

"Beg all ye like, lad, but that lass isn't goin' tae wait forever." He gave me a sly grin and then strolled off—presumably to harass some unsuspecting militia officer.

I took a steadying breath and made my way toward Bingley, who was still waving like a madman. If I couldn't avoid this disaster, I could at least pretend to be invested in polite conversation. *Polite* being a relative term.

"Darcy, my friend!" Bingley boomed as I approached. "Isn't this evening simply perfect? I was just talking to Miss Bennet about planning more festivities this winter."

"I'm sure it will be agreeable," I replied, hoping I sounded more convincing than I felt.

Bingley beamed, entirely oblivious to my discomfort. "I was thinking we might have some ice skating on Meryton's pond, or maybe even a bit of caroling around the fire. What do you think, Miss Elizabeth?"

I nearly jumped out of my skin. I'd thought she was on the other side of the room! But as I turned my attention, I found her standing at my elbow, her head tilted as she regarded me in a way that seemed... both curious and cautious. "That does sound delightful," she said. "I am quite certain that anything Mr. Bingley plans will be met with pleasure by the neighborhood in general."

"Splendid!" Bingley cried. "Why, as soon as the ice is thick enough, we shall make merry."

"Have you ever been skating, Mr. Darcy?" Elizabeth asked.

"I... I have," I stammered, the words coming out far more stiffly than I intended.

"Ah, but can ye stay on yer pins?" Ewan quipped from behind me, no doubt smirking like the fool he was.

I shot a glance over my shoulder but found nothing, just the maddening hum of party conversation. Still, the ghost lingered—right in my ear, apparently determined to ruin what little composure I had left.

"Darcy?" Bingley's voice broke through my haze. "Someone you were looking for?"

I straightened up, forcing a tight smile. "No, of course."

"Ye certain aboot that, lad?" Ewan's voice came again, closer this time. "Yer posture's stiffer than a pike."

Suddenly, what felt like a hand—*his* hand—clapped me firmly on the back. It wasn't visible to anyone—probably not even me, if I had twisted round to look—but the force of it made me lurch forward, nearly stumbling into Elizabeth. She stepped back, startled, and Bingley's brow furrowed in confusion.

"Mr. Darcy!" Elizabeth scolded. "Have you lost the last manner you possessed?"

"Ach, there he goes!" Ewan laughed from somewhere behind me. "Still standin' there like ye've a stick up yer backside!"

I managed to recover myself—barely—but I could feel all three of them watching me now. Bingley and Miss Bennet exchanged puzzled glances, and Elizabeth's eyes narrowed as if trying to solve the puzzle that was *me*.

"I—" I cleared my throat, forcing out a laugh that sounded horribly strained. "Just a misstep. A sore muscle... from riding yesterday. I'm afraid it has been troubling me some. Perhaps some fresh air would do me good. If you'll excuse me."

Elizabeth's frown deepened, and I could feel her eyes following me as I hurried toward the nearest exit. Behind me, Ewan's laughter echoed, growing fainter but no less humiliating.

I didn't stop until I was halfway to the terrace, heart pounding, my mind racing. It was only by sheer willpower that I hadn't made a complete spectacle of myself... yet.

But if I lived to see another day without being committed to an asylum, it would be a miracle.

Elizabeth

I WAS BEGINNING TO wonder if there was any corner of the room where I could stand without running into someone I was trying to avoid.

The Netherfield Ball had been exactly as expected—grand, lively, and packed with half of Meryton. I had successfully dodged Mr. Collins for most of the evening—a triumph in itself—only to find myself now dodging another, far more intimidating figure.

Mr. Darcy.

The man had been acting oddly all evening—though to be fair, his definition of "odd" was quickly becoming "business as usual." I'd caught him glancing in my direction at least a dozen times, each time with a look that was part confusion, part fascination, and wholly unsettling.

It wasn't that I thought he meant any harm. He looked more like he was trying to figure out *what* I was, rather than who. The way he stared sometimes—well, it was as if he were seeing something I couldn't.

I spotted him across the room now, standing near Mr. Bingley, looking as though he'd rather be slopping hogs than dressed in formal attire. His gaze flicked to me, just briefly, before he looked away again, and I felt a strange, unsettling pang of pity.

Poor Mr. Darcy. What must it be like to be trapped inside your own head?

Charlotte had once said that it was better to be poor than to be mad. You could climb out of poverty, but madness? That would follow you forever. And here I was, watching it unfold before my very eyes.

I sighed and turned my attention to Lydia, who was still holding court near the punch bowl with Lieutenant Denny and Mr. Wickham. The latter had, unsurprisingly, charmed half the room already, and Lydia, of course, was completely smitten. As I approached, she let out an excited squeal, nearly spilling her drink in the process.

"Oh, Lizzy!" she cried. "Mr. Wickham has just been telling us the most delightful story about—"

"I'm sure it's riveting," I cut in, offering Mr. Wickham a polite smile before glancing back at Mr. Darcy, who had somehow managed to inch even closer.

He was acting stranger than usual—looking at me, then at Mr. Wickham, then back again, as if trying to decipher some unsolvable riddle. His jaw was tight, and his posture even stiffer than usual, which I hadn't thought possible.

"Excuse me for asking," I began, unable to resist, "but have you noticed anything... off about Mr. Darcy tonight?"

Mr. Wickham's expression changed ever so slightly. He glanced over at Darcy, then back at me, before offering a slow, knowing smile. "No more than usual. Stiff as a fire poker, is he? Oh, I wouldn't worry, Miss Elizabeth. I doubt he's capable of harm. Just a man... well, not quite right in the head."

I raised an eyebrow. "You seem awfully confident about that."

"Oh, I am," Wickham said, his voice smooth as silk. "I've known him for quite some time. Seen him in... shall we say... less than favorable circumstances."

"Such as?"

Wickham's eyes gleamed. "Let's just say that Mr. Darcy has a history of erratic behavior. I'm not surprised you've noticed it." He paused, his gaze shifting briefly to Darcy, who was now standing almost directly behind me, his expression dark and brooding. "His poor sister, though. Imagine having a madman for a brother!"

Sister? Oh! That was right. I vaguely recalled Miss Bingley saying something about Mr. Darcy's younger sister when I was staying at Netherfield. I wondered where she was now. Probably as far from him as she could get.

I looked at the gentleman again, my heart softening just slightly. Whatever his faults, I couldn't shake the growing suspicion that he was less a villain and more... well, a victim of something I couldn't quite understand.

Mr. Darcy caught my eye and, after a moment of hesitation, walked toward me. His steps were measured, but there was an intensity in his gaze that made me straighten in response. Wickham, sensing the approach, took a step back, his usual charm replaced by something colder.

"Miss Bennet," Darcy said, his voice lower than usual. "May I have the next dance?"

The question caught me so off guard that I almost didn't respond. *Mr. Darcy*, asking *me* to dance? In the middle of all this?

I hesitated, glancing between him and Mr. Wickham, who looked entirely too pleased with himself.

"Well," I said, trying to keep my voice steady, "I suppose—"

Before I could finish, Mr. Darcy gave a short, tight bow and walked off, leaving me standing there, completely bewildered.

Mr. Wickham watched him go, concealing a faint smirk behind his glass of punch. "Odd fellow, isn't he?"

I didn't respond. My mind was already racing in a dozen different directions. What had just happened? Why had Darcy approached me like that, only to flee? And why, despite everything I knew of him, did I keep feeling sorry for him?

Darcy

I WAS AN IDIOT. There was no other explanation for it.

What else could possibly explain why I was striding toward Miss Elizabeth Bennet, hand half-raised in a gesture that was supposed to look polite but probably resembled a man about to shield his face from a punch?

Of all the ridiculous things I'd done lately—nearly decapitating myself in the militia's presence, fleeing conversations like a schoolboy—I had decided that asking Miss Elizabeth to dance, right in front of Wickham, was somehow a good idea. Why? Because I was tired of Ewan's endless goading? Because she was practically the only woman in the room who didn't bore me to tears? Or because I clearly had a death wish?

"Mr. Darcy?" Her voice was amused, curious. I snapped my arm the rest of the way up before it could collapse to my side like a damp rag.

"Miss Bennet," I said stiffly. "Would you... do me the honor of a dance?"

She blinked at me, as if she hadn't quite heard me correctly. Probably because *I* wasn't sure I'd heard myself correctly. "You already asked that once, and the dance is about to begin, sir."

"You did not sound sure."

Her brows raised. "You did not stay to *hear* my entire answer. Shall I go in search of another partner, sir?"

Her eyes flicked to the dance floor, where a few couples were already pairing off. I saw the hesitation there, the slight lift of her brow. I wouldn't have blamed her in the least if she did seek another partner. In fact, I might have had a chance to flee the room if she'd done so. But instead, she took a deep breath and looked back at me, waiting for me to pull my head out of my arse.

It was too late to back out now, so I offered my arm, and she accepted with a grace that made me feel about as steady as a horse on ice.

Ewan, of course, appeared the moment we stepped onto the dance floor. "Och, lad, look at ye! Finally showin' some spine—if ye dinnae look like ye'd rather be grape-shot."

I nearly tripped over my own feet.

"You are distracted again, Mr. Darcy," Elizabeth said, glancing up at me as we took our places. Her voice was light, teasing. But there was a flicker of something else in her gaze. Suspicion, perhaps? Or maybe amusement.

"Yes, I... I apologize," I muttered, trying to ignore Ewan as he sauntered up beside me, leaning in to inspect Elizabeth as if she were a prize horse at market. He let out a low whistle. "Bonny lass, that one."

"Shut. Up," I whispered under my breath.

Elizabeth blinked. "I beg your pardon?"

I forced a smile that probably looked more like a grimace and immediately turned my focus to the music starting up, desperately trying to find something to say that wouldn't make me look even more insane. "Drying up—the weather," I blurted out. "It's... a fine evening."

Ewan snorted, leaning against a pillar as if he'd been there the entire time, and I saw him roll his eyes and make an obscene gesture. When was I going to stop letting him goad me?

Elizabeth's lips twitched, and she shot me a sideways glance. "Indeed. It's remarkable how much the weather can change in such a short time."

"Yes," I agreed, desperately clinging to the thread of conversation like a drowning man clinging to a piece of driftwood. "Remarkable."

We began to move, and for a few moments, I managed to focus. The rhythm of the dance helped. The steps were familiar, and I'd always been a competent dancer. In fact, I found myself relaxing slightly. Elizabeth moved with a grace that was both effortless and captivating. She wasn't as oppressive for me to be in company with as other ladies—no fussy affectations, no coy glances. Just an unpretentious confidence that was impossible to ignore.

"Why so stiff, lad?" Ewan called from the sidelines, twirling a glass of claret in his hand. "Och, ye're meant tae enjoy it, lad! It's a dance, no' a bloody funeral march!"

I ground my teeth, determined not to let him get the better of me. Elizabeth's eyes were already too perceptive; the last thing I needed was to draw her attention to the fact that I was having a conversation with thin air.

To my surprise, the dance was going... well. Elizabeth's steps were light, playful even, and I found myself relaxing into it. Maybe, just maybe, I could manage this without tripping over my own awkwardness.

Then, out of nowhere, a voice chimed in next to my ear: "Ach, lad, yer footwork's all wrong! Let me help ye."

Before I could react, Ewan had materialized beside me, his ghostly hand hovering right over mine. "What are you—" I hissed, barely managing to keep my voice low.

He grinned, completely oblivious to the fact that I was already on edge. "Just a wee nudge in the right direction. Like so—"

That was when my foot tangled with Elizabeth's.

She stumbled, gasping softly as I scrambled to catch her before she fell. I failed. Miserably. Instead, we both nearly toppled over. Somehow, she righted herself, but not without sending me a puzzled look. "Mr. Darcy, are you—"

"Will everyone stop asking me if I am well? I am bloody well *not* well!" I snappped. And then I instantly regretted it.

Elizabeth blinked, clearly unsure of what had just transpired. "Perhaps... you would like some refreshment?" she suggested, eyeing me as though I might collapse at any moment.

I nodded, desperate to escape before anything else went wrong. "Refreshments," I managed to say. "Perhaps some... punch."

As I escorted her toward the refreshment table, Ewan sauntered ahead, weaving through the crowd, still taking the opportunity to shove any redcoats he happened to pass. Old grudges, perhaps. I could only thank whatever shred of luck I had left that no one could say I was close enough to those men to be the reason they suddenly lurched into their dance partners.

I prayed he'd stop there. But, of course, he wasn't done.

Just as I was handing Elizabeth a glass of punch, Ewan reached out with a grin, plucking one for himself from the sideboard. I watched in growing annoyance as he lifted it lazily to his lips, as if he were the guest of honor. And then... horror set in.

The glass wasn't invisible. It was just... floating.

I froze. Elizabeth's eyes fixed on the glass. Then they flicked to me. Then back to the glass.

I opened my mouth, but nothing came out. All I could do was stare back at her, wordless and useless.

For a second, I thought she might faint. Instead, without a word, she took the glass from the air, her hand trembling slightly, and placed it firmly back on the table—much to Ewan's consternation.

"Ach, ye've some nerve, lass! I wasna done with that!" he sputtered. I prayed he would not pick it back up.

Elizabeth Bennet swallowed the rest of her drink in one swift gulp, set her own empty glass down with a quiet clink, and hurried off—no doubt faster than propriety would allow.

I didn't stop her. I couldn't.

Meanwhile, Ewan burst out laughing, clutching his sides. "Well, that went better than expected! She didnae even scream! Ye've got yerself a brave lass there, lad."

I stared at the glass Elizabeth had set down, still feeling the ghost of her fingertips on mine, and did the only thing I could think of. I grabbed the glass, hoping it was rather heavily laced with spirits, and downed it in one go.

Sixteen

Elizabeth

I GLANCED OVER MY shoulder as I scurried away. Mr. Darcy was still standing by the punch table, his eyes fixed on the far wall, his back far too rigid for someone who had just offered me a drink. I suppose that was *technically* what had happened, though what I'd actually seen left me questioning whether I should ever accept a refreshment from him again.

That glass... it had *floated*. I was certain of it.

I'd stared at it, wide-eyed, not even bothering to hide my shock. And when I looked at Mr. Darcy, all he could do was stare back, his expression nearly as bewildered as mine. He hadn't said a word, hadn't even tried to explain himself, and yet I knew he had seen it too. That ridiculous glass of punch had hovered between us, as though it were suspended by invisible hands.

And I knew it was real because I had touched it. Lifted it from the shelf of air upon which it had rested and set it back on a firm surface.

My heart was still galloping like a runaway team. I'd swallowed the rest of my drink as quickly as possible and then fled—not because I was afraid of *him* exactly, but because... well, *what* had just happened?

Now, standing on the fringes of the ballroom, I glanced around, trying to steady my breathing. No one else seemed to have noticed. There was no frantic whispering, no murmured gossip about floating drinks. Just the same endless swirl of gowns, polite laughter, and music.

"Lizzy, are you quite all right?" Charlotte's voice broke through the fog in my head as she appeared beside me, her brow furrowed in concern.

"Am I all right?" I repeated, blinking at her. "Yes. No. I don't know."

Charlotte gave me a look, half puzzled, half amused. "You've gone pale. What happened?"

I opened my mouth to answer, but what was I supposed to say? That I'd just witnessed a glass of punch floating through the air? That Mr. Darcy might actually be possessed by some unseen spirit? She would think I'd lost my mind.

"I... don't know," I muttered. "Something strange."

"Strange?" Charlotte repeated, raising an eyebrow. "Mr. Darcy again?"

I hesitated, the image of that floating glass still fresh in my mind. "How did you guess? Yes... no. I mean, it's just—he's—oh, I don't know what to think!"

"Mr. Darcy always seems a little strange," Charlotte said with a shrug. "But he's hardly dangerous."

"I don't think he's dangerous," I said quickly, though I wasn't sure why I was defending him. "He's just... odd. *Very* odd."

Charlotte gave me a skeptical look, but before she could question me further, another voice cut in.

"Well, Miss Bennet," came Lieutenant Wickham's smooth tones as he approached, all charm and smiles, "you've been quite the object of attention this evening. I daresay you've caused Mr. Darcy no end of confusion on the dance floor."

I narrowed my eyes at him. "Mr. Darcy? Confused?"

Wickham's smile widened, though it didn't quite reach his eyes. "Yes, it seems he's rather easily thrown off balance, wouldn't you say?"

"Thrown off balance." *That* was one way of putting it.

I stared at him, trying to make sense of what he was implying. "Mr. Wickham, I am becoming truly concerned about our neighbor. The man has... troubles. Deep, serious troubles."

"That is not quite correct," Mr. Wickham said slowly, his gaze sharp. "More accurately, Mr. Darcy has secrets. Dark ones. And sometimes, Miss Bennet, those secrets start to show."

My stomach knotted. Dark secrets? Was Mr. Wickham suggesting what I thought he was?

I shook my head, trying to dismiss the absurd notion, but I couldn't shake the image of that floating glass. Had I imagined it? Was there some explanation I had missed? Or was Mr. Wickham right? Could Mr. Darcy truly be hiding something more... sinister?

"I don't know what you mean," I said, though my voice sounded less certain than I'd hoped.

Mr. Wickham smiled faintly, almost as though he pitied me. "I hope, for your sake, that you never find out."

A chill crept down my spine, and I glanced once more toward the spot where Mr. Darcy had vanished. Whatever was happening with him, it wasn't just awkwardness or arrogance. There was something much stranger going on, something I hadn't even begun to understand.

Charlotte cleared her throat. "Shall we take some air, Lizzy? You look like you could use it."

I nodded, still half-distracted by my racing thoughts. "Yes... yes, I think I could."

As we made our way toward the terrace, I cast one last glance back toward the refreshment table, half-expecting to see that cursed glass floating in mid-air again.

Nothing. Just the usual swirl of the ball, people chatting, laughing, unaware of the absurdity that had unfolded only moments ago.

But I knew what I'd seen. And whatever it was that haunted Mr. Darcy, it wasn't finished with him yet.

"MISS ELIZABETH," MR. COLLINS began, clearing his throat in that pompous, slightly phlegmy way he always did before launching into a speech. "I must confess that there is a matter of great... importance I have been meaning to discuss with you."

I already knew what he was about. He'd been loitering around me all morning like a moth around a candle, and I knew, without a shadow of a doubt, what he had in mind. His manners were, after all, far from subtle. He had been building to this moment ever since he'd set foot in Longbourn. The way he looked at me as if I were a prize ham at a village fair—it was impossible to miss.

But there was absolutely no way I was going to let him get started on whatever speech he'd been rehearsing in his head. Not if I had anything to say about it.

"Oh, Mr. Collins," I interrupted, feigning a sudden, dramatic realization, "how careless of me. I forgot to mention something terribly important."

His mouth hung open, words unsaid, but I pressed on. "It's about my... my clumsiness, you see." I sighed deeply, looking mournfully toward the ceiling, as if my very existence were a burden. "You are a parson, are you not? You hear confessions from burdened souls, I imagine?"

His mouth closed, and he smiled. "But of course, fair cousin. And how may ease your cares? For the confession of sins, one to another, is one of the finest tenets of our faith—it keeps one pure, you see."

"Ah. Well, then, I fear I must confess to the sins of envy and pride."

He tilted his head and eased into a chair—regardless of the fact that I was still standing. Not to be dissuaded, I chose a seat nearby. "And... upon what matter does this... envy of yours trouble you, Cousin?" he asked.

"Oh, it vexes me in so many ways, I've hardly had the time to count them," I gushed. "Especially now that I've seen how elegant all the other ladies in town are. I cannot help but feel entirely inadequate compared to them. Just yesterday, I tripped over a perfectly flat carpet, and as for my handwriting, well... it's barely legible. I'm hopeless, really. What chance have I, clumsy as I am, to compare with the refined young women you must meet elsewhere?"

Mr. Collins blinked at me, thoroughly perplexed. He had clearly prepared for many scenarios, but self-sabotage wasn't one of them. "Miss Elizabeth, surely you don't mean to suggest—"

"But I do!" I insisted, my voice tinged with just the right amount of dramatic despair. "I'm afraid I lack the grace, the... *je ne sais quoi* that makes a woman truly attractive. The other ladies in Meryton—so elegant, so poised! And yet here I am, a poor imitation of refinement." I shook my head sadly. "It must be a disappointment for you, I'm sure."

He stared, trying to digest this unexpected detour. "N-no, Miss Elizabeth. You mustn't be so... harsh on yourself. Lady Catherine herself has often remarked that—"

"Oh, Lady Catherine!" I exclaimed, cutting him off again. "She would take one look at me and instantly know what a disaster I am. Imagine! What would she say if she saw me falling flat on my face on the skating pond in Meryton?"

"Skating pond?" Mr. Collins repeated, his face blank.

"Yes!" I said, my voice rising with a sudden burst of inspiration. I glanced out the window and spotted my younger sisters, Lydia and Kitty, happily trudging along with their skates in hand. "You see, our housekeeper returned from Meryton only this morning with the news that the ladies in town are already out on the ice. My sisters were just heading there themselves! Oh, Mr. Collins, I cannot think of a better opportunity for you to see for yourself just how clumsy I really am."

Mr. Collins' mouth opened, then closed again. I could practically see the cogs turning in his mind. On one hand, I had just given him an excuse to avoid the unpleasant task of proposing to me. On the other, skating was undoubtedly an activity of dubious grace, and as a gentleman of good breeding, he probably hadn't the faintest idea what to do with a pair of skates. The thought of watching me fall and flounder, however, seemed to intrigue him.

"Er... Miss Elizabeth," he began, "I—I must admit I've never skated myself, but if you wish for me to accompany you—"

"Oh, but you must!" I declared, doing my very best to look pathetic. "I insist! After all, how could you possibly make a well-informed decision about my—er—*suitability* without first making a fair comparison to other ladies? Dancing—why, anyone can accomplish that, but it takes a true lady of breeding to master the art of skating well."

His brow furrowed, and I saw the hesitation creep into his expression. He was starting to second-guess himself. "Well... I suppose... if it's what you truly wish..."

"Oh, it is!" I assured him, already heading toward the door. "We shall meet the ladies in town, and you'll see for yourself how little I possess in the way of grace or charm. My only fear is that you'll find far more accomplished ladies there who would be much more suitable for a man of your standing."

Mr. Collins' mouth flapped open, but no sound came out. I could tell he was grappling with the confusion of having a woman practically reject herself before he'd even had the chance to offer. But his feet shuffled toward the door, and I knew he was hooked.

With a grin hidden safely from his view, I grabbed my shawl, thinking to myself how fortunate it would be if he took a fall on the ice. And, if I was especially lucky, perhaps he'd break something important—perhaps even his tongue.

Darcy

"D ARCY, YOU LOOK DREADFUL." Bingley's voice dragged me out of my stupor. I hadn't realized I'd been staring into the empty hearth, my mind stuck replaying every humiliating moment from the ball the night before.

I blinked, shaking my head slightly. "Do I?"

Bingley grinned, all bright-eyed and cheerful as ever, despite the late hour. How he managed to look so fresh after a night like that, I'd never understand. "You do. A bit pale. Perhaps some fresh air would help? The pond in town is frozen over, and I hear there's already some skating. Fancy that! I thought it would be another fortnight, at least."

"Skating?" I repeated, blinking again, still half-dazed from lack of sleep. "You're suggesting skating after dancing all night?"

"Why not?" Bingley replied, as though it were the most obvious solution in the world. "Fresh air, a little exercise—it'll clear your head. Good for the nerves, you know." He paused, then added with a sly grin, "Miss Bennet seemed to think it was a fine idea."

Of course. Miss Bennet. I stared at him, realizing the true motivation behind his suggestion. It wasn't the fresh air or the skating; it was her.

"Come, Darcy, it is not the time for gloominess. Do you know," Bingley continued, waving a letter in his hand, "I've just had word from my solicitor in town. Some business that requires my attention, but I've decided it can wait. Much better attractions here, and surely old Robert can manage without me for a few more days."

At this, Miss Bingley, who had been lurking by the window in a state of perpetual boredom, turned sharply. "Charles, you *must* attend to your affairs. Meryton is hardly a place to linger when there are matters of importance awaiting you in London."

Bingley waved her off with a good-natured chuckle. "Nonsense, Caroline. I'm enjoying my time here immensely. I'm sure my solicitor can manage just fine without me for a little while longer."

Caroline's lips pressed into a thin line, but she didn't argue further. Clearly, she had hoped to drag him back to London as quickly as possible, but Bingley was not to be moved. His thoughts were clearly in Meryton—and more specifically, with Jane Bennet.

"I see," I muttered, staring down at my hands, which had curled into fists at some point. Bingley was free to stay here, free to enjoy himself, free to court Miss Bennet. Free, in every way that I was not.

The truth of it was, I didn't know where I belonged. Here? In London? It hardly seemed to matter. I was cursed in either direction.

I could go back to London, escape this place, leave Wickham and his unsettling presence behind. Leave Elizabeth Bennet behind. But I would still be haunted—literally—and at least here, I wasn't making a fool of myself in front of my family.

Well, not yet, anyway.

"Darcy," Bingley's voice softened, a touch of concern creeping into his usual cheer. "I know last night was... well, not to your liking. I know you do not enjoy balls, and you seemed terribly out of sorts when last I saw you. But staying cooped up here all day won't help. Come skating with me. We'll make a day of it."

I glanced at him, the temptation to decline already forming on my lips. But then I thought of London. Of Georgiana. Of the chaos that awaited me there—and the very tangible ghost who would follow me wherever I went.

Here, at least, the madness was contained. Mostly.

"I suppose," I said slowly, "it wouldn't hurt to join you."

Bingley grinned again, clearly pleased with himself. "That's the spirit! We'll leave within the hour."

As Bingley bounced off to inform the rest of the household of his grand plans for the afternoon, I leaned back in my chair, staring into the cold hearth once more.

London or Meryton—either way, there would be no escaping this purgatory.

Elizabeth

"L IZZY, COME ON!" LYDIA's shout echoed across the frozen lake, her voice high-pitched with excitement. "The ice is perfect today!"

I tightened my scarf and took a deep breath, watching my breath cloud in the air as I pulled my skates tighter. "I'm coming, Lydia, don't wear yourself out before you've even begun."

"Not possible!" she sang, already spinning circles with Kitty, their laughter mingling with the other skaters gliding across the ice.

Charlotte, standing beside me, raised an eyebrow. "Do they ever slow down?"

"Only when they run out of breath," I said dryly, my eyes scanning the crowd. "Or, you know, when they crash into something."

Charlotte smiled as she tightened her own skates. "Well, I suppose we're in for quite a show then."

Mr. Collins had barely stepped onto the ice before disaster struck. He teetered for a full two seconds before his arms flailed wildly in the air, and with a resounding *thud*, he landed flat on his backside.

"Good heavens, Miss Elizabeth!" he yelped, trying and failing to pull himself back up. "I fear I have injured... something."

I stifled a laugh, offering him a sympathetic look. "Perhaps, Mr. Collins, it would be best for you to rest a while. There's a bench right over there. You mustn't overexert yourself."

"Y-yes," he wheezed, wincing as he hobbled off the ice, holding his lower back. "I shall supervise from the sidelines. A prudent decision, I'm sure Lady Catherine would agree."

Charlotte nudged me, her eyes twinkling with amusement as we watched him shuffle awkwardly toward the bench. "Well, that's one way to escape a conversation."

I grinned. "I have my methods."

With Mr. Collins safely seated on the sidelines, I allowed myself a moment of triumph before Charlotte's gaze drifted toward the ice once more. That was when I saw it, too. The wobbling, stiff figure attempting to maintain some semblance of balance just a few paces ahead. There, struggling to stay upright, was none other than Mr. Darcy himself, his face set in that familiar scowl of concentration.

"Oh no," I muttered, half to myself.

"Lizzy, what is it?" Charlotte asked, pulling up beside me.

"Just... that." I jerked my chin in his direction.

Mr. Darcy was attempting to stay upright, but it was a losing battle. His legs splayed out at awkward angles, and his arms flailed in every direction like a windmill in a storm.

"Oh dear," Charlotte said, covering her mouth to stifle a laugh.

"More like 'oh disaster,'" I sighed, trying not to wince as he stumbled again, narrowly avoiding a group of young children who skated past him with the ease of seasoned professionals. He might have managed to stay upright if not for whatever invisible force seemed to be tormenting him.

He got his feet again, and for a moment, he seemed to be doing tolerably well. Better than tolerably, in fact. It was Mr. Bingley who looked like the clumsy one as Mr. Darcy glided circles around his friend. Now, how did that man go from bumbling worse than Mr. Collins one minute and looking as though he could give a lecture on skating technique the next? But as he rounded the top of his circle, his eyes strayed to me, and all his grace evaporated.

Without warning, Mr. Darcy suddenly lurched forward as though he'd been shoved from behind, his arms flailing wildly. He muttered something under his breath—something about someone being drawn and quartered, it sounded like. I couldn't help but wonder if he was muttering at *me*—or to someone no one else could see. Indeed, that notion sounded crazy, but it was less crazy than certain alternative explanations.

"Is he... quite all right?" Charlotte asked, watching Darcy's odd movements.

I shrugged. "Who can say? Mr. Darcy's been acting strangely for weeks. This might just be the grand finale. Charlotte, do you suppose a mad man's brain actually explodes before he perishes of his insanity?"

"Oh, Lizzy, stop it." Before I could stop her, Charlotte waved at him. "Mr. Darcy! Care to join us?"

He managed to throw a tight smile our way, but before he could respond, he stumbled again, his skates slipping out from under him. I winced as he nearly collided with a tree. He might have managed to stop himself, but his eyes widened as though someone had done something—something only he could see.

"Well, I've never seen him quite like this," Charlotte said, frowning.

I bit my lip, trying to stifle a laugh. "You haven't been paying attention."

Darcy somehow managed to wobble his way toward us, his expression a strange mix of determination and dread, his eyes darting about as though he was expecting something—or someone—to jump out at him.

"Miss Bennet," he gasped, tipping his hat and inclining from the waist. There, see? A man truly as clumsy as he had looked a moment ago would have fallen when he tried to bow to a lady. "And Miss Lucas," he continued. "Lovely day for skating, isn't it?"

Charlotte blinked. "If you say so."

I couldn't resist. "Mr. Darcy, you appear somewhat winded. I quite understand, sir. After dancing all night, and then rousing for a bracing afternoon on the skating pond, anyone would be fatigued and... stiff. Perhaps you should rest."

Mr. Darcy's eyes flashed. "I am perfectly well, thank you."

"Well," I said, turning slightly so Charlotte wouldn't see the smirk tugging at my lips, "if you're certain, Mr. Darcy. But I must say, I am impressed with your stamina. That was a remarkable performance just now."

He looked as though he was about to respond when he suddenly jumped again as if someone had pinched him—or worse. His face flushed, and he muttered something unintelligible, his eyes darting around wildly. He glanced behind him, then back at me, clearly struggling to maintain his composure.

"Perhaps I should... excuse myself," he said, his voice strained. Without another word, he turned abruptly and skated off—if you could call it that—his movements looking more like marching steps than fluid glides.

Charlotte glanced at me, her expression mirroring my own confusion. "Well, that was... odd."

"*Odd* doesn't even begin to cover it," I muttered.

Seventeen

Darcy

I STRODE INTO THE bookshop, head down, hoping the wind from the door might blow me out the way I'd come. How had it come to this? Walking into Meryton—a town I had no love for, on a fool's errand to track down books that wouldn't be of any use if they ever arrived. But I had to try something. At least it gave me an excuse to leave Bingley and his endless prattling about Miss Bennet.

"Mr. Darcy, sir. Good afternoon!"

I grimaced. Old Mr. Stone, the bookseller, popped out from behind a towering stack of books like a rabbit from its hole. He peered at me with watery eyes, the smile of someone who'd been in business a bit too long.

"Do you have word from London?" I asked, trying to keep the desperation from my voice. Desperation was for people who still believed in miracles. At this point, I'd settle for a decent suggestion on how to rid myself of a drunken ghost.

The old man blinked at me, shuffling toward his counter. "Not quite yet, sir, not quite. They did say the shipment was delayed—something about a miscommunication with the delivery. But rest assured, Mr. Darcy, the books you've requested should be here in about a fortnight."

A fortnight. Fantastic. I'd be lucky if I still had my sanity by then. "I cannot wait a fortnight. I need them as soon as possible."

The old man gave me a strange look as if my life didn't depend on a few worn-out pages of Highland superstitions. Which it did. "Well, sir, did you ever ask Mr. Bennet? They say his library is one of the largest in the area. Might be something there on... er, unusual subjects."

Bennet. I swallowed. That was the last thing I needed. To owe him something. And worse, to have any reason to go to Longbourn, where his daughter—the one who already thought me mad—could eye me with the baleful cynicism of a judge at the Old Bailey. The mere thought of entering that house made me itch.

I opened my mouth to decline politely when the bell over the door rang behind me, and in walked the very person I had been trying, unsuccessfully, to avoid for weeks. The one person who, regardless of my efforts, seemed privy to all my most embarrassing moments, courtesy of one Ewan McLean.

Elizabeth Bennet.

My first thought was to make a run for it. Surely, I could bolt past her, pretend I'd seen some disaster in the street, and come back later.

Too late. She spotted me, and I felt my spine stiffen as if Ewan himself had just prodded it with that rusty Highland dirk he liked to poke me with.

"Mr. Darcy," she greeted me, her voice filled with what I could only describe as cautious politeness. The kind one might use on a wounded animal that could still bite.

"Miss Bennet," I managed, nodding stiffly. My brain scrambled for something more intelligent to say. Nothing came.

She regarded me curiously. Her eyes darted to the stack of books on the counter, then back to me. "You're here for... a purchase?"

What else would I be doing there? "Unfortunately, what I came to purchase is unavailable."

Her eyebrow lifted, and I could tell she was already suspicious. The woman could smell evasion like a hound on the hunt. But just as quickly, she brightened and turned to Mr. Stone. "My father asked me to collect the book he ordered last week. I trust it is here?"

Mr. Stone beamed and reached under the counter. "But of course, Miss Elizabeth. I sent the order express myself, and it arrived only this morning."

I narrowed my eyes. So, Mr. Bennet got his order in a week, but I offer enough gold to gild the entire shop, and I must be kept waiting? Either my order was harder to obtain than I had imagined, or the shopkeepers in Meryton were starting to decline to do business with me. I wasn't sure I wished to know which one it was.

Elizabeth thanked Mr. Stone for the book he handed to her, then turned back to me. "Are you in search of anything in particular, sir?"

I could practically hear Ewan's mocking voice in the back of my head. *Aye, tell her, lad. Tell her yer lookin' for a book on how tae get rid o' yer drunken, dead Scotsman.*

I cleared my throat. "Just some reading material. Nothing... of importance."

Elizabeth studied me for a moment, then glanced at the old bookseller, who was watching our exchange with all the subtlety of a hawk.

"You've been in Meryton much more frequently of late," she observed, her tone casual, but her eyes sharp. "I thought you did not care for our town."

She was not wrong, but I wasn't about to confess that the only reason I was in Meryton was to avoid the fact that my current residence, Netherfield, was a haunted prison.

I glanced back at Mr. Stone, who had taken it upon himself to study the fine details of his bookshelves, giving us the illusion of privacy. "I've had business here," I said. Technically, that was true. If by "business" I meant trying not to lose my mind.

Her gaze didn't waver, and I could feel her assessing me as if she were looking for cracks in my façade. "You seem... troubled again today, Mr. Darcy."

Was it that obvious? I thought I'd done a remarkable job hiding the fact that I was rapidly unraveling, but perhaps I'd overestimated my skill in masking madness.

"I assure you, Miss Bennet," I said, trying to keep my voice steady, "I am quite well."

That eyebrow of hers arched again. "Are you?"

No. Absolutely not. But I couldn't say that, could I?

Before I could deflect any further, she glanced at the door and said, "Well, it seems we're both headed in the same direction. Might I suggest we walk together?"

Walk? *Together?* She must be joking. I could hardly manage civil conversation with her in controlled situations, let alone on the open road, where my mind would undoubtedly betray me halfway through, and I'd be left muttering about ghosts. And Heaven only knew if Ewan would decide to make an appearance.

"I... suppose," I said, hating how unsure I sounded.

To my increasing horror, Elizabeth smiled and stood poised as if she expected me to offer her my arm like a regular gentleman. I *used* to be a gentleman. Now... I wasn't sure what one would call me.

I nodded stiffly and exited the shop, wondering if my legs would suddenly forget how to function properly. To my great relief, they worked. But walking alongside Elizabeth

Bennet was no easy feat. I could feel her presence beside me, calm and curious, waiting for me to speak—likely expecting me to, at any moment, blurt out something unintelligible.

For a few blessed seconds, the only sound was the creaking of carriages up the street and distant voices. I might survive this—see her safely on the path to Longbourn, then escape to Netherfield without further incident.

Then she spoke.

"I must admit, Mr. Darcy," she began, her tone measured, "you are a bit of a mystery."

There it was. The probing. The gentle pressing for answers that she already half-suspected. I stared straight ahead, determined not to look at her.

"I don't see how that could be," I replied, though I knew full well what she meant. "I am no more mysterious than any other gentleman."

She let out a soft laugh, and the sound hit me like a jab to the ribs. "Come now, Mr. Darcy. You can't expect me to believe that. Forgive me my bluntness, but I cannot help but wonder—are you quite well? And before you reply, take care. I am not Mr. Bingley, who can be swayed by easy platitudes, nor am I Miss Bingley, who believes you can do no wrong, so long as you compliment her. I want to know, sir. Are you *well*... in a medical sense?"

I stopped in my tracks, my throat so dry it was sticking to itself. I turned to face her, my heart thrumming so quickly I feared my ribs would break—*not from attraction*, I assured myself, but from sheer dread of what she might already know.

"Do you... feel safe in my company, Miss Bennet?"

Her eyes widened in surprise, and then something softened in her expression. "Safe? Why wouldn't I?"

I hesitated, unsure how to answer without admitting too much. "There are... things you don't know, Miss Bennet. Things that would explain my behavior."

She tilted her head slightly, her curiosity now fully engaged. "Then perhaps you ought to tell me, Mr. Darcy."

I stared at her, feeling the weight of that challenge. I was cornered. No escape. If I didn't tell her something—*anything*—she would surely press further.

"What I'm about to say will sound... incredible," I began slowly, "but I assure you, it's the truth."

Her expression remained unchanged, save for that one eyebrow that ticked upward.

"There is... someone I must deal with. Someone I cannot get rid of."

She blinked, clearly not expecting that. "Someone? You mean, a person?"

"Yes. And no. It's difficult to explain."

Her brow furrowed. "And is this... person... a familiar of yours?"

"If by that, you mean someone with whom I share a friendship, I would have to say no. You..." I blew out a breath. "You have never met this... person, but he has been with me constantly."

"I used to have an imaginary friend," she declared with a playful pucker to her lips. "A rag doll, if you must know. Alas, I lost her in the cow pasture due to a bit of my own carelessness, and I never—"

"It is not a figment of my imagination," I growled. "Would that it were."

She sighed. "Is this why you've been acting so strangely?"

"I am afraid so," I admitted. "It's... complicated."

For a moment, she said nothing. Then, to my surprise, she nodded. "I believe you, Mr. Darcy."

That threw me off entirely. "You... do?"

"It is the only logical explanation. I've seen enough oddities myself to know that not everything is as it seems."

My quick hope cooled to ash. "Then it is not from any confidence in my character but some detached puzzle you have determined to piece together that makes you credit my words."

Elizabeth laughed. "Come, come, Mr. Darcy. What character have you ever shown me, apart from being a reluctant conversationalist and an even more reluctant—though occasionally skilled—dancer? No, I have questions, and the only way for me to have them answered is to help you."

I frowned. "Help me? There is nothing to be done, and if you are quite through insulting me—"

"You were in the bookstore searching for something, and I have seen you tearing books off Mr. Bingley's shelves like a man possessed. You are trying to learn something, are you not?"

I hesitated, then nodded.

"My father's library is quite extensive. If there's anything you're looking for, perhaps we could find it there."

I was stunned. "You'd... do that for me?"

"Of course," she said. "I am too curious not to."

Elizabeth

P APA'S LIBRARY.

I had spent many an evening rooting around in there, much to his bemusement. While my father delighted in his eclectic collection, his taste in books ranged from the arcane to the absurd, most of which he rarely touched. Just the kind of volumes Mr. Darcy might be desperate to get his hands on—and I couldn't help but want to offer my help, if for no other reason than to observe the oddity that was Mr. Darcy up close.

I waited until Papa had retreated to his study after breakfast, as was his custom. No one ever disturbed him then—least of all me. Still, I tiptoed into the library, pausing at the door to listen for any sign of servants or sisters nearby. All was quiet.

It was far too early in the morning for a heist, but here I was, crouched in front of a dusty old shelf like a common burglar.

My fingers danced over the spines of countless forgotten volumes: *Human Pathology, Superstitions of the Highlands, An Account of Strange Apparitions in the British Isles, Disorders of the Mind* and one book that was simply titled *Ghosts*. Well, those seemed promising enough.

I stacked the books quickly, one on top of the other, until the pile was almost comically high. There was no need to be choosy when half of these would probably be useless. It was a good thing Papa wasn't here to see me now, or else I'd be in for another long lecture about how dull I was becoming with my obsession over "tedious" historical facts.

Clutching my armful of books, I scurried back to my room. Then I realized... where was I supposed to meet Mr. Darcy? I certainly wasn't about to march up to Netherfield and invite myself in like some stray dog. And there was no way I was letting Mr. Darcy into our home, either—my mother would have him married to one of us within the hour.

Then it struck me. The old gamekeeper's cottage, just on the edge of Netherfield's grounds. It had been abandoned for years, and no one ever went near it. If Mr. Darcy could discreetly make his way there, we could work in peace.

M R. HILL HAD ALWAYS indulged my whims, and today was no exception, when I begged him to have a note carried to Mr. Darcy at Netherfield under the guise of my father's name. Surely, even suspicious Miss Bingley would sense nothing unusual if the gentleman received a note from a doddering old neighbor. Papa would never hear of it, either, so I scrawled out the details of the plan and waited. After about an hour, when my younger sisters had gone to town, and Papa was closeted with a book, I pulled on my cloak and headed for the cottage, an odd sense of excitement bubbling up inside me. Sneaking around wasn't exactly becoming for a lady, but there was something thrilling about it all.

When I arrived at the moss-covered stone cottage, I glanced around. The place was as lonely as ever, with ivy creeping up the walls and a thick mist clinging to the trees. Inside, it was musty and cold, but serviceable enough for our purposes.

A creak from the door caught my attention, and I turned just in time to see Mr. Darcy step inside, looking more like a man on the run than one meeting a lady for a quiet rendezvous. He glanced around warily, his shoulders tense. I half-expected him to pull his coat tighter, as though the very air were conspiring against him.

"Ah, Mr. Darcy," I greeted him. "You are looking remarkably sane at the moment."

His eyes narrowed. "If you invited me here merely to insult me, Miss Bennet..." He *sounded* annoyed, but his eyes were busy scanning the room as if expecting something—or someone—to jump out at him.

"You needn't look so alarmed. No one knows we're here."

"On the contrary, Miss Bennet, it is precisely that fact which alarms me," he muttered, eyeing the rough wooden table in the center of the room.

I set down the books with a thud, watching as he flinched ever so slightly. "Afraid I'm luring you into a trap, Mr. Darcy?"

His eyes flickered with something close to exasperation. "It's *your* reputation I'm concerned about, not mine."

I laughed. "You think anyone would believe I'm alone with you of my own accord? Honestly, if you tried to tell them, I would simply have to declare that Mr. Darcy has lost his mind, and no one would ever take your side. You're worse than harmless. You'd sooner do *yourself* harm than me."

"That is hardly reassuring."

"Isn't it? But you must give me some credit for my courage, sir. What if you're plotting to trick me into a compromising position so that I'll have to marry you? I am taking a terrible risk here, you know. And are you entirely certain that *I* mean *you* no harm?"

His expression shifted almost imperceptibly. "I think I'll take my chances."

For a moment, he said nothing, only glanced at the books I'd brought as though grateful for the distraction. I started to unstack them, laying them out in a disorganized sprawl on the table.

"I've pilfered these from my father's library. Don't ask me how I'm going to explain their absence, but I imagine he won't notice them missing for a week or so."

Darcy's brow furrowed as he picked up one of the tomes, his fingers brushing the cover with the kind of reverence that only a man utterly desperate for answers could muster. He flipped through the pages, his expression softening ever so slightly as he realized they might actually be of some use.

We sat down at the table, the musty air thick around us, and for a moment, there was silence as we both stared at the books. "I suppose," I said, breaking the quiet, "it would help if you told me exactly *what* we are looking for."

He glanced up, meeting my eyes for a moment longer than necessary. "Yes," he murmured, almost to himself. "I suppose it would."

Eighteen

Darcy

O F ALL THE PLACES to meet a young lady, an abandoned gamekeeper's cottage wasn't high on the list of acceptable venues. It was drafty, musty, and isolated, not to mention... highly improper. But it wasn't as if I had much choice.

Miss Bennet—Elizabeth—had chosen the location, and with good reason. Neither of us could afford to be seen together like this, but the circumstances left me with few alternatives. My options had dwindled down to precisely none, and now I was sitting in the middle of a decaying stone cottage, surrounded by stacks of stolen books, trying to convince myself that the best chance I had now was to confess the entire absurdity of my situation to the one person I least wanted to think I'd gone mad.

I stared at the stack of books, but the words on their spines blurred together, slipping out of focus. I needed those books to hold the answers. I needed anything—anything—to make sense of this curse that had taken over my life. But before I could ask for Elizabeth Bennet's help, she needed to hear the truth.

The real truth.

I exhaled, the air heavy in my chest. She was sitting across from me, her posture relaxed but her eyes keen, watching me with a kind of curious patience. I could only imagine what she was thinking. This would be the moment that confirmed for her, beyond any doubts, that I truly had lost my mind. That Mr. Darcy of Pemberley had finally cracked.

I reached for one of the books, stalling for a second longer, running my thumb along the worn leather spine.

"It started with a brooch."

The words felt foreign on my tongue, strange and absurd. Elizabeth raised an eyebrow, her head tilting ever so slightly to one side.

"A brooch?" she echoed, her voice even, though I could see the flicker of doubt in her eyes.

I nodded, staring at the book in my hands. "An old brooch. One I that was bequeathed to me by some... connection... I still do not quite understand the nature of it, but the end of it was that I acquired a collection of trinkets and curios that seemed perfectly unremarkable." My grip tightened. "Until one of them wasn't."

"Who was this... connection?"

"I don't know. Some spinster named Isobel McLean who claimed a friendship with my grandmother—I've not the least idea if that is even true. But the brooch itself once belonged to her brother, a Jacobite soldier," I said, my voice low, each word feeling like it cost me something. "Ewan McLean. A man who died at the Battle of Culloden."

Her eyes narrowed, her expression unreadable.

"But he didn't die—not properly," I went on, swallowing the lump in my throat. "Or perhaps he did. It's... difficult to say. All I know is that ever since I found that brooch, he's been... haunting me."

The word "haunting" hung in the air between us, and I half-expected her to laugh, to scoff, to tell me how ridiculous I sounded. But she didn't.

She blinked once. Twice. And then: "I beg your pardon?"

I clenched my fists, fighting the urge to stand up and flee the cottage altogether. "He's been with me constantly. He talks, he meddles, he... interferes in my life. He was at the ball."

Her mouth opened, then closed again. "At the ball?"

"Yes," I said, the word coming out sharper than I intended. "He was there. You saw him—or, rather, you saw the effects of him."

Her brow creased further. "I'm afraid you will have to clarify somewhat."

"The glass, Miss Bennet. The punch glass that you took from him. He was... rather put out about it, in fact."

For a moment, Elizabeth was silent, her gaze fixed on me as if trying to gauge my sincerity. And her eyelid started to twitch. Finally, she spoke. "I was terribly curious about that, sir."

I swallowed and closed my eyes. "I know how it sounds. If it were anyone but myself who had seen it, I—"

"Back up the carriage for a moment," she interrupted. "Are you trying to tell me that you are not only plagued by the specter of a long-dead Highlander, but that this... person?... also has a predilection for punch?"

I lifted my shoulders. "Punch, claret, whiskey... I rarely see him but that he does not have some sort of alcoholic beverage in his hand. And when he is not drinking, he smells like he has been."

Her eyes widened in a flash. "He smells!"

"And leaves muddy footprints across my bed chamber whenever it pleases him. Believe me, Miss Elizabeth, if I had any explanations for it, I would surely offer them, but I do not."

Her mouth was starting to fall slack by now, but not for breathing. I was fairly certain she had not taken a breath in quite some time. Sure enough, before she spoke again, she was required to take a fresh gulp of air.

"Excuse me, Mr. Darcy, but how is it that nobody else sees this... character? Surely, you do not expect anyone to believe—"

I clenched my jaw and glared at the wall. "I am *not* mad. I am a rational, thinking man, Miss Bennet, who just happens to be beset by something I cannot explain."

"Oh," she said gently, her brows arching, "I can see that."

My gaze centered back on her. "If you mean only to mock me, you may as well leave. I know you are going to spread the rumors all over town, so do not let me cause you any delay."

Elizabeth tilted her head, her mouth puckering. "Is this Mr. McLean... present now?"

It was a trap, and I knew it. She wanted to watch me leaping at shadows again so she could have something to laugh over with her friends. But I could not resist sliding my gaze to the corners of the room, just to make sure...

"I do not see him just now, but that does not mean he is not listening at the windows, or whatever the ghostly equivalent is of being a peeping Tom."

Elizabeth suddenly flushed, tensing her shoulders and casting about as if she, too, could search for Ewan and that her modesty was in some jeopardy.

"Calm yourself, Miss Bennet," I said. "While I have known him to..." I cleared my throat. "*leer* at a lady... namely you... I believe he only did so to provoke me. Your dignity is quite safe... as far as I know."

Her eyes rounded even further. "That is hardly comforting, Mr. Darcy! Are you saying this... this thing was rattling about Netherfield while Jane and I stayed there? How can you now give your assurances that he did nothing unseemly while we were in our private rooms?"

"He's a ghost, not a deviant." My brow creased. "I think."

Elizabeth held both hands in the air, shaking her head and looking down as if trying to collect her thoughts. "So, that morning on the lawn, when you were screaming and running as if someone had set your trousers on fire?"

I swallowed. "I had cherished some small hope that you might have forgot all about that."

"Not bloody likely, Mr. Darcy. What about the rumors of you losing control of your horse and running through some laundry line in the middle of town?"

I sighed. "Are you going to name every embarrassing incident that miscreant has caused me?"

"That depends. How many are there?"

"More than I can number. Please, Miss Elizabeth, at this point, either you credit my words somewhat, or you mean to pat me on the head like a harmless eccentric and go your way."

"Not necessarily. There is always a third option. Have you ever heard of a nice little estate called 'Bedlam'? I fancy you could meet any number of fine new friends there."

I glared at her with a deadpan expression. "This is the trouble with trying to ask for help from one who considers herself a wit."

"Oh, come, Mr. Darcy, I was only teasing. Very well, back to the brooch, where it all began. You say this Ewan person began appearing to you after it came into your possession? Why not simply get rid of it?"

"Would that it were that simple. No matter what I've done—no matter how I've tried to rid myself of him—he remains."

Elizabeth's fingers brushed against the edge of one of the books, but she didn't pick it up. Her gaze stayed on me, her lips pressing into a thin line.

"And this Ewan... what does he want?"

I leaned back in my chair, my hands trembling despite myself. "That's what I've been trying to figure out. He's given me vague hints, but nothing certain. All I know is that he had someone—someone named Elspeth. And somehow, she's connected to this."

Elizabeth's eyes widened slightly. "Elspeth?"

"Yes. And before you ask, he claims that you remind him of the lady, but I am not certain if that can be true. How can I trust the memory of a man who is not even alive? And even if I trusted his memory, I doubt I can trust his intentions. He delights in getting a rise out of me."

"Well, in that respect, he and I think somewhat alike. You are perfectly diverting when thrown off balance."

I gestured toward the door. "You are still free to leave, Miss Elizabeth."

But she acted like she hadn't even heard me. Her fingers tapped lightly on the table, her eyes darting to all corners of the room as she seemed lost in thought. "So," she began slowly, "we're looking for... what exactly? Information about this Ewan McLean? About his connection to the brooch? To this... Elspeth?"

I nodded, swallowing hard. "Yes. That's what I'm hoping these books might tell us. If we can find out who Elspeth was and what happened to her... perhaps we can put an end to this."

Her gaze switched back to me, and for a moment, she just stared, as if she were trying to divine the truth. As if I had not already told her everything I knew. Then she took a deep breath and opened one of the books. "Well, Mr. Darcy, it seems we have our work cut out for us."

I watched her begin to flip through the pages, her brow furrowing as she scanned the text. She was taking this seriously—more seriously than I could have hoped for. But there was still a part of me that feared she didn't truly believe me. That she was humoring me, just waiting for the next time I jumped out of my skin or did something entirely uncivilized, just so she would have the pleasure of laughing about it.

I cleared my throat, my heart hammering in my chest. "Miss Bennet," I said carefully, "I understand that this must sound..."

"Completely insane?" she finished for me, a wry smile tugging at her lips.

I winced. "Yes."

She looked up from the book, her eyes locking onto mine. "Mr. Darcy, you are many things. Stiff, brooding, and occasionally insufferable... but I don't believe you're a liar."

The words hit me harder than I expected, and for a moment, I couldn't speak. She believed me—or at least, she believed that I believed myself.

"Thank you," I murmured.

Elizabeth's smile softened. "Besides," she said, turning back to the book, "I don't think you're nearly clever enough to invent something like this."

Elizabeth

I TURNED THE PAGE of the latest book I'd picked up from the stack—an ancient tome on Highland folklore—with a sigh. It was an account of banshees, ghosts, and various other Scottish superstitions, all intriguing in their own right, but none of it was helping us unravel the puzzle of Ewan McLean or why he was bound to Mr. Darcy.

Mr. Darcy sat across from me at the table, scanning yet another book, his brow furrowed in concentration. He had been enough of a gentleman to scavenge some firewood for us and had even found an old flint among the dusty stones of the mantle. Now, a fire crackled merrily in the hearth. It was the only sound in the room, and for a moment, I allowed myself to glance at him, just once.

There was something oddly... calming about him now. He wasn't the aloof, haughty man I'd first encountered in Meryton. He was still stiff, still proud in many ways, but I was beginning to see flashes of something else beneath the surface—something far more complex. I was no longer sure if I found him intriguing or infuriating. Both, most likely.

But we were here for answers, not distractions.

A sudden thought struck me, and I looked up from the page. "Mr. Darcy?"

He glanced up from his book. "Yes, Miss Bennet?"

"There's something we've overlooked." I closed the book in front of me, leaning forward slightly. "We've been so focused on Ewan, but why did Isobel McLean make you her heir? Surely, that's unusual—especially if she had no direct connection to your family beyond what you've told me."

His expression shifted—just the barest flicker of surprise, followed by a thoughtful frown. "I've wondered the same myself, but I never found a satisfactory answer."

I drummed my fingers on the table, thinking aloud. "Do you think that question might be part of this... mystery? Could it help us understand why all this is happening to you?"

Darcy's eyes darkened slightly as he considered my words. "It's possible. I hadn't thought to investigate that aspect in much depth. I was more focused on ending Ewan's presence altogether."

"Well," I said, reaching for another book, "perhaps we should try a different approach. Isobel McLean must have had some reason to favor you. Maybe her family history holds a clue."

He leaned back slightly, nodding. "You could be right, Miss Bennet. I will send a letter to my solicitor at once to ask him to report any and all details of Miss McLean's life and circumstances. He gave me very few details before, but I am sure there are some that I have forgotten."

"You said she was your grandmother's friend?"

He lifted his shoulders. "That was the claim. Perhaps my grandmother..." He narrowed his eyes, and then an inspired light shone in his eyes. "I shall write to my housekeeper at Pemberley to have my grandmother's journals sent to me. Excellent notion. Thank you, Miss Bennet."

I couldn't help but smile a little. "Good thing you've got me here, then."

The corner of his mouth twitched, almost—but not quite—a smile.

We resumed our search, but after that, we were both more vocal about our findings. Any curious notion, any strange little fact, was sufficient cause for an uttered musing, which was usually received and considered by the other. It was strange, really—sitting across from Mr. Darcy in a deserted cottage, poring over dusty old books and grunting at our discoveries like a pair of conspirators. I hadn't realized until now just how accustomed I'd become to his presence, and even more so to the strange... warmth that came with it.

As I reached for yet another book, my hand brushed against one of the larger volumes I had brought, one I'd nearly forgotten about in the shuffle. It was a thick, heavy book—likely one of the oldest in Papa's collection—titled *An Account of the Glorious Fight at Culloden, with a Record of the Fallen and Imprisoned, Collected from Reliable Sources*.

I pulled it toward me and opened it, the old pages crackling slightly under my fingers. As I flipped through, my breath caught. "Mr. Darcy... look at this. What luck! Fancy me grabbing this when I did not even know what I would be looking for."

He leaned forward, and I pointed to the page in front of me. It was a list—long and detailed—of the names of those who had died or been imprisoned after the battle of Culloden. Ewan McLean's name should be here.

Mr. Darcy scanned the page, his frown deepening as he read. "There it is. Clan McLean... Not Ewan, though."

I shook my head, biting my lip. "Interesting. But I doubt this is the complete list. The book says there were more than fifteen hundred dead, and this looks like it is only heads of clans. Perhaps there is a more exhaustive list further on."

He stared at the page for a moment longer, then glanced at me. "May I...?"

I hesitated for a brief second, then nodded. "Of course. You can take the book with you, if you like. My family will be wondering where I am, and I imagine you'll want more time to go through it carefully."

Darcy's expression softened slightly, and he gave me a small, grateful nod. "Thank you, Miss Bennet. I appreciate your help more than you know."

I stood, brushing a stray curl from my face. "I'm only curious about what else we might uncover. Perhaps we'll discover that this mystery has a very simple explanation after all."

"I hope so," he murmured, closing the book and rising to his feet as well. His height struck me again—as it always did when I stood this close to him—and for a moment, I felt a strange flutter in my chest. It was disconcerting, this odd awareness of Mr. Darcy as more than just an irritating puzzle to be solved.

He lingered by the door, holding the book under his arm. "Miss Bennet," he began, his voice softer than usual, "I know you've humored me throughout all this. And for that, I... thank you."

I raised an eyebrow, half-smiling. "If I didn't believe *something* was going on, Mr. Darcy, I wouldn't be here."

For the first time, he offered me a real smile—small, but sincere. "Then I shall consider myself fortunate."

He left the cottage, disappearing into the night, and I was left standing alone, still feeling the strange way my heart had stuttered when he smiled. This was a man I had once thought insufferable, and yet... I couldn't help but be drawn in. Not just by the mystery, but by him.

Nineteen

Darcy

I SLAMMED THE DOOR to my room and tossed the book onto the desk. The chair creaked as I fell into it, not wasting a moment before cracking open the pages. *An Account of the Glorious Fight at Culloden...* Thanks to Elizabeth Bennet, it was the most promising lead I'd found since this nightmare began, and I wasn't about to squander it. Oh, but first, I had those letters to write.

I reached for my pen and scratched out the letter to my solicitor—my handwriting barely legible in my haste. I needed details. Why Isobel McLean had named me her heir was a mystery I had neglected for too long, but it could hold the key to this madness. The letter done, I moved straight to the next—one to Mrs. Reynolds at Pemberley, instructing her to send anything of my grandmother's she could find. Letters, journals—anything that could give me answers.

But even as I sealed the letters, my eyes kept drifting back to the book. I hadn't seen Ewan McLean's name in it yet, but surely, it was only a matter of formality. There were hundreds of names listed after the battle—soldiers who had died, clansmen taken prisoner—but no Ewan yet.

I flipped through the pages again, scanning for any hint of Ewan's name, but nothing stood out. McLeans, yes—but not him. It didn't make sense. Ewan had sworn he'd died at Culloden, and yet there was no trace of him here. Had he lied? Or was this list incomplete?

That seemed the most likely case. Too many bodies to count—it was a wonder there was a list of names at all. The whole thing was maddening. I rubbed a hand over my face, wondering if there was any end to this insanity.

It was Elizabeth Bennet's voice that interrupted my thoughts—a memory of her questioning tone from earlier. *"Why not simply get rid of it?"* She had made it sound so simple, as if tossing away the brooch would end everything. As if I hadn't tried it already! But it was not the obvious question that made my thoughts keep returning to her. It was the pragmatic way she had asked, with such honest curiosity that, for a moment, it had made the madness seem... like she believed me. And somehow, that alone made the whole thing feel somewhat more manageable.

Elizabeth Bennet. The afternoon with her had been... revealing. And not entirely unpleasant. Her sharpness, her refusal to accept things at face value, had been a surprise, but perhaps not as much as the fact that she had taken me seriously at all. She had looked at me as if she wasn't sure whether to pity or believe me, but she had still helped. That alone was... unsettling. She'd not only humored my tale but had brought real help, something tangible, like the book that now sat in front of me.

I flipped through the book again, my patience wearing thin as I scanned page after page. Ewan's name wasn't there. My pulse quickened.

"Where are you?" I muttered, flipping through the pages faster, frustration mounting with every name I scanned.

"Ye'll no' find it, ye ken."

I froze, the now-familiar brogue making my skin prickle. Ewan leaned against the bedpost, arms crossed.

I didn't look up from the book. "You told me you died at Culloden. Your name should be here."

"Ach, it's there," he replied with a shrug. "Ye're just no' lookin' right."

I scowled, scanning the list of McLeans again. No "Ewan" in sight. "I've looked twice."

Ewan stepped forward, peering over my shoulder. "That one there—aye, could be me. Or that one," he added, tapping the name of another McLean. "My..." he squinted. "My brither."

"Eoghan?" My tongue twisted as I tried to wrap it around the word.

"Nay, ye've got it wrong. Say it like 'Ohh-wen.' Aye, but it looks like my name, does it no'?"

"But it is not your name," I snapped, glaring at him. "You're not even listed."

Ewan waved a hand dismissively. "Wee bit of confusion is all. Happens when ye've got half a clan fightin'. Hard tae keep us all straight, aye?"

I slammed the book shut and stood up. "You expect me to believe that?"

Ewan's grin didn't waver. "What else d'ye think, lad? I told ye I was at Culloden, didn't I? I'm dead, nae matter. Not my fault if some scribe forgot to put me down proper."

"Not your fault," I echoed, seething. "That's convenient."

"Aye, it is. Now quit yer fussin' o'er that wee book an' get on wi' it."

I narrowed my eyes. "And I suppose you have nothing more to offer me? No more half-truths or obnoxious riddles?"

Ewan's gaze flickered, just for a moment, but then he shrugged again. "Truth's there if ye've got the eyes to see it, lad."

I was about to demand more when his expression softened unexpectedly. "So... the lass gave ye the book, eh?"

My jaw tightened. "Miss Bennet helped, yes."

Ewan's grin returned, though it seemed a touch wistful. "Ah, Elspeth..."

I frowned. "What?"

"Elspeth," he repeated, his voice almost distant. "Reminds me o' her."

"Elspeth," I repeated, taking a step forward. "Who was she?"

Ewan's eyes darkened as he straightened up. He reached forward and slammed the book cover closed. "Ach, keep yer nose out, lad. Some things are best left buried, ye ken?"

And with that, he was gone, leaving me to stare at the closed book on the desk and wonder if I'd ever get a straight answer from him.

Elizabeth

As I stepped into the warmth of Longbourn, the familiar clamor of home greeted me—a combination of Kitty and Lydia's shrill laughter and Mama's inevitable fussing. The contrast was jarring. After the eerie stillness of the gamekeeper's cottage, where Mr. Darcy had just shared his outlandish tale, the noise here was almost too much. I shook the cold from my cloak, willing myself to act as if nothing had changed—though, in truth, everything had.

What had I gotten myself into?

"There you are, Lizzy," my father's voice floated out from his study. "A word, if you will?"

I cringed inwardly. I bet I knew exactly what this was about. With a deep breath, I approached his open door and peeked inside. He was sitting at his desk, spectacles perched on the end of his nose, leafing through what remained of the stack of books I had until recently pillaged.

"Papa?"

"Ah, yes," he said, without looking up. "I couldn't help but notice a rather curious gap in my library. Several books on history and even a handful on paranormal curiosities seem to have taken a walk—on their own, I presume, since no one in this house would ever dream of sneaking them out without asking." He raised an eyebrow, finally meeting my gaze.

I bit my lip, trying to concoct a reasonable lie. "I... thought they might be helpful for—research."

"Research, is it?" His other eyebrow joined the first. "Is that what they're calling pilfering these days?"

I shifted uncomfortably. "A little harmless reading, Papa. Surely you don't begrudge me that?"

He leaned back in his chair, his expression turning bemused. "As long as it's harmless. But do tell, what is so fascinating about folklore that you've turned historian overnight? And is it merely a coincidence that my books on mania have also disappeared?"

"I—" I fumbled, trying to piece together something believable. "It's just an interest. I-in Scottish superstitions, to be specific... you know, all the things that Mama would call nonsense."

Papa snorted. "Well, as long as it's not too serious. But do try to return them in one piece, my dear. I don't fancy a ghost turning up to demand his books back."

Ghosts. That was Papa being facetious, but if only he knew how close he was to the truth.

I managed a weak smile before escaping the study, only to find myself immediately ambushed by Lydia and Kitty.

"Lizzy, you're just in time!" Lydia said, her cheeks flushed with excitement. "We're going to Meryton again to see the officers!"

I groaned inwardly. "Didn't you just see them yesterday?"

"That's hardly the point!" Kitty chimed in. "We need to show our faces. If we don't, they'll think we're dull, and I refuse to be thought dull."

"I doubt anyone could accuse either of you of dullness," I muttered, casting a glance toward the front door.

Before I could find an excuse to escape, Mama's voice rang out from the sitting room. "Lydia, Kitty! You mustn't go without your new bonnets. Only wait a moment until I have finished this ribbon."

Lydia rolled her eyes. "Oh, nonsense, Mama! The officers adore us with or without our bonnets. We could have any of them wrapped around our fingers if we tried!"

"You're delusional," I said dryly, earning a playful shove from Lydia.

"You're just jealous because Mr. Wickham has eyes for me," she teased. "Oh, he was so handsome yesterday, wasn't he, Kitty?"

I had to resist the urge to roll my eyes. Mr. Wickham. He certainly seemed gentlemanly enough, but there was no way he would indulge my sisters honorably. They could not conceive that a man, even a handsome man, must have something to live on as well, and they had nothing that might attract him besides themselves. Hardly a prospect I wished to see them entertain, but not one I could utter aloud in this house. I'd sound as mad as... well, as Mr. Darcy.

And that was a problem I wasn't ready to face.

Still, the idea of Darcy lingered in my mind as Lydia chattered on. His confession had been... unsettling, to say the least. I could hardly make sense of it all myself, and yet there was something in the way he'd spoken, in his quiet desperation, that made me want to believe him. If it was a lie, it was a deeply convincing one.

But what if it wasn't?

The floating glass. All those times I had seen Mr. Darcy looking like something had shoved him, tripped him, dragged him... And Mr. Darcy himself—a man I had first thought only proud and arrogant—seemed genuinely haunted and entirely earnest.

I shook the thought away. I didn't have time to dwell on Mr. Darcy's plight. At least, not right now. Lydia was tugging on my sleeve.

"Come on, Lizzy! You'll come with us, won't you? You never know what fun we might have!"

"Fun," I echoed. "Is that what you call it?"

"Of course!" Kitty chimed in. "Besides, there are more than enough officers to go around. We need someone to keep them all entertained."

"Well, I can assure you I'm not volunteering for that particular task."

Lydia grinned. "Oh, but you'll come anyway."

And with a sigh, I allowed myself to be pulled into the fray, all while wondering how on earth I was supposed to balance this absurd mystery with my equally absurd family.

But then again, what else was new?

Darcy

A KNOCK AT THE door.

I turned just in time to see Bingley step inside, his usually bright expression tempered by a touch of concern.

"Darcy, I—well, I hope I'm not disturbing you," he said, hesitating a little at the door. "You've been quite... preoccupied these past days. I haven't seen you for dinner, and we missed you at shooting yesterday."

I blinked, caught off guard. How many days had it been? I'd been so buried in papers, sending letters, scouring through what little information I had, that I'd nearly forgot the world around me. "Yes, I've... had much to attend to," I muttered, feeling a wave of guilt.

"You have," Bingley agreed, his brows drawing together. "I don't mean to intrude. Only, Colonel Forster has been asking about you—wondering when we might call on him."

"Forster..." My heart swirled in dread. I'd managed to avoid any face-to-face encounters with the colonel during the ball, and my last brush with him in town had been... somewhat less than dignified. "Why... er... would Colonel Forster be asking about me?"

Bingley came all the way into the room, wandering toward the mantel with his hands clasped behind his back. "Oh! Nothing particular. But any good militia colonel would like to know all the principal gentlemen of the neighborhood—it helps him to keep the peace, of course."

"Well, I am not the master of any of the local estates."

"Come, Darcy, you know perfectly well what I mean! Forster is in town today, and I thought it might be a good chance for us to mend fences after... well... last time."

Last time. When Ewan had made a spectacle of me in front of the entire square.

I resisted the urge to groan. "Must we?" I asked, rubbing the back of my neck. "I doubt Colonel Forster is waiting with bated breath for another encounter."

"He is a fair-minded man," Bingley said diplomatically. "I'm sure he holds no grudge against you for an accident. Besides, it's been a few days since you've been in company. A little conversation might do you good."

I stared at him for a moment. Bingley had no idea of the storm that was brewing inside my head. He knew nothing about my outing yesterday afternoon, when I had spent hours cloistered with Elizabeth Bennet. And here he was, as polite as ever, practically begging me to make myself sociable... to join him in town. He didn't deserve to be ignored. And it would be impolitic of me to alienate him, for he was the one gentleman in all of Meryton who was still speaking to me—though Heaven only knew why.

"You're right," I said finally. "I owe the Colonel—and you—a call."

Bingley brightened. "Splendid! We can leave within the hour."

"Within the hour?" I grimaced. It seemed a bit sudden, but then, if I didn't go now, I'd probably put it off for another week, or never. "Very well. I'll be ready."

THE MARKET SQUARE OF Meryton was bustling when we arrived. Townsfolk moved about in their usual hurried manner, while a handful of officers milled about near the shop fronts. Colonel Forster was among them, standing with his hands clasped behind his back, his sharp gaze surveying the crowd.

As we approached, Bingley waved a hand in greeting. "Colonel Forster! Good to see you, sir!"

The Colonel turned, his face lighting up in recognition. "Ah, Mr. Bingley! And Mr. Darcy as well!" His gaze lingered on me for a moment, and though his expression remained polite, I could sense the lingering memory of our last encounter.

"Colonel," I said stiffly, nodding my head in greeting. "I trust you've been well."

"Quite," Forster replied, though there was a curious gleam in his eye. "I'm glad to see you out and about again, Mr. Darcy. We were beginning to wonder if you'd taken permanent refuge at Netherfield."

Bingley chuckled lightly. "Darcy's been buried in work these past days, but I finally managed to drag him out for some fresh air."

"Yes, work," I muttered, though the lie tasted bitter. "A number of letters, you see."

"Well," Forster said, clasping his hands together, "you'll be pleased to know that Meryton has been peaceful lately. No runaway horses or flying laundry lines to speak of."

I swallowed a groan. So, the rumors still lingered. Of course, they did. I glanced over Forster's shoulder, hoping against hope that Ewan wouldn't take this moment to make a scene.

But then, as if summoned by my very thoughts, a familiar voice chimed in behind me. "I'd no' stand fer such an insult tae my face, lad."

I froze, my knuckles tightening on the reins as my shoulders drew back.

Forster tilted his head, watching me with a raised brow. "I certainly did not mean to offend you, Mr. Darcy. Only a bit of a jest, sir."

"No offense taken at all," I managed to choke out, though Ewan's presence was now unmistakable, lingering far too close for comfort. "Just... a chill in the air this afternoon."

Forster nodded slowly, but I could tell he wasn't entirely convinced. He gave Bingley a pointed look before saying, "I trust we'll see you both at dinner with my officers next week?"

"Of course!" Bingley answered with a broad smile. "Darcy and I wouldn't miss it."

I glared sideways at him. Dinner? When was this invitation accepted? I gritted my teeth, offering Forster and Bingley a tight smile. "I wouldn't dream of missing it."

Forster nodded, though I caught the brief flicker of amusement in his eyes. "We look forward to it, Mr. Darcy."

Wonderful. More time in the company of Colonel Forster, Wickham, and every other person who now suspected I was teetering on the brink of madness.

Bingley tipped his hat to the colonel and turned his horse. He clapped me on the shoulder as we walked our mounts back up the street. "See, Darcy? It wasn't so bad."

I gave him a weak smile, praying that the afternoon would pass without further incident.

Twenty

Darcy

A FEW DAYS LATER, I had another note from "Mr. Bennet." And for once, I actually looked forward to meeting the person who wanted to meet with me. Besides, I had something to show her.

I arrived at the gamekeeper's cottage, the letter from my solicitor in hand. I ducked inside to find that Elizabeth had been busy. The fire crackled warmly in the hearth, and there was already a fresh pile of books stacked on the table—some of them opened, pages spread with scribbled notes and bookmarks. Elizabeth was hunched over one of them, her brow furrowed in concentration.

She glanced up, smiling. "Mr. Darcy, you've brought news?"

I dropped the letter on the table. "It's from my solicitor, but it's not what I hoped for."

Her face brightened, and she picked up the letter. "Oh?" She scanned it quickly, her brow furrowing.

"Nothing new. Isobel McLean left no direct heirs, no children, which I already knew. Never married, and just the one brother. A few scattered properties in the Highlands and England. But no clear reason why I was named her heir."

Elizabeth frowned, tapping her fingers against the table. "Odd. No family at all?"

"None. It's as if she lived in isolation." I stared at the fire. "I can't figure it out."

She tilted her head. "It is strange. You don't leave a fortune to someone without a reason."

"Well, it was not much of a 'fortune,' as fortunes go. But indeed, you are correct. The solicitor found very little. She's a mystery. My grandmother may have known her, but even that must be a weak connection."

Elizabeth leaned back, thoughtful. "Could it be that the key to all this is not who Isobel was, but what she wanted?"

I blinked. "What do you mean?"

"Perhaps it wasn't about family or obligation. Maybe her choice had more to do with... something else."

I nodded slowly. "Maybe." It was more than I had considered. "It will be some days yet before I have the journals from Pemberley, but hopefully they will yield some answers."

"Well, that's a start," she said with a small smile. "Meanwhile, I believe I've found something."

I dropped into the seat across from her. "Found what?"

She glanced up, her eyes shining with the faintest hint of excitement. "A connection. Possibly."

I raised an eyebrow, moving toward the table. "Go on."

"This book—Highland Traditions and Mysteries—talks about spirits bound by unfinished business. Particularly, it mentions Christmas as a time when spirits are more... active."

"Christmas?" I couldn't help the doubt that crept into my voice. "What could that possibly have to do with Ewan?"

"Well," she said, flipping through the pages, "according to this, it's a time when... if a spirit is tied to the mortal world by something unresolved, they can find peace during the Yuletide. Some kind of... restoration, or balancing of wrongs."

I leaned over the book, scanning the lines she pointed to. It was full of old superstition, no doubt—but still, something about it seemed to click in place with everything I'd been experiencing.

"So, you think," I said slowly, "that this is about... justice?"

Elizabeth shrugged lightly, but her eyes stayed fixed on the book. "It would explain why he's still here. Maybe he needs you to help him... put something right."

I sighed, stepping back and rubbing the bridge of my nose. "I already asked him about that, and he was entirely impossible. If only it were that simple."

Suddenly, a familiar voice chimed in from the far corner. "Aye, too simple fer me, lad. Whit'd I be needin' yer help for? I've been rightin' wrongs just fine on me own, I have."

I froze, clenching my jaw. Ewan was slouched against the wall, arms folded lazily as he smiled and tipped his hat at Elizabeth. Not that she could see him.

"I suppose you'll claim this has nothing to do with you?" I asked.

Elizabeth, sitting across from me, blinked in confusion. "Are you... talking to him?"

Ewan chuckled, his voice low and tired. "She's catchin' on, Darcy. Maybe ye should let her in on the joke."

I scowled at him. "I have already distressed the lady enough."

Elizabeth narrowed her eyes. "Mr. Darcy, if you're having another conversation with... him... would you kindly include me in this?"

I shot her an apologetic glance, then turned back to Ewan. "She can't hear you, can she?"

Ewan snorted. "Does it look like I care, lad? I'm well past explainin' things tae the likes o' ye."

I sighed, sitting down heavily in the chair across from Elizabeth. "I don't know how to explain this."

She leaned back, crossing her arms. "Then don't try. I'm already watching you argue with thin air—there's no explanation that can make that seem reasonable. Let's focus on what we can understand."

I hesitated, then nodded. "Very well. According to him, I'm not needed for anything. No 'injustices' to set right, no unfinished business... we have argued before about it until I ran out of breath."

Elizabeth raised an eyebrow, flicking her gaze to the same space on the wall where I'd been looking at Ewan. "If *you're* not needed, Mr. Darcy, then why is he still here?"

Ewan's grin widened, but it was tinged with something that looked almost... weary. "Ach, lass, that's the real question, aye? Why am I still hangin' aboot? Aye, a right honorable soldier I was. Did nothin' tae deserve this, I'll tell ye that."

I glared at him. "Don't play coy, Ewan. I've been over that list of names. Yours wasn't there. You claimed it was your brother's name put down instead of yours."

Ewan's expression faltered—just for a moment, but long enough for me to catch it.

"Eoughen McLean," I pressed. "That was your excuse. You said he was your brother, and they got your names confused."

Elizabeth sat up straighter, her eyes darting between me and the empty space near the wall. She couldn't hear Ewan's side of the conversation, but she didn't need to. She raised a hand. "Wait... brother? Mr. Darcy, you just told me that Isobel McLean only had the one brother. Are they..." She looked back and forth between me and the empty corner. "Are they brothers, or are they not?"

Egad, she was right. How had I blurted both those facts out without noticing how they contradicted each other? Perhaps I could blame it on my lack of sleep. I whirled on him. "Explain yourself. The lady is right—according to everything I've found about Isobel McLean, she didn't have another brother, so how do you?"

Ewan's smile faded, and for the first time since I'd met him, there was something like regret in his eyes. But he said nothing.

"Perhaps," Elizabeth suggested, "a half-brother? Some... adoptive relationship?"

She couldn't see Ewan's face, but I could, and the guilt I read there... Indeed, that was precisely what I needed to see.

I leaned forward. "You lied."

His posture sagged, his usual bravado nowhere to be found. "Aye. I've nae brither."

Elizabeth's brow furrowed, and she glanced at me. "Did he admit it? About what?"

I shook my head slowly, still staring at Ewan. "Everything, I imagine."

Ewan sighed, scuffling his boots on the floor, and I caught the way Elizabeth gulped when a mud stain suddenly appeared on the stone.

"It wasnae supposed tae matter. Nothin' was supposed tae matter. But here we are, aye?"

Elizabeth leaned forward, her eyes darting between me and the space where Ewan stood. "What is he saying?"

I dragged my gaze away from Ewan and met Elizabeth's eyes. "He... he lied about his death."

She tilted her head. "What?"

"Ewan McLean didn't die at Culloden." I leveled a long look at him. "Did you?"

He leaned heavily forward, one hand massaging the other as though his knuckles were sore. "Nae."

"Let me guess. You ran. Deserted. You've been lying this whole time."

Ewan's face was pale—no, I've no idea how a ghost suddenly looked pale, or like he was struggling to breathe properly. But he did. He tugged the Balmoral off his head and slouched. "Aye, I ran. Slipped away the night before the fight. Left my clan behind. Bonny Prince Charlie... the lot of them."

I glanced at Elizabeth and nodded to confirm his confession.

She blinked. "That... that is horrible. I mean... I can certainly understand. So many died, but... why lie about it?"

I stood, the frustration and confusion boiling over. "I don't know. I don't know what to believe anymore."

Ewan's voice cut through the room once more. "Some things... they're too precious tae share, lad. Even now."

I turned to face him, my fists clenched. "You owe me the truth."

But Ewan just shook his head, retreating into the shadows.

Elizabeth

I TUGGED MY CLOAK tighter against the cold, quickening my pace as I left the game-keeper's cottage behind. There was a fresh blanketing of snow, and my tracks—as well as Mr. Darcy's—would stand out for all to see until more snow had fallen. Fortunately, it was doing just that, filling in the cups of my footprints almost as quickly as my feet made them. But that would not continue to be the case—we were bound to be discovered if we kept meeting over our books, and I found myself glancing over my shoulder more than once.

It wasn't just the fear of discovery—it was the lingering strangeness of what I had just witnessed. Mr. Darcy had sat there, talking to no one, yet answering as if he were engaged in a real conversation. Not muttering nonsense, but speaking in full sentences, responding to questions I couldn't hear. The more I relived it in my imagination, the less it made sense.

That... thing... that apparition he claimed was haunting him—it must be real. I'd tried to believe him before, if only because no other explanation made sense, but now? Now, I was certain. Mr. Darcy wasn't mad. He couldn't be. His thinking was far too logical, his reasoning sound. If anything, I was the one questioning my own sanity.

And then there was the mud. The unmistakable streak across the floor of the game-keeper's cottage that just *showed up*, as though something—or some*one*—had scuffed it there. Someone I couldn't see.

A chill ran through me as I recalled the way Mr. Darcy had glanced at that same patch of floor, his gaze following something invisible to my eyes. He'd looked so sure, so certain, as if it was all perfectly real to him. And now... well, it seemed more and more likely that it was.

As I reached Longbourn, my thoughts still tangled in a mess of disbelief and reluctant acceptance, I spotted Mr. Collins pacing in the drawing room. The sight of him only added to my unease. He had been acting strangely all day, muttering cryptic things about "certain expectations" and "Lady Catherine's advice." I couldn't shake the feeling that he was still planning something involving me—something I had no desire to be part of.

I edged quietly toward the library, hoping to deposit a few of Papa's books without being noticed. They hadn't been particularly useful in our research, and returning them now seemed like a safer course of action than encountering Mr. Collins in the hall. The last thing I needed was for him to accost me with another tiresome speech about his "humble abode" or his "fortunate situation." I feared he still intended to propose.

As I reached the door to the library, I paused, listening. Silence. Good. If Papa was in the study, I could slip in and out without attracting any attention. But just as I placed my hand on the doorknob, I heard a voice behind me.

"Elizabeth," my father called from the next room. "I'm not blind to your attempt at stealth. Do come in, will you?"

I cringed, caught in my tracks. Slowly, I turned and made my way to the study, peeking inside to find Papa sitting behind his desk, watching me with a raised brow.

"Papa," I greeted him, stepping into the room with a sheepish smile. "I was just—"

"Pilfering my library again, no doubt," he interrupted. "You've been disappearing with my books quite often lately, my dear. Care to explain what curious project has you so enthralled?"

I hesitated, unsure how much to say. I could hardly tell him about Mr. Darcy's ghostly visitor—not without sounding like I had gone mad myself.

"Well... I have been... assisting with some research," I said, cautiously skirting around the subject.

Papa raised an eyebrow. "Research? You? And here I thought you spent your days reading novels." He leaned forward in his chair, his voice dry with amusement. "Whose research, might I ask?"

I hesitated, my fingers toying with the edge of my cloak. "Just... someone who required a bit of help."

His eyes glinted, and he looked far too confident for my liking. "And this someone has a name, I presume?"

I bit the inside of my cheek. "Yes."

Papa chuckled, but his eyes narrowed. "It wouldn't be one of our neighbors, would it? Someone with a slightly... peculiar reputation as of late?"

My heart stuttered and died in my chest. Right there. *He knew.* Oh, dash it all, I was caught. Visions of fatherly consternation and forced engagements began screaming through my mind. "Po-o-s-ssibly," I mumbled.

"Elizabeth." His voice held a note of gentle demand now. "Who is it?"

I sighed. "It's Mr. Darcy."

"There, now, how difficult was that?"

I cocked an eye at him. "You sound as if you expected that."

He chuckled. "Oh, come now, Lizzy! What I 'expect' is for you to be intrigued by mysteries and curiosities, and can there possibly be a more 'curious' person in all of Meryton at present? Here, now, out with it. What puzzle has our good Mr. Darcy got you piecing out for him, hmm?"

I shifted uneasily, unsure how much to reveal. "It's... complicated."

Papa raised an eyebrow, a slight smile tugging at the corners of his mouth. "Complicated? That does sound intriguing. Does it have anything to do with the madness that seems to have beset our poor neighbor?"

I winced. Of course, he would jump to that conclusion. Everyone in Meryton seemed to think Mr. Darcy had lost his mind. Including me, until a few days ago. "I... don't think he's mad, Papa," I said carefully. "He's... troubled, certainly, but I wouldn't call it madness."

He chuckled, leaning back in his chair. "No? Then what would you call it?"

I glanced down, choosing my words with care. "I think... he's dealing with something very real, but difficult to explain."

Papa's eyes narrowed, his amusement fading slightly. "Real, you say? Hmm." He tapped his fingers on the arm of his chair. "And do you plan to continue assisting him with this... something?"

I hesitated. "Am I... forbidden?"

Papa laughed, shaking his head. "Of all the gentlemen in the neighborhood I might worry about with my daughter, Mr. Darcy is the least troubling. If anything, he's far too honest for his own good. A man who wears his demons so openly would never be able to lie to a lady."

I blinked. "You think Mr. Darcy is... honest?"

He shrugged. "In his own way, yes. The man may be burdened with oddities, but I suspect he is as forthright as they come. I doubt he could lie to you if he tried. But," he added with a sly smile, "he might work upon your sympathies+."

I rolled my eyes. "I assure you, Papa, I am not vulnerable to Mr. Darcy's... particular charms."

He studied me for a long moment, his gaze thoughtful. "Perhaps not. But I will say this: the only real danger I see in Mr. Darcy's company is that it might compromise your reputation. And then, my dear, you would be forced to marry the poor fellow. I cannot think which of you two I would feel the most sorry for."

I groaned. "Papa, really."

"Only think how pleased your dear mother would be! I daresay she would make the most of it. Oh, I imagine it would be quite the scandal—marrying a madman. But surely it would still be preferable to marrying Mr. Collins?"

I laughed despite myself, shaking my head. "I think I should rather stay unmarried forever."

"Well," Papa said with a twinkle in his eye, "I shall leave that decision to you. But do try not to drive the poor man mad. He seems to have quite enough voices clamoring in his head already."

With a final smile, he waved me off, leaving me to return the books and escape back into the hall. As I walked away, I couldn't help but mull over Papa's words.

Mr. Darcy... honest. The thought lingered, tugging at something deep inside me. For all his strangeness, all his mystery... Papa was right. He *was* honest—at least in his own peculiar way.

But what did that mean for me?

As I passed through the drawing room, Mr. Collins' pacing stopped abruptly. He turned to face me, an expectant look on his face. My stomach dropped, but before he could utter a word, I offered him a hasty smile and continued walking, hoping to avoid whatever dreadful speech he had been preparing.

Some things, after all, were far worse than encountering a madman.

Twenty-One

Darcy

W HEN I OPENED THE door to my room, Ewan was already there—lounging in *my* chair at *my* desk, scribbling away with *my* quill, looking for all the world like he owned the place. The fire crackled, casting shadows that made him seem even more obnoxiously at home.

I didn't even bother to wonder how he was casting a shadow. I just ground my teeth, barely resisting the urge to shout. "What in Heaven's name are you doing now?"

"Dinnae fash yersel, lad," he said without looking up. "Just finishin' up a wee note. Won't be a minute."

"A note," I repeated, half disbelieving. "For what?"

He sanded the paper, gave it a shake, and tucked it into his coat pocket. "Ye'll see soon enough."

I wasn't in the mood for his games. "Get out of my chair."

Ewan stretched, arms over his head, utterly unbothered. "Ach, calm yersel, lad. I'll be out o' yer hair in a few wee weeks. But I reckon ye've got some questions I ought tae answer, aye?"

I glared at him, pacing the room because I couldn't stand still. Not with this infuriating ghost lounging around like it was perfectly normal for a dead man to be writing letters at my desk.

"You lied to me," I said finally, stopping in front of the fire. I kept my back to him. "You said you died at Culloden."

He was quiet for a long moment. Too long. I turned, and for once, he wasn't smirking. He looked—what was it? Embarrassed? No, something deeper. Regret.

"Aye," he said, barely above a mutter. "I lied."

I folded my arms. "About what?"

Ewan shifted uncomfortably, running a hand over the back of his neck. "'Bout the whole lot. Culloden... the fight, how it all played out."

I stared at him, waiting.

Ewan sighed heavily. "We got our orders that night, the night before the battle. It was cold. Cold enough ye could feel it in yer bones, and the sky... och, the sky was hangin' heavy, like even it kent whit was comin'." He paused, his gaze far away as though he were seeing something long buried.

He ran a hand over his face and continued. "We all sat roond the fire, me an' the lads. The bravest men ye could ever ask tae fight by yer side. They tried tae joke, tried tae laugh like it was just another day, but there was nae denyin' it—we all kent we were walkin' intae doom. Prince Charlie? He had our loyalty, aye, but we kent he had nae chance. The English were ready, better armed, better fed, better prepared. But none o' that mattered. We were Highlanders—men who'd die for our clans, for our country, an' fer our prince."

He paused, his voice growing quieter. "But really, it wasnae the prince we were fightin' for. It was the ones we left behind. The women, the bairns... Our wives, our mothers, sisters. Like Elspeth. Aye, that's what kept us there, starin' down the English, ready tae die. We'd fight fer them."

His expression softened, and for the briefest moment, he looked almost human again, as if he were remembering something far too personal to share.

"That night, as we sat waitin'," he murmured, "I pulled out the brooch Elspeth had given me. It was small, ye ken? Ye've seen it, Darcy. Just a wee thing, silver and polished up nice, but... it was hers. She'd given it tae me the night before I left, made me promise I'd come back. That I'd find my way back tae her, no matter what happened on that battlefield."

He swallowed hard, his voice thickening. "I kissed it, held it in my hand like it was the last thing I'd ever touch from her. I made a vow that night. Swore tae it. Swore I'd come back tae her, dead or alive. Thought I'd be a right hero, ye ken? Thought I'd die like the others, and my name would be spoken wi' honor, and maybe Elspeth would remember me as some gallant fool."

Ewan's fists clenched slightly, his knuckles whitening as the memory seemed to tighten its hold on him. "We sat there, makin' grand plans—how we'd storm the enemy, how we'd take as many o' them doon with us as we could. We kent we were walkin' intae death, but none o' us cared. What mattered was how we died, aye? Die wi' honor, wi' pride. Die wi' yer sword swingin', die fer yer clan. That was the dream."

Ewan's voice cracked just slightly as he continued. "I looked 'round at the lads. Every one o' them had someone they were fightin' for—some lass they'd left behind, some family waitin' on them tae come home. That's what we told ourselves, what we held onto. We werenae fightin' for Charlie, not really. We were fightin' for the folk at home. The folk that needed us."

He closed his eyes, shaking his head. "But then... then I saw it. Saw the redcoats marchin'. Slipped away from the camp, just a bit, tae get a look over the hill. An' what I saw... the sheer size o' them, their weapons glintin' in the moonlight... It was like starin' at the end o' the world, lad. I kent, right there, that none o' us would see the mornin'. That every one o' us was marchin' tae a slaughter. An' somethin' broke in me that night. I dinnae ken what it was, but somethin' snapped. I'd promised her I'd come back, alive or dead, but I couldnae keep that promise. I couldnae die wi' the rest o' them."

He swallowed hard, his voice now barely above a whisper. "Ran like a coward. Abandoned my clan, my brothers. Left them tae die. An' I've regretted it every day since."

He dropped his head into his hands, his entire body slumped in a posture of defeat. "I should've died wi' them. Should've died wi' honor. Instead, I lived wi' shame. Hid from the world. Hid from her. Elspeth... she deserved better."

His voice broke on the last word, and for the first time, I saw the weight of that promise—how it had clung to him even after death. He wasn't just a ghost tied to some worthless brooch. He was a man bound by his own cowardice.

He stopped, his breathing ragged, like just telling the story was pulling him back to that night.

"And you ran," I finished.

"Aye," he whispered, his voice rough. "I ran. My legs took me before my brain caught up. Ran 'til my feet bled, 'til my lungs gave out. Didn't even know where I was goin'. Just away."

"And when you stopped?"

"I went down, slept where I dropped. When I woke, it was done. The fight, my clan—everythin'. Should've died that day, lad, same as my brothers. But... I wasnae there."

The words hung heavy in the room. This wasn't just about a lie to cover up his cowardice—*cowardice!* As if any rational man would not quake in his boots at that. But this was about the life he had lost—the honor he could never reclaim.

"And Elspeth?" I asked, my voice catching.

Ewan's face twisted, and he clenched his fists at his sides. "She... she waited for me. Thought I was comin' back tae her. Thought I was dead. And when I didnae come back... they said she... she drowned hersel'. Threw hersel' off the rocks, into the loch."

The room seemed to spin for a moment, and I had to grip the back of a chair to steady myself. "She... drowned herself?"

"Aye," Ewan whispered. "She reckoned I'd be there waitin' for her in Heaven. Thought I'd be there, ready an' all."

I closed my eyes. Egad, this was no ordinary ghost story. This was a tragedy, one that had consumed one life and left another trapped in the wreckage.

"But why lie about it?" I could hardly find it in me to be angry anymore. I was just... lost. "What do you think I care about a battle that was fought forty years before I was born? Why not tell the truth?"

Ewan let out a bitter laugh. "Tell the truth? Och, lad, how could I? How could I face me sister, Isobel? Face any o' them? I didnae die wi' honor—I ran. Hid like a whipped dog, I did. An' by the time I crawled back tae find Isobel, fifteen years had passed. Fifteen years o' livin' wi' the shame. It was her that told me aboot Elspeth." He hid his face in his hands.

"So, how did you die?" I asked, stepping closer. "How did it finally end?"

He turned to face me, his expression hollow. "It was Elspeth's loch. The same place she jumped. I went back there, tried tae throw mesel' in after her. But I wasnae as lucky as she was. I slipped, broke my leg on the rocks. Infection took me after that."

My mouth dropped open at the horror of it. "And Isobel? Did she know?"

He gave me a crooked smile. "Aye, she tried tae nurse me back, but I was gone before she could do anythin'. Gave her ma brooch before I passed."

I swallowed, staring at him. "And after that? Did you haunt her, too, or am I the first one to be so lucky?"

Ewan's smile faded, and he glanced at the floor. "Aye. At first. Had a laugh or two, ye ken? But after a while, it just... got old."

I took a breath, my mind racing with questions, but one pressed to the front, demanding an answer. "Why me? Why was I her heir? Surely you know something, Ewan."

He shrugged, his face a mask of confusion—or indifference. "Dinnae ken, lad. Maybe the brooch had its eye on ye. Always seemed like it was huntin' for its rightful keeper, it did."

I frowned. "The brooch's rightful owner was you, Ewan. So, how did that help?"

Ewan shook his head slowly, his voice dropping to a near whisper. "The brooch was never mine, lad. It belonged tae Elspeth. Always did."

Before I could press him further, he tipped his hat, a tired smirk on his lips, and vanished.

Elizabeth

"OH, LIZZY, DO HURRY up!" Lydia called back to me, skipping ahead like a child. Her bonnet, already askew, flapped precariously as she trotted toward Aunt Philips' house. "Mama says we mustn't keep Aunt Philips waiting."

I sighed and adjusted my gloves. "She won't even notice if we're five minutes late. She'll be too busy talking."

Kitty, trailing beside me, grinned. "Aunt Philips does love her gossip."

"She does," I agreed. "Which is why I can only imagine what wild tales we're about to hear today."

Ahead of us, Mama had already linked arms with Mary, who was grimly holding her prayer book as if she might be ambushed by sinners at any moment. But, at least, there would be no ambushes by Mr. Collins. He had remained at Longbourn to read, saying he must prepare his sermon for when he returned to Kent. So long as he was not with us, I did not care what he did.

As we approached Aunt Philips' house, Lydia had practically broken into a run, barely knocking before bursting through the door, her laughter echoing down the street.

Inside, Aunt Philips welcomed us with open arms—and, true to form, immediately launched into conversation.

"Ah, Sister, and my dear nieces! Come in, come in! I was just telling Mr. Philips the most delightful bit of news! Oh, you'll never guess what I heard at the butcher this morning!" Aunt Philips practically dragged us into the parlor, her hands framing the air.

I exchanged a wary glance with Kitty. Whenever Aunt Philips started a sentence with "you'll never guess," it usually meant some far-fetched rumor was about to make the rounds.

"What is it, Sister?" Mama asked, eyes wide, already readying herself to feast on whatever morsel of gossip was about to be served. "Do tell!"

"Well!" Aunt Philips sat down, smoothing her skirts. "Mr. Bingley's cook was at the butcher this morning, placing the largest order I have ever seen—absolutely staggering amounts of beef, poultry, and game. You know what that means, don't you?"

Mama gasped. "A ball! Oh, it must be a ball! What else could it be?"

Kitty and Lydia squealed in delight, clapping their hands. "A ball! A Christmas ball at Netherfield!" Lydia cried. "It's too perfect!"

I folded my arms, narrowing my eyes. "It seems like quite a leap to assume that, Aunt. Mr. Bingley just hosted a ball. It seems odd he would so quickly be planning another. It could be for any number of reasons. A large gathering of guests from Town, perhaps. Or something festive for his tenants."

But Aunt Philips waved away my objections with a flourish. "Nonsense, Lizzy! Everyone knows an order *that* large from the butcher is the surest sign of a ball being planned. And at this time of year? It simply must be a yuletide celebration!"

"But there have been no invitations, no calls to that effect—"

Oh, what was the use? Everyone was talking over me, anyway.

"It *has* to be a ball, Lizzy," Lydia insisted. "After all, with such a fine house, where else would we all have a Yuletide party? Mr. Bingley loves dancing, and with so many eligible ladies in the neighborhood, he'd be mad not to host one."

"And if Mr. Bingley hosts a ball, surely all the officers will attend again!" Kitty declared.

I was already shaking my head. Only the previous afternoon, I had been with Mr. Darcy, and he had given no indication that such an event was being planned. He, of all people, would certainly be wary of another such event in the offing.

"I'm not sure," I said slowly, choosing my words carefully. "If Mr. Bingley were planning such an event, surely... his friends would know of it. It would not be a matter for speculation. Jane, you have heard nothing of this from Miss Bingley, have you?"

Jane shook her head. "No, and I took tea with her yesterday."

Lydia pouted. "Oh, Lizzy, you always have to be such a voice of reason. Why can't you just let us be excited?"

"Because excitement is best saved for actual events, not imagined ones," I replied, earning a scowl from both Lydia and Kitty.

But my mother was having none of it. "Now, Lizzy, let your sisters have their fun. After all, Mr. Bingley is a man of considerable means, and Christmas is the perfect time for such festivities. If I know anything about the world, it's that wealthy young men don't need much excuse to throw a ball."

"Indeed!" Aunt Philips nodded sagely. "Mark my words, Lizzy, you'll see the invitations soon enough."

As much as I wanted to argue further, I knew it was a lost cause. There was no stopping this runaway carriage once it had gained momentum. Mama and my sisters were already giddy with anticipation, whispering excitedly about the gowns they would wear, the gentlemen who might attend, and—inevitably—who might propose to whom.

I sighed, resigned to the madness, and followed them out into the street, where we continued toward the shops. I was still pondering the alleged ball when we nearly collided with Lieutenant Denny and Mr. Wickham.

"Miss Bennet!" Wickham's voice was warm and charming as he greeted us with a smile. "What a pleasant surprise!"

Before I could reply, Lydia had already launched herself in between us. "Mr. Wickham! Have you heard the news? There's to be a Christmas ball at Netherfield!"

I winced. "Lydia, we don't know that for certain."

Mr. Wickham raised an eyebrow. "Another ball at Netherfield? How delightful. Though I must say, Miss Bennet," he added, turning to me with a slight grin, "you seem rather apathetic about the prospect."

I met his gaze evenly. "I prefer to wait for facts, Mr. Wickham. Rumors, as you know, can be misleading."

"Quite right," he agreed, still smiling. "But sometimes, a bit of anticipation can make the eventual truth all the sweeter."

"Oh, Mr. Wickham, you must attend! I only got one dance with you last time, and Lizzy got two. It is not fair, you know. You simply *must* come!"

He chuckled. "If there is another ball, Miss Lydia, I will do my utmost to attend."

Kitty beamed. "And then you can dance with all of us!"

Mr. Wickham bowed slightly. "I would be honored."

I tried not to roll my eyes as the younger girls practically swooned at his charm. Mama was no better, encouraging them with enthusiastic nods and murmurs of approval.

And there I was, the lone voice of reason in a sea of wild speculation. As much as I wanted to believe that there would be a ball—and that Mr. Bingley and Jane might find themselves perfectly paired on the dance floor—something about the whole situation left me uneasy.

"Come along, girls," Mama said at last, practically pulling Lydia and Kitty away from Mr. Wickham. "We've much to do before the ball if there's to be one!"

And with that, we were swept off again, leaving Mr. Wickham and Lieutenant Denny behind, the rumor of a Christmas ball growing ever larger in my family's imagination.

Twenty-Two

Darcy

D INNER WITH COLONEL FORSTER and his officers was exactly as dreadful as I had
expected.

Bingley, of course, had agreed to the evening with enthusiasm, while I had spent the
entire carriage ride into Meryton contemplating whether I could feign a sudden illness
to escape. Hurst had been little help, already half-asleep in the corner of the carriage, and
I'd been left alone to grapple with the fact that I'd soon be sitting down to a meal with
Wickham.

Wickham.

It was as if fate took some dark delight in torturing me.

By the time we arrived at Colonel Forster's residence, my mood had soured entirely.
The officers were already gathered—Lieutenants Denny, Saunders, and Wickham among
them—and my spine went rigid as we were led to the dining room. Forster regaled us with
the usual pleasantries, his deep voice carrying easily over the clinking of glasses and idle
conversation. His wife, young and sprightly, was nowhere to be seen, but Forster assured
us she was engaged with friends. I had no doubt those "friends" included a gaggle of
Meryton's young ladies, no doubt discussing which officers would make the best suitors.

Dinner began with forced cordiality, as these things often do. Bingley, all smiles as
usual, complimented Forster on the spread before us. I merely nodded in agreement,

grateful I hadn't been placed next to Wickham. Unfortunately, he was only two seats away, and the moment I sat down, my mood soured like week-old milk.

"Lovely evening for dinner," Bingley said, grasping at the obvious. He kept sliding uncomfortable glances toward me as if waiting for me to embarrass him again. I prayed he would be wrong, just this once.

"Indeed," Forster agreed. "Though we're expecting the weather to turn before morning. I'll have to keep a close watch on the clouds."

Saunders, seated across from me, added with a smile, "Better than marching in the rain, sir. Though I daresay our boys wouldn't mind a little fresh air."

It was the kind of talk that lulled me into a sense of false security—the quiet before the storm. I should have known better.

Just as Colonel Forster stood to propose a toast, I felt a familiar presence at my side. Ewan, slouched casually near the fireplace, arms crossed, grinning like a cat who had found a particularly amusing mouse. I froze, my wine glass halfway to my lips.

"Aye, lad, look at them all. Bunch o' proud roosters struttin' aboot," Ewan drawled. He cast a disdainful glance at the officers, particularly at Wickham. "I dinnae care fer redcoats, but ye knew that."

I clenched my jaw, determined to ignore him. He had to know I couldn't respond, not here, not in front of these men.

But Ewan wasn't the type to take a hint. He waggled his eyebrows at me. "Clap yer eyes on this."

Just as Saunders shifted in his chair, it jerked backwards out from under him, sending the poor man flailing. He went down in a heap, limbs flailing like a beached fish.

Wickham chuckled. "Perhaps too much wine already, Saunders?"

I nearly choked on my drink as Saunders scrambled back to his feet, glancing around as if searching for an explanation. The other officers laughed it off, but there was an unmistakable flicker of confusion in their eyes.

Ewan, of course, found it delightful. "Och, laddie, ye see that? Like a fish floppin' out o' water!"

I shot him a warning glance, but he only winked in response.

Dinner continued, with idle conversation turning to politics and the latest news from London. Bingley managed to steer the topic toward the local militia and their drills, much to Forster's pleasure.

Wickham took every opportunity to insert himself into the conversation, spinning tales of his "adventures" and "heroism." I had to grit my teeth through every insufferable word.

And then, of course, Ewan struck again.

Forster, mid-sentence about troop movements, reached for his wine glass—only to find it empty. His brow furrowed, clearly puzzled, as he looked down at the drained glass. He hadn't taken more than a sip from it. With a grumble, he refilled it, casting a glance at his men as if one of them had somehow pilfered his drink.

I nearly laughed out loud but caught myself just in time. Ewan, however, was shaking with silent laughter beside me.

Forster cleared his throat, apparently deciding to move on from the strange occurrence, and turned to Bingley with a smile. "So, Mr. Bingley, I hear there's to be another grand event at Netherfield soon. A yuletide ball, if the rumors are true?"

Bingley blinked, his smile faltering for just a moment. "A... ball?"

Forster chuckled heartily. "Yes, my wife and her friends have been talking of nothing else since they heard of the butcher's delivery. Apparently, your cook placed quite the order."

Bingley sent me a wide-eyed glance, and I shrugged slightly, just as mystified as he was. But true to Bingley's polite nature, he recovered quickly.

"Ah, yes, well... perhaps the ladies are planning something," he said with a laugh, although his eyes remained confused. "You know how they are. Always keeping us men in the dark."

Forster laughed along, but I could see the wariness in his men. It wasn't just the ball. It was the strange chair, the empty wine glass... and now, as Forster was speaking, his wig began to slip ever so slightly to the left.

I bit the inside of my cheek, trying desperately not to react. Forster did not appear to even notice as the wig shifted further and further, until it sat at a ridiculous angle on his head.

"Aye, he looks like a teapot aboot tae tip o'er," Ewan snickered.

I couldn't help it. I choked on my wine, sputtering in an uncharacteristic fit of laughter. Every eye at the table turned toward me.

"Mr. Darcy," Forster said, raising a brow. "Are you... quite well?"

I coughed, struggling to compose myself. "Apologies, Colonel. The wine, it must have gone down... the wrong way."

Forster nodded slowly, but his eyes lingered on me for a moment longer. Wickham, of course, was watching me with that smarmy, knowing grin of his, as if he suspected far more than I would ever admit.

I sent Ewan a murderous glare, but he only looked more amused. "Och, lad, ye should be thankin' me! I've gone an' made yer evenin' a sight more entertainin', haven't I?"

The rest of the meal passed in a blur of half-hearted conversation and strained smiles. Glasses moved just beyond the officers' reach, legs of pheasant suddenly vanished from their plates, and the fire from the hearth kept blustering up, then going cold all at once, as though "someone" was tampering with it. It was when the shutter on the window suddenly blew open, leaving the panes flapping in a stiff breeze from outside, that even Hurst began glancing about nervously.

Ordinarily, we'd have stayed for port and cigars. Bingley had told me that was how he had passed his last meal with the colonel. But tonight, Colonel Forster, clearly uncomfortable with the odd occurrences, cleared his throat as Saunders jumped up to lock the window. "It seems the weather is turning. Terrible shame, sir. We have drills early in the morning, and I'd hate for the drive back to Netherfield to be unpleasant."

Bingley nodded immediately. Poor chap, he had no idea that we had brought the trouble with us, and must have thought we would escape it when we left. "I... I think you are right, Colonel. We, ah... we wouldn't want to keep you."

The officers seemed relieved to see us go, and I could hardly blame them. As we said our farewells, I caught Wickham's gaze lingering on me, his eyes sharp and calculating. But for once, I didn't care.

Ewan had made Wickham the butt of more than one of his pranks that evening—more than the others had noticed—and I could only imagine what Wickham's face would have looked like if he'd known. I almost smiled at the thought.

Almost.

T HE NEXT DAY AT Netherfield brought an odd calm. Ewan had been conspicuously absent, though I doubted for a second that meant he wasn't meddling somewhere. I suspected he was behind the rumors of the ball, but why he would orchestrate such a thing remained a mystery.

Bingley, however, was utterly baffled.

"I just don't understand it, Darcy," he said, pacing in front of the study window. "The butcher confirmed the order—enough provisions to feed an army! Yet, no one in the house knows anything about it." He paused, throwing his hands up in frustration. "I've spoken with Cook. She's just as confused as I am. She swore up and down she placed no such order!"

I sat back in my chair, watching him with the calmness of a man who was fairly certain he already knew the culprit. Ewan's interference was written all over this, but why he was intent on hosting a grand event at Netherfield on Christmas Eve? That remained maddeningly unclear.

Bingley paused his pacing long enough to look at me, eyebrows raised. "You're sure you didn't...?"

I shot him a pointed look.

He nodded. "Right. Of course not."

He resumed pacing, his brow furrowed deeply. "I was almost resolved to put a stop to the whole thing," he admitted, "but then I started thinking... Well, why not? I've been invited to no fewer than ten dinners over the Twelfth Night season, but as it happens, no one around here has any major plans for Christmas Eve. It might be nice to host something festive."

There it was. The exact moment Ewan had been waiting for, no doubt. Bingley, the most easily guided man alive, was now halfway to embracing the idea of this ball as if he'd thought of it himself.

I sighed, leaning forward slightly. "Bingley, are you sure this is wise? I can't shake the feeling that someone—" a ghostly Scotsman, perhaps— "is pulling strings here, and you may regret this decision later."

He waved a hand dismissively. "I don't see the harm. The provisions are already being prepared, and truly, a Christmas Eve ball would be splendid. Just think of the atmosphere—dancing, caroling, good cheer!"

I could think of other things. Ewan, lurking in the shadows, plotting something devious. Wickham, probably charming every unsuspecting guest in attendance. And the potential chaos that would ensue when both of those elements collided in one ballroom.

Before I could press the issue further, the door creaked open, and Williams, the footman, entered with a slight bow. "Mr. Bingley, Mr. Darcy, I've been asked to inform you that Miss Bingley and Mrs. Hurst are currently entertaining the Bennet ladies in the drawing room."

I turned sharply to Bingley. Why on earth would we be alerted about that? It wasn't as if Miss Bingley and Mrs. Hurst hadn't entertained female guests before—far from it. The Bennet ladies had been here on more than one occasion without requiring an official notice.

But the way Bingley's face had gone from pleasantly confused to a rather vivid shade of red told me there was something more at play.

"Why," I asked, narrowing my eyes, "would we need to be informed of that particular visit?"

Bingley scratched the back of his neck, clearly flustered. "Well... I... may have asked Williams to fetch me any time the Bennets called."

I raised an eyebrow. "The Bennets. Specifically."

Bingley gave a sheepish nod.

"Jane Bennet," I said flatly.

He turned an even deeper shade of crimson, which at least answered that question.

I sighed and stood, straightening my jacket. "Let's go, then. You can't very well leave Miss Bennet waiting, can you?"

Bingley beamed at me. "Right! Yes, of course." He moved toward the door, eager to follow Williams to the drawing room.

I, on the other hand, was less enthusiastic. There was only one hope that would make this surprise visit remotely tolerable: Elizabeth.

If she was there, perhaps she could help smooth matters over—especially if this ridiculous ball was brought up.

Heaven help us all.

Elizabeth

Miss Bingley was doing her best to play the perfect hostess, which meant wearing a smile that looked as though it might crack at any moment. She had greeted us with such warmth, you'd think we were old friends, but her eyes told a different story altogether—especially when Lydia and Kitty began chattering about the officers.

"Oh, Miss Bennet," she purred, turning to Jane with an almost predatory smile, "we were so delighted to hear of your visit today. It's been far too long."

Jane inclined her head. "We're always pleased to call at Netherfield, Miss Bingley."

Caroline and Mrs. Hurst exchanged a glance over Jane's head, their lips tight in the universal language of sisters who pretend to smile while silently begging for rescue. They were marvelous at it, though, not a crack in the veneer as Kitty launched into a description of some rather dramatic spectacle involving Lieutenant Denny and a misfired musket. If either hostess found the story tiresome, they hid it behind a mask of politeness, though I suspected Caroline's cheek twitched a little too much.

"It was the most thrilling thing that's happened in weeks," Lydia declared, her hands gesticulating wildly. "And I'm sure we'll see something even grander at the ball!"

Miss Bingley blinked. "Ball?"

At that moment, the door opened, and the gentlemen entered.

Bingley was all smiles, as usual, but I scarcely paid him any mind. My attention, as always of late, went straight to Darcy, who followed closely behind, looking like he was holding his breath. His eyes scanned the room, searching—no doubt for Ewan. He was nearly twitching with it, and when his gaze finally found mine, I raised my brows in silent question.

Darcy gave the barest shake of his head. No ghost, no nonsense. Not right now, at least. That settled, I shifted my attention to my mother.

Mama made a flurry of herself greeting the gentlemen, and before long, she was in full form, exclaiming loudly about the ball Lydia had so casually let slip.

"Oh, Mr. Bingley!" she said, clasping her hands together, "we're all so delighted about the ball! It's going to be such a tremendous event. I must make over my gown, of course, but I think Jane shall have a new one. She's so beautiful—she deserves to look her best, don't you think?"

I winced. There it was, laid out as plainly as possible for all to see. The plan. The expectation. My mother might as well have pulled out a contract and handed it to Bingley with Jane's name on it, ready for his signature.

I glanced toward Caroline Bingley and Mrs. Hurst, whose eyes had gone noticeably glassy. They still wore their hostess smiles, but they were brittle at the edges, as if the idea of Jane in a new gown, dazzling their brother at a ball, was a fate worse than death.

"I hadn't realized we were hosting a ball," Caroline said, her voice as smooth as glass, though I didn't miss the undercurrent of irritation. "I had thought we'd be in London by the end of the month."

I turned my gaze to Darcy, seeking some sort of explanation. His expression was... well, tight was the only word for it. His lips pressed together as if holding back some dreadful piece of news, and when my eyes met his, he gave me the faintest, almost imperceptible eye roll.

I sensed a ghost afoot.

Poor Mr. Bingley looked like a man juggling too many glass balls at once. His smile had wavered for just a second when his sisters expressed their dismay, but he quickly recovered.

"Well," he said brightly, "we're to have so many lovely dinners this season, I think a Christmas Eve ball would be just the thing! A perfect way to celebrate, don't you think?"

I had to give him credit—he said it with such conviction, you'd think this ball had been planned all along.

Jane smiled at him—that particular smile, the one she reserved only for Bingley—and, if I wasn't mistaken, that was all it took. Bingley's mind was made up.

"There *will* be a ball," he said, looking directly at her.

Caroline's smile barely held. Mrs. Hurst's teacup rattled just the tiniest bit on its saucer.

And Darcy? Oh, Darcy was frowning. He glanced at me, then raised his brows in that way of his—the one that said, "I don't like this, and I'm sure you don't either." I could read him as well as I could read any book, and at that moment, we were both on the same page.

I didn't know exactly what was happening, but I had a strong suspicion that this mysterious ball had everything to do with Ewan. I could practically hear the ghost cackling in some invisible corner of the room, rubbing his hands together in delight.

The rest of the conversation blurred as Mrs. Bennet continued to gush about gowns and preparations, Lydia babbled on about the officers, and Kitty joined in with her own suggestions for the ball. But I kept glancing toward Darcy, whose eyes met mine each time with that same unspoken understanding.

Something was definitely brewing.

Twenty-Three

Darcy

THE BENNET LADIES WERE preparing to leave, a flurry of cloaks and chatter as they gathered at the carriage. I stood a short distance from the door, doing my best to keep out of the way, while Bingley hovered near Jane, still glowing from the victory of his declared ball.

Miss Bingley and Mrs. Hurst, however, were far less enthusiastic about the whole affair, their polite smiles barely hiding their displeasure at Bingley's impulsive decision.

I watched from the edge of the entryway, half-expecting Ewan to make his presence known again at any moment, but the ghost had been suspiciously absent since the previous night. My relief was tempered by the knowledge that this calm wouldn't last. Ewan was up to something—I just didn't know what.

As I turned to follow Bingley back inside, movement from across the courtyard caught my eye.

Elizabeth.

She stood at the carriage, adjusting her shawl, but her eyes met mine in a brief, secret glance. No one else seemed to notice—her sisters were too busy fussing over who would sit where, and Mrs. Bennet was too focused on reminding Jane of something—but Elizabeth held my gaze for just a moment longer than necessary. Then, with a subtle tilt of her head, she glanced toward the woods. It was so faint, so perfectly timed between movements, that no one else would have noticed.

But I did.

My heart lurched in my chest. It was a signal. She wanted me to meet her at the gamekeeper's cottage again, where we could speak freely.

It was unwise, incredibly so. Her reputation could be jeopardized if we weren't care-ful—if anyone saw us. This was not like a few days ago, when fresh snow promised to cover our tracks. There wasn't a cloud in the sky today, and our footprints would stand out clear as a bell—but the temptation to talk to her, to unburden myself of everything I knew about Ewan, was undeniable.

Before she could turn away, I mouthed, "One hour."

She caught my meaning immediately, gave the smallest nod, and stepped into the carriage, her face calm and unreadable as the Bennet party departed.

WHEN I ARRIVED, ELIZABETH was already waiting. She stood near the small table, her back to me, her hands tracing absentmindedly over the spines of the books that littered the table—no doubt the latest pillaging of Mr. Bennet's trove. She didn't startle when I entered, and I could tell by the slight tilt of her head that she'd heard my approach.

"I was beginning to think you might reconsider," she said, turning to face me with a half-smile.

I closed the door softly behind me. "I nearly did."

Her eyebrow arched slightly. "And yet, here you are."

I gave a short nod, moving to stand opposite her. "I needed to tell you the rest. About Ewan."

Elizabeth's expression softened instantly. Her sympathy for the ghost—a man she had never seen, who wasn't even real to her—was remarkable. I hadn't expected that when I first confided in her.

"All I knew was that he fled the battle at Culloden. Did he tell you why? Anything else?"

I nodded, running a hand over my face, trying to organize the pieces of Ewan's chaotic confession into something that made sense. "Yes. He told me the story. He wasn't proud of it, but he didn't mince words. He was... trapped between loyalty to his clan and the knowledge that staying would mean certain death. The fighting was over by the time he turned back, and he carried the shame of it—of not going down with the others."

Elizabeth frowned, her fingers resting on one of the books. "I can't imagine the guilt, even though I... I am certain I would have done the same." She paused, her brow furrowed in thought. "He told you all of this himself?"

I nodded. "In his own way, of course."

A soft sigh escaped her, and she leaned against the table. "I am sorry for him."

I blinked at her. Sorry?

"You pity him," I said, more a statement than a question. "He's not even real... not in the traditional sense... and you pity him."

"I do. If you hadn't told me about him, I would have never known he existed. But he's real enough to you, Mr. Darcy, so he's real enough for me."

The warmth that spread through me at her words caught me entirely off guard. It wasn't just what she said, but how she said it—without hesitation, without questioning my sanity or doubting me. Her belief, even in something as absurd as a meddling ghost, stirred something deep inside me.

I let the moment settle before I spoke again. "I've been wondering how Ewan plays into all of this. Especially given the matter of the ball."

Elizabeth's eyes narrowed, and I could see the wheels turning in her mind. "Ah yes, the ball. I have my suspicions as to how that came about, but I'd like to hear it from you first." She folded her arms, a smile tugging at her lips. "Mr. Bingley seemed just as surprised by the whole affair as I was."

I sighed. "That's because he was. None of us placed the order with the butcher, and yet, the provisions for a ball are being prepared." I glanced around the room, half expecting something to materialize out of thin air. "It seems we have a third party pulling strings."

Elizabeth's eyes twinkled with amusement. "I wonder who that could be."

Before I could respond, there he was.

Ewan, sitting on the table between us, his legs swinging over the edge as he perched atop one of Mr. Bennet's books like it was the most natural thing in the world.

"Well, I cannae leave ye tae fumble through this ball without a bit o' help, now can I?" he said with a grin, folding his arms across his chest. "Ye'll thank me yet."

Elizabeth

I HADN'T MEANT TO laugh, but when Darcy lurched backward in his chair as if something invisible had yanked at his coat, the sound just slipped out before I could stop it. Almost at once, a book slid across the table toward me, stopping just before it toppled over. Something—or rather, some*one*—had shifted it.

I reached out to steady the book, biting back another laugh. "He's here, isn't he?"

Darcy shot me a look that could only be described as long-suffering. "Yes."

"Good. Then I'd like to ask him a few questions."

Darcy's brow furrowed, clearly not thrilled with being the middleman in this conversation, but after a deep sigh, he relented.

"Ewan," I said, keeping my voice even though I felt slightly ridiculous speaking to an empty room, "why are you manipulating this ball?"

Darcy crossed his arms and turned to the space where I assumed Ewan was lingering. "Yes, I'd like to know that as well."

There was a pause, during which Darcy's expression shifted to one of growing irritation, and then he let out a low, frustrated groan. "He says... if I want to be rid of him, I'll need to play along."

I raised an eyebrow. "Play along with what?"

Darcy's gaze flickered to the table, where the corner of another book lifted slightly, then settled again. I could see him trying to parse out Ewan's words, clearly as confused as I was.

Darcy finally sighed. "Christmas Eve is a... magic time, according to him."

I tilted my head, considering. "I've read something like that in one of my father's books. There are myths about spirits walking freely on Christmas Eve. The time between worlds is... thin. But honestly, Mr. Darcy, is any of that..." I was going to say "true" or "possible", but the fact was, I was speaking to a ghost, so those questions went out the window already.

Darcy shifted uncomfortably. "Yes, well, he's certainly acting as if it's his magic time."

I leaned forward, intrigued. "What does he mean?"

Darcy pressed his lips together before turning back to the empty space. "Ewan, what happens on Christmas Eve? What exactly are you planning?"

The room fell quiet as Darcy focused on whatever response Ewan was giving him. His brow furrowed deeper.

Finally, Darcy relayed what he'd learned. "He says Elspeth will be waiting for him. And... the brooch."

I frowned. "The brooch?"

Darcy nodded. "Apparently so. Though what exactly that means is as much a mystery to me as it is to you."

There was another pause, followed by Darcy's sudden stiffening and a deep red flush spreading up his neck. He spluttered, his hands flying up in frustration, and I knew instantly that Ewan had said something else—something Darcy did not want to repeat.

"What did he say?" I asked, amused.

Darcy's response was immediate and adamant. "*No.*"

I bit back a smile. "Come now, Mr. Darcy. What was it?"

He clenched his jaw and avoided my gaze, muttering something under his breath that I couldn't catch, then refused to speak any further on the subject. Whatever Ewan had said, it was clearly embarrassing, and there was no prying it out of him. I made a mental note to ask Ewan directly if I ever had the chance.

Still, I wasn't ready to let the conversation end on such a mysterious note, so I tried another angle. "Very well. We'll leave that for now. But regarding the ball, Ewan clearly has a hand in it. Are there... any unusual requests? Anything he expects us to do?"

Darcy blinked, clearly reluctant to ask the question, but after a moment's hesitation, he tilted his head slightly, listening for Ewan's response. He sighed. "He's being difficult."

"It sounds as if that is rather the norm, sir. Well, at least we will have dancing. Perhaps you'll redeem yourself on the dance floor, Mr. Darcy."

His head snapped toward me, cheeks flushing again. "There were reasons for... my previous lack of coordination," he said, his gaze darting pointedly toward the empty space where Ewan was likely still sitting.

I chuckled. "Oh, I'm sure. But if you do find yourself indisposed, I'll have to look elsewhere for a dance partner. Perhaps my cousin Mr. Collins? Or... Mr. Bingley, of course." I paused, letting my voice drop teasingly. "Or perhaps... Mr. Wickham?"

As soon as the name left my lips, Darcy stiffened. The way his eyes flicked immediately to the far wall, glaring at it as though he might burn a hole through the plaster, told me everything I needed to know.

I *knew* there was something between them. Something more than Darcy had let on before.

I crossed my arms, waiting him out. "Mr. Darcy?"

His gaze snapped back to mine, but the look on his face was different now—graver, more like the first night I met him.

"What happened between you and Mr. Wickham?"

For a long moment, Darcy said nothing, his jaw tight. I could see the internal struggle playing out in his mind. Finally, he let out a long breath, as though resigning himself to the truth. "You already know enough to ruin me in all good society," he muttered. "What's one more thing?"

I stayed silent, sensing that this was not a moment to press. Darcy seemed to gather himself, then spoke in a tone that was quieter than I'd ever heard from him.

"Wickham was my father's steward's son. He was given every advantage—every opportunity. My father was... too generous." Darcy's eyes darkened. "Wickham squandered his inheritance, then returned again and again, demanding more. Eventually, it came to this: he tried to elope with my sister last summer. She was fifteen."

A chill ran through me. I could only imagine the scandal—how it might have destroyed his sister, his family. "That's... horrible," I managed.

Darcy nodded. "Yes. And the worst part is... she trusted him. He played the part of the charming suitor, the knight in shining armor." He broke off, his gaze hardening as he glanced again at the empty space where Ewan presumably lingered.

Whatever Ewan said next, I couldn't hear it, but I saw Darcy's reaction clearly. His eyes narrowed at the invisible specter, and he said through gritted teeth, "Not another word, Ewan."

I frowned. "What is it?"

Darcy shook his head. "It's nothing. I wish for you to keep this in strict confidence, Miss Bennet. It could destroy my sister."

I nodded immediately. "Of course, Mr. Darcy. I give you my word."

His posture relaxed slightly, though I could still see the tension in his shoulders. He glanced around the room, clearly frustrated, and muttered, "That is why I did not try to return to London when this all started, much as I wanted to. He would have just followed me. I'll keep him entertained at Netherfield forever if I must, so long as my sister is safe."

Before I could respond to Darcy's heartfelt confession, I saw him tense again, his eyes narrowing as though he was listening to something only he could hear. His expression darkened for a moment, and then, through gritted teeth, he muttered, "That will not be necessary."

I tilted my head, amused. "I take it Ewan has something to say about all this?"

Darcy shot me a look—half irritated, half resigned. "He's offering... assistance."

"Assistance?" I repeated, a smirk already forming. "And what exactly would that entail?"

Darcy cleared his throat and shifted uncomfortably in his seat. "Apparently, Ewan would be happy to... throttle Mr. Wickham. Or any other redcoat, for that matter."

The image of an unseen Scotsman going after Wickham, with Darcy caught in the middle trying to maintain his composure, was too much. I let out a laugh that echoed through the quiet room.

Darcy gave me a pained look, but I could see the corners of his mouth twitching, as if he couldn't help but be slightly amused himself. "It is not as funny as you think."

"Oh, but it is," I said, biting back another giggle. "At least it seems Ewan is on your side."

Darcy's eyes flicked toward the empty space again, and he muttered under his breath, "It's not loyalty to me. He just hates redcoats."

"That is understandable, given his history."

Before Darcy could respond, his body stiffened again, and his eyes suddenly shifted toward the far corner of the room. He went still, like a man holding his breath.

"He's gone, isn't he?" I asked, having learned by now to read the signs. The sudden stillness, the change in Darcy's gaze—it all pointed to Ewan's abrupt departure.

Darcy exhaled slowly and nodded. "Yes. For now, at least."

"Well, that's something, I suppose," I said, leaning back slightly in my chair. "Though I must admit, I rather enjoy watching you squirm when he's around."

Darcy shot me a look, but there was no real heat behind it. "You would."

"You know, you still haven't told me what he said to you earlier. That thing that made you turn so... red."

Darcy's face colored again just at the mention of it. "Miss Bennet, I assure you, not everything that comes out of Ewan McLean's mouth is fit for a lady's ears."

I raised an eyebrow, half expecting him to elaborate, but he clamped his mouth shut. "Ah, I see," I said lightly, leaning forward with a conspiratorial smile. "I suppose I'll just have to ask him myself, then. If he is capable of writing notes, perhaps he will write one to me."

His eyes widened, and he sputtered slightly. "You will do no such thing."

I couldn't help but laugh again. "Oh, don't worry, Mr. Darcy. I wouldn't dream of putting you in such an uncomfortable position. For now, I'll let it remain a mystery."

"Thank you," Darcy said, though he still looked slightly uneasy, as if Ewan might return at any moment to resume his antics.

I stood up from the table and adjusted my cloak. "Since our 'chaperone' has disappeared, I suppose I should take my leave as well."

Darcy rose from his seat, ever the gentleman, though I could see a flicker of relief in his eyes. Perhaps he wasn't sure how much longer he could maintain his composure with both me and a meddlesome ghost in the room.

"Miss Bennet," he said, his voice softer now. "Thank you. For... listening. For everything. You've given me more grace than I deserve."

I smiled, but there was an undercurrent of seriousness in his tone that caught me off guard. "It is I who should thank you, Mr. Darcy. You've entrusted me with something very important, and I assure you, I will keep my word."

His gaze lingered on mine, and for a moment, there was something unspoken between us—something that felt deeper than the playful teasing or even the strange circumstances that had brought us here.

I nodded once more, then turned toward the door. "Until next time, Mr. Darcy."

He inclined his head. "Until next time."

Twenty-Four

Darcy

T HE BOX ARRIVED UNCEREMONIOUSLY one chilly afternoon, left in the drawing room by a footman who hadn't bothered to mention it until I asked if the post had arrived.

I stood there for a moment, staring at the unassuming wooden crate. Inside it were pieces of my past I hadn't realized I missed so keenly until this very moment—my grandmother's journals, bound in worn leather, the spines surely creased from her careful hands.

It had been years since I'd thought of those journals. Even longer since I'd seen her handwriting—elegant but steady, the kind of penmanship that spoke of discipline rather than flair. Grandmother had always been practical, always composed, even when recounting the most sentimental of things. I remembered that well from my childhood.

I took the box upstairs to my room, waving off the offer of help from a servant. This was a task I wanted to handle alone. There was something deeply personal about unwrapping these small relics of my past, and I found myself uncharacteristically eager to sit down and leaf through them.

Once inside my room, I set the box on the desk, cutting through the twine that had held the lid in place. The scent of aged paper and faint lavender—her favorite fragrance—drifted up to greet me, pulling me back in time before I even laid eyes on the journals themselves. My fingers stilled on the wood as a pang of nostalgia hit me.

Lavender. I had never cared for it much as a boy, but now... now it felt like home.

And reminded me of another lady—one who was *not* my grandmother.

The journals were stacked neatly inside, just as I had remembered them—leather-bound, faded in places, but still intact. There were six volumes in all, neatly organized by date. I sat down, taking the first journal in my hands and running my fingers over the cover.

Her name, A. Darcy, was inscribed on the front in gold leaf, almost worn away from years of use.

I took a deep breath, turned the cover, and began to read.

June 12th, 1788

The roses in the garden have bloomed early this year, a welcome sight after the wet spring we've had. Fitzwilliam came to visit today, full of energy and curiosity. I had hardly finished my tea when I saw him climbing the oak tree in the garden, completely disregarding my warnings. He has such confidence for a boy of his age. His father would have laughed, I am sure, though I suspect George will have words with him about the state of his clothing.

He did not fall, thankfully, but he did manage to ruin his shirt in the process. When I suggested that perhaps his father might be displeased, he simply smiled that sly little smile of his, as if he already knew he would not be punished.

I smiled as I read, though the memory was hazy now. Climbing trees? I wondered what Mother and Father thought of that. They must have permitted it, surely, but I could hardly remember being given leave to indulge in such exploits. When Georgiana was born, all such permissiveness immediately became hers, while I was groomed for weightier duties. But it seems that when I was young—well, I had found trouble in the smallest of places. And grandmother had written about it with a certain level of loving exasperation.

December 23rd, 1788

The snow has fallen heavily, and it appears Pemberley may not, after all, host the Fitzwilliam family this Christmas. Dear Anne will be terribly disappointed. But she came with Fitzwilliam to call this morning, and it is such a joy to have them here on these wintry mornings.

Fitzwilliam brought me a gift—a collection of pastoral poems. I suspect he chose it because it was the only book in the shop that was not on warfare or politics. What can a child of four comprehend of such things? I shall treasure it. He pretended to be uninterested when I opened it, but I could see the way his eyes darted over to watch my reaction.

I paused, feeling a lump form in my throat. Christmas at Pemberley had always been a grand affair, but the memories were distant now, clouded by time. I could almost hear Mother's... and, later, Georgiana's delicate fingers on the pianoforte, playing the soft melodies that filled the drawing room, her face flushed with the quiet pride of someone who loved to play but hated to be watched.

I closed my eyes, letting the sweetness of those memories linger for a moment before turning the page.

As I continued through the journals, the entries were full of small, personal moments—glimpses of my childhood, memories of family gatherings, Christmases at Pemberley. I had forgotten how much time we spent at the dower house, how often we visited my grandmother, and how much those small, seemingly insignificant moments had shaped me.

But they were also mundane in a way that was beginning to annoy me. I had come looking for something specific, and I found myself growing impatient as I skimmed through pages that held nothing of real consequence.

But then I found her.

September 2nd, 1797

Today, a new companion arrived—a woman by the name of Isobel McLean. George found her through his brother-in-law, Matlock. I understand she was living in Edinburgh. I was quite cynical of her at first, but he said he was sure the woman would suit me well. She does have a very proper look about her, though she has a rather superstitious way of drinking her tea. Though she hails from Scotland, I suspect she has traveled more than she lets on.

She speaks little of her past, though there is a sadness in her eyes that she cannot quite hide. She said she once had a brother but now tells me she has no family left, which is hardly surprising. Too sad of a tale these last fifty years. I suppose that is why she has come so far to seek employment.

She is a little... odd, but she seems capable enough. I have given her quarters in the house, and she has taken to her duties well enough, though I have noticed that she tends to speak to herself when she thinks no one is listening.

That was her—Isobel, Ewan's sister. I could feel a prickle of anticipation as I read. I turned the page, eager to find more, but what followed were several weeks' worth of entries detailing nothing more than garden improvements and social calls. I kept reading, more intently now.

October 7th, 1797

Fitzwilliam visited today, and it was such a joy to see him growing into a fine young man. He has his father's serious nature, but there is a lightness about him as well, a curiosity that keeps him asking questions and seeking answers. I find him thoughtful beyond his years, though I worry that he carries too much weight for someone so young. The loss of his mother last year, I fear, has quite taken the shine out of his eyes, but he dotes on little Georgiana. I daresay his father is quite proud of him.

Miss McLean was quite taken with him. She watched him closely throughout his visit, almost too closely. Several times, I caught her muttering to herself—something about "that's the lad," though I could not make out the full meaning of it. It was rather peculiar, and I wonder if perhaps she is not entirely well. I will speak to George about it if this behavior continues.

My heart stilled.

I remembered none of this. Grandmother always had a companion of sorts, but I never paid them any mind. Isobel McLean—Ewan's sister—had been watching me even then? I turned another page, half-expecting some revelation, but the next entries were disappointingly mundane. There was nothing else about her peculiar behavior, nothing more about "the lad."

Had Ewan been communicating with her even then? Had I somehow been part of Ewan's plans since childhood?

The question gnawed at me as I flipped through the rest of the journal, scanning for any other mentions of Isobel. There were a few—passing comments about her competence, her occasional oddities—but nothing more of the sort that had been written on that strange October day.

May 20, 1799

Miss McLean has become more withdrawn in recent days. She speaks even less than usual, though her work remains impeccable. Today, as we sat for tea, she seemed distracted, her eyes constantly flicking to the window as if she were waiting for someone.

I asked her if something was amiss, but she only smiled politely and said that all was well. I do not believe her. There is something she is not telling me.

Fitzwilliam has been asking more questions lately—about his father, about Pemberley, about the future. He has a sense of responsibility that I did not expect at his age, though I suppose it is only natural. He will one day take over the estate, and I can already see the mantle of that knowledge settling on him. So much like his father, that lad.

Again, that sense of waiting. Isobel was waiting for something—or someone. But who? Or what? The tension in my chest grew as I read, each entry pulling me further into a mystery I hadn't even known existed.

November 15th, 1799

Miss McLean spoke to me today about her brother. Nearly two years under my roof, and it was the first time she has mentioned him in any detail. She said that he had been involved in the Jacobite rising, just as George suspected. I daresay the fool met with a swift and brutal end. Little wonder Miss McLean speaks of him sadly. She also mentioned that at one time, he was to be married to a friend of hers, though the name slips my mind. I believe it began with an "E". Alas, the poor child apparently drowned herself in the winter of '45.

I wonder if this is why she has been so unsettled lately. Perhaps the memories of her brother weigh heavily on her mind, especially now as winter approaches. There is a certain sentimentality, I suppose, in coming into one's sunset years. I have the joy of seeing my family growing, while she lost all hers to that futile Uprising.

I turned the page, my breath catching in my throat as I reached the next entry.

December 5th, 1799

There is a strange aura in the house lately. Miss McLean has been acting more peculiar than ever. She still performs her duties, but there is a distracted air about her, as if her mind is elsewhere. I have caught her speaking to herself

*more frequently, though when I ask her who
she is speaking to, she only smiles and says, "my
brother."*

*It is unsettling, to say the least. I have spoken
to George about it, but he assures me that there
is no need for concern. He believes that she is
simply homesick and that her behavior will pass
in time.*

*But I am not so sure. There is something very
troubling about her now. As if she is not entirely
present in the room with me... nor, indeed, in
the same world.*

The air in the room seemed to grow colder as I read those words. Otherworldly. My grandmother had sensed it too. Isobel had been communicating with her brother—even then, even after his death. But how? And why?

I kept reading, my fingers trembling slightly as I turned the pages.

December 15th, 1799

*Fitzwilliam came to visit today, and again, odd
behavior from Miss McLean. She has been so
quiet and reserved for the past few weeks, but she
seemed almost... animated in his presence. She
watched him closely, her eyes following his every
movement, as if she were seeing something in
him that I could not. I begin to fear she intends
to do him some mischief.*

*At one point, she approached him and spoke to
him in a low voice. I could not hear what she
said, but Fitzwilliam looked confused, and she*

quickly retreated. I think it would be wise if I did not leave him unattended in her presence.

December 25th, 1799

Christmas Day has come again, and the house is full of warmth and laughter. I spent the day at the manor house with Fitzwilliam and Georgiana. Dearest Georgie brings such cheer to the house, particularly after her mother's passing.

Fitzwilliam and I had tea by the fire today, just the two of us. He is a fine young man, and I know he will grow into someone worthy of Pemberley. He has always had the weight of the world on his shoulders, even as a boy, but I see something in him now—something that seems rather masterful.

Miss McLean finally seems to have settled in well. It is as though whatever once troubled her suddenly ceased, and she is become most decent and sedate, indeed. She is a dutiful companion, and for that, I am grateful. But occasionally she still gets an odd look about her. She will take to staring into her teacup or fingering some old brooch and will spend hours staring off into the hills. At times, I feel as though I am caught in the middle of a story I do not understand, a story that began long before I was aware of it.

I stopped reading. *"A story that began long before I was aware of it."* It wasn't just my grandmother who had been caught in this story—it was me. I had been part of this, tied to Ewan and Isobel and Elspeth, long before I had ever known their names.

The realization hit me like a cold wind, sharp and unforgiving. Ewan had chosen me—somehow, for some reason—and his sister had known it. She had seen something in me, something that had tied me to her brother's fate.

I set the journal down, my heart hammering like I had just run for miles.

Pricking my finger on that brooch had been no accident. I had been part of this all along.

Twenty-Five

Elizabeth

W HEN I REACHED THE cottage, I wasn't surprised to find Mr. Darcy already waiting—leaning casually against the low stone wall. He wasn't exactly the sort to be late. What did surprise me was the ease in his posture, a marked difference from the stiff, guarded man I had come to know over the past two months. He straightened when he saw me, brushing off his coat as if to shake off the winter cold, though something in his expression softened.

"Miss Bennet," he said with a bow.

"Mr. Darcy." I gave him a teasing smile, tugging my gloves off and dropping them on the table. "I wondered if I would see you here today. I came to collect the last of my father's books, as he was rather eager to have them back before mildew took the pages."

Something like a smile warmed Mr. Darcy's face, and he was rather fetching when he looked like that. A pity I had more often seen him flinching and looking over his shoulder. But today, he seemed relaxed and very much at peace.

"Tell me," I said, "has Ewan left you alone for once?"

Darcy's lips twitched into a reluctant smile. "Yes, for nearly two days together. Miss Elizabeth, have you any experience with small children?"

I pursed my lips and tilted my head. "Mr. Darcy, you have met my younger sisters. What do you think?"

He quirked a brow. "Indeed. Well, then, you may be familiar with the concept of 'if it is quiet, there is trouble.'"

"Ah." I started to collect some of the books on the table and stack them neatly. We had no further need for some of these, so I would carry them back today. "Does that mean you are concerned that your friendly neighborhood ghost is up to some mischief?"

"When is he not up to mischief? Usually, he delights in destroying my life up close, but for now, at least, it seems he's found more... amusing distractions."

"For now?" I raised an eyebrow. "I must admit, I half expected him to be waiting here, making books fly off the table for daring to meet with you unchaperoned."

"He'd likely enjoy it too much," Darcy muttered. "But no, thankfully, he's spared us that particular... intrusion."

"Well, I suppose we should consider ourselves lucky," I said, laughing softly. "A conversation without being interrupted by an invisible Scot sounds almost... pleasant."

Darcy looked at me, his gaze lingering a little too long. "It does."

There was something in the way he said it that made me pause. It wasn't just the words, but the timber of his voice when he said them. Darcy had always struck me as serious, almost somber at times, but there was a quietness to him now that felt different. Warmer, somehow.

I swallowed. "You've learned more from Ewan, haven't you? You have an odd look on your face just now."

"More so than usual?"

"Oh, indeed. For your 'usual' expression is one of terrified paranoia. Now, you just look annoyed."

Darcy sighed, then chuckled, his breath misting in the cold air. "Not from him directly, but yes. My grandmother's journals proved... enlightening, though I'm not sure how much of it is relevant."

"Relevant to what?"

"To... everything, I suppose." He looked down, avoiding my gaze for a moment. "It seems I've been involved in this tangled story much longer than I ever realized."

I set down the books I'd been collecting. "What do you mean?"

"My grandmother had a companion," he said slowly, "a woman named Isobel McLean. Ewan's sister. She lived at Pemberley's dower house for some time, though I have no memory of her. Apparently, I met her when I was only four years of age."

I blinked, trying to piece it together. "Your grandmother's companion? Interesting."

Darcy nodded. "Grandmother died in January of 1800, so Isobel McLean would have only been at Pemberley for about three years. I've no idea what became of the woman after that, but I was able to find entries about Isobel in Grandmother's journal... odd ones. Strange things she said, strange behavior. Sound familiar?"

I raised a brow. "Indeed. Strange how?"

"Well, as you might expect, she used to talk to herself. Or rather, she talked to someone who 'wasn't there.' My grandmother wrote it off as harmless eccentricity at first, but then there was an entry that caught my attention. Apparently, Miss McLean used to watch me. Every time I visited Pemberley as a boy, she would mutter under her breath, saying things like, 'That's the lad.' As if she were expecting me."

I stared at him, trying to absorb it all. "So you've been... fated to cross paths with Ewan's ghost since you were a boy?"

"Apparently."

"That's... quite a long game to play for a ghost," I mused, biting my lip as I tried to imagine how a decades-old plan could unfold so subtly.

Darcy shook his head. "I've given up trying to make sense of it. There's too much we don't know. Too many pieces missing."

"Have you considered," I started, stacking more books into the basket, "that perhaps Ewan doesn't even know the full story himself? Maybe he's just... improvising."

Darcy's lips twitched, but his eyes remained contemplative. "Improvising, Miss Bennet? I do wonder if you give him too much credit. I suspect Ewan's version of improvisation would involve throwing more objects at my head."

"Yes, but think about it," I said, warming to the idea. "He might believe he's orchestrating something grand, but he might also be as lost in all of this as we are. What if he only knows half the reason he's still here, and he's making it up as he goes along?"

Darcy considered this, the crease in his brow deepening. "That would explain his constant meddling."

"And the ball!" I added. "He practically forced Mr. Bingley into it, but other things seem so chaotically random that I doubt he had a plan. If Ewan were really in control of this whole fate business, wouldn't he have done something a little more... direct?"

Darcy raised a brow. "Direct like...?"

"Oh, I don't know," I said, smirking. "Perhaps making you wear a kilt and a Balmoral and sporran, then thrusting a bagpipe into your arms. That seems more Ewan's style."

Darcy snorted—an actual snort of amusement, which I did not expect. "Well, it's a relief he hasn't gone that far."

"Indeed! Although I think if it does, I should like to see it."

Darcy—Fitzwilliam Darcy, the proudest man in Hertfordshire—actually laughed at that. His eyes lingered on me for several seconds, and then he cleared his throat and glanced at the books I was collecting, his expression turning serious again. "And what of you, Miss Bennet?" he asked. "Do you have any ideas about how we should proceed?"

I tilted my head, pretending to consider it. "Well, the obvious choice would be to gather everyone at the ball, have you make a dramatic speech about Scottish folklore, and then we all run out at midnight to bury the brooch somewhere. Or maybe throw it in a lake or make everyone take some sort of blood oath... whatever it is, it's all very romantic."

Darcy chuckled. "I imagine that would go over well with the redcoats."

"I'm sure Colonel Forster would lend you his sword to cut your thumb for the oath."

He smiled, shaking his head. "I'll pass."

"But in all seriousness," I said, softening my tone, "we don't know enough yet. We'll just have to play along, won't we?"

Darcy nodded, though he still looked as though he were carrying the weight of the world—or at least, the weight of a particularly stubborn ghost. "Yes," he agreed. "We'll have to see what Christmas Eve brings."

I gathered the last of the books, stacking them into the basket I'd originally carried them in. Darcy, still watching me with that quiet intensity of his, seemed to hesitate for a moment, then cleared his throat.

"Allow me to help you carry those back to Longbourn," he offered, taking a step forward.

I raised a brow, suppressing a grin. "Oh, I wouldn't dream of it, Mr. Darcy. If you show your face at Longbourn, my mother will shackle you to a chair until you propose to one of us."

He blinked, taken aback, and then the corner of his mouth twitched. "A reasonable concern."

"Exactly. It's for your own good." I gave him a bright, teasing smile and hoisted the basket onto my arm. "Unless you *want* a leg shackle?"

His lips quirked again. "I think I'll pass."

"Good choice." I turned toward the door, throwing one last look over my shoulder. "After all, Christmas is still a few days away. Plenty of time for trouble."

WHEN I RETURNED TO Longbourn, the first thing I noticed was Mr. Wickham's familiar figure through the window of my mother's sitting room. I paused at the door, my hand tightening on the latch. I hadn't expected to see him today, especially after everything I'd learned.

A wave of unease swept over me. In all my distraction over Mr. Darcy's ghostly troubles, I had failed to mention anything about Wickham's true nature—to Jane, or even my father. Now, he was here, comfortably ingratiating himself into our household like an honored guest.

I stepped inside, brushing the snow from my cloak, and was immediately greeted by the sound of Lydia's too-loud laughter echoing through the drawing room. There he was, Wickham, surrounded by my younger sisters, holding court like some sort of genteel prince. Kitty and Lydia were practically draped over the furniture in their eagerness to hang on his every word.

"Miss Elizabeth!" Wickham exclaimed as I entered, standing with a flourish that was as smooth as it was practiced. "What perfect timing."

"Mr. Wickham," I replied, forcing a smile to mask my unease. "I see you've been well received in my absence."

He gave a lazy, charming grin, his eyes gleaming with that false warmth I now recognized. "Ah, but the household shines brighter now that you've returned."

Lydia giggled at that, thoroughly taken with his flattery, and even Kitty couldn't resist glancing in his direction with wide, adoring eyes. I, however, remained still, my thoughts dark with the warning Darcy had given me just days ago.

Wickham's gaze lingered on me for a fraction too long before he gestured toward the window as if continuing some light conversation that had begun before I arrived. "I happened to pass through the woods earlier. A peaceful place for a stroll, don't you think?"

My stomach twisted. "Yes. Very peaceful," I said, keeping my tone steady despite the implication behind his words.

His smile widened, but it was too sharp to be friendly. "Of course, it pays to be vigilant. One never knows what one might encounter in the woods."

I met his gaze head-on, refusing to flinch. "I imagine only the occasional fox."

"Or something equally... unexpected," Wickham replied, his voice still light but the meaning beneath it unmistakable. *He knew*. Somehow, Wickham had stumbled across my footprints or—worse—Darcy's.

I forced another smile, unwilling to let him see me falter. "Indeed."

"Well, then, it is unfortunate that I missed you before you set out for your outing. I believe I have stayed my welcome already, and I shall about-face and take me back to my quarters."

Mama gasped in dismay. "But you have only just arrived, Mr. Wickham! You simply must stay for dinner. I insist! It would be our greatest pleasure to have you."

I clenched my jaw, watching as Wickham's smile slid back into place with effortless ease. "I wouldn't dream of imposing, Mrs. Bennet," he said, though we all knew he would hardly decline the invitation.

"Nonsense!" my mother declared. "You must stay, Mr. Wickham, you must! We shall have a delightful evening together."

I caught Wickham's glance as he cast me another look—this time more smug than playful, as if he'd already won some unspoken victory. And I, for once, had no clever retort. Not in front of my mother, and certainly not with my sisters fairly swooning in their slippers.

It was too late to warn anyone now. Wickham had already embedded himself too deeply into our lives, and while my family basked in the glow of his charm, I stood frozen, trapped between my knowledge of the truth and my inability to speak it. Before I could formulate an escape plan, the door to the drawing room opened, and in marched Mr. Collins. He looked about until his eye settled on me, and then he brightened, hurrying forward.

"Cousin Elizabeth, what exceeding luck to find you. It is so rare that I have had the leisure of seeing you about and unoccupied that I feel I must, even in the presence of company, impose upon your good nature to relay to you some bit of news. I have received a most urgent letter from Lady Catherine herself."

I stifled a groan and prepared for whatever nonsensical praise he was about to heap on his benefactor.

"She requires my presence back at Hunsford with immediate effect, due to certain pressing matters. However..." His eyes took on that familiar glint as he leaned in slightly, lowering his voice. "I deeply regret that there is a *most*... important matter I had hoped to secure during my visit, and time is slipping away."

Ah, of course. That again.

I folded my hands in front of me and gave him my most attentive smile, though my mind was already working out how to divert him. "Mr. Collins, how tragic for you that duty must call you away from such pressing personal concerns. Lady Catherine's word is, after all, as close to law as one might hope to follow."

"Indeed, Miss Elizabeth, you understand perfectly!" he said, beaming at what he assumed was my complete submission to the conversation.

"Well, Lady Catherine's needs must always come first, Mr. Collins. How unfortunate that she requires your return to Hunsford immediately, when there was still something... dear to you left unsecured." I clasped my hands with exaggerated sympathy. "But surely such matters will keep, won't they? Kent needs you."

Mr. Collins blinked, his mouth opening and closing like a fish gasping for air. "Well, I... I—"

"And imagine Lady Catherine's disappointment should you tarry here any longer!" I continued, as though I hadn't noticed his growing confusion. "Surely, she would be beside herself knowing you're delayed when she needs you so. Why, I dare say Kent might collapse without you."

His brow furrowed, and for the first time, he appeared uncertain. "But... Miss Bennet, I had intended—"

"You mustn't allow such trivial matters to weigh on you, Mr. Collins." I smiled brightly, stepping past him with a polite nod. "Duty calls, after all! Lady Catherine must not be made unhappy by any delay, even for a moment."

Without giving him a chance to recover, I dipped my head and turned toward the stairs, leaving him frozen in the middle of the drawing-room, utterly baffled by how the conversation had slipped from his grasp.

As I ascended the stairs, my basket full of books balanced carefully on my hip, I bit back a triumphant grin. If nothing else, today had been a success in keeping Mr. Collins, Mr. Wickham, and my sanity at arm's length.

Twenty-Six

Darcy

I T HAD BEEN, OVERALL, a less than tedious afternoon. Bingley had tried to drag me out skating in the Meryton Square again, but the thought of another humiliation before the entire town had been too much to bear. So, I talked him into a brisk ride instead.

The winter weather was fair for a change, the horses were swift, Bingley only mentioned the words "Miss Bennet" and "Angel" a couple of times, and we had not seen even one of the militia officers on our outing. I daresay, it ought to have been everything pleasant to set my thoughts at ease.

But the ride had not done what I had hoped—clear my head and rid me of some of the more inconvenient notions nagging at my mind. By the time I dismounted, I was in no mood for pleasantries. The last thing I wanted was an invitation to take tea with Bingley's sisters as soon as we returned. Yet, as ever, Bingley was enthusiastic about it.

"Come, Darcy!" he called, far too chipper for my taste. "Caroline was lamenting only yesterday that we hardly see your face. She will start to think you are avoiding her."

Perhaps because I *was* avoiding her. Tea with Miss Bingley and her sister was about as appealing as having my boots tied together, but I could hardly refuse outright. So, I followed him into the drawing room, dreading what was sure to be a painfully long half-hour of simpering smiles and inane conversation.

Caroline Bingley was already seated, her eyes lighting up the moment I stepped inside. "Mr. Darcy, how lovely of you to join us. I trust the ride was invigorating?"

I gave a curt nod, offering nothing more.

Her smile tightened, but she persisted. "Would you care for some tea?" She already had the teapot in hand, a cup half-filled before I could even open my mouth.

"None for me, thank you," I said quickly, settling into the farthest chair I could find. The fire seemed a better conversationalist than anyone in this room.

Caroline's lips twitched. "Oh, but surely after such a ride, you must be in need of refreshment." She extended the cup toward me with a forced smile.

This—*this* was why I avoided these situations. She was relentless, forever seeking to find favor with me, despite my best efforts to remain distant.

"No, really," I replied, sharper than I intended. "In fact, I am hardly decent to be in company. I would not like to make myself an unpleasant presence in your drawing room."

Beside her, Mrs. Hurst looked up from her embroidery, a knowing smirk tugging at her lips. "Mr. Darcy has been... distracted lately," she said, in a tone that made it clear she thought she was clever. "Preoccupied, perhaps?"

Distracted. That was one way to put it. The dead quiet from Ewan over the past three days had me on edge. His presence was irritating, but his absence was perfectly unnerving. If Ewan was silent, it meant he was planning something.

Miss Bingley beamed, clearly pleased that her sister had noticed my "distraction." "Indeed, Mr. Darcy has much on his mind, I'm sure," she said, her eyes gleaming. "With the ball and... other matters to think about."

I stifled the urge to roll my eyes. The ball. She would, no doubt, be expecting me to open the evening with her, just like the last time.

"And how fortunate that we'll have such an event to look forward to," Mrs. Hurst added, with a glance at me. "Though I do hope Mr. Darcy will save a dance or two for the deserving ladies."

"Quite," I muttered, though I had no intention of discussing the ball any further. If I had my way, I'd be far from the dance floor.

Bingley finished his tea and set the cup aside, looking pointedly at my cup where it sat on the table beside his, still steaming. "Well, I've some letters to write. I believe I shall attend to some business before I retire to dress for dinner. Caroline, Louisa, you'll excuse us?"

I followed Bingley out of the drawing room without a second glance, grateful to escape the stifling atmosphere of simpering smiles and forced pleasantries.

"Darcy." Bingley wheeled on me the moment the door closed behind us. "Are you unhappy here at Netherfield?"

I straightened in alarm. "Good heavens, no. What gave you that idea?"

"It is plain as the nose on your face. You avoid my sisters, you hardly speak to me, and your behavior of late has been waffling between distant and irrational. Really, Darcy, is something the matter?"

I sighed. "No. Nothing that is within your power to correct, at any rate. Forgive me, Bingley, but you are correct that I have not been entirely myself lately. Nor have I been a very gracious guest. I shall attempt to remedy that."

Bingley studied me for a few seconds, then his face brightened as if the matter were settled. "Well, do be sure to tell me if there is anything you need. I could send for Mr. Jones, of course."

"That will not be necessary."

"Oh, well, then, very well. But the offer stands, should you choose." I thanked him, and we parted for our separate rooms.

Dash it all. That blasted Scotsman had nearly made a very good man think I despised him and disdained his home and family. How I longed to be rid of the nuisance, once and for all!

Where in blazes was he?

I shrugged out of my coat and tossed it aside, already anticipating the relief of solitude. Perhaps I was only tired. I'd hardly slept since October, and a brisk ride on a cold day certainly set the chill into my bones. A bath would be just the thing, and since there had been no Ewan to loiter about to humiliate me in a state of undress, why... I stepped to the bellpull and rang for my valet.

I WAS HALF-LISTENING AS the valet set about his usual tasks—hanging up my coat, preparing evening clothes for later, directing the maids on the bath water—but my mind wasn't on any of that. Oddly enough, it was the wisp of lavender fragrance that kept capturing my attention.

I opened my hands to stare at my palms and sniffed them surreptitiously. I had not handled the journals since yesterday. Where was that fragrance coming from? I had no notion, but it no longer reminded me of my grandmother. It was another lady who also favored that scent, one with dazzlingly fine eyes...

My valet cleared his throat, drawing my attention back to the present. "Sir, the bath is prepared. Shall I assist you?"

I nodded, not bothering to glance at him as he opened the door to the next chamber, where the last maid was just leaving with her bucket. The scent of lavender steam rose through the room—the answer to my question, I suppose, but I'd no notion why that fragrance had suddenly been added to my bath water.

I assured my valet I needed no further assistance and made quick work of stripping off my clothes. My skin prickled with gooseflesh and I felt obscenely exposed until I hurried into the tub to restore some measure of my modesty. It was tempting to rush through the whole thing, but the warmth of the water as I slid into the tub forced a reluctant sigh from me.

I leaned my head back, trying to relax. If only I could wash away the thoughts of Ewan as easily as the mud and grime from the ride.

For a few moments, the room was blissfully silent, the heat soaking into my bones, the water rising just below my chin. Perhaps—just perhaps—if Ewan did decide to reappear, he would have the goodness to wait until I had enjoyed an hour of peace.

A thought that lasted precisely three minutes.

As soon as I heard the window creak open, my body tensed, the splash of water shifting in response. The gust of cold air that followed sealed my fate.

"Yer lookin' quite... soft, laddie. And pink like a wee piglet."

I sat up with a start, the water sloshing over the edge of the tub, and turned to find Ewan perched casually on the windowsill. He grinned, swinging his legs as if he hadn't just burst in on a very private moment.

"Ewan!" I sputtered, grabbing for the nearest towel to cover myself.

He only raised an eyebrow. "Aye, ye missed me, then?"

"This is hardly the time!" I hissed, trying—and failing—to keep the water from soaking the towel as I struggled to shield myself from his amused gaze.

Ewan chuckled, hopping down from the window. "Oh, I'd say it's the perfect time, lad. Ye're all nice an' relaxed, open tae a wee bit o' conversation, aye?"

"I'll be open to tossing you out that window," I muttered under my breath, hastily trying to gather my dignity. "Where have you been?"

Ewan ignored my question, sauntering over to the desk as if he owned the place. "It's a fine thing, isn't it? A wee break from me fer a few days?" He paused, looking me up and down with that insufferable smirk still plastered across his face. "But I knew ye'd come crawling back."

"I did no such thing!" I snapped, water dripping from the towel as I tried to wrap it around my waist before standing. "You've been scarce for three days, and I have questions. I need answers."

He sauntered over to the fireplace, ignoring me entirely as if my current predicament was of no consequence to him. "Aye, aye, now ye're wantin' answers, eh? Funny how that works."

I was too furious to care anymore about my current lack of clothes, stepping out of the tub as I pointed an accusatory finger at him. "I found my grandmother's journals."

That stopped him in his tracks. His face flickered with something I hadn't seen before—guilt, perhaps? Annoyance?

"Aye," he finally muttered. "Thought ye might."

My patience was running thin, and I grabbed for my robe, securing it around myself. "You've known me since I was a boy, Ewan. Since Isobel—your sister—was at Pemberley. You've been tied to my family for years. Why? What is your game?"

Ewan, for once, didn't crack a joke. Instead, he stared at the flames, silent. The playfulness was gone, and for a moment, I saw something darker lurking behind his eyes.

Finally, he sighed, his voice losing its usual edge. "It was never aboot ye, Darcy."

I blinked, not understanding. "What?"

"It's not *ye*, lad," Ewan repeated, turning toward me. "It's *her*."

"Her?" My heart thudded in my chest as I tried to make sense of his words. "Miss Bennet?"

Ewan's lips twitched into something resembling a sad smile. "Aye. It's always been aboot her."

"What does Elizabeth Bennet have to do with any of this?"

He rubbed a hand over his face, and for the first time, I saw something almost... regretful in his expression. "'Cause she's got the same spirit as Elspeth. The love o' my life."

My head swam, my hands gripping the edges of my robe to keep my composure. "Elizabeth... is Elspeth?"

"Nah, not exactly. But they've the same... light," he said softly. "Same soul, ye might say. The moment I clapped eyes on her, I kent."

I folded my arms as the thin garment soaked more water from my skin. I was already dripping all over the floor, but this was a matter beyond niceties, beyond modesty and manners and good breeding. "What, exactly, did you know?"

Ewan leaned against the desk, his gaze far away for a moment, as if seeing something I couldn't. "It's in the way she moves, lad, the way she laughs. A fire in her, same as Elspeth had. Hard tae put in words, but soon as I laid eyes on her, I kent it. Her soul's bound tae mine. Like the auld stories say—two souls yoked, no matter the time nor space between."

I stared at him, still trying to make sense of it. "You think Elizabeth is... what? A reincarnation?"

He shook his head, his expression softening, almost reverent. "Nay, lad, not that. It's deeper than that. It's as though my Elspeth's spirit lives on through her—no' in flesh, but in essence. There are some bonds that dinnae break. Fate's seen fit tae bring her tae me... and tae ye."

"But if that were the case, why did you not simply hunt her down yourself? Why was *she* not Isobel McLean's heir? Why do I have any part in this?"

"How was I tae find her mesel'? I needed *ye* for that, lad."

I shook my head. "Why?"

Ewan rolled his eyes. "Are ye deaf as well as blind? Because she's your *dìthchail*. Ye and her, yer fates are bound—two lives linked across time, meant tae meet. It's no' a choice, no' a passing fancy. It's in the blood, in the spirit. Elspeth's essence found its way tae Elizabeth, just as ye were meant tae find her."

I stood there, reeling. My mouth opened to speak, but no words came. *Her?* Elizabeth? My mind stumbled over itself, trying to grasp the enormity of what Ewan had just said. Fated? Bound by some ancient connection to his long-dead lover? I didn't even *believe* any of this stuff, and yet, here I was, entertaining it!

"What if I don't want any part of this?" I shot back. "What if I don't want to become... whatever it is... *bound* to Miss Bennet?"

"Too late fer that, laddie. She's meant fer ye, an' if ye'd just pull yer heid outta yer arse, ye'd see ye've already gone an' handed that wee sassenach heart o' yers tae the lass."

I swallowed, but my throat wouldn't work. Blinked until my eyes were dry, and struggled for breath until there were spots in my vision. Ewan thought *I*... and *Elizabeth*...?

Heaven and earth. This whole time, I had thought I was the one tied to Ewan's fate, that I had been caught in the middle of some cosmic joke. But no—Elizabeth. It had always been her.

"You... you could have told me this from the start," I managed, though my voice came out somewhat strangled. My pulse hammered in my ears, and heat crept up the back of my neck, embarrassment warring with confusion.

I'd dealt with Ewan's interference before, his relentless schemes and cryptic nonsense, but this? This was beyond anything I could possibly imagine. Elizabeth—*my* Elizabeth—was somehow tied to this tangled web of fate? It was absurd. Impossible.

And yet...

I swallowed hard, my gaze drifting to the window where the last traces of daylight bled into dusk. Some part of me—some ridiculous, utterly foolish part of me—was intrigued. Drawn in by the thought of it. Could it be true? Was there some reason beyond mere attraction that I couldn't seem to get her out of my mind, that no matter how much I tried to convince myself otherwise, she was the one I...

No. I clenched my jaw, forcing the thought back. This was Ewan's madness, not mine. And yet the idea pulsed there, at the back of my mind, as if teasing me with some truth I wasn't ready to accept.

"Tell ye? And ruin all the fun?" He quirked a brow, though it lacked its usual mischief. "Ach, ye wouldn't ha' believed me anyhow. Ye don't even believe me now, do ye?"

The blighter was right. I... I was in love with Elizabeth Bennet. And it took some miscreant figment of my imagination... or whatever he was... to make me realize it.

"And the ball," I muttered, my voice tight. "What happens at the ball?"

Ewan's grin returned, a glint of that old mischief creeping back into his eyes. "Ah, lad, that's where it gets interesting."

I groaned, running a hand through my wet hair. "You know, I'm starting to hate that grin."

He winked at me. "Ye'll see soon enough."

Twenty-Seven

Elizabeth

M R. COLLINS CLEARED HIS throat in the drawing room, and I immediately braced myself. There was no escaping him this time. The rest of the household was busy elsewhere, and the moment he approached me, I knew exactly what was about to happen.

"Cousin Elizabeth," he began, puffing his chest up as though Lady Catherine herself had placed a medal of valor upon it, "I trust you understand why I wish to speak with you in private."

I suppressed a sigh, pasting on my most patient smile. "Mr. Collins, I do believe I have an inkling."

His chest inflated even further, if such a thing were possible. "Indeed, indeed. I am sure you are not unaware of the... admiration I hold for you. And I come now with an offer that I believe you will find most advantageous—"

Ah, there it was. The moment I had been dreading, unfolding before me like one of those awful plays where the ending is known from the start, but one is forced to sit through it anyway.

"Miss Bennet, it is with the greatest respect and the most *ardent* affection that I humbly offer you my hand in marriage," he declared, beaming as though he'd just handed me the keys to a kingdom.

"Oh, Mr. Collins," I began, voice dripping with sincerity, "I am truly honored that you would even consider me for such a position. But..." I paused, glancing down as if I were filled with doubt. "I fear I may not live up to the high expectations that Lady Catherine de Bourgh surely has for your future wife."

His smile faltered. "I... beg your pardon?"

I pressed on, adding a note of regret to my tone. "Indeed, a woman of my limited refinement might bring embarrassment to such a distinguished household as Lady Catherine's." I gave a small, sorrowful sigh for effect. "I trust she will not be too disappointed with me, knowing you could have done so much better."

"I..." He tilted his head. "Why, Cousin! Whatever do you mean?"

"Oh, surely, Mr. Collins, you must know that I cannot cook. I do not even know how to boil water without scalding myself."

"Well, naturally, Cousin, that skill could be learned in time."

"And I can hardly read."

He narrowed his eyes. "I beg your pardon?"

I shrugged. "I'm afraid it is all a sham—every bit of it. All the times you have seen me with my Papa's books, the things I try to say to Mary—fake. All of it. I can barely make out my own name, and it is not for want of effort. I believe there is something wrong with my eyes—it must be hereditary, for Mama is the same. The letters swim all over the page, and *poof.* I cannot make heads of tails of them. Fancy *me* being good enough for a parson's wife, illiterate and unable to cook! Good sir you are *too* kind."

"Well!" He swallowed and glanced to the side. "I... ah... Surely, Cousin, that would matter little once we are married."

"Oh, I dearly hoped you would say that. You are too good," I gushed. "Mama told me never to say a word of it to anyone, and I *almost* never have, but you are so terribly generous and kind-hearted that I doubt you shall even be disappointed that I cannot have children."

Mr. Collins blinked, clearly thrown off course. "Miss Bennet, I... I had not considered—" He gulped and leaned toward me with a questioning look. "Ah... you will forgive my indelicacy, Cousin, but... exactly *how* are you aware of this... infirmity?"

I shook my head mournfully. "I was not 'usual' like my sisters when they came into womanhood, and Mama brought in a midwife to confirm it. But truly, what is that in light of a lifetime of happiness? Oh, Mr. Collins, you have made me the happiest woman alive! I daresay even Lady Catherine will become accustomed to me in time. You know I can hardly hold my tongue in company, but as she is such a great lady, I've no doubts that she will bring even my stubborn tongue to heel."

The wheels in his head started turning, and I could see the moment he began reconsidering his offer. His mouth opened and closed a few times before he spoke again. "Yes, well... Lady Catherine does prefer a certain... level of decorum, that is true. And I had hoped..." He cleared his throat and bit his lip. "Of course, in my position as your father's heir, I had hoped for a son of my own one day."

I let my face collapse in sorrow. "Then... are you saying I am not good enough for you? That you would put me aside for such a little thing?"

"Well! It is hardly a little thing when it is one of my chief requirements in... That is to say, I had certain expectations, and... well..."

I nodded in understanding. "That is what the last gentleman said. Oh, I really ought to have listened to Mama and not said a word. But truly, Mr. Collins, I would absolve you of any wrong if you chose to retract your offer. I think perhaps you should seek a lady of... quieter manners. Someone truly worthy of Hunsford."

He nodded, looking increasingly convinced that this was all his idea. "Exactly as I was thinking, Miss Bennet. I see now that, in my eagerness, I may have overlooked certain... qualities. It is possible Lady Catherine would prefer someone with... greater refinement."

I smiled sweetly. "You are wise, Mr. Collins. I'm sure you will find someone more suitable in no time."

By the time I excused myself from the room, Mr. Collins was nodding so vigorously that I feared he might dislodge his wig. But at least he was no longer proposing.

I MADE MY WAY straight to my father's study after that little debacle. A victory like that deserved an audience, and Father would certainly appreciate the performance.

I knocked once, not bothering to wait for a response before slipping inside. "Papa, I have important news."

He glanced up from his book, an amused eyebrow raised. "Well, Lizzy, what could possibly be important enough to interrupt my reading?"

"I have just refused a very eligible offer of marriage. I believe it is now your duty to denounce me as the most ungrateful daughter in all of Hertfordshire."

Papa's lips twitched, but he held his composure remarkably well. "Ah, yes. I have long awaited this moment. And how shall I go about denouncing you? Shall I send you out into the snow to fend for yourself? Perhaps your mother will build a gallows in the back garden."

"Only if there's room beside her gardenias," I quipped, settling into the chair across from him.

He chuckled and set his book aside. "Come now, Lizzy. Who's the poor soul who had the misfortune of proposing to you? Mr. Collins, I presume?"

I nodded. "Indeed. I believe I handled him quite well."

Papa leaned back, smirking. "I imagine you sent him running for the hills?"

I shook my head, feigning modesty. "Not at all. I simply... encouraged him to realize that he was the one who should retract the offer."

Papa let out a bark of laughter. "Good girl. Well done, Lizzy. I feared for a moment I might actually have to approve of the match. A relief, truly. I daresay you've spared him a lifetime of misery, though your mother may never forgive you for it."

"I'm certain I shall recover," I said airily. "But now that I am officially off the market—at least in Mr. Collins' mind—what am I to do with the rest of my time?"

Papa leaned back, his eyes gleaming with mischief. "Well, you could always come back to the serious business of returning my books. Are you quite finished with them yet, or have you found yourself compromised by the same scoundrel who's stolen them away?"

The words, spoken in jest, made my smile falter. Papa noticed, of course. He always noticed. His gaze sharpened, the lightness in his tone fading just slightly.

"What is it, Lizzy? You look troubled."

Compromised... I hesitated, the memory of those snow-covered woods flickering in my mind. The footprints Wickham had surely seen. My heart twisted at the thought, but I pushed it down. Surely, he would not have followed them for over a mile to learn where I had gone.

But how to explain all my dealings with Mr. Darcy? Papa was whimsical, to be sure, but he was also a rational man. He wasn't the sort to take kindly to talk of ghostly happenings, and I could hardly confess all that was on my mind. But there was something else I could admit.

"It's not about Mr. Collins, Papa," I said, choosing my words carefully. "I've... come to rather like Mr. Darcy."

Papa's eyebrows shot up in surprise. "Oh? Well, this is news indeed. Your mother will be over the moon."

I rolled my eyes. "It's not like that. I just... he's not the man I thought he was."

Papa leaned forward, the corners of his mouth twitching in amusement. "I see. So, you've given up all hope of ruining yourself with a good-for-nothing officer like your sisters and have taken a fancy to the idea of letting a fine, upstanding gentleman disappoint you instead?"

"It's not a fancy," I protested, though the heat creeping up my neck betrayed me. "I simply... he's been through a great deal, and I misunderstood him at first."

Papa gave a slow nod, though his eyes were still twinkling with mischief. "And does he return your admiration, or is this a strictly one-sided affair?"

I narrowed my eyes, refusing to rise to the bait. "I've no intention of getting my heart involved, thank you very much. Mr. Darcy and I have simply... reached an understanding."

Papa's smile faded slightly as he studied me, his expression more serious now. "An understanding? You've never spoken like this before, Lizzy. What has changed?"

I bit my lip, searching for the right words. "I suppose... I've seen another side of him. He's... vulnerable, in a way. He's been dealing with more than anyone realizes."

Papa leaned back in his chair, his gaze still on me. "And this other side of him... do you like it?"

I hesitated, unsure of how to answer. "I don't know. It's complicated."

"Lizzy, if there's one thing I know about you, it's that you never do anything halfway. If you've come to like this Mr. Darcy, then there's more to it than simple admiration. You always see things through to the end, even if it's uncomfortable."

I stared at him, taken aback by his perceptiveness. "I'm not sure it will come to anything, Papa. He's... well, he's Mr. Darcy. And after the ball, everything might change."

He chuckled again, though this time there was a note of sympathy in his voice. "Ah, yes. The grand ball. And what will happen after all the Christmas festivities have ended? Will Mr. Darcy vanish back into his world of riches and responsibilities?"

I shrugged, trying to appear indifferent. "Perhaps. Or perhaps he'll be freed of all the... distractions that have been plaguing him. Either way, I don't know what the future holds."

Papa studied me for a long moment, then finally nodded. "Well, whatever happens, Lizzy, I trust you'll make the most of it. Heaven knows you've more sense than the rest of your sisters combined."

I smiled, though the unease still lingered in my chest. Father had a way of simplifying things, of making them seem less daunting. But in this case, I wasn't sure sense had anything to do with it.

L ATER THAT EVENING, BEFORE bed, Jane and I were laying out our gowns for the Christmas Eve ball. Jane leaned over hers, adjusting her ribbons and inspecting any flaws in the lace with serene concentration, while I fussed unnecessarily with a shawl, pretending it needed far more attention than it did.

"I confess, Lizzy," Jane began, "I believe I've quite lost my heart to Mr. Bingley."

I glanced up, watching her reflection in the mirror. Her cheeks were a soft pink, her eyes sparkling. I smiled, setting aside the shawl entirely. "I'm so happy for you, Jane. He's a good man, and it's clear he cares for you."

She blushed, her lips curving into a shy smile. "It's almost too good to be true, isn't it? Sometimes I wonder if it's all a dream."

I chuckled. "Dream or not, you deserve it. More than anyone I know."

Jane turned to face me fully, her expression soft but filled with that unmistakable glow of someone very much in love. "You're kind to say so, but I still can't believe he seemed to choose me. He could have had any of the fine ladies in town, and yet..."

I waved off her modesty with a flick of my hand. "Oh, Jane. He didn't 'choose' you like you're some dish at the local tavern. He fell for you. Thoroughly, completely, and probably before you even batted an eyelash his way."

She gave a small laugh, fiddling with the ribbons in her lap. "Perhaps. But it's still overwhelming. I've never felt this way before. I never knew it could be like this."

The soft vulnerability in her voice made my heart warm. "Mr. Bingley is the lucky one, and if he has any sense, he already knows it."

Jane glanced at me, then gave me a sly look, her eyes sparkling mischievously. "And what about you, Lizzy? I've noticed something between you and Mr. Darcy. There's... something there, isn't there?"

I nearly dropped the ribbon I was holding. "Jane, don't be absurd. Mr. Darcy and I are... acquaintances, nothing more."

"Acquaintances?" she repeated, her tone sweetly disbelieving. "Yet his eyes seek you out whenever you're in the room. He always seems to look for you, doesn't he?"

I waved her off, though my heart gave a little flutter at the thought. "You're imagining things. Mr. Darcy seeks no one out."

"Am I?" Jane tilted her head, her soft teasing laced with gentle curiosity. "Lizzy, I think you care for him more than you let on."

I busied myself with my gown, smoothing out non-existent wrinkles and adjusting the sleeves, anything to avoid Jane's knowing gaze. "You're reading too much into it."

Her eyes twinkled. "Lizzy, I've seen the way he looks at you."

I bit my lip, trying to ignore the tug of truth in her words. Over the past few weeks, my feelings for Darcy had shifted in ways I wasn't ready to admit, even to myself. First, I thought him a madman, then a reluctant partner in this bizarre ghost business. But now... now I feared something else entirely had taken root.

The thought terrified me.

"It doesn't matter," I said quietly, finally meeting Jane's eyes. "After the ball, everything will change. He'll be... free. Free of all this. Free of me."

Jane frowned, concern softening her features. "Free of you? Lizzy, why do you say that? You speak as though he's trying to escape."

I let out a long breath, dropping the pretense of fiddling with my gown. "Once Christmas Eve is over, he'll have no reason to stay. He'll go back to his life, to London... and to whatever future he had before all of this."

"What is all this nonsense about Christmas Eve? As if we've not twelve more days of festivities after Christmas! You think Mr. Darcy will suddenly leave all his friends in the middle of the season? Do you honestly think he'll forget you?"

I hesitated. "Perhaps he won't forget me... but that doesn't mean there's a future for us."

Jane reached out and took my hand, her grip warm and reassuring. "You don't know that, Lizzy. He... he may not be as indifferent as you think."

I tried to smile, but it felt strained. "We'll see. But for now... let's focus on the ball, shall we?"

"If you insist. But don't give up hope just yet."

I turned back to the vanity, adjusting the ribbons on my gown for the third time. "Hope? I didn't think I had any left to lose."

Jane gave a soft laugh, standing to help me with my shawl. "I'm sure you have more than you think. I've never seen a man as serious as Mr. Darcy quite so... serious about you."

"Oh, he's serious, that is certain," I muttered, rolling my eyes. "Serious about frowning. I'm not sure he even knows how to smile properly."

"I think you've seen him smile more than you'll admit," Jane teased, adjusting my shawl. "And I think he cares for you more than he'll admit."

I snorted, though a flicker of warmth stirred in my chest at the thought. "We shall see about that. Now, come on, let's focus on you and Mr. Bingley, shall we? We wouldn't want you to lose your sense before this ball."

"Lose my sense?" Jane echoed, laughing softly as she tucked a stray curl behind my ear. "I think I've already lost it. To him."

Twenty-Eight

Elizabeth

THE BALL HAD BARELY begun, and already I was regretting the decision to wear new slippers. They pinched my toes like an overzealous aunt at Christmas dinner, but I forced a smile as I followed Jane into the grand ballroom at Netherfield.

"Mama was right," Jane whispered beside me, her cheeks pink with excitement. "This really is the event of the season."

I glanced around at the crowd gathering inside—the well-dressed, the well-mannered... and Mr. Wickham. Naturally. At least Mr. Collins had returned to Kent—without a bride, mind you—but we still had *that* vulture in our midst.

Before I could begin tallying how many times Wickham would try to lie to us all tonight, I caught sight of Mr. Darcy standing near the far wall, looking as tall and forbidding as ever. He was watching me. Of course, he was.

"Lizzy," Jane said softly, glancing between us. "I do believe he means to speak with you."

"Is that so?" I said lightly, though my heart had begun thumping a little faster. "Well, I suppose there's no avoiding him. He does look rather determined, doesn't he?"

Jane smiled. "Perhaps because he's not as terrifying as you think."

I arched a brow. "You're not the one who's had to make excuses for him all over Meryton. Did you even hear that conversation I had with Aunt Philips yesterday? She was *sure* he was for Bedlam, and I w—"

"*Go*, Lizzy," Jane commanded, giving me a little push forward.

Before I could continue, Darcy had arrived. He greeted us with a crisp bow that made my skin flush. "Miss Elizabeth," he said, his voice low and far too delicious for my nerves. "And Miss Bennet," he added with a nod to Jane, who returned it with all her sweetness. "I hope you find the ball to your satisfaction."

"Who could not, Mr. Darcy? I was just saying as much to Jane, was I not?"

Jane's eyes were already fixed across the room, and she hummed distractedly. "Indeed, you were. If you will excuse me, Lizzy, I... I think I should like some punch."

Mr. Darcy bowed again as Jane left us, and we both watched her path—directly toward Mr. Bingley, who was already moving to meet her halfway.

"Your sister appears to be somewhat... emboldened this evening," he observed.

I pinned him with a look. "Precisely what is that supposed to mean, sir?"

"Nothing more than surprise on my part, I suppose. I had not previously noticed any symptoms of peculiar regard from her."

"That is because you have been too twisted in knots to notice much of anything apart from your own concerns."

Mr. Darcy narrowed his eyes at me, but there was that flicker in his cheek that gave away his efforts at not smiling. "Touché, Miss Elizabeth. It seems that for once in my life, I cannot presume the right to claim the superiority of my own observations. I trust I may rely on your counsel in... certain matters?"

"On that one, at least. And if you should decide to take it upon yourself to meddle in my sister's affairs, I shall start telling everyone that you talk to spirits, and do not for an instant think I won't."

"I would not dream of it, Miss Elizabeth. There are few beings in this world... or the next... who frighten me quite so much as you do."

I fisted a hand at my hip and surveyed him archly. "*I* frighten *you?* And you, a big, strong gentleman who would never, in a thousand years, dream of running screaming across the Netherfield lawns in abject terror? Certainly nothing twitchy or nervous about *you*, Mr. Darcy."

He arched a brow. "I will give you ten thousand pounds to never repeat that episode to another living soul."

"Oh, I will take you up on that offer, Mr. Darcy. I suppose you expected me to modestly protest that I could never take advantage of you like that, but I could, and I will. Do you prefer a bank cheque, or hundreds of ten pound notes that no one will ever trace back to you?"

His lips twitched, and his eyes twinkled in mirth, though it still wasn't quite a smile. "I submit to the lady's preference."

"Well, *this* lady's preference is to sort it out over a dance. And since we have been standing here for several minutes and you have yet to tender your offer, I shall simply claim it. Shall we dance the first set, once the music begins, or the supper set?"

He looked me directly in the eyes. "Yes."

That caught me by surprise. His gaze was so focused just now—the light in his eyes so intense and his posture suddenly listing toward me in such a way that I felt like we were alone at that gamekeeper's cottage again—and he was still pleading for me to understand, to accept what made no sense.

It was that look that said he would have crawled inside my winter cloak with me and simply hidden away from the rest of the world, clinging to me like I was his only friend... or a lover. Either notion made my blood heat in a way that was probably indecent in a crowded place. Indecent *anywhere*, I suppose, save a bedroom—another idea that made my skin prickle with wild notions.

I tried to swallow but found little success. "Well, sir," I rasped. "I believe the first set is about to begin. And as you have said, 'yes,' that amounts to a contract, so I shall demand my due."

This time, Mr. Darcy did smile, and it did something to break off the look with which he had been searing me. A relief, to be sure, but not altogether a pleasant one. I rather liked the way he had been looking at me.

He cleared his throat and gestured toward the ballroom. "It seems I've been dragged into festivities against my will."

I narrowed my eyes slightly, catching the flicker of something—someone—just over his shoulder. Oh, of course. *Ewan.* I couldn't see him, but Darcy's posture stiffened, his eyes flickering to the side, telling me all I needed to know. The ghost was back, and no doubt, he was up to something.

"Dragged against your will, Mr. Darcy?" I tilted my head in mock sympathy. "Whatever could have convinced you to agree to such torture?"

Darcy's eyes flicked momentarily to a spot over my shoulder, the barest hint of exasperation crossing his face before he composed himself again. "It's a long story, Miss Bennet. One that involves... more than just my own volition."

I bit back a laugh. "I'm sure it does."

Just as I spoke, a loud crash echoed from the refreshment table. Every head in the room turned toward Wickham, who stood frozen next to what had once been a perfectly intact bowl of punch. He looked down at his soaked waistcoat, blinking in shock.

Wickham's gaze darted around the room, searching for someone to blame, but as far as everyone could tell, the punch bowl had simply toppled of its own accord.

I smirked. "Well, Mr. Darcy, it seems the festivities are already off to a... lively start."

Darcy cleared his throat. "I fear there may be more of that to come."

"Oh, don't be so dour," I teased. "It's a ball. What could possibly go wrong?"

Just then, a shriek rang out from the far side of the room as one of the younger militia officers' cravats tightened dramatically, choking him so suddenly that he flailed about like a startled duck. Darcy's hand clenched slightly at his side, and I could almost see him resisting the urge to roll his eyes.

I blinked at him. "On second thought, you might be right."

Darcy

THE BALLROOM WAS A blur of movement—twirling skirts, laughter, and the bright hum of conversation—but all I could focus on was Elizabeth. She stood across the room, speaking with her sister and Bingley, her eyes alive in the candlelight, her lips curved in a faint, secret smile that seemed meant only for herself. I had barely looked away from her all evening.

It wasn't just her appearance, though. Egad, I had not expected to be so thoroughly undone by the scent of lavender surrounding her, or the way her curls framed her face. Her smile, her laugh, her ease among the crowd—the way she commanded attention without demanding it, that effortless grace tempered by something fierce and untamed. And every so often, she glanced in my direction as if checking to see if I was watching. And by Heaven, I always was.

Ewan had claimed she was meant for me—destined even.

I hadn't taken him seriously at first. But now—every look, every laugh—it was clear that fate or no fate, I wanted her as I'd wanted nothing else. She would be mine—that had become my only hope. Every glance she cast my way only set my resolve firmer. The rest of the evening didn't matter. It was all leading to one thing: Elizabeth Bennet in my arms, and willing to stay there forever.

"Mr. Darcy," a familiar voice interrupted my thoughts, one that grated on my nerves as easily as nails on slate. I turned to see Wickham, his smile more predatory than pleasant, approaching me with a lazy confidence that made my blood boil.

"Wickham," I replied, stiffening. Elizabeth was still visible just over his shoulder, her laughter a light melody on the air. But now, my mood had shifted. Wherever Wickham went, the air turned sour.

"I trust you're enjoying the evening?" Wickham asked. He stepped closer—close enough for me to see the evidence of still-drying punch framing an unsightly circlet across the front of his waistcoat. "I couldn't help but notice you and Miss Elizabeth Bennet have become quite the subject of interest tonight."

I raised a brow, refusing to rise to his bait. "I wasn't aware my dance partners were of such concern to you, Wickham."

He chuckled, a sound that sent a jolt of irritation through me. "Oh, I think they concern more than just me, Darcy. After all, I overheard a rather intriguing conversation earlier. Seems Miss Bingley wasn't best pleased by your choice of partner to open the evening. She seemed quite... put out, if I may say."

I resisted the urge to roll my eyes. Caroline Bingley's wounded pride was the least of my concerns. But Wickham had a knack for turning any situation to his advantage, and I could sense there was more to his visit than idle gossip.

"You see," Wickham continued, his smile widening, "there's been talk. After all, it's quite rare for a man like you to take an interest in a lady like Miss Bennet. Some might say... unusual. Others might even think there was more going on than meets the eye."

"There usually is."

"Could be lust, of course. I certainly could not blame you—she *is* a fetching specimen. But I know you better than that, Darcy, and I have another theory."

"Oh, do tell."

He raised his brows. "Madness?"

I kept my expression deadpan, staring at him until his questioning look relented into a grin.

"Come, Darcy, I have known you too long. Either this is your cleverest ploy yet to evade matchmaking mamas, or there is something..." he tapped my lapel... "*very* wrong with the master of Pemberley."

"I suppose that would be a matter of opinion."

"The Lord Chancellor's opinion, I daresay. If Fitzwilliam Darcy is mad, then what, I do wonder, must become of his dear sister?"

I tensed, my fists clenching at my sides. "Get to the point, Wickham."

"Why, Darcy, you wound me! Are we not old friends?"

"No."

He laughed and leaned to the side to pluck a wineglass from the tray of a passing waiter. "Very well, I shall come out with it. A thousand pounds, Darcy. Enough to keep me quiet about your darling sister and your..." He took a drink from his glass. "... Shall we say 'oddities.'"

I studied him, then forced a fake smile. "Suppose I refuse to pay you off for... what, I do not know. It is not as if giving you money has ever proved a sound investment before. Why should I even entertain your threats?"

Wickham shook his head. "You do not believe I would bother confronting you if I only held one trump card, do you?" He leaned in, his voice dropping to a near whisper. "I noticed something curious a few days ago—a lady's tracks in the snow, leading into the woods from Longbourn. And not just a simple woodland wandering was it—no, no, those tracks continued on a straight path for better than a mile to an abandoned cottage in the woods. Someone was on a mission. I'd hate for anyone to misunderstand what those tracks might mean. Especially when another set of tracks in your boot size led back to Netherfield."

My heart hammered, but I kept my expression neutral. This was exactly the kind of trap Wickham excelled at—dangled just close enough to ensnare me, but not enough for me to bite back.

"And?" I said coolly, refusing to give him the satisfaction of a reaction.

Wickham's eyes gleamed with malicious delight. "And, Darcy, people notice things. They talk. A gentleman like you wouldn't want his name linked with scandal, would he? Especially not a scandal involving a lady's honor. That would be... most unfortunate. Oh, you are welcome to your dalliances, I care not. But I daresay you have your sights set somewhere higher for a wife than a country lass from Hertfordshire." He leaned back and tilted his head. "Unless, of course, you are fond of the chit. Is that it, Darcy?"

Before I could respond—likely with something less than polite—something odd caught my eye. Wickham's cravat. It twitched.

Just slightly. At first, I thought it was a trick of the light, but then, unmistakably, it shifted again, loosening ever so slightly as if someone was untying it with invisible hands.

I blinked, and sure enough, there he was. Ewan. Standing just behind Wickham, his hands working deftly at the cravat, untying it with such precision that Wickham hadn't noticed yet.

Not now, I thought, glaring at him, but Ewan only grinned.

Wickham, oblivious, continued. "Now, of course, I'm sure it's all innocent. But you know how people love to talk. And a word from me, well... I could either quell those rumors of madness or liaisons, or I could let them spread like wildfire. All it would take is a whisper."

The cravat loosened further, the knot now barely holding, but Wickham still hadn't noticed. Ewan stepped back for a moment, admiring his handiwork, before reaching out again—this time, more deliberate. His fingers tugged gently at the fabric, making it slip down just enough for Wickham to feel the shift.

Wickham frowned, his hand moving to his neck, brushing at the loose ends of his cravat. "As I was saying, Darcy, it would be in your best interest to—"

And then, without warning, the cravat unraveled completely, the silk fabric slipping free and fluttering to the floor in a soft heap.

Wickham's hand froze, his face flushed with confusion. He stared down at the cravat, utterly baffled, and I had to bite the inside of my cheek to keep from laughing.

"Something the matter, Mr. Wickham?" Elizabeth's voice cut through the room, her tone sweet and innocent as she stepped beside me, her eyes gleaming with amusement.

Wickham flushed an even deeper shade of red, scrambling to pick up the fallen cravat and fumbling to retie it. "I... it's nothing," he muttered, clearly flustered.

Elizabeth's lips twitched. "Perhaps you should take more care, Mr. Wickham. It wouldn't do to have your attire... misbehave."

Wickham, still flustered, tugged at the cravat, his hand shaking slightly as he tried to loop it back around his neck with only one hand free. "As I was saying, Darcy," he stammered, his composure all but shattered, "I think you understand the... delicacy of the situation."

I raised an eyebrow, taking full advantage of Wickham's momentary disarray. "Delicacy, Mr. Wickham? Perhaps you're the one who should take care with such... delicate matters. You wouldn't want to make a fool of yourself, would you?"

His eyes flashed with anger, but before he could retort, Ewan struck again. This time, Wickham's wineglass tilted—slowly at first, then more deliberately—until the red wine sloshed over the rim, splashing across his loosely hanging cravat and his already-stained waistcoat.

Wickham let out a strangled sound, staring down at the crimson stain spreading across his chest. His hands flailed uselessly, trying to dab at the mess with his sodden cravat, but only succeeded in smearing the wine further.

Elizabeth stifled a laugh beside me, and I could feel my own lips twitching as I watched Wickham's mounting frustration.

"Goodness, Mr. Wickham," Elizabeth said, her voice laced with mock concern. "You do seem to be having a rather difficult evening."

Wickham sputtered, his face now a deep, furious red. "I—I don't know what's happening, I—"

"I think it's clear," I said, my voice steady, but the amusement was impossible to hide. "You are either in your cups, or there is something *very* wrong with Lieutenant George Wickham. Perhaps you should retire for the evening before further humiliation strikes."

Wickham glared at me, his chest heaving with rage, but before he could respond, the button at the top of his breeches gave a sudden twitch. My eyes widened as I watched in disbelief. *Ewan, don't you dare...* There were ladies present!

Wickham opened his mouth to respond, but at that very moment, the final button of his breeches gave way, and the fall slipped, exposing... egad, *too much*, even to the tops of his garters. He fumbled, his hands flying to hold his breeches together, his face now a deep shade of crimson.

Elizabeth covered her mouth, but a gasp escaped her. I had to bite the inside of my cheek to keep from joining her outright. "Mr. Wickham! How dare you expose yourself in public? Turn away, Miss Elizabeth—you needn't look on something so distressing."

"Oh, I daresay this is not the first time Mr. Wickham has *exposed* himself to a lady." Elizabeth did not, as I had hoped, look away. Instead, she crossed her arms... and laughed. "I cannot see why you are so concerned, Mr. Darcy. There is nothing worthy of looking at."

"This is absurd!" Wickham sputtered, furiously buttoning his fall and glaring at me with venom in his eyes. "You'll regret this, Darcy."

"Regret what? I never touched you. All I see is the careless efforts of a lazy soldier coming to fruition. You really ought to take better care of your wardrobe, Wickham."

"You... you did something!" he accused. "I don't know what, but I'll find out, and everyone will know! You've some sorcery or... or your sort of madness is catching!" He clutched at his clothing again, sweeping Elizabeth with his gaze. "You'll be a pariah, Darcy. It's dangerous just to be around you!"

"Oh, I doubt that," I replied calmly. "Miss Elizabeth, do you feel in any danger in my company?"

She frowned and lifted a shoulder. "None whatsoever. Really, Mr. Wickham, this sort of conduct is unbecoming of an officer. What *will* Colonel Forster say when he learns of it?"

With one last scowl, Wickham gathered what was left of his dignity and stormed out of the ballroom, his breeches hastily fastened and his wine-soaked waistcoat still dripping.

Elizabeth turned to me, her eyes alight with laughter. "Mr. Darcy, I must say, that was the most... eventful conversation I've witnessed all evening."

I couldn't hold back anymore. Laughter—genuine and unrestrained—spilled out of me. I do not think I had laughed that long or that hard since I was a boy. And if anyone present wished to declare me mad for laughing until tears sprang into my eyes, they were welcome to it.

Twenty-Nine

Darcy

I THOUGHT I'D SEEN the last of Wickham for the night, but Ewan clearly wasn't done having his fun. As I watched Wickham march out of the ballroom, half-undressed and fuming, I turned my attention back to Elizabeth, who had barely managed to stifle her laughter.

"Miss Bennet," I said, offering her my arm. "Would you care for a walk? I think we've both earned some air after that... spectacle."

She hooked her hand through the loop of my elbow. "Lead the way, Mr. Darcy."

We made our way toward the grand terrace doors, where the December air awaited, crisp and refreshing. As we passed through the ballroom, I caught sight of Ewan hovering by the refreshments table, pretending to inspect a tray of mince pies. The moment our eyes met, he gave me a wink and disappeared through the wall. I couldn't suppress a sigh of relief.

"Ah, there it is," she said softly.

"There what is?"

"That sigh. You've been holding your breath all evening—laughter notwithstanding. I was beginning to think you would turn purple from keeping that upper lip of yours so stiff."

I smirked. "It's become a necessity, I'm afraid. I keep waiting for some sort of disaster to strike, and so far, I have not been disappointed."

She shivered slightly, pulling her shawl tighter around her shoulders. "Disaster seems to follow you, Mr. Darcy. But I must admit, tonight has been... eventful."

"Eventful, indeed," I agreed, glancing around the terrace. The night was clear, the stars scattered across the sky like diamonds. And, to my immense relief, Ewan was nowhere to be seen.

For the first time all night, I felt a strange sense of peace. Standing here with Elizabeth, away from the madness of the ball, the world felt... quieter. Simpler. And for a moment, it was just the two of us, with no ghosts, no Wickham, and no distractions.

"Thank you," Elizabeth said suddenly, her voice softer now. "For what you did earlier."

I let my hand trail down the edge of her laced glove to catch her hand. "I don't know what you mean. What did I do?"

She let her fingers curl around mine. "Oh, well, when I saw Mr. Wickham approaching you, I came closer. I overheard some of what he said about the tracks in the snow. I had some inkling that he had seen something, but that he could have followed them all that way—I had been concerned about being found out. Such a thing would be... difficult."

"Difficult is a charitable way of putting it," I replied dryly, earning a soft laugh from her. "But you need not thank me, Miss Bennet. I'm merely trying to make it through the night without strangling him."

"You showed admirable restraint. Especially considering what he tried to imply."

"What, the madness? Or..." I raised my brow. "The *other* thing?"

She sucked in a breath, and her cheeks suddenly went crimson. "I... I would not presume to think..."

I released her hand to touch her chin, lifting her eyes back to me. "Elizabeth Bennet, you were the only person to see me—truly *see* me. You were the only one courageous enough to confront me and the only one who trusted me enough to believe me when all I had to offer sounded like madness. You may presume anything you want, and you will be right. You have made me wholeheartedly yours, and I can only hope—please tell me it is not in vain!—that you may, someday, come to feel the same for me."

Her eyes rounded, and her lips parted softly, and for once, Elizabeth Bennet had no clever retorts. No witticisms or pert replies to set me back on my heels. Just... awe.

She swallowed. "Mr. Darcy, I..."

But before she could choke out another word, a soft rustle sounded above us. I looked up and, to my horror, saw a sprig of mistletoe floating down from the terrace overhang. No one had placed it there, of course. This had Ewan's ghostly fingerprints all over it.

Elizabeth followed my gaze, her eyes narrowing in confusion. "Is that...?"

"Mistletoe," I confirmed, as my face heated.

Elizabeth looked at me, the corner of her lips twitching as if she were trying to suppress a laugh. "Did you... arrange this, Mr. Darcy?"

"Not at all," I said quickly, stepping slightly to the side. "This is not of my doing, I assure you."

The mistletoe hovered ominously between us, swaying gently as if to remind us of its presence. I could practically hear Ewan's laughter echoing in my head. Elizabeth, meanwhile, was watching me with a gleam of amusement in her eyes.

"Oh, come now, Mr. Darcy," she teased. "Surely you know the tradition."

I swallowed hard. *Elizabeth Bennet. Mistletoe.* Ewan meddling in the background, likely doubled over in ghostly laughter. This was not how I envisioned confessing my love to Elizabeth. I'd wanted words, true feelings, a moment of quiet reflection and honesty.

And what I got was Ewan McLean.

"I... suppose I do," I said cautiously, glancing upward as the mistletoe bobbed slightly closer. "Though, under the circumstances..."

Elizabeth took a step closer, her face illuminated by the light spilling from the ballroom. "Under the circumstances, I think a kiss wouldn't be entirely out of place, don't you?"

My breath caught. For a moment, I could hardly think—my mind too full of the sight of her, standing before me, her cheeks flushed from the cold, her eyes glinting with amusement.

Before I could even respond, I felt a soft nudge at my back. I nearly stumbled forward, catching myself just in time. Elizabeth's eyes widened in surprise as I closed the distance between us, mere inches away.

I didn't need to look to know Ewan was responsible for that gentle shove.

Elizabeth arched an eyebrow, clearly trying to contain her laughter. "You... seem eager, Mr. Darcy."

I cleared my throat, trying to regain some semblance of dignity. "*Someone* certainly is."

Her lips curved into a smile, and for a moment, the rest of the world seemed to melt away. The night, the cold, the oddity of the mistletoe floating above us—it all faded into the background. There was only Elizabeth, standing before me, her gaze holding mine in a way that made my heart race.

I leaned in, slowly, giving her every chance to pull away. But she didn't. Instead, she tilted her chin slightly, her breath mingling with mine as I closed the last of the distance between us.

The kiss was brief, barely more than a brush of lips—but it was enough to set my pulse racing, enough to make the ground feel unsteady beneath my feet. When I pulled back, Elizabeth's eyes were still closed, but she was smiling.

She opened her eyes slowly, her gaze meeting mine, and for a moment, neither of us said anything. The air between us felt charged, like the calm before a storm.

But before I could speak, before I could even process what had just happened, I heard a faint, mocking applause from behind me. I turned, and sure enough, there was Ewan—sitting on the stone railing, clapping slowly, a self-satisfied smirk on his face.

"Took ye long enough, lad," he said with a grin. "That was doonright romantic."

I sighed, shaking my head, but I couldn't help the smile tugging at my lips. "You are insufferable, Ewan."

Elizabeth gave me a playful nudge. "Well, it wasn't the worst mistletoe kiss I've ever had."

I chuckled softly, my heart lighter than it had been in weeks. "Then I'm honored, Miss Bennet. If you don't mind... what do you say to a second attempt?"

She leaned slightly closer to me, tilting her head up and fixing me with a seductive pout. "Why?"

"Because," I whispered as my lips lightly touched hers, "before the evening is out, I want mine to be the *only* mistletoe kisses you will ever remember."

Her lips smiled under mine. "Challenge accepted, Mr. Darcy."

Elizabeth

WE WERE STILL ON the terrace—well, our bodies were, but I was fairly certain my heart was in the clouds—when I heard a faint giggle, then the unmistakable click of heels on stone.

Oh, no.

I pulled back from Darcy just as Jane appeared with Bingley, her eyes going wide as she took in the scene. Bingley, bless his heart, just blinked at us, looking somewhat bewildered. Darcy, in a rare display of composure, barely cleared his throat and nodded to our spectators.

"Oh, Jane! Mr. Bingley!" I started, scrambling to summon my usual aplomb. "You know, they really should post a guard at the mistletoe. It's become an utter menace tonight, throwing people into all sorts of, er, compromising positions."

Jane's lips pressed together, her eyes dancing as she held back laughter. "Is that so?" She tilted her head at me, clearly amused.

Darcy stepped in smoothly, offering a gracious nod to Bingley. "Entirely innocent, I assure you, Bingley. Just the... mistletoe's doing."

Bingley squinted, looking around the terrace as if expecting the elusive sprig to pop out from somewhere. "Really?" he asked, puzzled, scanning the empty air. "I don't see any. You are claiming it was here a moment ago?"

"Oh, without a doubt," I said. "A fleeting thing, mistletoe, like good intentions."

Bingley nodded as if that explained everything, but he was looking at Darcy strangely. "Are you sure everything's all right with you tonight, Darcy? You're... a little unsettled again."

Darcy chuckled, finally letting the faintest hint of mischief show. "I can assure you, Bingley, there's nothing to worry about. You could say I've been... persuaded to embrace the spirit of the evening."

"You *both* appear to be in fine spirits," Jane murmured, trying to keep a straight face.

We all laughed, and, eager to escape further scrutiny, Darcy and I followed them back inside, arm in arm. The warmth of the ballroom enveloped us, along with the din of laughter, music, and an ongoing ripple of excited chatter. People were too wrapped up in their own merriment to notice us returning, which was a relief, though I noted that a certain soldier was conspicuously absent.

It wasn't until I heard Lady Lucas murmuring that I knew why.

"Yes, yes! Lydia Bennet, of all people, went to fetch Wickham for a reel, but he was bolting right out of the room like the devil himself was after him! Haven't seen him since."

"Oh dear," I whispered to Darcy, catching his eye. "So much for his threats."

Darcy smirked, his brow lifting as he watched the guests swirling about the ballroom. "It appears Wickham had his fill of theatrics for the night."

Just then, a roar of laughter erupted from the other side of the room. One of the officers, a Lieutenant Saunders, was valiantly trying to lead his partner in the dance, but his feet were simply not cooperating. His movements were jerky, his steps misaligned, as though someone—or something—was tugging at him from every direction.

"I say, Saunders!" someone shouted, holding back laughter. "Steady on, man!"

But Saunders could do nothing to steady himself; instead, he found himself spun in an unexpected twirl, his feet tripping over one another until he spun right out of his partner's grip and collided headlong with a waiter, knocking the poor man's tray of wine glasses to the floor. A crescendo of gasps and laughter rose up as Saunders struggled to regain his footing, his face a mixture of confusion and embarrassment.

Darcy pressed a hand over his mouth, but I could see his shoulders shaking. "Ewan does have a sense of theatre, I'll give him that."

"And a healthy dislike for redcoats. Oh, look," I whispered, nudging him as I saw a matronly woman turn to her astonished husband. She was muttering furiously, clutching at her collar as her brooch flew open and dangled, spinning like a pendulum.

"What on earth?" she cried, grasping at it as though it had a life of its own. "Harold, I told you these pin clasps were useless!"

Her husband stared, speechless, while the brooch snapped itself shut just as suddenly as it had opened, leaving her gasping as though the thing had simply come to life.

But not all the chaos was of Ewan McLean's making. After all, Lydia and Kitty were in the room, as well. I sighed as Lydia stole one officer's sword and twirled it about with a flourish. From across the room, it looked as if she were challenging the poor fellow to a duel. I could only pray that Mr. Darcy was looking the other way... but he wasn't.

He pressed his lips into a thin line, and for a moment, I feared he was about to disengage my arm from his, and that would be that. But instead, he leaned close to my ear. "Come, let us find some refreshment. You look as though you could use it."

I smiled gratefully and let him lead me away. I think I would have let him lead me anywhere.

The ballroom thrummed with elegance, a swirl of silk and laughter as guests danced, chatted, and basked in the warmth of Netherfield's candlelit splendor. Jane and Mr. Bingley were swept up in a waltz nearby, absorbed in their own world, a sweet image of holiday cheer that could have graced any winter portrait. I watched them, my heart a little fuller at Jane's happiness.

But then, across the room, a young redcoat officer executed a smooth turn—only to stumble wildly forward as if someone had shoved him. His face flushed as he just barely missed colliding with a lady's chair, grinning sheepishly at his partner, who only laughed and brushed it off. But I could have sworn I'd seen the fabric tug at the back of his coat.

Darcy, standing beside me, shook his head, his own restraint slipping into something that might almost have been called a smile. "Ewan, it seems, hasn't exhausted his tricks."

I raised an eyebrow. "If anything, I think he's just begun."

No sooner had I spoken than the wine tray beside the refreshment table listed slightly, tipping a decanter over with a distinct splash. A few officers turned to find their boots newly christened with mulled wine, leaping back in surprise. In the same moment, a lady next to me suddenly found herself whirled into an elegant, unexpected twirl. Her partner's hands had been nowhere near her waist, but she moved with the grace of someone being led, giggling all the while. She staggered a bit as she tried to regain her bearings, clearly wondering who had taken her for that lovely turn.

And then it happened. A light gust stirred the air above the floor, catching our attention. Out of nowhere, a small sprig of mistletoe drifted down, hanging suspended in the middle of the ballroom. Guests gasped, looking up as another sprig appeared, then another, until mistletoe sprinkled down like confetti, dusting heads, shoulders, and the tops of coats with green and white.

"Oh, my," Jane murmured from beside me, her eyes round with delight. "How magical!"

"Bingley!" called one guest, clapping him heartily on the back. "What a display! I might have known you'd surprise us with something so grand."

Bingley's polite, puzzled smile told me he had no idea what his guest was talking about, but he offered a gracious nod all the same. "Ah, yes, of course... glad you're enjoying it," he replied, casting a quick glance at Mr. Darcy with a raised eyebrow. He mouthed, "Did you plan this?"

Mr. Darcy shook his head. "Not I, I assure you," he whispered back.

"Marvelous!" another guest exclaimed, clinking glasses with Bingley. "Such a holiday spirit!"

"It's beautiful, Charles," Jane said softly, her cheeks aglow from the kiss Mr. Bingley had just bestowed on her cheek. Bingley's expression wavered between bewilderment and gratitude as he returned her smile, clearly pleased despite his confusion.

Everywhere I looked, the guests had taken full advantage of the holiday greenery. Couples began pairing off beneath the mistletoe, laughter and stolen kisses spreading through the room like wildfire. A sprig drifted down near a pair of elderly ladies, who glanced at one another with a laugh before each placed a sisterly kiss on the other's cheek.

One of the militia captains, noticing a sprig above him, reached gallantly for the hand of a nearby matron, bestowing an exaggerated kiss that had her blushing furiously. Her husband, across the room, took one look at the captain's theatrics, chuckled, and pointed upward, indicating another sprig dangling over his own head. The captain's face turned nearly as red as his uniform.

"Brilliant idea, Bingley!" someone shouted again, and the guests all erupted in applause, clinking their glasses in toast to their bewildered host.

A few seconds later, there was a stir at the punch bowl. I did not see how it began—I only heard a yelp and looked over just in time to see the ladle tipping unnaturally, sending a generous splash of punch directly into the open collar of a nearby lieutenant. The poor man squealed like a little girl, leaping back and fanning his dampened cravat while his friends roared with laughter.

"What in—who did that?" he sputtered, patting at the wet fabric with his handkerchief.

A chorus of laughter erupted from the other side of the room, where yet another young officer had nearly tripped over his own feet, staring down at his shoes with a look of deep confusion. Darcy sighed. "Ewan truly has an odd sense of humor."

Just then, the violinists struck up a new, lively tune, prompting several guests to clap in rhythm. Two militia officers took this as a cue to join a spontaneous jig, much to the delight of the onlookers. But before they could fully commit, one of them stumbled forward, nearly colliding with his partner as they both burst into laughter, unable to keep their footing as something invisible tugged playfully at their sleeves.

"Bingley! You've outdone yourself!" one guest shouted with a laugh, taking the merriment in stride. "First the mistletoe, and now invisible jesters!"

Another sprig of mistletoe floated down, landing above a particularly stoic elderly gentleman. His companion—a lady who must have been seventy if she were a day—leaned in to peck his cheek with a mischievous grin. The poor man went beet red, coughing politely into his handkerchief.

Around us, guests took turns pretending to look around for the floating mistletoe, as if expecting it to land on them next. Meanwhile, I spotted Ewan at work again near the refreshments. A portly gentleman reached for his punch cup, only to find it empty with a mystified look, while his friend beside him discovered his drink vanishing before it reached his lips. They exchanged puzzled glances, muttering about mischief as they refilled their glasses yet again.

A loud cheer went up as another sprig of mistletoe drifted above Kitty and Lydia. And to my everlasting mortification, Lydia bowled Kitty over as she jumped in the air to catch the thing first... and then ran straight for Lieutenant Denny with the greenery clutched in her fist.

But at least hardly anyone was paying attention to Lydia by now. More floating mistletoe sprigs kept appearing, each descending slowly, gliding and drifting through the room as though carried by invisible hands. The guests looked up in awe, their faces lit with delight and curiosity. Mistletoe seemed to appear from thin air, and each new sprig brought its own flurry of surprised laughter and delighted chatter.

"Oh, it's like magic!" a young woman nearby exclaimed, clasping her hands together.

At the far end of the room, I saw Colonel Forster glance up with a skeptical frown as a sprig of mistletoe drifted down toward him, seeming to hover just above his head. His partner at the moment, one of his wife's friends, as it happened, seized the opportunity, leaning forward to peck him on the cheek with a mischievous smile.

The colonel's eyes widened, his cheeks going red as he stammered, "Madam! I... I wasn't expecting—"

"Oh, don't be so coy, Colonel!" she laughed, patting his arm, as he blinked, completely out of sorts.

I turned to Darcy, who was watching this unfold with unrestrained amusement. "I don't know whether to applaud Ewan or to be horrified."

"It appears he's making full use of his freedom tonight," Darcy replied. "A last hurrah, I suppose. I daresay it's all rather harmless."

"Oh, harmless indeed," I agreed. "Unless, of course, you count Saunders' shattered dignity and Colonel Forster's complete mortification."

Before Darcy could reply, we both turned as a towering display of fresh Christmas greenery near the window seemed to sway. One of the taller branches leaned forward slightly, before pulling back like it was caught in an invisible breeze. Just as a young lady and her mother were admiring the greenery, it bent forward again, as if in a bow, and tipped one of its sprigs directly between them.

"Oh, heavens!" the young lady squealed as the mistletoe dipped, nudging her cheek in a feather-light touch as if she'd just been kissed.

"My stars, it's bewitched!" her mother gasped, clutching her daughter's arm in surprise.

And on and on it went. Drinks vanished from people's hands, officers found themselves pinwheeling into one another, and more than one lady swore someone had kissed her, but no one ever saw who. And the mistletoe—it was everywhere. How had Ewan pulled off such a feat? All I could think of was that Darcy *did* say his "visitor" had been scarce of late. Perhaps he had been out plundering the woods.

Meanwhile, couples continued to gather beneath the floating mistletoe, laughter, and kisses filling the room as each sprig seemed to have a mind of its own, hovering above pairs before disappearing as swiftly as it had come.

I looked up at Darcy, my heart pounding as the festive chaos unfolded around us. It felt as though we were the only two people in the world, standing amidst the wild revelry, utterly captivated.

His hand found mine, and he gave it a gentle squeeze. "I do believe this is our cue, Miss Bennet."

I glanced back at him, a mischievous smile on my lips. "Well then, Mr. Darcy, let's not keep our friend waiting."

Thirty

Darcy

I GUIDED ELIZABETH INTO the library, closing the door quietly behind us. The noise from the ballroom faded to a soft hum. Here, we were alone—or as alone as anyone could be with an invisible Scotsman lurking about. The library seemed warmer, with faint shadows dancing in the lamplight, casting an amber glow over the books and the crackling fire. Elizabeth's eyes were alight with curiosity, glancing around as though the library itself held the secrets we'd come to uncover.

I cleared my throat, suddenly aware of the small brooch in my pocket. Ewan's brooch. I'd kept it with me, a faint insurance policy against whatever strange magic might occur tonight. Slowly, I took it out, holding it between us.

"Ewan gave this to me. It's his lost love's brooch," I said softly, studying her reaction. "It's... well, it's complicated."

Elizabeth took a step closer, her eyes fixed on the brooch. Her gaze softened, almost hesitant. "So, this is it?" she asked, her voice barely more than a whisper. "The very thing that binds him to you?"

"To *us*, it seems," I replied, managing a faint smile.

She narrowed those glorious eyes and looked up at me, her fingers falling away from the brooch. "Us?"

"Yes." I pulled in a breath and wondered how much of Ewan's madness I should repeat to her. "It... well, apparently, *it*... as if it has its own will, I suppose... was looking for *you*, all the time."

Elizabeth's expression deepened with skepticism. "I don't understand."

"Well, that makes two of us."

She chuckled and reached out, fingers brushing mine as she took the brooch and turned it over in her hand. "It doesn't look like anything special," she mused.

"Oh, trust me. Don't underestimate it. And take care with the point on the back, for that is what got me into this mess."

She flipped it over in her hand once more, then she gave me a wry smile. "We're here at midnight, holding a haunted brooch, so I must ask, Mr. Darcy—do you have the slightest idea what we're supposed to do?"

"Not a clue." I attempted to laugh but realized I was practically sweating. "Ewan just said to make sure we were alone together at the stroke of midnight, as though that explains anything. And knowing him, it could involve anything from a blood oath to a series of ritual chants. But I absolutely draw the line at sacrificing a goat."

She laughed. "A blood oath? Truly?"

"Desperation breeds ideas, Miss Bennet." I couldn't help but grin back.

Elizabeth's laugh faded, and her expression grew serious. Her gaze sharpened on something behind me, and she swallowed. "Mr. Darcy?"

I turned, and there he was—a faint silhouette at first, then clearer, his face materializing with a look that was both hauntingly familiar and slightly confused. Ewan's gaze landed on Elizabeth, and he seemed to take a step closer, his eyes widening.

"Elspeth?" His voice, still a whisper, filled the room. He reached out a hand, brushing it over Elizabeth's shoulder. She shivered, looking up at him with a shock that mirrored my own.

"You can see him?" I gasped.

Elizabeth's eyes were wide and fixed on Ewan's face so intensely that they bobbed as she nodded. "I can. Is it because I'm holding this?" she whispered, her palm flattening under the brooch as if she were eager for Ewan to take it back.

For a moment, Ewan was frozen. He seemed lost in the memory, his hand falling to his side as he met her eyes. He shook his head. "Nay, I've muddled it again. Elizabeth," he said softly, letting the name settle as he looked at her with an odd sort of recognition. "But there is somethin' o' her spirit in ye, lass. I'll no' forget that."

Elizabeth's hand was still stretched flat as she stared at him, but then she did something curious. She blinked, finally shifting her attention back to me, and closed her fingers around the brooch, as if claiming it as her right. I suppose it always was. "What... what do we do, Ewan?"

Ewan turned to me with that half-exasperated, half-amused look he wore so well. "Ye see, lad? I told ye she's a bonny, canty lass, an' nae mistakin'. Got fire in her, she does, an' a fair sight more spine than ye'll ever muster."

"Thank you for noticing," I retorted dryly. "But you are right about her. I suppose you knew that all along."

"An' ye've still nae clue o' any of it, have ye, lad?"

"Yes, well, I'm still in the dark, if you must know. For once, perhaps you might tell me what's expected of us—without any more riddles."

Ewan sighed, looking heavenward as if I were a particularly dense child. "Och, I'll lay it oot plain fer ye. All ye need tae do is what ye were fated tae from the start—just make yer pledge tae her, lad. That's all it takes."

Elizabeth glanced at me, her brow furrowing. "Pledge...?"

"Aye," Ewan said, nodding to her. "A 'dùrachdan'—your vow, spoken in earnest, wi' all your heart."

Elizabeth blinked. "I... I don't understand, Mr. Darcy. What vow? And what is a... doorak... I don't even know what that word was."

"A *dùrachdan*, lass," Ewan said softly, "is a love fated by the very bones o' the earth—bindin' ye tae each other in this life and the next."

Her face flushed and her chest started rising rapidly as she sent a shy glance my way. "Oh," she said softly.

"Ye cannae deny it, lass. The brooch kent it, long afore ye did. Go on, Darcy—tell her what ye came here tae say."

I blinked, staring at him, uncomprehending. "That's all? I've endured everything—from my windows rattling at ungodly hours to utter humiliation—and now you're telling me I just... say *that*?"

Elizabeth, who was trying to stifle a grin, gave me a nudge. "Rather dramatic, whatever it is," she murmured.

I gave her a slightly exasperated look, but the truth was, my heart was pounding, the words already crowding at the edge of my mind. If I had to make this vow—to make her mine now, tonight—I'd do it gladly.

Turning fully to her, I took a deep breath. "Elizabeth," I began, "I—"

"Not yet, ye daft fool! Ye've got tae wait till the stroke o' midnight!"

All the pent-up urgency in me collapsed as if a pin had pricked a bubble in a rising loaf of bread. "You have *got* to be joking," I growled.

"Not a whit o' it!" Ewan grabbed the watch from my waistcoat pocket and raised his hand in the air. "Fifteen more seconds."

"Are you s—"

"Nae, lad!" he bellowed with laughter. "I just wanted tae see if ye'd go through wi' it. Go on, then."

I sucked in another breath and determined to do it right this time. On my knee—that was the only way to make a pledge like this to the woman I loved. I sank down, clasping her hand, my voice trembling despite my resolve.

"I..." My voice shook, but I found my footing. "Elizabeth Bennet, be it in this life or the next, I will always come back to you. Will you—will you marry me?"

There. The words hung in the cold air between us, solid and irreversible.

I hadn't planned this, not here, not tonight—but Heaven and earth, it felt right. Every hesitation, every doubt that had plagued me for weeks—months—had evaporated the moment I spoke. I realized then that I had been preparing for this for far longer than I'd known.

Elizabeth stood frozen, her breath caught, and then she laughed—soft and breathless, a sound I wanted to wrap myself in forever.

"I—Mr. Darcy..."

She was stunned. I had stunned Elizabeth Bennet. But I saw it—the warmth creeping into her eyes, the incredulous smile on her lips, as if she couldn't believe this was happening.

I couldn't believe it myself.

Her smile wavered for a moment, and I felt my heart lurch in my chest. What if I'd been wrong? What if—?

"Yes," she whispered, her voice barely more than a breath.

I blinked. "Yes?"

"Mr. Darcy..." Her voice caught, and I saw the warmth in her eyes grow. "Yes. Yes, I'll be yours. I already am."

A rush of warmth surged through me, and I felt a smile tug at my own lips, as though the entire world had shifted beneath my feet and righted itself, all at once. My hands shook, and I reached for her—hesitant, unsure whether I should—but she clasped my hands and urged me to my feet. And then her body was wrapped into mine with a sweetness that felt as natural as breathing.

"Ye did it, lad." Ewan's voice drifted over us, softer now, with an odd tremor that hadn't been there before. "Ye've found yer dùrachdan, and now I'll hae mine. Oh, Elspeth!"

I turned, Elizabeth still close against me, and caught a final glimpse of him standing by the doorway, his features softened with an expression I could only describe as peace. He nodded, one last look of recognition, and then his form began to fade.

And then he was gone.

Elizabeth and I were left standing in the quiet, surrounded by the warmth of the room and the gravity of the promise I'd made. She looked up at me, a spark of laughter returning to her eyes.

"So, Mr. Darcy," she murmured, "when did you plan to tell me all of this?"

I chuckled, brushing a stray curl from her cheek. "Honestly? I hadn't quite planned on telling you anything tonight."

"Then it's fortunate Ewan's meddling has finally come to good use," she whispered, her lips turning up in a mischievous smile.

"Is that what you call it?" I asked, drawing her even closer, feeling as though I might never be ready to let her go.

"Of course. How else would I be able to kiss you and wish you a Merry Christmas, my own Mr. Darcy?"

I let her pull me down to her, losing myself in the power of her caress. "Well, when you put it that way..."

Her laughter filled the space, warm and rich, echoing through the library as we stood there, caught up in the glow of something I could never name—something that felt, at long last, like coming home.

Epilogue

Darcy
Twenty-Five Years later

THE STRAINS OF A lively reel filled Pemberley's ballroom as guests swept in, their laughter mingling with the clinking of crystal and the joyful hum of voices. Elizabeth turned from a conversation, her gaze meeting mine from across the room with that mischievous sparkle that I had come to know so well. She raised an eyebrow, a slight nod telling me she had her eye on our son Bennet.

"Why, Mr. Darcy," she called to me with a playful smile, "aren't you going to see to your guests? They'll say you're slacking in your old age."

I chuckled, crossing the room to join her. "Slacking? I have greeted no fewer than half the county, my dear," I replied, reaching for her hand. "And yet you seem to have won all their attention, as usual."

She laughed softly, squeezing my hand, before her gaze shifted to our son, who stood by the refreshment table, shifting his weight from one foot to the other, his eyes fixed on a particular figure in the crowd. Elizabeth sighed and shook her head.

"Ah, but I wonder if he's found someone a bit more captivating than his parents tonight," she murmured. "I do believe our Bennet has his mother's nerve for love."

"Let us hope he has more of his mother's fortune," I replied, my own gaze following Bennet's. He stood, half-concealed in the shadows, doing his best impression of a bashful suitor—no easy feat for a Darcy. He tugged at his coat sleeves, casting an anxious look toward the ballroom's opposite side, where Miss Eliza Bingley stood in animated conversation with her aunt Catherine. Sweet-natured, poised, and possessing every whit of her mother's grace, she was as kind as she was lovely. And Bennet, for all his attempts at composure, looked as though he were teetering on the edge of a great precipice.

"Poor boy," Elizabeth murmured with a soft laugh. "I don't think he's drawn breath since she walked into the room."

I smiled, clapping my hand over hers. "He may have taken more after me than you'd think. There's no denying it: he's well and truly besotted."

"Then perhaps it's time he learned a thing or two about love."

He hadn't yet noticed me watching, too lost in his own world, but I saw him reach one hand toward his pocket and then pull it back, hesitating. I caught Elizabeth's gaze, and we both shared a knowing smile before she moved to his side. She reached up to her gown and unpinned a brooch—an ancient, worn thing, the silver tarnished and the stones dim, yet still beautiful in its own way. And then she pressed it into Bennet's hand.

He glanced down, then back up at her, a bewildered expression on his face. "Mother... forgive me, but why are you giving me this... thing?" He looked up sheepishly. "I only mean—well, it's rather ugly, isn't it?"

Elizabeth chuckled, unfazed. "Perhaps it is. But it holds more worth than you might think. I thought there might be a special lady in the room you would like to give it to."

Bennet looked even more confused, glancing between us as if searching for answers. "I do not... will any lady... appreciate it?"

I stepped closer, placing a hand on his shoulder. "Sometimes, Bennet, the most precious things come from the most inauspicious beginnings." I tilted my head toward Miss Bingley, who was still speaking with her aunt across the room. "If you truly love her, if you believe in your heart that she is meant for you, then give her that brooch at the stroke of midnight."

He looked down at the tarnished pin in his hand, his brow furrowing. "But... why?"

"Because, son," I said, my tone growing solemn, "that brooch is bound by an old vow, one meant only for those with steadfast hearts. If you pledge yourself to her with it, if you promise to come back to her in this life or the next, that promise will hold you to it."

Bennet glanced up, uncertainty in his eyes. Elizabeth reached out, brushing a hand over his cheek. "Do you love her, my son?" she asked softly.

The young man snapped his gaze to hers, resolve flaring in his eyes. "Yes, Mother. More than life itself."

"Then know this—such a vow can be a curse, or it can be a blessing. For me, it has been nothing but blessing." She nodded as if reassuring herself as much as him. "And I am certain it will be the same for you."

I squeezed his shoulder. "Go on, Bennet. No time to waste. And do us proud."

He hesitated only a moment, clutching the brooch tightly in his palm before he took a steadying breath and nodded. "Thank you, Father. Mother." With one last glance between us, he turned, his shoulders squared with purpose as he made his way toward Miss Bingley.

Elizabeth and I exchanged a quiet, knowing smile, watching as he wove through the crowd, finally reaching her and leading her toward the doors to a quiet corner of the hall. The glow of the ballroom faded as he took her hand and guided her, both of them sneaking glances back, their laughter hushed in excitement.

The clock began to chime, marking the approach of midnight.

Beside me, Elizabeth slipped her hand into mine, her fingers warm and her grip as sure and steady as it had ever been. I turned to her, the light in her eyes reminding me of every year we'd shared, every Christmas since that first, wild ball that had bound us in ways neither of us could have ever foreseen. She tilted her head, her eyes brimming with emotion.

"Do you think," she whispered, her voice just for me, "that Ewan McLean would be proud?"

I chuckled, drawing her closer. "I think he'd be insufferably smug." Then, more tenderly, I added, "But aye, ma *dùrachdan*. I'd wager he'd be right proud."

The final chime of midnight rang out, echoing through the hall. From across the room, Bennet's laughter mingled with Eliza Bingley's as he slipped the brooch into her hand, sealing his promise.

"Merry Christmas, Fitzwilliam," Elizabeth whispered.

"Merry Christmas, my love," I replied, holding her close, feeling the blessing of our shared life wrap around us, warm and sure as ever.

A RE YOU READY FOR another Darcy and Elizabeth Christmas story? ***Follow my newsletter and you will be in for a November surprise!***

Also, keep reading for a preview of ***How to Get Caught Under the Mistletoe.***

From Alix

T HANK YOU FOR INDULGING with me and spending a little time with Darcy and Elizabeth.

I hope you've had a delightful escape this Christmas! I'd love it if you would share this family with your friends so they can experience a love to last for the ages. As with all my books, I have enabled lending to make it easier to share. If you leave a review for *The Scotsman's Ghost* on Amazon, Goodreads, Book Bub, or your own blog, I would love to read it! Email me the link at **Author@AlixJames.com.**

And if you're hungry for more, including a free ebook of satisfying short tales, stay up to date on upcoming releases and sales by joining my newsletter: https://dashboard.mailerlite.com/forms/249660/73866370936211000/share

How to Get Caught Under the Mistletoe

Chapter One
26 November

IN MY DEFENSE, CHARLOTTE kicked me.

Oh, very well, perhaps it was not a kick. Charlotte is too civilized for that, but it was a very firm nudge. The sort of nudge that will probably leave a bruise.

I recovered myself somewhat and blurted out the first words to tumble into my mouth. "I thank you, yes." And then I died a little.

Mr. Darcy bowed. "I look forward to it, Miss Elizabeth."

As the gentleman walked away, I groaned and rolled my eyes to the ceiling. "Why did you do that?" I whispered to Charlotte.

Charlotte smothered a smug little grin. "I daresay you will find him very agreeable, Lizzy."

"More would be the pity! Tragic indeed to be forced to admit that I enjoyed dancing with a man I swore to despise."

"Despise! Do not let your fondness for Mr. Wickham let you make yourself disagreeable to a man of ten times his consequence. Every lady in the room is pining for a set with Mr. Darcy."

"Well, how unfortunate for him that he chose to ask the one woman who is not." I sighed and drew back my shoulders. "I require a little more punch before I stand up with him. Charlotte, are you well? You are looking somewhat out of breath."

She fanned her face, and indeed, she did seem paler than usual. "Oh, 'tis nothing, Lizzy. I should like to sit for a few moments, though. You know, I do not dance as often as I used to, and I suppose the exertion..."

Movement just beyond Charlotte caught my eye, and I gave her a tug at the elbow. "Yes, yes, keep on with that. You are frightfully out of breath, and your feet hurt and you require some time in the ladies' retiring room. Repeat after me."

She gave me a quizzical look as I rushed her toward the door. "But Lizzy, I said nothing about my feet hurting. It is only that I feel rather faint just now, and—"

"Faint, yes, that is very good. Say something about feeling feverish, too. Oh!" We stopped short as my cousin, Mr. Collins, deposited himself in our path. "Excuse us, cousin. I was just escorting Miss Lucas out for a respite."

He bowed deeply, sweeping his hand from his chest to the air in a ridiculous flourish. "Forgive me, fair cousin. I had hoped to beg a set of Miss Lucas, and, dare I hope, another from you before the evening is complete?"

Charlotte opened her mouth, but I gave her a little push in the shoulder, propelling her forward. "I fear now is not an opportune time, Mr. Collins. My friend is feeling unwell, and I have only a few moments before I must return for my set with Mr. Darcy. Some other time, I hope."

His disappointment was keen, and he was still lamenting about it as I dragged Charlotte from the room. "Lizzy, I would have said yes," she chided me.

"Charlotte, even *your* kindness can extend only so far. My toes are still tender from my set with him, and truly, you do not look like you can sustain half an hour of his conversation." I dragged her away. "There are far more agreeable men."

"But Lizzy, what if none of them mean to ask me? I do not entertain as many offers as you or Jane."

I stopped. "Jane and I only danced with him because we had no choice."

She put a hand on her hip. "You are purposely missing my point."

"Indeed, I am, and I still say you ought to count yourself fortunate that you were spared the trouble. The very idea! It is not as if you would consider anything else with the man."

"Well..."

"Come. Here is a nice seat, and let me fetch you a glass." I swiped one from the tray of a passing footman and placed it in her hand. "There. I shall return straightaway to tell you how odious a half hour I passed."

"Be careful not to accidentally enjoy yourself, Lizzy."

EVERYONE WAS STARING AT me. I swallowed and lifted my chin against the aghast expressions all around—all my neighbors who either knew of my dislike of the gentleman or thought me so far beneath him that they must have assumed it all a good joke. I drew back my shoulders and hoped Mr. Darcy didn't have sweaty palms or clammy fingers.

In point of fact, his hands were quite nice. Just what I might expect from the rogue. And he seemed to know his way about the dance floor, for which my toes blessed him. But he was excruciatingly silent all the while, and the way he stared at me did nothing to settle the flutter of nerves that suddenly tickled my stomach. Why would the man just gape blankly into my eyes, with no thought for conversation or admiration or even a jolly good row? Terribly disconcerting.

Very well, if he would not say something, I would do it. I waited until he stepped forward to lead me down the set. "Mr. Walton's fingers have recovered admirably."

Mr. Darcy's face jerked down to me as we stepped apart. "What?"

"Mr. Walton. He is the violinist, do you see? There. Bitten by a horse last week, I'm afraid. One would never know by his enthusiasm for the piece this evening."

"Er..." Mr. Darcy adjusted his cufflinks. "Indeed. He plays very well."

"There. Now we may be silent until we must step together again." I turned my head to watch a servant replacing a set of nearly guttered candles at the edge of the room, but when I looked back, Mr. Darcy was still staring at me. Oh, bother.

"Do you find the tempo a little fast this evening, Mr. Darcy?"

He looked at me strangely. "I find it precisely as it should be. Do you not?"

"Oh, no, I think it accurate in every way. For, you see, it took us exactly one measure to traverse the line, just as it ought. I only wondered because you look displeased by something."

"Nothing at all, Miss Elizabeth."

"That is very fine. Now, it is your turn to think of something to speak of, Mr. Darcy. Might I suggest observing something about how much pleasanter it is to attend a private ball than a public one? Or perhaps you could comment on the flavor of the soup."

He stepped forward and took my hand to lead me around the next couple. "The soup?"

"Just as you please. The pheasant was done to a turn. Do you not agree?"

"Indeed."

"Oh, come, Mr. Darcy! You must give me something better than one-word answers."

A ghost of a smile touched his lips. "I would be happy to discuss anything you prefer. Pray, tell me what you would most like to speak of."

I considered his question as he marched me around, then returned me to my place. "It must be difficult to settle on a topic, is it not? For I have noted that you, like myself, are usually unwilling to speak at all unless you can say something profound indeed."

"I would argue that *you* possess no such difficulty," was his dry retort. "And I cannot control how my own words are perceived."

"There, an answer that I must think on for a moment. That will do for the present."

He stepped back, but his face did not look so grave as it had. In fact, he almost appeared to be amused, and searching for something to say. "Do you often walk toward Meryton?" he ventured.

That was a piteous attempt. But at least it was a question that evoked a response, so I smiled. "Yes, often. In fact, we had just been meeting a new friend yesterday when you happened upon us."

My heavens! I did not know Mr. Darcy possessed so many feelings, but a great cascade of them blasted over his face all at once. His jaw rippled, his throat bobbed, and his eyes glittered to a fearsome black. "I do not wonder that Mr. Wickham was able to *make* a friend of you. Whether he deserves to *keep* your friendship is another matter."

"A friend is a valuable thing to have, would you not agree?"

His nostrils flared slightly. "I would."

"Then you must also agree that the loss of a friendship is a tragic thing, indeed. The material harm in such a loss cannot be measured."

He moved toward me and caught my hand for another march, and his voice dropped to a low growl. "Unless the 'friend' is shown to be deficient in character, in which case, the loss ought to be his burden to bear, not mine to regret."

I stopped mid-step. "You are very hard, Mr. Darcy. With such high standards, it must be difficult, indeed, for anyone to win *your* friendship."

He tightened his grip on my hand and pulled me out of the way of the next dancers. "Not so difficult as you might imagine. I believe the fault you would assign to me is not lack of civility, but an unwillingness to revise my opinions once they are fixed."

I pivoted into my place. "One must wonder what measure you use. I trust you are exceedingly careful in the forming of these opinions?"

"Exceedingly."

And with that one word, our conversation was done. I fell to silent fuming, and he to dark brooding. The very cheek of the man! To stand here with me and all but tell me to my face that I was being deceived in Mr. Wickham's character, when *he* was the disagreeable one and everyone knew it! For surely, it was for *his* pleasure that Mr. Wickham had been excluded from this evening's enjoyment. And not because the rest of the neighborhood liked Mr. Darcy, but because he was Mr. Bingley's friend, while the other was not.

I was too practical to think myself in love with Mr. Wickham after only two meetings, but I will own that his happy manners and the hope of a dance with such an amiable man had been my balm since Mr. Collins demanded the first set. And now, because of Mr. Darcy, I was to be denied the pleasure of a cheerful man's company.

But there was always tomorrow. Surely, we would see him walking up the lane with Denny, and he would humbly describe some perfectly acceptable excuse for his absence. And then, he would ask to walk our party to Meryton, or call on us again in the following days.

It was only a pity that for nearly every amusement to be had in the neighborhood for the foreseeable future, Mr. Darcy's glowering face would be my company instead. For surely, *he* would be invited everywhere, and Mr. Wickham nowhere. Such a disappointment! For a lady likes to think that as the season approaches for stealing kisses under the mistletoe, she might look forward to an agreeable partner.

Mr. Darcy was not so ungentlemanly as to neglect to escort me from the floor, but it was not with a happy countenance that he did so. I matched his curt bow with an equally impudent curtsey, and finally let go a breath as he turned away. There! That unpleasantness was done for the evening. I spun round to find Charlotte before Mr. Collins could make his way across the room to ask for my hand once more.

"Did you enjoy yourself, Lizzy?" she asked from her chair.

"If I did, you ought to see it in my face. There, what do you think?" I turned my cheek from one side to the other, framing my chin with my hands and fluttering my lashes. "Do I look like a girl who just relished her dance with the most valuable bachelor in the room?"

"Not a bit of it. I hope you did not tease him, Lizzy."

I sank into the chair beside her with a sigh. "No, we argued instead."

"Oh, Lizzy!" Charlotte shook her head and rested a hand on her stomach. "You would do better to keep quiet altogether than to provoke such a man as Mr. Darcy."

"Come, Charlotte, you know I might as well try to stop the sun in its tracks as my mouth. But do not worry—I said nothing he did not deserve, and richly."

She sighed and brushed her forehead with the back of her hand. "Just be careful not to make an enemy of Mr. Darcy. I should think his regard to be something worth having."

I snorted rudely into my glass.

Chapter 2

27 November

I HAVE ALWAYS ADMIRED the notion of love. Romance to sigh over, devotion to curl a girl's toes, and passion enough to shatter a heart in two. The sort that is not even spoken about in polite company because it might cause a lady to sweat inconveniently. Perhaps I had read too many novels, but a gallant sir knight to sweep away the princess and promise to spend the rest of his days making all her dreams come true—that was *my* idea of a romantic proposal.

This, however... no.

"My fairest cousin, allow me to protest the sincerity of my feelings, the ardency of my devotion, the depth of my affection—"

I pressed my fingers into my temples. "Mr. Collins, you are simply repeating yourself. I have declined your offer as many times as you have tendered it, and I mean to continue doing so, as long as you keep drawing breath. There is no possible scenario where we would suit one another. In fact, I am quite certain that your esteemed Lady Catherine would be appalled by me."

He clasped his hand over his chest. "Oh, not so, cousin! Why, she is eminently gracious and welcoming. Her condescension is everything magnanimous and splendid, and the advantages of her friendship are too numerous to be counted. I flatter myself, any young lady would—"

"Any young lady but this one. I am sorry, Mr. Collins, but my answer remains unchanged."

I pushed up from the sofa, nearly knocking him backward as I did so—for keeping a polite distance was not something he seemed to understand—and marched out of the room.

It was no mystery what would happen next. He would apply to Mama to try to make me see reason. Mama would weep and mourn about what a foolish, headstrong girl I was, and she would batter the door of Papa's study until he grew tired of the hullabaloo and heard her out.

I would be forced to stand by while Mama sobbed she would never speak to me again unless Papa made me marry Mr. Collins, while Mr. Collins continued with his delusions about his passionate romance and how insensitive I was to the delicacy of my own position. Papa would roll his eyes and declare he would have nothing to do with the matter. And...

That was why I was already on my way out the door toward Lucas Lodge, still buttoning my pelisse and tying my bonnet as I scampered away from the house.

"W HY, LIZZY! WHAT BRINGS you so early?"

Maria Lucas was the only one in the drawing room, and I looked round as I let her take my hat and gloves. "Oh, nothing, I... I wanted to ask how Charlotte was this morning. She seemed rather worn last night."

Maria frowned. "Why, I suppose she is well enough. But now that you mention it, she has been rather late to rise. Shall I call for her?"

"No, no, that will not be necessary. I will call again later." I turned back for my gloves once more, but the memory of what no doubt awaited me at home gave me pause. "You don't suppose I could look in on her myself, do you?"

"Oh, I don't... why, she probably would not mind. Shall I...?" She gestured up the stairs, offering to lead me.

"Thank you. No, that is not necessary. I will show myself up."

Charlotte was slow to answer my knock. Perhaps she had a little too much punch last night. I waited for a moment, then tried again. "Charlotte? It's Lizzy."

Her voice sounded rather thin when she called, "Come in, Lizzy." *Odd.*

I pushed the door open and nearly gasped. Charlotte, usually so robust and cheerful, reclined on her bed, her nightgown rumpled and her face unnaturally pale. The sunlight filtering through the windows cast a warm glow on her, but it couldn't mask the weary shadows beneath her eyes.

"Charlotte?" I moved to her bedside and brushed her forehead. "Are you ill? Was it something you ate last night?"

She managed a feeble smile, her hand gesturing for me to sit beside her. "I am just... not feeling well, Lizzy."

I sat on the edge of the bed and took her hand into mine, feeling the coolness of her skin. "You are more than 'not well,' Charlotte. You look... positively ill."

Charlotte sighed, her eyes drifting towards the window. "I've not been strong for some time now. I've tried to hide it, but I fear after last night, it's caught up with me."

"Some time now?" I repeated. "Why did you not say anything?"

She shrugged weakly. "What would it have done but worry my family? Besides, I did see Mr. Jones."

"And?"

Her eyes met mine, and there was a depth of sadness there that I'd never seen before. "He was concerned. Very concerned."

"Charlotte, no..." My voice was barely above a whisper.

"Headaches, stomachaches, dizziness," she listed off, her voice oddly detached. "I often feel as though I can't catch my breath. And there are some other things I'd... rather not mention."

"But you'll get better," I insisted. "Surely, you only want rest. You must take care to eat properly and not overtax yourself."

She shook her head and looked away. "It's more than that. Mr. Jones thinks I have a wasting disease, Lizzy. There's nothing he can do."

The world seemed to tilt beneath me, and blood pounded in my ears. "No," I whispered. "That can't be right."

Charlotte rested a hand on my arm. "I'm not afraid, Lizzy. Well, perhaps a little. It's not as if I had grand prospects awaiting me."

I couldn't hold back the tears. "Charlotte!"

"I know it's hard, Lizzy. I didn't want to say anything. Please don't tell Mama!"

"But she ought to know! And Jane and Maria... they should all know."

"Oh, yes, do tell Jane. She could keep it to herself, but please, don't tell my family. They don't need that sort of burden." She sighed, her eyes wistful. "Truly, Lizzy, it will be all right. I did wish for a bit of romance, though. Just a taste."

My throat tightened. "Charlotte, you deserve so much more than just a 'taste'."

She chuckled. "I always said I did not care about such a thing, but after watching Jane with Mr. Bingley, I think it would be very fine indeed just to sample a little. That would be enough for me."

I shook my head. "No, it isn't. It's not right, Charlotte."

She thinned her lips and sighed. "Well, I suppose it's not up to us to decide that, is it? Now, why did you rush over here so early the morning after a ball? Don't tell me Mr. Darcy presented himself on your doorstep this morning with an offer of marriage."

I sniffed and blubbered a laugh, then wiped my nose. "Mr. Collins, actually."

"And what did you say?"

I scoffed. "Well... I refused him! What else could I do?"

Charlotte shrugged. "I suppose that is a matter of opinion."

"And I made mine known." I laced my hand in hers. "What can I do for *you*, Charlotte? Shall I bring a book up and read to you?"

She smiled and shook her head on the pillow. "I will be well enough later, Lizzy. These bad spells come and go. I just need a little rest, and I will be downstairs by the time Mama begins to look for me. Go on—I am sure your mother is searching for you, too."

I huffed and shook my head. "That is precisely why I came here. Are you sure you will be well?"

Charlotte tightened her grip on my hand. "Well enough."

THE MOMENT I ENTERED Longbourn, Mama's familiar wails echoed from the drawing room, louder and more harrowing than any I'd heard before. She was inside Papa's study with the door open, but I managed to slip past without either of them seeing me. What had become of Mr. Collins? I knew not, nor did I mean to stop and ask. It all felt distant, secondary to the fears turning in my stomach after my visit with Charlotte.

"Lizzy!" Lydia's voice called out as I passed the drawing room, but I had no patience for her now. I clutched my skirts and ran up the stairs to Jane's door, and pushed it open without pause. "Jane, I've just come from Charlotte. You'll never believe what I..."

I stopped. Jane sat on her bed, a letter in hand, her face a study of distress. And when she looked up at me, she was blinking away tears.

"Jane?" Could this day take more frustrations or grief? I glanced at the letter, then examined her face. "What is it?"

"Lizzy," she choked. "It's from Miss Bingley. They..." She stopped, closed her eyes, and blew out a slow, shaky breath. "Oh, I am sure it is nothing, truly, but she says that by the time I receive this letter, they will already be on their way to London. Mr. Bingley departed at first light, but the rest of them have decided to follow."

"What?" I took it from her and scanned Miss Bingley's fine script. "For how long?"

Jane sniffed. "She does not say. Only that she is most eager to see Mr. Darcy's sister in London, and that she was pleased to make my acquaintance while they remained in the neighborhood. That does not sound like a farewell to you, does it?"

My lip curled as I read. "It sounds to me like Miss Bingley did not like her brother's fondness for you, and she meant to whisk him away."

"Oh, Lizzy, you do not know that. I am sure he only left on business, but it does seem odd that the rest of the party went after him. London must be so much more diverting at this time of year, but he will come back."

I handed the letter to her. "Yes, with a bride, no doubt. I understand Miss Darcy is a perfect peacock."

Jane's eyes widened. "How did you hear that?"

"Mr. Wickham."

She shook her head and folded her letter, then opened it again to re-read Miss Bingley's words. "No, I am sure you are wrong. The way I read this, she says only that she and Mr. Darcy are eager to see Miss Darcy again. She says nothing about..." She sagged, and her breath left her. "Oh, dear. Lizzy, can it be true?"

"You can count on it. And I think she is doing her brother a tremendous disservice, taking him from a lady he loves and forcing another upon him."

"Oh, Lizzy. Mr. Bingley was never... well, he was friendly. Kind." She looked up to the ceiling, her shoulders slumping and the letter falling to her lap. "I did fancy one or two times there that he might kiss me—you know, when he would escort me for a walk or when Mama would leave us alone in the drawing room. Is that not silly? He never did, of course. He is too much the gentleman for that."

"He is still a man, and a man in violent love, if I ever saw it. Would you truly let Miss Bingley take that away from you?"

"But what am I to do about it?" She tossed her hands, then swiped at a tear. "He is gone, and I cannot know when he will come back."

I frowned and sank onto the bed beside her. "It is not fair, you know. I mean, not fair to him. To have to leave behind a lady he clearly loves, and be forced to make himself amiable to a snobbish bore of a girl just to please his sister and Mr. Darcy."

Jane bit her lip and looked at me, her brow crumpled with hurt. "What do you mean?"

I just lifted my shoulders. "Only that Mr. Bingley seemed quite happy as he was. What a shame to have his hopes stolen, because they did not please someone else."

She dashed another tear from her face. "Oh, Lizzy, to hear you talk, one would think you want me to chase after him. Go to London and seek him out!"

"I suppose that it is very much what I am saying."

Jane shook her head. "No. It seems likely that I was simply misled. If he cares for me, he will come back. I am sure of it."

I thinned my lips and sighed. "Let us hope. Does Mama know about this yet?"

"Oh." Jane clapped a hand over her face. "Did you not hear all the crying downstairs?"

"Yes, but I thought I occasioned that by refusing Mr. Collins. Poor Mama! She truly is having a day of it."

"Indeed."

Grab your copy now!

Also By Alix James

The First Impressions Collection:

All Bets Are Off

———————

The Measure of a Man Collection:

The Measure of Love

The Measure of Trust

The Measure of Honor

The Measure of a Man Box Set (Coming December 2024)

———————

The Mr. Darcy Collection:

Mr. Darcy Steals a Kiss
Mr. Darcy and the Governess
Mr. Darcy and the Girl Next Door

Mr. Darcy: Swoonworthy Collection

––––––––––––––

The Heart to Heart Collection

These Dreams
Nefarious
Tempted

Darcy and Elizabeth: Heart to Heart Box Set

––––––––––––––

The Sweet Escapes Collection

The Rogue's Widow
The Courtship of Edward Gardiner
London Holiday
Rumours and Recklessness

Darcy and Elizabeth: Sweet Escapes Box Set

————————

The Sweet Sentiments Collection:

When the Sun Sleeps
Queen of Winter
A Fine Mind

Elizabeth Bennet: Sweet Sentiments Box Set

————————

The Frolic and Romance Collection:

A Proper Introduction
A Good Memory is Unpardonable
Along for the Ride

Elizabeth Bennet: Frolic & Romance Box Set

————————

The Short and Sassy Collection:

Unintended

Spirited Away

Indisposed

Love and Other Machines

Elizabeth Bennet: Short and Sassy Compilation

<u>Christmas With Darcy and Elizabeth</u>

How to Get Caught Under the Mistletoe: A Lady's Guide

The Scotsman's Ghost: Or How to Wreck a Yule Party

<u>North and South Variations</u>

Nowhere but North

Northern Rain

No Such Thing as Luck

John and Margaret: Coming Home Collection

<u>Anthologies</u>

Rational Creatures

Falling for Mr Thornton

Spanish Translations

Rumores e Imprudencias

Vacaciones en Londres

Nefasto

Un Compromiso Accidental

Reina del Invierno

Una Mente Noble

Cuando el Sol se Duerm

A lo largo del Camino

Reina del Invierno

Una Mente Noble

El señor Darcy se roba un beso

Italian Translations

Una Vacanza a Londra

Printed in France by Amazon
Brétigny-sur-Orge, FR